And so thy thoughts, when you art gone

Love itself shall slumber on

— Percy Bysshe Shelley
"Music, When Soft Voices Die"

The Last Train to

HULL

Arthur Aughey

SHORELANDS PUBLISHING

Published in the UK by SP (Shorelands Publishing) 2023

ISBN 978-1-7399568-2-0 (Paperback)

ISBN 978-1-7399568-1-3 (Hardback)

Typesetting: Derek Rowlinson

Cover image: Strickland Street (Stricky) Bridge to William Wright Dock, Hull, 5th December, 1977. Photograph courtesy of Dr Alec Gill.

A Shorelands Publishing Book

CONTENTS

PART ONE

Going

CHAPTER ONE

Edward Sweeney stood at the window of the first floor flat where he'd lived for the past three years. A feeble light of early morning wearied into his room. The house was empty now. His neighbours had left some time before. No clacking typewriter keys, no rhythms of jazz, no slippers flapping on the hallway floor, only silence. On Park Road everything was still. No one was about at this hour, no sound of footsteps, and no noise of traffic heading towards the city centre. Hull was dreaming, deep in a slumber which had eluded him. Looking onto wet streets and urban emptiness, Sweeney felt the approaching indifference of things, as if this flat, this house and this city were beginning to turn their backs on him. Once he set his keys on the table and pulled shut the front door, everything would continue as before and without him.

Yet hadn't he said love meant she would be always bound to him, and he to her? Wasn't it true of places as well as of people? He could never feel she was lost to him. He could never think Hull was lost to him either. Hadn't he joked that he had to come all this way to find her? Those who didn't believe in fate lived unimaginatively. That's what he wanted to think. His story of Hull, half memory, half fantasy, might be a lie. But it might as well be true – and it suited his temperament to believe so.

. . . .

He would never have thought of studying in Hull without the persistence of Dr Rodney – 'call me Rod' – Thomas. Rod was a young lecturer, a product of the expansion of higher education in the sixties who was determined to unsettle university culture in the seventies, even if he had to begin with the English

Literature Department in Belfast. When Malcolm Bradbury's *The History Man* appeared in 1975 students drew comparisons with Howard Kirk, inevitably earning Rod his nickname 'The English Man'. He came from somewhere in the Midlands, an accent reminding Sweeney of a character from *Crossroads*, an accent at once serious in deliberation and comic in tone. Wearing tight denims, collarless cheesecloth shirts and colourful waistcoats, Rod adopted a friendly rapport with students. He was nothing if not self-consciously progressive and the only habit linking him to the stereotype of university professor was his pipe. 'None of your Beowolf bollocks or Chaucer chunter on my courses,' he'd say. His specialism was the working-class novel in post-war Britain.

In lectures he would tell them things like 'I'm going to put you in touch with the modern world' and Sweeney couldn't help hearing the lines of Jonathan Richman's song. Rod wasn't joking. He was serious about revolution or at least his idea of it, measured by what appeared the most significant moment in his life, occupation of the administration building on the Hull campus in 1968. 'Solidarity with comrades in Paris' – Rod looked into the far distance as if imagining barricades and tear gas on the Boulevard Saint Germain – 'we were a bit late, a month late to be exact, but we changed things. Direct action' – his voice rose as he warmed to the subject – 'it's the one thing the establishment is afraid of' – and he would look meaningfully at students shuffling feet or doodling on pads. Only a few, Sweeney being one, were polite or interested enough to give Rod their full attention. It was obvious 'direct action' for Rod didn't go much beyond a rather civilised affair of unarmed Bobbies shoving against a crowd of high-spirited protestors, their helmets knocked askew, the sort of thing you saw on TV at picket lines in England. No one assumed by 'direct action' he meant the sectarian mayhem happening outside the walls of his university office and depriving students, Sweeney included, of their youthful freedom.

'My main purpose in teaching you,' he would go on, 'and your main purpose being here is to understand what cultural progress means.' Sweeney took such remarks as enjoyable theatre, entertaining rather than educational, but was smart enough not to let his scepticism show, and sufficiently engaged to convey an impression of intellectual solidarity. He did want to be modern, after all, and enjoyed the novels, Sillitoe, Braine, Dunn, Storey, the lot. His enthusiasm made Rod look upon him with particular favour. In conversations after class the merits of studying in Hull were made.

'Eddie, you don't want to get drawn into the toff-infested literary world of Oxford or Cambridge. Believe me, it would corrupt you. Anyway, Oxbridge dominion will soon be over.' Rod said these words with the confidence of someone believing himself on the right side of history. 'Maybe London would suit someone of your obvious talents but let me tell you something, it will feel like you're nobody, like you're studying in the academic equivalent of rush hour. It can be very alienating. Hull – and I speak from experience as you know – has a great library, Philip Larkin's doing. Lecturers are approachable, the campus is small enough to feel intimate but there's enough going on for you to get the most out of your time there. An excellent balance, if I may say so. You won't lose touch with the radical spirit which inspired us in 1968.' That last thought pleased Rod and he sat back in his chair waving away a cloud of pipe smoke.

'What's the city like?' Sweeney asked. He had images of back streets in *Saturday Night and Sunday Morning*, the multi-story car park in *Get Carter* and the pub in *Coronation Street*. He also had a vague impression of a television documentary about Larkin in Hull but the only scene he recalled was the poet riding his bicycle in a rain-sodden overcoat, trousers bicycle-clipped and passing by gravestones. It wasn't much to go on.

Rod puffed reflectively. 'You'll not find it praised by the likes of Kenneth Clark and you'll never find it in a programme like *Civilisation*. But Hull's a fine city and you'll discover it's a charming city. And the people, you'll like the people, they're unpretentious ... like Hull itself you could say.'

'Clark never came to Belfast either so I suppose I should feel at home there.'

'That's the stuff, Eddie. You can help put Hull on the new map of civilisation, the *people's* civilisation this time ... Think about it. If you want help with your application – you are going to apply for doctoral study, aren't you?'

'It seems the natural thing to do,' Sweeney replied.

Becoming what the press still liked to call a 'don' was what he considered, in moments of vague vanity, worthy of his talents. Studying was all he knew and thinking it the 'natural thing to do' also meant lack of interest in or imagination for anything else, the aspirant intellectual's incapacity for what his parents knew as 'real life'. Moreover, he couldn't help feeling flattered by Rod's encouragement and his faith in him.

'Good! When you're ready and would like some guidance, let me know.'

What Rod had said about Hull seemed to make sense. But in truth, he made no decision at all, allowing himself to be borne along by recommendation. Sweeney's personal curse of intelligence was simple. For every good reason to do or not to do something, he could imagine its equal and opposite, every choice a torment of decisions taken or not taken. So why not let fate give randomness meaning? It was as good a way to live as any, he thought. Eventually he worked up a research proposal with the title 'Imagining the North of England in Post-War Literature' and asked for Rod's advice.

GOING

As his tutor studied the handwritten pages, Sweeney said, 'You can see how I've incorporated your reading of the literature. Also, how I've taken on board your warning to avoid all the old clichés.' Rod only nodded. 'I know it needs re-worked. Any help gratefully received ...' Sweeney's voice tailed off. He worried he'd written nothing of interest.

When Rod finished, he tapped the pages with the back of his hand. 'This is very good indeed. Well done.' He shuffled the papers, handed them back and said, 'As the vet might say, you'll enjoy being doctored in Hull.' Clearly an old and well-practised line and Sweeney laughed along. 'If you decided to apply there, of course ...'

'I intend to, yes. I checked the university prospectus, the library, facilities, accommodation and all that. It looks good to me.'

'I told you. You'll fit in there well.' He paused. 'Look, if you go ahead with the application, why don't you let me take you to have a look around the campus, after your finals that is. It would give you a feel for the place. But if you think I'm pressuring you ...'

'I don't think that at all. It's a very generous offer. Thank you. And you really think my proposal is okay?'

'I made a mental note of a few changes you might make. I'll write them up. If you need a reference, put my name down.'

Sweeney incorporated Rod's suggestions, sent off the application, and was accepted provisionally without an interview, possibly on Rod's reference. He sailed through his finals, got the First everyone expected and a scholarship. The university confirmed his place at Hull. Shortly after graduation, both of them set off for Hull.

. . . .

THE LAST TRAIN TO HULL

On the dockside at Larne they sat in Rod's blue Hillman Imp waiting to board the Stranraer ferry. It was unusually warm for seven in the morning.

'It will be good to see Hull again,' Rod said. 'We'll be staying with some old friends of mine. You can come and go as you please. I've got people to see so feel free to do your own thing.'

'Thanks, I will.' Sweeney wasn't sure what that own thing would be but didn't take Rod's words as a diplomatically-phrased brush off. 'It'll give me an opportunity to look around.'

Rod told him as you get older you appreciate these little escapes from normal life. 'So don't tell my wife you heard me coming in late,' he laughed.

'You can rely on me.' And he could because Sweeney had never met Rod's wife and never expected to.

He remembered little about the journey and even less about the drive back. All that stayed in his mind was the heat. The summer of 1976 had been the hottest on record and they'd driven through a scorched landscape. Rolling down the car windows provided only temporary relief because the air blowing through made the Imp vibrate alarmingly. Anyway, Rod was convinced drafts were more dangerous to health than being boiled slowly.

'Isn't it just great being on the road, our next crazy venture beneath the skies,' Rod said with a knowing glance.

Sweeney observed the English countryside flashing by on either side of the Great North Road, fields and hills veiled in a bluish haze, animals finding shelter where they could. 'It's difficult to believe we're in England at all,' he said.

'Eddie, we gotta go and never stop going till we get there ... don't worry,' he said acknowledging Sweeney's obvious discomfort, 'we'll take plenty of breaks.' However, Rod usually found a reason for 'pushing on'.

When they arrived, it was equally difficult to believe they were in Hull. Its inhabitants seemed unable to believe it either.

GOING

The city basked and baked and it felt like the everyday had been suspended. Life had slowed, the young lingering in the sun, the old dawdling in the shade. Shoppers and office workers took the opportunity to sunbathe in Queens Gardens, rather self-consciously he felt, some lying, some sitting, shirts opened, skirts pulled up, primly though, not much thigh revealed. Strangers were happy to talk to one another. A plague of ladybirds, their red and black splashing on street signs and tree boles made an exotic contribution to a feeling of geographical otherness. 'Doing his own thing' when Rod was 'seeing some people', Sweeney was plunged into popular cheeriness, a cheeriness he later came to think distinctive of English life. At home people always talked of English reserve, of how impersonal they were, how distant. There was some truth in that quality of indifference, a quality which he didn't think a failing at all. He took it as a mark of civility. But it was only a partial truth and it wasn't his impression in those few days in Hull. He strolled about the old town in the press of cheery people, taking his time, seeking the cool of shadow, looking around. In this summer's light, nondescript buildings appeared stately, familiar storefronts colourful, everything seeming more dignified and more interesting than at home. He imagined not just him but everyone was seeing the city for the first time.

One thing Sweeney had heard of was the Land of Green Ginger. In first form English class at school they'd read a short story with that title by Algernon Blackwood. He could picture his copy of *Short Stories of the Twentieth Century* and its series title, *Heritage of Literature*. He'd liked the idea of absorbing 'heritage' as a cultural rite of passage. He couldn't remember anything about the story but their teacher had told them there was a Land of Green Ginger in Hull (even if no one knew where Hull was exactly). Maybe Blackwood's story had nothing at all to do with this shaded passage in the Old Town but Sweeney was pleased to discover the street sign. Only it wasn't the *Land* of Green Ginger. Someone, by adding a spray-painted double loop, had changed the L to a B. It had become the *Band* of Green Ginger. The po-faced side of Sweeney's character registered outrage but he had to smile as he imagined a late night sortie, two local youths, one hoisting the other on his shoulders, a quick daub, then running off laughing towards the docks. In the three years Sweeney spent in Hull, no one saw fit to restore the name to its original. Band of Green Ginger it remained, gently mocking, or so it seemed to him, affectations of 'heritage' in Hull.

He liked that self-deprecation – if that's what it was – self-deprecation as self-perception. Hull appeared unconcerned how it appeared to others. This heatwave was enough to be getting on with. The thought made Sweeney feel at ease among these people and their good cheer. It could have been anywhere that summer. It could have been Oxford. It could have been London. But it wasn't. It was Hull. And he said to himself, so be it. Hull. It must be providential.

. . . .

Finding his flat was equally providential. Rod had taken him to the campus to meet his prospective supervisor, Mr Dawson. When he'd first told him, Rod had sighed. 'Dawson is old school in every way, minor public school and Oxford. I don't know much about him. Few do seem to know much about his personal life. From what I gather, as you would say in Belfast, "he's not too bad", a sound enough academic. He is a bit of a "chap", though. You'll soon pick up on these English class distinctions.'

Dawson's major publication – so far as Sweeney could find out, his one and only publication – was a study of Evelyn Waugh's Second World War trilogy *Sword of Honour*.

GOING

Sweeney hadn't bothered to read the book but supposed he should eventually. The only review he'd found was a paragraph in *The Times Literary Supplement* devoted to a clutch of new academic publications. There he'd found that 'Dawson's *Memories of Things Like This* rarely excites but is workmanlike and though the author, a lecturer at the University of Hull, breaks no new ground it will be welcomed by readers looking for a reliable guide to Waugh's trilogy.' Sweeney thought 'workmanlike' and 'reliable' recommendation enough. He was confident of his own ability to do better.

As Rod and Sweeney walked around the university grounds, many of those compelled to be in work had escaped from indoors to congregate in small groups shaded between the walls of red brick buildings or to sit on benches around the plaza. Others lingered, as if summoning the physical effort to go further, on steps giving access to an elevated walkway joining the Students' Union with low-slung grey concrete and glass blocks comprising offices, lecture theatres and tutorial rooms. Sweeney couldn't blame anyone for their absence or their wish to abandon daily routine. It was just too hot.

Rod pointed to a window over the entrance to the Brynmor Jones Library. 'You might be lucky and get a glimpse of Larkin. He's known to observe people from his vantage point up there.'

'If I make a spectacle of myself do you think he'll put me in a poem?'

'It's not the spectacular but the commonplace which appeals to Larkin.'

The English Department's corridors were silent and deserted. In the main office, they found only one secretary on duty. She was young and slim, seemingly cool despite the heat, her long blonde hair waving in the breeze of a noisy electric fan. Sweeney registered her smooth creamy skin and blue eyes. She seemed glad of their interruption.

'Are you here to see someone?'

She was obviously new for Rod had to introduce himself. 'And this is Edward Sweeney.' Rod put his hand paternally on Sweeney's back. 'He's taking up a postgraduate studentship in the department. It would be good if he could have a word with Mr Dawson.'

She looked directly at Sweeney. What was the expression his French school teacher Miss Bell had mentioned? *Coup de foudre?*

'Oh dear, I'm sorry. I have a message for you. Mr Dawson sends his apologies.' With long red-polished nails she drew from under a telephone, perched on its raised pivot, a pencilled page. She laid it carefully on top of a typewriter from which the grey dust cover hadn't been removed.

'Mr Dawson called to say he's delayed in London,' she said as she placed a finger on the lines of explanation. 'He was attending a function at the Waugh Society yesterday evening.' She looked to them for confirmation they had understood so far and looked down again at the note. 'Mr Dawson says he intended to take the early train and meet Mr Sweeney for lunch.' She paused to decipher her handwriting. 'Unexpectedly something has come up and he has to attend this morning's AGM.' She looked at them once more to make sure this made sense. 'He regrets the change of plan.'

At this point she looked again at Sweeney – not, he thought, to estimate intellectual potential but to appraise his looks. At least, he hoped she had. Did he detect in her glance an intimation of approval? He liked to think her eyes conveyed a judgment of 'not bad'. That was all the endorsement he needed for now. 'Mr Dawson', she went on, 'liked the proposal and looks forward to Mr Sweeney getting doctored in due course.' When they laughed, the secretary looked worried as if she'd made a mistake.

'Sorry,' Rod apologised for both of them. He asked her name.

'Julie,' she said.

'Julie, Mr Dawson is making a silly academic joke.' He said this so sweetly, so flirtatiously, Sweeney suspected his tutor, like him, was hooked. He felt an absurdly competitive urge as well as moral censure – a married man indeed!

'Ah, I see.' Julie smiled vaguely and continued to read out another line of banal apology.

Sweeney wasn't listening to what was being said. He couldn't care less about Dawson now. He was charmed by Julie's Hull accent, flat like the East Yorkshire landscape but flowing like the Humber tides, convinced life in Hull would be good. He associated it with this young woman, like he associated London with Twiggy.

The main purpose of the day gone, Rod suggested Sweeney should look around the campus while he went to see someone in another faculty. They arranged to meet up again at the office an hour later. Sweeney thought he'd breeze around the bookshop and Students' Union and return early to chat with Julie. His day had new meaning. He considered Dawson's non-appearance providential.

In the bookshop no customers browsed. Even with its doors fully opened the atmosphere was stifling and a few staff fussed around lethargically and, it seemed, resentfully. He asked a thin middle-aged woman in a green linen dress and sandals, glasses hanging from a cord around her neck, if Dawson's book was available. She conducted Sweeney to shelves of literary criticism, pointed to three copies and left without saying a word. The effort seemed to exhaust her. He took down one hardback and flicked through pages liberally padded with passages from either Waugh's trilogy or from commentaries on it. Workmanlike indeed, he thought. If Dawson had got his manuscript into print with a reputable publisher then Sweeney judged his own chances of writing a decent thesis equally good. With that encouraging wager on his talent, he wandered out without buying. Dawson's book he could read in the library, certain his future supervisor had ordered multiple copies.

The Union next door was as somnolent and vacant of activity as the bookshop but at least it was cooler. Passing along dim hallways Sweeney scanned noticeboards where only the ragged debris of the past academic year remained – notifications about Student Council meetings, an International Marxist Group debate on 'The Crisis of Capitalism' and some sports team sheets pinned but not removed. Nothing of interest detained him. From the shuttered bowels of the building he detected the faint but unmistakeable aroma of stale beer, lingering long after students had gone. Finding a shop still open, he bought himself a packet of Embassy Regal and climbed the stairs again onto the elevated walkway. Stopping by the metal railings, he took a cigarette, fished in his trouser pocket for matches and lit up. Below him was a neat area of grass toasted by weeks of relentless sun, the earth around saplings parched and cracked. Beyond it in the half empty car park, windscreens of Morris Marinas and Austin Allegros reflected blindingly, making him squint, while roofs and bonnets appeared to shimmer. He retreated to what little shade there was and leaned against the wall. Smoking idly, he thought once more of Julie. He checked his watch. Half an hour had passed. He pushed himself from the wall, flicked the butt nonchalantly, and walked back to the department. If he was lucky – and today he did feel lucky – he would have Julie's company to himself.

. . . .

The office door was wedged open and he could see her attending to papers in the drawer of a filing cabinet. Sweeney stood and watched for a few seconds as her red T-shirt rippled slightly in the breeze of the fan. She was singing to herself as she worked. Above the fan's hum he could hear faintly the words of Candy Staton's 'Young Hearts Run Free', one of the summer hits. As Sweeney listened, charmed by the voice, he thought the lyrics too sad for someone as perfect as Julie.

'Sorry, it's me again,' he said. She stopped singing, turned her head towards him, one hand holding a sheaf of papers and the other marking the appropriate space in the drawer. Strands of blonde hair blew across her eyes.

'Just a moment please … Mr Sweeney.'

She'd remembered. 'Edward,' he replied, 'you can call me Edward … or Eddie.'

She smiled with the same appraising look as before and finished what she was doing. 'I'm glad you're back so soon. Raymond has been looking for you. He'd like to have a word.'

Sweeney was mystified. 'Is he a member of staff?'

'No, Raymond Blanche, one of our research students.'

'I see. Is it important do you think?' He'd never heard of Raymond Blanche and had no idea why he should want to talk to him. He wanted to talk to Julie.

'Everything's important for Raymond,' she laughed. There was a tolerant inflection to her reply which Sweeney considered another challenge. 'He says he's in a bit of a rush and would you mind popping in to see him.'

'Do you know what it's about?'

'I don't know,' she said, her words drawn out languidly. 'It's best you ask him.' He wasn't sure if these words were dismissive. She gestured with the palm of her hand. 'He's in the postgrad room which is three doors along the corridor on your right.'

'I suppose I'd better see what he wants. I didn't know my fame had preceded me,' he joked but she looked unsure if he was being serious or not. 'By the way, I do appreciate all your help, Julie.'

He detected a recovery of interest because of the compliment but before she could reply, the phone rang. Turning to go he heard her answer, 'Hello? Nooo, this is Julie. Jan's at home today. Sorry, Jo's away n'all.' She said this with a hint of resentment suggesting Julie wanted to be away at home too.

The postgrad door was shut. Sweeney could hear someone moving about, dragging an object across the floor. He thought it best to knock.

A voice called out, 'You may enter'.

Pushing open the door he saw a plump young man of medium height, light brown hair, thinning already on top, with a neatly trimmed beard. He was wearing a checked blue and white short-sleeved shirt, his plumpness straining against the buttons, a pair of knee-length white shorts and brown leather sandals with no socks. Around his neck was a blue spotted silk cravat, reminding Sweeney of the sort of thing his mother used to wear at the seaside. However, this neckerchief, unlike his mother's, looked expensive and, equally unlike his mother's, a fashion item. The noise Sweeney heard had been the dragging of a large and well-stocked cricket bag – he could see in it bat, pads, gloves, jumper and whites – in the course of which a plastic chair had been knocked over. The struggle with the bag and chair had brought a little colour to the man's pasty cheeks. Sweeney felt his competitive instincts relax. He couldn't imagine Blanche, if this were Blanche, being the object of Julie's desire.

'You are the new man, I take it? Raymond Blanche, pleased to meet you.' Sweeney had expected the accent to be aristocratic but it was Middle England of uncertain geographical provenance – but not Rod's Brummy tones – middle class and well-educated. He wasn't from Hull that was for sure. 'Do come in, do come in.'

'Edward Sweeney, pleased to meet you too.' They shook hands.

GOING

'You're from Belfast, aren't you? We're familiar with the accent these days, of course. You've chosen to take a few years RnR with us, I see, getting away from all the mayhem? I can't say I blame you.' Sweeney was waiting for an addition of 'old boy' but it didn't come. 'It can't be much fun,' Blanche continued. 'You'll find life better here on the mother ship.'

Sweeney had never heard that description before. 'Julie told me you had something important to discuss?'

'Ah, Julie, you don't need good weather like this for Julie to brighten your day, now do you?' Blanche appeared to take Sweeney's silence as assent. 'Yes, indeed … lovely girl. Well, let's just say my proposal could be – no, *would* be – beneficial for you and for me.'

Sweeney, none the wiser, felt obliged to say, 'That sounds intriguing. I'm all ears.'

Blanche smiled at the expression, walked behind his desk and sat on an upholstered swivel chair. There were three other desks in the graduate room with signs of occupancy, a book here, a box file there, but only Blanche's had a comfortable chair. The rest had to make do with the sort of moulded plastic seat his cricket bag had knocked over.

'Do have a seat,' he said and indicated the fallen chair.

Sweeney righted it and tested its stability before sitting. The man's presumptuous behaviour was beginning to irritate him but something beneficial might be worth his remaining civil. Noticing a glass ashtray on his desk sitting atop a neat pile of photocopied articles, he offered Blanche a cigarette.

'Thank you, no.' Blanche put up his hands. 'I only smoke Sobranie Black Russian. I'm being disciplined this morning. I've had my after breakfast one. As you can see,' he indicated the cricket bag, 'I have a match this afternoon.' He laughed. 'My self-denial is the only training regime I need.' He took an exaggerated breath and exhaled slowly. 'But please, do smoke.' He

15

pushed the spotless ashtray across the desktop towards Sweeney. 'Thank you. Sure you won't have one?'

'I'm sure.' Blanche eyed warily the packet of Embassy Regal. Sweeney pictured Blanche in a few years' time when youthful 'plump' would have become middle-aged 'portly'. He was well on the way already. It did seem his natural destiny and would complement Blanche's old-fashioned manner of speaking. At least it seemed old-fashioned to Sweeney. Then again, it might be an English class thing.

'I was on the point of leaving,' Blanche went on, 'so I will, as they say, cut to the chase.' He smiled benevolently and picked up one of the pens arranged neatly on a decorative oblong plastic dish printed with the Hull University logo. Beside it was a framed photograph of Blanche in graduation gown and mortarboard, proudly showing off his degree certificate. There was also a tea mug with a stylised picture of an English country cottage, a sheepdog asleep on its porch. Blanche seemed the sort to make himself feel at home.

'First a question – have you arranged accommodation yet?' He tapped the pen once against the palm of his hand.

'No, I haven't. I believe the university arranges something for new students? I'm still waiting details.'

Blanche leaned back in his chair dismissively. 'Believe *me*,' he said, tapping the pen vigorously, 'you do not want to put any faith in what they will offer. Most likely you'll be placed in a shared room at some student house on the Avenues or Cranbrook here.' He waved his pen loosely in the direction of somewhere off-campus. 'It's a lottery and you may draw the short straw of some loud-mouthed lout. Imagine being woken at two in the morning. Imagine someone staggering in like a madman doing the guitar riff from "Smoke on the Water".' Blanche shuddered as if recalling a bad memory. 'Or horror of horrors they could ship you up the road to Cottingham and shove you in The Lawns.' Blanche waved in the opposite direction. 'You'll feel like you're in an army barracks and you don't want that, do you?' He smiled knowingly. 'You can't imagine the number of students who go AWOL up there.' He shuddered once more. 'No, you most certainly do *not-want-that*' and tapped the pen at each word.

As Blanche spoke, Sweeney remembered *Carry On Sergeant*, a Nissen hut and a wind-swept parade ground, and suppressed a shudder himself. And he'd never considered the possibility of having to share a room with a noisy, possibly football-obsessed, or even worse, heavy metal-obsessed, youth. And now that he did consider it, no, he did *not* want either of these things.

'If you put it that way …'

'I do. It is a real possibility.' Blanche's face conveyed how uncertain life could be. Then it conveyed hope. 'Here's my proposition. I know you might think it a little sight unseen, maybe a bit of a pig in a poke,' he continued, as if no one would ever think such a thing, 'but my flat will be free by September – you are coming over in September, aren't you?'

'I am, yes.'

'It's no Mayfair apartment but I can assure you it's in a decent big house, a self-contained flat mind you, first floor, large living room, adjacent kitchen, comfortable bedroom, decent bathroom and your neighbours are quiet. They won't bother you.' He cleared his throat. 'They're interesting too in their own way. We all get along terribly well.'

'Are they students?'

'They are alumni of this great institution. The chap at the front is an aspiring novelist. The couple at the back, let's say, are enjoying un-married bliss.'

As Blanche seemed to reflect on what such bliss could be, Sweeney asked, 'Where is this flat?'

'It's on Park Road, do you know it?'

Sweeney shook his head. 'I haven't got my bearings in Hull yet.'

'Well, it's just about as convenient as you can get. And by that I mean it's half way between the campus and the town centre, only fifteen minutes' walk, either way – well, if you put an inch to your step. Plenty of shops nearby, Pearson Park right next door – Larkin lived there until recently, you know – and there are good pubs around to choose from ... well some are better than others. You'll soon find one to your own taste.' He had been tapping his palm for each of these selling points and when he'd finished, set the pen delicately back in place, perfectly aligning it with the others. 'What do you say? Would you be interested?'

The offer had been unexpected and Sweeney was uncomfortable with surprises. There was a silence. His reticence may have suggested to Blanche there was a hardman side to Sweeney which needed appeasing or a business-like side which needed convincing. He put both of his palms on the desk.

'Look, truth to tell, you would be doing me a big favour – as well as getting yourself a topping place to live. My lease runs to the end of the year – I anticipated taking an extra few months to finish my thesis – but I've bagged the job I really want. It's with the British Council – in London, of course. They want me to start as soon as possible and let's say it puts me in something of a bind.' He grimaced. 'My landlady Mrs Herdecka, she's a bit of a tough cookie, Polish you know, takes no prisoners as it were, but she's actually being rather decent about it.' His tone modified to the slightly pleading. 'The thing is, if I can get someone to take the flat from September she'll not keep my deposit or, God help me, make me pay the months to Christmas. As you can imagine, life in London will be much more expensive than here.'

Blanche adjusted his cravat slightly as if imagining himself being hung out to dry financially, those Russian cigarettes denied him. He was a man, Sweeney judged, who liked his

GOING

luxuries, a thought which predisposed him to say yes to his proposal. He couldn't believe, looking at the neat row of pens in the dish, that twee teacup, the upholstered chair, his cravat, Blanche would live anywhere unwholesome.

'Before I say yes, what sort of rent are we talking about?'

'It's £36 a month. You'll not do any better in university accommodation. And if you can get yourself a few teaching hours in the department – they're always trying to offload first year classes in the name of giving you experience – you'll not make much of a hole in your grant either. You'll be able to live very comfortably indeed – as I have.'

'And if I do say yes, how do I go about arranging everything?'

He could see Blanche felt he'd done the deal. 'You don't have to worry about a thing, not a blessed thing. Leave all the details to me. I'll be obliged to you.' He leaned forward. 'I'll put in a word with Mrs Herdecka, sort out all the bibs and bobs and get her to post the paperwork, pronto. I know from experience you'll want these things in place as soon as possible – for peace of mind that is.' Sweeney scrutinised Blanche for hints of sharp practice. He couldn't spot any. He was innocent of tenancy and its obligations but he supposed the landlady, if she was as tough as Blanche claimed, wouldn't let Blanche slip out of his contract if there was a problem. He looked to providence to favour him once more.

'Okay, let Mrs Herdecka know I will take the flat.' He stubbed out his Embassy Regal, dizzy at his unaccustomed decisiveness.

'Marvellous! Good man! May I call you Edward?' Sweeney nodded, thinking Eddie would be too common. Blanche put his hand to his chest. 'And call me Raymond. I've spent happy years in Park Road, Edward, and I'm sure you will too. Shall we call our arrangement a gentlemen's agreement for now?'

'Let's do that,' Sweeney replied. After all, that's exactly what it was.

Blanche stood up, came around the desk and shook hands again, more firmly this time. His palm was surprisingly cool and dry.

Sweeney asked for the number of the house. 'Just for my records, Raymond,' he said. But he intended to ask Rod to drive him there to look it over, at least from the outside. If there was a 'side' to Sweeney's character it was a suspicious one.

Blanche tore a page from his desk pad and handed it to Sweeney to write down his own contact details. Glancing at the address, folding the page carefully and putting it into a drawer, he murmured, 'Better keep it safe and sound.' Both of them faced one another across the desk. 'Well,' said Blanche more loudly than Sweeney expected, 'that was a very good morning's work.'

'For both of us, I hope.'

'Have no worries on that score. And now, Edward, I must dash. I'm opening the batting and need to get in a few practice shots before the start of play.' He grabbed his bag, staggering for a step as he lifted it. 'By the way, you don't happen to play cricket, do you?'

Sweeney had played cricket at school, a 'make up the team' nonentity who couldn't bowl or couldn't bat but who was reasonably nimble in the outfield, saving runs rather than scoring them. Like Oscar Wilde he considered cricket a form of organised loafing. He was partial to loafing but could think of better ways to loaf than cricket.

'I'm a bit of an all-rounder,' he lied.

'Good show, I can recommend a few decent clubs if you like.' Sweeney's look implied a lack of interest. 'No matter, there's always the annual staff-student match, always great fun. Just watch out for Dawson smuggling in a ringer or two.'

'And what's your opinion of Dawson? He's down to be my supervisor.'

'He's a decent enough old stick. I can't say he's an outstanding scholar but he's, well, workmanlike you might say.' Sweeney noted that word again. He pulled the door open for Blanche to struggle through. 'Thank you, Edward. It's been a pleasure.' They were now outside in the hallway and Blanche stopped. 'Just one word of advice, don't expect Dawson to be all that diligent. Let's say you might find him a little hard to pin down.'

'I have noticed that.'

'Splendid! You're getting the hang of the place already.' Blanche headed off down the corridor, bag in hand, raised his free arm in farewell and, without turning his head, called out, 'You won't regret taking the flat. I'll be in touch anon.'

. . . .

When Sweeney got back to the departmental office, Julie was gone. A typewritten note pinned to the door read, 'The office is closed for lunch and will re-open at 2pm.' He pictured Julie sitting somewhere alone, eating a meagre sandwich. He wanted to rescue her, to make her happy, to make her feel wanted, and knew he was foolishly stricken.

'Seen all you want to see?' Rod asked when he met him lounging in the corridor.

'I have, yes. And I seem to have got myself somewhere to live too.'

'Is that so?' Rod took a step back. 'No, please don't tell me you're moving in with Julie? You are a fast worker.' Winking, he nudged Sweeney's arm.

If only, thought Sweeney. 'No. I met someone called Raymond Blanche who's just got a job in London. He needs to offload his flat as soon as possible.' He feared Rod might think him rash. 'It's only a gentleman's agreement so I'm not committed. I can always back out.'

'Old Raymondo! I forgot he'd still be here. We overlapped

for a while. He was starting his research as I was finishing. Is he in the postgrad room?'

'He went off to play cricket a few minutes ago. Do you think I can trust him?'

'Raymondo will be a suitable candidate for re-education come the revolution. We will have to reform his bourgeois habits.' Rod chuckled at the thought. 'To answer your question, he's as straight as they come ... is it the old place on Park Road?'

'Yes, Park Road.'

'I used to live on Park Grove, which connects with it.' Rod made a T-junction with his hands. 'We shared the same landlady.'

'Mrs Herdecka, the Polish woman?'

'That's her, the very same. What a stroke of luck you've had! We can drive by if you like. It's memory lane stuff for me.' Rod looked at his watch. 'Let's go now. Afterwards we'll find a pub. What do you say?' He slapped Sweeney on the shoulder and guided him gently along the corridor. 'I'll introduce you to your first Hull tradition, drinking at lunchtime.'

So, on that day in the heatwave of 1976, they braved again the metal furnace of the Hillman Imp, seats scorching their backs and legs as they drove down Newland Avenue, the air thick with exhaust fumes. At Pearson Park, Rod took a detour for Sweeney to see where he'd live for the next three years.

'I love this area,' Rod said, his voice almost breaking with emotion, his eyes moist.

What Sweeney saw was a row of down-at-heel Victorian terraced villas, desperately clinging to vestiges of former respectability. Yet in the early afternoon haze these houses appeared softened, mellowed, like a Renoir street painting, inviting him to wonder.

PART TWO

Here

CHAPTER TWO

A few weeks after his return to Belfast a letter arrived from Blanche telling Sweeney arrangements for the flat had gone *swimmingly*. There was no need to worry about bringing domestic *chattels*, they were all included, pots, pans, kettle, *the whole kit and caboodle*. There were added details about gas and electricity. *When you arrive*, Blanche wrote, *ring the bell for Pearl and Simon. It's the only bell that works so you can't go wrong. If you can be bothered, ask Mrs Herdecka to fix yours. It never caused me any problem. Roland isn't concerned about his – he's your other neighbour on the ground floor – for he never has anyone calling. By choice, I hasten to add. He's writing the great novel de nos jours or says he is. Interesting fellow (I wouldn't want to give you the wrong impression). Apologies for the digression. I will leave your keys – front door and flat – with Pearl. Make sure you get there before 8 o'clock to be on the safe side. She and Simon are keen bridge players and seem to play most nights. Remarkable dedication if you ask me. They're both marvellous. You will get on splendidly.*

As Sweeney read the letter he wondered if the British Council required its staff to write and speak like Blanche. It reminded him of the public school argot in the *Jennings* stories (which he disliked), overly mannered as well as overly chummy. Did people abroad still expect the representative voice of the country to sound like this?

The letter concluded, *I have left you my duvet (dry-cleaned, naturally). It will make life so much easier – you only have to take the cover to the launderette.*

Sweeney had never heard of a duvet and had never visited a launderette. He looked up the meaning of duvet. It sounded *chic*, modern, befitting his aspirant status of a bohemian intellectual. Perhaps Blanche wasn't such an old fogey after all. He noted a home address in Worcester, pleased to have the location of Blanche's middle Englishness. Shortly after this letter, he received a brief message from Mrs Herdecka asking him to acknowledge *by return* his tenancy with a request for a deposit of £36 *herewith*. Attached to the note was a typewritten page, constituting a lease for twelve months *renewable*, which he was required to sign *as per instruction*. His landlady's language wasn't Blanche's at all.

. . . .

'So that's it then?' his mother asked.

'That's it, no pulling out now,' he replied.

She enquired about the 'chattels'.

'The flat has everything I need. And you can trust me to cook for myself.' He'd mastered the basics, the rest he would improvise.

'Do you have towels, bedding, that sort of thing?'

'Not sure about towels, better take some along, tea towels too if you can spare any. The previous tenant left his duvet.' He had to explain to her what it was.

Duvet appeared an uncomfortable reminder her son was leaving for a strange new world. After a brief silence she added, 'You'd better buy a pair of pyjamas. Make sure they are good and warm.'

Sweeney had abandoned pyjamas. He considered them old fashioned. No one in those French *avant garde* films he'd watched ever wore pyjamas. He couldn't imagine anyone truly modern in a pair but mumbled assurance anyway. He never bothered and, in the end, his mother had bought a pair of heavy red and black flannel ones and, still in their Marks and Spencer packaging, slipped them into his suitcase without saying a word.

'So that's it then?' It was his father this time.

HERE

'More or less,' Sweeney said as he carried down from his bedroom a brown faux-leather suitcase and yellow nylon, metal-framed, rucksack.

'All your worldly goods safely stowed? Here, I'll take the suitcase, you take the rucksack and we'll stick them in the car.'

A cigarette hung from his father's lips and he squinted to avoid the smoke. He was driving his son to the docks for the overnight ferry to Liverpool. The weather was miserable, a stiff breeze and the clouds ominously dark. Rain had fallen heavily all day.

'You'll need your sea legs tonight, Eddie.'

'It was your idea to travel on Saturday to avoid the football crowd.'

'It was and I'm right.'

His father took a last drag before flicking the butt into the gutter where it drifted in rainwater towards the grating. He shoved the case into the boot of the second – or was it third? – hand Hillman Hunter, a troublesome car, prone to stalling and unpredictable when starting. Sweeney hoped there would be no problem tonight.

'Don't look so worried. I tried the engine a while ago. I told your mother we have to make sure we get rid of you.'

His mother closed the front door of their terraced house, double checked the lock as she always did and slid into the back seat beside the rucksack, shaking raindrops from her hair. 'Now you're certain you have everything?'

'Yes, mum. Shall we head on?'

His father turned the key in the ignition. The engine spluttered. They looked at one other. The key was turned again and the engine fired into life. His father revved the engine like he was about to race. 'What did I tell you? Car's running like a dream.'

His mother said, 'Okay James Hunt, you heard the boy. Let's head on.'

THE LAST TRAIN TO HULL

. . . .

Their farewell at the dock was undemonstrative. They were not a family to make a show in public. They didn't do that in private either. An undramatic people, their culture associated sincerity with a still small voice.

His mother gave him a quick hug, no kisses and, suppressing tears, told him to come home if he didn't like it, to eat properly, to call if there was any trouble, to write as often as he could. 'Postcards would be nice. We don't even know what Hull looks like. At least you'll be safer in Hull than here. This place has gone crazy.'

He closed his eyes in agreement to all requests. 'I will.'

His father held back, letting his wife do emotion. As Sweeney was about to turn away, he said, 'Hang on.' He offered his son a Gallaher Blue. He'd always said you have to earn the right to smoke 'a quality cigarette' and used to tell Sweeney he hadn't earned it yet. 'If you want one, buy your own.'

Unfiltered brands weren't fashionable any longer. They were the choice of an older generation. His father's refusal to share – and he was a generous man – was one of those comic rituals of family life. Sweeney took one from the proffered pack, lit it and inhaled.

'It was worth waiting for,' he said.

'Look after yourself, son.'

And that was it. They turned, he turned, they were gone and he was gone.

Sweeney boarded The Ulster Queen and lingered at the railing on the deck. So this is what departure is like, he thought – rain clouds lowering over hills, oily scum on the water between quayside and ship, floating debris, twisted shapes of wood, a child's soft toy which had been in the water so long it was almost unrecognisable, hawsers and ropes on the quayside coated in slimy sheen. He entered through the main hatchway. The damp, tangy, sea air was replaced by stale on-board warmth and by odours of polish, metal, paint, disinfectant, diesel, fried food and, very faintly, of vomit.

He had saved money by not booking a cabin and sat in a row of high-backed orange vinyl seats. Leaving the shelter of Belfast Lough and heading into the Irish Sea, the engines of The Ulster Queen throbbed louder, the roll of the boat became more pronounced, the bulkheads shuddered, the fittings vibrated noticeably, the deck swelling and falling. Sweeney felt only a mild queasiness which thankfully never crossed the border into nausea. He tried to sleep, attempting to ignore the ship's pitching and creaking, thinking of Julie again, imagining the look of recognition in her face when he returned, their meeting later as she waited for a bus, inviting her for a drink, her hesitant acceptance. They would sit together in a crowded bar, Julie saying she was late and really had to run, he walking her to the bus stop, asking if she would like to go out together some evening and Julie would say yes. His father liked to croon 'I'm a Dreamer, aren't we all?' Sweeney thought how right he was but chose to ignore the line 'And I'm a fool, aren't we all?'.

. . . .

In a busy café in Manchester Piccadilly, he was waiting for his connection to Hull. The Ulster Queen had docked in Liverpool at six. He had been questioned about his destination and purpose by a detective, obviously irked to be on duty so early on a Sunday morning. Sweeney's face fitted the profile of a likely terrorist, young male with moustache, longish dark hair, of slight build, medium height, apparently innocuous but travelling alone. When he showed his letter from the university confirming a studentship at Hull, the detective had waved him through dismissively.

Later, buying his train ticket at Lime Street Station, he was told by the booking clerk there were delays on the line and he would have to wait. 'Take the next available Manchester train. Change there for Hull,' the man mumbled and yawned. He probably resented working so early on a Sunday morning too.

In Manchester the Hull train was also delayed. Seated at a rickety wooden table, on an uncomfortable wooden chair, Sweeney nursed the dregs of a cup of tea gone cold. He pretended to sip, worried he'd be thrown out, for his suitcase and rucksack forced other customers to negotiate awkwardly around him. He'd ordered a meat pie with his tea. It had been tasteless and left an unpleasant soapy aftertaste. The din of the Piccadilly concourse muscled in every time the café door opened. The accents he heard were new to him. Mancunian, Lancastrian, they sounded harsher than those in Hull.

'Is this seat taken?' It was a middle-aged man in a beige raincoat, the fabric greying with age, its cuffs mottled with a mixture of grease and grime, its shoulders damp with rain. Columbo, Sweeney thought at first, but no – Colombo had a good head of hair and looked tanned. This man was balding and overweight. He had a pale, jowly face with broken veins on cheeks and his chin showing traces of blood congealed after shaving. Columbo always had a cigar. This man had a bar of KitKat.

'No, it's free.' Sweeney felt obliged to add apologetically, 'I was just about to go.'

The man sat down heavily and put a cup of coffee on the table.

'Is that a Scottish accent?'

'No, I'm from Northern Ireland … Belfast.'

'I see, from over there.' He ripped the paper wrapping from his KitKat, laid the chocolate wafers delicately in their opened foil, took out a handkerchief and loudly blew his nose. As he did so, he looked directly at Sweeney as if to say, this is what I think of Northern Ireland. He put his handkerchief back in his pocket and sniffed.

'And where are you off to?' The man nodded at Sweeney's luggage.

'I'm going to Hull. If and when I can get a train, that is. All these delays drive you mad, don't they?' He wanted to divert onto safe conversational territory, be it weather, British Rail, anything but the Troubles.

'Let me get this straight. You are leaving one godforsaken place and going to another? Well, well, that's the best thing I've heard in a long while.' The man laughed and shook his head. It wasn't playfulness, though, it was bitterness. An air of resentment clung to him, a history of failure and disappointment, Sweeney imagined, and it wouldn't have surprised him if he was always on the look-out for opportunities to take revenge on a hostile world. Today Sweeney was his opportunity.

'What are you intending to do in Hull?'

'I'm going to university there.'

'Now I've heard it all.' He slapped the table with the palm of his hand. 'You are going there by choice? Is this some kind of Irish joke? Frank Carson couldn't do any better. You've actually *chosen* to go to Hull? That's a cracker!' He said the phrase in a terrible Belfast accent and then looked around to see if anyone else in the café appreciated his wit. No one had taken any notice.

Sweeney told himself not to be provoked. Better such prejudice, if that's what it was, should take the form of a bad joke than a punch in the face. And what was the point of taking offence at every offhand remark or barbed comment? In England he wanted to be Edward Sweeney and not 'that guy from Belfast with a chip on his shoulder'. He had warned himself against becoming some sort of stage Ulsterman. Some fates were unconscionable.

'Name me one good thing that ever came out of Hull? Go on, name me one thing?' The man snapped his KitKat, pointing a wafer at Sweeney.

Only Philip Larkin came to mind, but Larkin, Sweeney knew, wasn't *from* Hull. He couldn't think of anything or anyone and stayed silent. A smug look appeared on the man's face as he put a piece of wafer in his mouth.

This calculated rudeness unsettled Sweeney. He felt defeated, humiliated, and made a hasty, awkward escape. Outside the café, he smoked to calm his nerves. As a porter walked by, he asked about his Hull connection.

'Should be leaving from Platform Three,' the porter said, looking up at the station clock, 'in twenty minutes.'

Sweeney didn't like the sound of 'should be'. Fortunately, 'should be' turned out to be 'was'.

. . . .

The carriages rattled out of Manchester across an industrial landscape of rail sidings lined with goods wagons, vast sheds of brick, metal and glass, factories, some of which stood derelict, fenced yards filled with junk and scrap metal, row upon row of terraced housing, now and then high-rise apartment blocks. They passed leafy suburbs and verdant parks becoming ribbon developments of semi-detached homes interspersed with supermarkets and car parks. In open country, the distinctive shape of power-station cooling towers could be seen, their emissions white against dark clouds.

Such sights were supposed to depress the spirit. Yet Sweeney could never appreciate England as a land of thatched cottages in quaint hamlets around greens with ducks on the pond. England to him meant something different. To him England represented progress, energy and industry. England was urban, England was science, England was motorways, and England was … well, modern. That's what he thought and that's what he wanted to be – modern. It was the reason he was here. If this was the filthy tide Irish romantics loathed, Sweeney was happy to float along with it.

It was late afternoon when the train began to track east towards the Humber Estuary. The day was fading, lights were on and rain fell steadily. The landscape here was different, flat, in places criss-crossed by drainage ditches, fields neat, tidy, and much larger than at home. He saw horses in waterproof coats grazing serenely in white-fenced paddocks, every now and then limestone churches standing prominently between hamlets shielded by ranks of trees, the odd tower flying the Cross of Saint George. In the far distance was a gathering of yet more cooling towers, unrepentantly secular in this, God's own country. And the sky – the sky seemed vast, shifting patterns of white, grey and black extending forever.

Suddenly, out of nowhere, Sweeney felt a rising anxiety. The words of the man in Manchester Piccadilly returned to mock his ambitions. The further the train travelled, the more distant his destination seemed. It was a ridiculous unease, he knew, and yet it possessed him. On the drive here with Rod he'd been unaware of this apparent endlessness, this terrible far-off-ness. He glimpsed the bullying Humber, dirty brown, its currents and eddies rippling across mud flats, struggling against one another, edging banks of scrub and wind-blown bush as it hurried to the North Sea. Land, sky, river, misted in rain, seemed to envelop him in a fog of insecurity. Larkin-land … he was in Larkin-land, swerving to the solitude of a city not his own. It wasn't homesickness he felt. It was self-doubt. It was fear of freedom, awareness that the independence he desired required worldly responsibility, a self-assurance he knew he didn't yet possess and feared he never would.

THE LAST TRAIN TO HULL

Then Hull appeared unexpectedly as the train rushed past warehouses, industrial buildings, waste ground, running by backs of terraced housing, a pub close to a level crossing, cars, cyclists, and pedestrians waiting to cross. He picked out the Royal Infirmary, a multi-story building of concrete and glass, its lights shining, its honeycomb slab dominating the surrounding streets. As the engine slowed and carriages swayed across a network of points, passengers stood up, gathered belongings from luggage racks and prepared to leave, heads lowered as if in prayer.

On the gable wall of a house Sweeney glimpsed a faded whitewashed advertisement for Tupper's Gloves and Hosiery. The name made him think of Anchor Alley under the railway arches and of his childhood hero from *The Victor*, Alf 'Tough of the Track' Tupper. Alf was hard as nails, a welder by trade, a runner for love, training on fish and chips wrapped in the sports pages of the local newspaper. Here was a sign, he imagined, a providential sign. His self-doubts – he would run them down, just like Alf did. It stilled his anxiety, almost. A signal box announced Hull Paragon and the train pulled into the station under an iron and glass canopy. It was the end of the line.

Evening was giving way to night, pavements wet and gutters awash, rainwater glistening under street lights. In his letter Blanche had provided directions. *When you leave the station, go onto Ferensway and head towards the junction of Spring Bank and Beverley Road. You can't miss it. There's little you can miss in Hull! Go up Beverley Road until you reach Cave Street. Turn left and in a skip and a jump you will be chez moi. Rather, chez toi.* Sweeney stood for a while and watched traffic filter along the streets. Only the swish of tyres and the rough sound of a diesel locomotive powering out of the station disturbed the quiet. It had stopped raining. He decided to walk.

In July's heatwave Hull had been an impressionist painting of people, buildings and trees, soft and flowing with colour. How different everything was in September. The season had turned. Everything appeared sharp, harsh and monochrome, a Hull folded into itself, mourning for that lost summer. Rain began to fall again. The suitcase was more awkward to carry than he imagined. Park Road seemed far off. Be like Alf, Sweeney said to himself, keep going, and be like Alf. The season will turn again.

. . . .

Blanche was right. Only one doorbell was lit. A white paper strip behind transparent plastic announced Pearl Spencer and Simon Rhodes. He decided there and then never to ask if she was the 'Pearly Spencer' in the David McWilliams song. No doubt she'd been asked many times. From the flat on the ground floor, its front window hidden from the street by a tall, bedraggled hedge, Sweeney could hear soft rhythms of modern jazz, punctuated by high-pitched saxophone tones. He pressed the button but heard no ringing. He wasn't sure if this bell was broken as well or inaudible from the doorstep. He looked at his watch. It was half-past six. Surely Pearl and Simon hadn't gone out already? He was about to ring again when he heard slippers slapping along the hallway. No light went on but the lock turned and someone struggled with the door, its bottom edge sticking to the tiles. After a couple of tugs, the door swung open more violently than expected.

He made out the shape of a woman in her late twenties, maybe early thirties, about his own height, dressed in a full-length, navy-blue satin robe that she was holding together at the waist. Her hair was unkempt and her face without make-up. Blanche would have probably have described her state as *au naturel*. She was good-looking. Even in this light Sweeney could see that. He was momentarily speechless, not only thrown by her appearance but also uncomfortable that Pearl – for he thought it couldn't be anyone other than she – would interpret his stare as indecent.

She didn't give him time to introduce himself. Noticing the suitcase by his feet, she pointed. 'You're our new neighbour, aren't you? Don't tell me, don't tell me.' She put a hand to her chin, looking upwards and finally directly at him. She clicked her fingers, appearing greatly pleased. 'You're Edward, right?'

Sweeney coughed. 'Yes, Edward, or Eddie, either will do, I don't mind.'

'Eddie, it is then. And I'm Pearl. But then you probably knew that already. I take it Raymond told you all about us, Simon and me that is.'

He might have replied it would be beyond Blanche's ability to describe Pearl but he didn't, of course. What he said was, 'I'm very sorry to intrude on your evening like this.' He thought he should start off with polite formality, unsure of English ways, even if Pearl didn't seem the formal type.

'Come in. Come in. We can't have you standing outside on a night like this,' Pearl said, glancing past him at the gloom and rain. 'It's your home now as well, after all.'

'Thank you, yes, I suppose it is.'

She pushed the door closed with difficulty. 'It's the weather,' she explained. 'The wood must have swollen in the wet. That Denis Howell certainly did his job, didn't he? Imagine this country wanting rain!' Pearl's tone suggested it wasn't her wish at all.

'I know. It's a nasty evening,' Sweeney replied, wiping raindrops from his cheek. 'Raymond said he'd left the key with you? Otherwise, I'd have …'

'Yes, we have it. At least we did have it somewhere. Simon will know.'

She brushed past him and Sweeney was half-relieved to see she wasn't naked under her robe. He glimpsed a knee-length skirt, black or blue he couldn't tell, and a white chemise.

'Why don't you leave your stuff here,' she nodded at the foot of the stairs, 'and you can carry it up later.' She pointed to the lampshade in the ceiling. 'We really must get Mrs Herdecka to fix the light in this hallway. You can hardly see a thing. Come on, I'll introduce you to Simon.'

The windowless hallway narrowed by the stairwell. Sweeney followed the satin robe and slapping slippers as Pearl spoke over her shoulder.

'Have you had anything to eat today, Eddie? You are welcome to join us for dins. There'll be nothing in your flat, I expect. Oh, and before you say yes' – her matter-of-fact voice lightened into humour – 'Simon does the cooking around here and he's trying out a new dish, so it might be a bit hit-or-miss.'

The door of the flat was ajar, light seeping into the gloom, and Pearl stood aside to let Sweeney enter.

'Thanks so much,' he said, bowing his head, unsure if he was overdoing the formality.

Now he could see clearly Pearl's shoulder length auburn hair, high cheekbones, almond eyes, straight nose and full lips. Her lack of vanity charmed – or was it disarmed? He supposed no vain woman would allow a strange man to see her *au natural*. But then he knew little about what women would or would not allow, though he hoped to find out.

In the kitchen off the living room, he could hear pots being shifted on a stove top and the sound of running water. A voice asked, 'Who was it, love?'

'It's our new neighbour, Simon. Come and have a quick word.' Pearl whispered to Sweeney, 'then he can get back to the kitchen where he belongs', winked at him and smiled.

Simon appeared at the door, wiping his hands on a tea towel. He was a big man, over six feet tall, powerfully built, but ex-uding affability. Over shirt and trousers he wore a blue and white checked smock. Sweeney had never seen a man wearing a domestic apron before, apart from James Dean's father in *Rebel Without a Cause*.

'Eddie – you did say I could call you Eddie? – this is Simon.'

They shook hands, saying hello simultaneously. Sweeney felt his own hand disappear within Simon's grasp and expected a crushing squeeze. He wondered if Simon suspected every man of wanting to steal Pearl from him. He would understand if he did and maybe a show of strength would be his signal to keep off? But his grasp was gentle. Even so, Sweeney thought it best not to let his gaze linger on Pearl too long or too often.

'You're moving into Raymond's flat, right?' Simon asked. Sweeney noticed Pearl raise her eyebrows as if the question was superfluous. It wasn't a cruel gesture but a gesture of familiarity. 'I'm sure he told you all about us?' There was that question again.

'I've asked him already,' Pearl interrupted, 'and he's not confessing – which makes me suspect Raymond *has* told him all about us.'

'We have a maxim back home. Whatever you say, say nothing.'

Pearl and Simon laughed and he considered he'd made the correct impression. His spirits improved and he relaxed.

'Simon,' Pearl said, 'I've invited Eddie to join us for dinner. Can you stretch the nosh to three?'

'That's nooo problem. I'll just put on more rice.' He looked at Sweeney. 'I'm making a curry, a bit experimental, a new recipe for me. Do you like curry?'

Sweeney thought of *Vesta Beef Curry*, emptying a sachet out of the box, adding water and heating it on the stove. He liked *Vesta* well enough, it was modern, but he'd never heard of anyone *making* a curry.

Pearl answered for him. 'Everyone loves curry.'

'It's very kind of you. If it's no trouble, that is.'

Pearl waved her hand as if nothing could ever be any trouble. Simon did a thumbs up and returned to the kitchen.

'Have a seat, Eddie, make yourself comfortable.'

The room was warm. He sat in an armchair arranged to one side of a large gas fire, its flickering blue and orange flame humming gently and soothingly. Pearl flopped down in the chair opposite, kicking off the leather slippers, stretching out her legs and wiggling her toes. Both her big toenails were varnished bright red. She sighed as if expecting Sweeney to say something.

'Would you like a cigarette?' he asked. He noticed ashtrays set on small wooden tables next to each chair.

'Oh, go on then, why not? Simon's always trying to get me to cut back and always losing.'

He slid open his packet of Embassy Regal. He leaned across to offer her one, struck a match, lit hers and then his own.

'Oh, I knew there was something,' she said. 'I was just about to make myself a gin. Would you like one?'

Sweeney had never drunk gin. It was something he associated with maiden aunts and retired colonels. Come to think of it, he associated gin with the sort of people who played bridge in Agatha Christie stories. But Pearl wasn't one of those people.

'Or you can have a beer if you like.'

'I'll have a beer, please.'

'I won't be a mo,' she said, 'sit tight.'

She rested her cigarette on the lip of the ashtray and walked on the balls of her bare feet into the kitchen. He heard muffled words, glasses being readied, bottles chinking and a beer cap falling onto the worktop.

Pearl reappeared with her gin followed by Simon carrying a glass of beer in each hand. 'Sorry, I should have asked you earlier,' he said. He set Sweeney's beer on a coaster he'd brought with him. 'Well then, cheers!' Simon said, lifting his glass in a toast. Sweeney stood up.

'Cheers!' they declared as one and touched glasses.

'Welcome to Park Road,' Pearl said, taking a sip from her glass and picking up her cigarette again. 'I think you are going to fit in here just fine, Eddie. Don't you Simon?'

'Yes, indeed', he replied, draining his glass in one go. 'Dinner will be on the table soon.'

'Sit, sit, Eddie,' Pearl gestured to the armchair. 'I'm still not ready. Simon fusses about being late and keeping people waiting. You don't mind being on your own for a bit?' She didn't wait for his answer. She patted her cheeks softly, theatrically, leaning her head to one side and pouting her lips. 'If I feel under pressure I always make a mess of my make-up. Better to do it before dinner and on my first gin. Men are lucky not needing to bother. So if you'll excuse me?' She took a final drag, stubbed out the butt, blowing the smoke slowly upwards, and disappeared with her drink into the bedroom.

After a few sips of beer Sweeney began to feel dizzy. Unused to alcohol on an empty stomach, he puffed out his cheeks, sensing his face redden from the heat of the fire. Drowsy too, he realised how stressed he'd been to avoid making a bad impression. He fought against sleep and lost.

A hand on his shoulder gently shook him back to consciousness. It was Simon.

'Oh, I'm really sorry,' Sweeney said, fearing he'd broken some convention. 'I didn't mean to be rude.'

'Don't mention it. You must be tired after your journey.'

Pearl was adjusting her hair by the mirror and turned to ask, 'And how did you get here, sleepy head?' Sweeney recounted his itinerary. 'I know Hull is hard to get to but that was quite a trek. You must really want to be here,' she laughed

'I suppose I must, yes.'

HERE

'Dinner is finally ready.' Simon announced.

Vesta Beef Curry it wasn't. Never had Sweeney tasted anything quite like it, or so good. Never would he have used the word 'exciting' to describe food at home but what Simon had served was definitely exciting.

'This is really great. I've never tasted anything so good.'

'Thank you,' said Simon, 'your endorsement is much appreciated. I get the ingredients from a wholefood store which has opened close by. It has brought to Hull something different, all sorts of wonderful stuff. Everything is vegetarian. So is dinner. Pearl and I stopped eating meat some time ago.' Here was another first. Sweeney had never eaten a vegetarian meal before, beans on toast excepted. This was a real taste of the modern world, he thought.

'Correction, Simon, *you* stopped eating meat some time ago. *I* was vegetarian long before we met.'

'I defer to the honourable lady. Anyhow, I can thoroughly recommend the shop. It's just where Princes Avenue turns onto Spring Bank West. You can't miss it, always full of hippies like Pearl here.'

She snorted, 'And I can thoroughly recommend a vegetarian diet … oh please stop me, I sound like one of those loud religious fanatics.' She looked at Sweeney. 'I'm sorry.' She put her hand to her lips. 'Sorry,' she whispered once more.

'No need to apologise. We aren't all religious. We aren't all interested in politics either. In Northern Ireland, I mean, if that's what you're saying sorry for. I'm definitely not. It's worth the trek from Belfast to get away from all that.' He said no more. If he was determined to reject playing up to the Northern Irish stereotype, he was equally determined not to disrespect his own people.

'I'm so glad I didn't offend,' said Pearl, touching his arm softly. 'Simon is a big Van Morrison fan. Isn't that right, Simon?'

'He's great. I have all his LPs. *Astral Weeks, Moondance, Saint Dominic's Preview …*'

'That's fantabulous,' Sweeney said.

'Ha!' Simon said and sang the line 'Well, it's a marvellous night for a moondance.'

'We shouldn't have got him started,' Pearl moaned. 'And Simon's the one for politics too. He studied politics at university, here in Hull.'

'They nicknamed our block the Kremlin but I think it was the sociologists they had in mind, not us.'

Conversation settled on life at the university. Sweeney gave a summary of his proposed thesis, rather groggily at first, then more confidently. Both of them nodded politely as he went through a list of novelists he'd searched out, some of whom he knew only by reputation. He'd already mastered one of the arts of the academy, talking with assurance about books he'd never read.

'So that's the connection with Raymond,' Pearl said. 'We wondered how you'd found out about the flat. We live in a house of literary geniuses! Roland, the person in the flat at front, he's writing a novel. At least that's what he tells us. He's a bit reclusive but we love him anyway, don't we Simon?'

Simon kept on eating and didn't reply.

'Raymond mentioned him to me,' Sweeney said.

'He's from Stratford-on-Avon, believe it or not. And you're going to love this, Eddie. He looks just like William Shakespeare.'

'Raymond never mentioned that.'

'Raymond would be too kind. It is uncanny, though. You think the same, don't you Simon?'

This time he did reply. 'It *is* uncanny but then I've never been to Stratford-on-Avon. Maybe everyone there looks like that, women as well as men.' He took another mouthful of curry. 'It was good of Raymond to tip you off about the flat. It's much better than the usual student accommodation.'

'He did say something along those lines, especially about The Lawns.'

'Who was that student with the double-barrelled name, Simon?' Pearl asked. She looked at Sweeney. 'It's quite a story, though I never believed all of it. These things take on a life of their own.'

'Oh, it was true alright. I heard it from a friend on my course who witnessed it first-hand. Well, he claimed he did.'

'His name was Jackson-Browne,' said Pearl.

'Jackson-Browne is a musician, love, and an American. This guy was a Geordie but not your average Newcastle Brown Ale type. He came from quite a well-to-do family, hence the double-barrelled name, Fenwick-Clark. He was kicked out of The Lawns for disruptive behaviour, drink-related, became one of the exiles as they liked to call themselves. He slept on various floors and couches and ended up in my friend's university house on Marlborough Avenue. It's close by. Can you guess where he slept?'

'I don't know,' Sweeney answered.

'Believe it or not' – Simon looked across at a sceptical Pearl – 'in the cupboard under the stairs. He used the common facilities, toilets, shower, kitchen, and so on. Then, my friend told me, they thought he'd gone. No one had seen him in ages. But he'd become reclusive, nocturnal and then paranoid, believing those going up and down the stairs were trying to get him. One night there was an almighty racket in the lounge and they found him with a hatchet chopping up the table and chairs.'

'Isn't that something?' Pearl asked.

Sweeney showed appropriate astonishment even though, if he had been living under the stairs for any length of time, he could imagine doing something similar. 'What happened to him?' he asked Simon.

'The parents came down and poor Fenwick-Clark was spirited away. As far as I'm aware, the university hushed it up as best they could, understandably of course. There would be no stain on his character, that sort of arrangement. It would allow him another chance.'

'Did he take that chance?'

'We haven't a clue.' Simon looked at Pearl for confirmation. 'I like to think he did. My friend tells me he was likeable enough. When he was sober, that is.'

'And not living under the stairs,' added Pearl. 'Eddie, doesn't that story, even if it *is* an urban myth, make you glad to be with us here in Park Road?'

'It is providential, I think,' Sweeney told them. By the look on their faces, he realised Pearl and Simon were not familiar with this distinctive outlook on life. 'I mean, I got lucky, Raymond getting a job just before I came to look around the university in July. It would be to our mutual advantage was how he sold it to me.'

'I'm sure he did,' Simon said. 'Things have a habit of falling to Raymond's advantage. To be fair to him, it's fallen to your advantage as well. So maybe it is … providential. That's your word?' Sweeney nodded. 'You'll find this is a very good place to live. We like it so much we've stayed on – here, and in Hull, that is.'

'It is true what they say,' Pearl added. 'Hull is a difficult place to get to – you know that now – but it's also a difficult place to leave.' She put a hand on Sweeney's arm again. 'That may have come across the wrong way. I mean, the city grows on you. It has its own peculiar charm. Some may say *very* peculiar charm, maybe a different rhythm, maybe another sense of time. We've been here, what, six years, love?' Simon nodded. 'It's not where we expected to be. But it's where we want to be.'

'The locals have a saying. "You should try living here". It's typical of Hull, you'll discover,' Simon said, 'grumpy about the place's deficiencies but pride in them as well. We tried living here and *we* like it.'

'Which part of England are you from?' Sweeney asked them. 'I'm trying to work out all the different accents.'

'I'm from Sale,' Pearl answered.

'I apologise for my ignorance but where exactly is that?'

'That's Manchester to you. Simon over there, he's from Prestwich. That's Manchester to you and also to him, but not to me.'

Simon put his fork down in mock protest. 'We're not Yorkies, that's for sure, Eddie,' Simon said, 'so we're not pushing the merits of Hull for love of the white rose.'

'A lot of people don't think Hull *is* in Yorkshire,' Pearl laughed. 'It's in North Humberside – allegedly. It's a sore point with the locals, isn't it Simon? I recommend you avoid the subject, Eddie, and never mention North Humberside outside this room ever again.'

'It all sounds familiar,' Sweeney laughed. 'It makes me feel quite at home.' He asked them what they did.

Pearl had studied mathematics, stayed on to do a Masters and considered studying for a doctorate. 'In the end I decided to work in the real world. I ended up in insurance dealing with risk management ... I see from your look, Eddie, that means nothing to you.'

As she explained it, assessing risk sounded to Sweeney like the skills a card player would need. Films like *Smart Money* and *The Cincinnati Kid* came to mind but Sweeney couldn't imagine Pearl as a card sharp. She seemed without guile or deception though bridge, of which he knew nothing, wasn't poker, of which he knew little. Perhaps seeming to be without guile or deception was astute practice when playing cards?

Simon, it turned out, was a house husband. 'My job is to

keep domestic life in good order and make sure Pearl here eats properly without drinking and smoking too much.' Pearl smiled at him.

Sweeney believed Simon must be doing everything for love and wondered how he managed to spend his days. But this was the 1970s, not the 1950s. Why not reverse traditional roles? Simon seemed to have reckoned precisely what was needed to keep Pearl happy – another sort of risk management – and seemed more than content. Sweeney watched and listened, appreciating Pearl's good looks, in awe of her spirit and delighting in her voice. He wasn't so unworldly to believe a rose was without a thorn. In another mood, someone with Pearl's vivacity might be inconsiderate and quarrelsome. But he detected no malice and understood exactly why Simon lived as he did.

Simon looked at his watch. 'Sorry to bring things to an end, Eddie, but we will have to leave soon.'

'Oh, we must, we must,' said Pearl, who didn't move but lifted an ashtray from the dresser near the table and opened a fresh packet of Benson and Hedges. 'Would you like one of these?' she asked Sweeney.

He was about to reach across and take one when Simon returned with a tray to collect the dishes. He felt he should help. 'Can I lend a hand? Do the washing up maybe?'

Simon stopped what he was doing and Pearl hesitated as she raised a cigarette to her lips. Then both of them together said emphatically, 'No, no, no, we wouldn't dream of it.'

'Your first night with us in Hull and we have your elbows in dishwater? Wouldn't hear of it,' Pearl wagged a finger, 'would we, Simon?'

'Certainly not, it would be exploitation.'

'Simon's the expert on the subject. He would have to leave the Labour Party if anyone found out. Taking advantage of non-unionised workers doesn't go down well here.'

Simon cleared the rest of the table and Pearl waited until he disappeared into the kitchen. They heard the remains of the meal being scraped into a bin, the clattering of plates in the sink and the running of water.

'I pay him over the going rate as it is,' she whispered, winked and took a luxurious drag on her B&H.

Returning, Simon said, 'I will leave everything to soak, be an easier job when we get back. Let's get our coats, Pearl, we don't want to keep Mark and Sal waiting.' As he spoke the doorbell rang. 'Now that's what I call perfect timing.'

Sweeney suddenly remembered why he was there. 'Can I have the keys, please, if it's no trouble?'

'What keys? Oh, cripes, the keys, yes,' said Pearl. 'Simon, do you know where I put the keys?'

He opened the door of a small extension leading into the back garden. Through its window Sweeney glimpsed the outline of a large tree. Simon took a set of keys from a wall rack, held them up for Pearl to see and handed them over to Sweeney.

'Thanks. And thank you both again for your hospitality. It was very kind of you.'

'You'll only embarrass us if you keep on saying thanks,' said Pearl. The bell rang once more as they hustled awkwardly out of the flat, putting on their coats as they did. 'Eddie, be a dear and pull the door shut after you.'

'Good luck tonight. I hope you win,' he called after them. He heard the sound of doors closing and a gear engaging as the car accelerated along Cave Street towards Beverley Road. As he gathered his baggage at the bottom of the stairs, the jazz music which had been playing stopped mid-track. Roland must be getting back to his novel, Sweeney thought.

The entrance and hall were an untidy no-man's-land. The tiled floor felt gritty under his boots. He noticed for the first time a waist-high wooden fuse box intruding awkwardly, its white paint scratched and flaking. Stacked haphazardly on the ledge were unopened circulars for long-departed residents. A threadbare reddish carpet ran up the stairway. Sweeney held on to the shaky wooden bannister and struggled up to the flat. When he was on the landing, he heard Roland's door opening softly, a shaft of light fell across the stairwell only to disappear quickly as the door closed again. He found the correct key and switched on the lights of the flat.

The main room was painted cherry-red. In one or two places the walls were spotted with the greasy residue of Blu-Tac. Maybe Blanche wasn't entirely fastidious after all. Blu-Tac seemed a little common for him. However, the shadowed outlines of a few frames suggested paintings had once hung there too. The Wilton carpet with intricate patterns of red, cream, blue and green which covered most of the dark-stained wooden floor had thinned and was fraying at the edges. Book shelves in an alcove were empty. A large sash window was hung with thick curtains, also cherry-red. In one corner stood a wooden standard lamp with a circular floral-patterned shade. Two wingback chairs sat either side of a gas fire set into a brown and white-tiled fireplace. In front of the fire was a low backless sofa bed over which a coloured cotton blanket had been thrown. Against the wall inside the door bulked a traditional chest of drawers, lacquered but scratched and which, like everything else in the room, had seen better days. Above it a plain rectangular wall mirror was secured by a metal chain. Like Pearl and Simon's flat, the room contained a large mahogany dining table but, unlike theirs, the four chairs were non-matching, something Sweeney considered un-Blanche-like.

This room gave directly onto a narrow galley kitchen with stove, fridge and kettle. Over the sink was a gas water heater with a long thin metal tap. He checked the cupboards for an abandoned packet of tea or jar of coffee, but there was nothing.

HERE

The back bedroom contained a wardrobe and two bedside tables on which sat matching lamps. He tried one. It worked. The bed was a double and sure enough, there was Blanche's duvet, in a light blue cover. Sweeney inspected it and sniffed the bed sheets. Everything was newly washed. The room was chilly but like the rest of the flat, as far as he could detect, there was no trace of damp. Its window overlooked an untidy paved alleyway leading to the garden, partly hidden by the rear extension. It wasn't a scene of beauty but his earlier despondency was gone. This is my place now, he told himself. Be like Alf, be like Alf.

CHAPTER THREE

'You should try living here,' Simon had said. Those words made sense to Sweeney now.

It rained for the next three weeks. If anyone had asked, 'What's your impression of Hull?' Sweeney would have answered, 'I've only seen the pavements.' Few did ask. As he soon discovered, acceptance was a characteristic of life here, especially in weather like this. Keeping his head down as he walked, the hood of his Peter Storm tied tight under his chin, he became acquainted with Hull's drain covers and cracked flagstones, its uneven kerbs and patches of sodden fallen leaves. He got used to damp denims clinging to his thighs, slowly drying during the morning, only to get soaked again later. He was grateful for his waterproof Doc Martins.

Living anywhere new at first feels like a hall of mirrors, he thought. Hull was no different. Sense of place was distorted, short was long, long was short, space compressed, space enlarged and nothing had a fixed shape. Only when he had established his own mental map would he consider Hull to be in perspective, his perspective, the solid bulk of things arranged to scale, his scale. That meant establishing a familiar network, a pattern of comings and goings. It meant devising a routine in which, literally and metaphorically, he would know where he was, recognising these streets as part of his life. To others Sweeney's regularity might seem a failure of ambition, a limitation, a settling for less when there was so much more. He didn't see it that way. He considered routine as an anchor, not fixing him permanently, not ruling out adventure, not denying possibility, but providing the necessary stability and perspective to do all of these things – even if he chose not to. Wasn't this everyone's way of trying to live anywhere? Didn't everyone make a bespoke world from many possible worlds? Out of the regulation of his days, out of his habits, and out of his choices, he set about making Sweeney-land, a Hull which conformed to his geography of character as the city became his place of living freely.

. . . .

Most days he walked to university from his flat, crossing Pearson Park and taking the diagonal tree-lined path towards Princes Avenue, passing the small serpentine lake with its fountain and greenhouse, beside it the children's playground. Larkin used to live in the top floor flat of 32 Pearson Park and from his window observed people. Sweeney never saw, as Larkin had, palsied old step-takers, hare-eyed clerks, or anyone deep in litter-baskets. But he did see plenty of young mothers, often 'thickening' as Larkin described them, prams parked around the sandpit, keeping watch on children, chatting, every so often calling out to chastise their offspring. Did they no longer feel at the centre of their own lives, as Larkin believed? It didn't appear that way to Sweeney. They had a presence which implied possession, a status unrelated to losing youth and beauty. He didn't pity them. He appreciated their apparent security in the familiar.

Reaching Princes Avenue, he passed a large town house with a prominent blue and white sign which read 'Conservative Workingmen's Club'. In this Labour Party stronghold, Sweeney believed it a mark of defiance. Well, he did until he became better acquainted with a people who could see no reason to be apologetic (and never tell them they were from North Humberside). Conservative working men they were so why hide the fact? Coming home in the evening Sweeney sometimes dawdled by the park entrance to watch figures in the upper room of the club standing with snooker cues in hand or hunched over a table, all framed in the soft greenish glow of shaded light. He felt comforted that everything was right with the world, a feeling tinged by melancholy that he would never share such conviviality.

He cut the corner opposite The Queens public house, from which one evening he had stolen a stylish yellow triangular glass ashtray advertising Ricard *anisette liqueur*. He considered it very Left Bank and *chic*, incongruous in this West Hull pub where nearly everyone drank mild or bitter or a combination of both. He hadn't felt guilty about taking it. Everyone did it. At least students did. Heavy ceramic ones for Fosters or Carlsberg, metal ones for Senior Service or Woodbine. They became trophies, like beermats, advertising the apprenticed dissipation of youth.

Rounding the corner onto Newland Avenue, he walked under the iron railway bridge across which heavily laden goods trains screeched and groaned. Beyond the bridge, a collection of small two-story red-brick shops unfolded for half a mile towards Cottingham Road. There were fruit and vegetable stalls, apples and oranges, cabbages and carrots, crowding the pavement on wooden boxes under canvas canopies. There were cake and bread shops with their distinctive yeasty, sugary aroma where Sweeney discovered Yorkshire cheesecake with its soft pastry shell, raisins in sweet curd filling. There were electrical shops with new or reconditioned washing machines, tumble dryers and fridges, many of them also set on the pavement, adjoining hardware stores full of keys, locks, hinges, buckets, hammers, hacksaws, power tools and plumbing supplies. There were clothes and furniture shops with second-hand goods alongside fishmongers, butchers, newsagents and a Jacksons supermarket on the corner with its front of blue mosaic panels and clock. Sweeney never tired of these commonplace stores, of wandering in the everyday, of enjoying the bustling resolve of others to get and spend, of window shopping, of pottering around shelves of discounted wares, of being asked by kindly middle-aged women shop assistants, 'What can I get you, me love?'

Weekdays provided purposeful activity when he could, if asked, give justification for his existence. Sweeney chose to spend most of his time at the university where, between post-grad room, library, departmental office and students' union, another pattern became fixed. There was much going on in the hinterlands of university life and if he felt so inclined always something to do in the evening, a public lecture, a reading, an event of some sort to attend. One thing he avoided was the student Celtic Cultural Society. He'd gone once and heard the Scots read from Burns, the Welsh from Dylan Thomas, and the Irish scuffle over playing 'The Sash' or 'The Soldier's Song', everyone either wallowing in their thick soup of identity or playing up to collective national clichés. Sweeney recognised how effortless this could be, how comforting, and also how seductive to differentiate himself from the English by indulging an exaggerated, self-conscious, otherness. But he judged it a cage in which to confine himself, a betrayal of his individuality and wish to be different on his own terms.

Saturdays involved exploring the other half of Sweeney-land, walking along Beverley Road or Spring Bank and into town. These routes too became part of a pattern, leading to new routine, new haunts. He would go by the statue of Amy Johnson on Prospect Street (if asked again to name one good thing to come out of Hull he could now say, 'Have you never heard of Amy Johnson?') and wander around the shopping centre there, idly browsing in W. H. Smith. In the main square he would cross at City Hall, briefly pop into the Ferens Art Gallery and afterwards mingle with shoppers on Whitefriargate. In the Hepworth Arcade, a small, late Victorian shopping mall with arching glass roof, tiled flooring and dark wooden frontage, he discovered a cramped second-hand bookshop. He saw there a set of Disraeli's novels, a beautifully bound nineteenth-century edition, and had to have it. He considered this find providential for it reminded him of the day he'd considered becoming an academic.

. . . .

In his first year, history was one of the subjects he'd chosen. Along with other students, he'd climbed the stairs to an attic room of the house on University Street for a seminar in Modern British History. Different members of staff had taken them week by week and since everything was 'introductory', the topic never seemed to matter. This time they found their tutor in his office sprawled on a well-worn chaise longue, looking just like an aesthete in an Edwardian etching. One of his spidery legs stretched along the couch, the other hooked down to the floor. In tweed jacket, light checked shirt, open collar with silk cravat, he leaned back against a cushioned roll. In one hand, raised languidly above his head, was a cigarette. With his other he wordlessly beckoned everyone to sit. Most striking was his footwear, a pair of green leather slippers with a silver decorative pattern. Sweeney assumed they were Persian because he remembered Sherlock Holmes kept one filled with shag tobacco on the mantelpiece of his lodgings. A student afterwards had giggled to her friend, 'Did you notice he was wearing a pair of Moroccan slippers?' He trusted her judgement more than his own literary hunch.

The seminar proceeded as a stream of consciousness. Their tutor made reference to a shifting cast of personalities from nineteenth-century Britain, punctuated by successive Silk Cut King Size cigarettes. With a flourish, he would blow out the match, drop it delicately into an ashtray on the floor, take a long drag, push back his head and blow the smoke lazily towards the ceiling. That it was possible to earn a living in such an eccentric and artful manner was nothing if not alluring even though Sweeney knew such style could never be his. If that was a moment of revelation, he also recalled vividly the tutor's commentary on Disraeli's novels.

'Each plot is a fantastical, egotistical rodomontade, filled with completely outrageous characters, scenes of romantic nonsense as gaudy as Disraeli's own clothing, myth-making of the most blatant kind with intimations of esoteric wisdom. And yet they are written with such panache, with such insight into human foibles! How can we not be seduced by his stories as Disraeli seduced large swathes of Victorian England?' There was a pause as he inhaled another lungful of smoke, exhaling this time in short puffs, his unkempt beard stained with nicotine. For the first time in almost forty minutes he turned to look at the class, as if he'd forgotten they were there. 'Reading Disraeli will disorder your senses,' he announced calmly.

Sweeney did read *Sybil* but that was it. Seeing the collection arranged on the owner's desk in the Hepworth Arcade, he was convinced his discovery was not *mere* coincidence. Just like Disraeli, he imagined his intellect seducing England. Hull would do for now, beginning with Julie. He glanced at the price. It was well beyond his means, at least in one transaction. Sweeney ran his hand over the tooling on the spines and picked up the first volume. It contained the novels *Vivien Grey, Contarini Fleming* and *Alroy*. He'd never heard of them. Opening the book delicately and turning the thin pages, they crinkled crisply.

'It's an excellent edition,' the owner said, appearing from behind a row of shelves, 'and each volume is in pristine condition. Do you collect books, young man?' He was well-spoken with only a hint of Hull accent, tall, heavily built, a full head of swept back silver hair. He was dressed in what to Sweeney looked like the uniform of a shabby country gentleman – well-worn brown windowpane tweed suit, checked shirt and mustard tie. He moved awkwardly, shuffling his feet, a habit which may have developed from years negotiating, for someone of his girth, the narrow passages between bookshelves.

'No, not a collector, but I am a reader.' He could have added that he was mainly a borrower not a buyer. His parents did possess a shelf of crime-club hardbacks as well as full set of Newnes Pictorial Knowledge. But they were library regulars, so regular that they would put a small distinctive mark in books to know which ones they'd read. Sweeney had followed in that tradition, generally buying only what was necessary for his studies.

'You're not from here, a student perhaps?'

'I'm from Northern Ireland. I'm just starting research at the university, looking at literature in and about the north of England … in the twentieth century, mainly.' As he said this, Sweeney once more considered it all a bit vague.

'It's not about Disraeli?'

'That would be too political for me.'

The owner raised an eyebrow but didn't respond. To explain his interest, Sweeney recounted the story of his tutor in Belfast. The man laughed. 'Yes, I can see why you might be interested in Disraeli.'

'When I saw this collection, I felt it was a sign – not sure of what exactly, but a sign nonetheless. I can't afford them … well, all at once. I suppose you wouldn't sell each volume separately?'

The man walked around the desk and sat down. His chair was a mid-back of green buttoned leather, the sort Sweeney associated with a banker's office in Western films. He made a steeple of his fingers in front of his lips.

'What do you say to this? Pay me for the Disraeli collection volume by volume when you can. I will set it aside for you. Your research topic – you will want to buy books for your own use I take it?'

'Yes. I have a grant. It's pretty basic but it does give me some money to spend.'

The owner tapped his fingers on the table. 'It will be an arrangement to our mutual advantage. You come here, pay off the Disraeli collection,' he put his hand on the volumes, 'and maybe you'll buy the books you need from me. I might even consider giving you a discount.' He pointed a finger at Sweeney and smiled. 'A bargain isn't what you expect from a Yorkshire man, is it?'

'There's a first time for everything.'

He wagged his finger this time and laughed. 'A first time for everything, you're right.' He tapped the table again. 'I always like to think my books will end up in good hands.'

And so was made another mutually advantageous deal, one fulfilled dutifully on both sides, begun as a purely transactional arrangement but which transformed into one of fellowship. They shook hands and the owner introduced himself as Mr Trammer. Sweeney was pleased to have a purpose for Saturday afternoons, somewhere to visit regularly and someone to chat to about literature.

Trinity Market was beside the Hepworth Arcade. After his visit to the bookshop, Sweeney picked up what he needed for the weekend and, burdened with his bags of fresh vegetables and meat, the odd book and a Yorkshire cheesecake (if they hadn't sold out already), he would make his way home via Lowgate and Queen's Gardens, wishing the licencing laws allowed pubs to open in the afternoon. He wanted to set down his bags, have a beer and stand at the ceramic counter of The Polar Bear on Spring Bank or sit at the open fire of The Station on Beverley Road. He wanted to rest in a mild fug of tobacco smoke, to hear murmurs of conversation and the occasional register of raucous laughter, to smell the beer from the taps as it foamed into glasses. He wanted to take a first sip of ale, to savour the flavour of hops, in the background to hear the soft thud of darts hitting a board, a score called out with derision or appreciation. By evening things would become frenetic, less accommodating of the solitary drinker, and he would be more exposed in a crowd. He regretted being unable to immerse himself in these sociable spaces and to feel more in step with the world than he usually did. Yet in his alone-ness he enjoyed the sense of being impermeable, of feeling things more intensely, experiencing life more sensuously, as if privy to secrets hidden from everyone else. There was always a 'but'. *But* alone-ness he feared becoming the curse of loneliness. Didn't everyone judge solitude sad, especially for someone young? It was harder to be at ease with solitude if society thought you *should* be sociable, surrounded by friends, believing solitude a kind of sickness to be avoided at all costs and the person deemed solitary to be avoided for fear of contagion.

. . . .

Sunday made that anxiety more intense. Sunday was a reminder of time in all its immensity, weighing down relentlessly. Sunday recalled the malady of life, the potential for absolute vacancy. Johnny Cash was right. There was something in a Sunday that made a body feel alone. On a Park Road Sunday, silence seemed deeper. Pearl and Simon always slept late and it was normally well after noon before Sweeney heard sounds of life, like the back door opening. From behind his bedroom curtain he might glimpse Pearl in the garden, wearing satin robe and slippers, hair untidy, scattering crusts for birds.

Sometimes he walked around quiet streets pretending he had something to do and somewhere to go. Sometimes he would linger in Pearson Park, now and then meeting Pearl and Simon out for a stroll. He worried they might think him needy, engineering these encounters for company. Often he failed to muster energy to do anything much, trying to make time pass pleasantly, holding demons of Sunday monotony at bay. In the armchair, wrapped in the duvet for warmth, he would read book reviews in the newspapers, listen to his portable radio (he never bothered to get a television), a play, perhaps a concert, rarely news (he didn't want monotony to become depression). The sash window was draughty and the thick curtains, whatever the weather, shivered constantly. Now and then, lying on the sofa bed beneath the white-swirled plaster ceiling, fashionable at one time he supposed, but greying slowly because of age, he would silently contemplate this and that. Or dream of Julie.

One Sunday morning, standing by his front window, Sweeney finally saw Roland. Before the hedge hid him from view, there was William Shakespeare checking he'd put the keys in his pocket. Pearl hadn't exaggerated. A more youthful version certainly, late twenties most likely, but his hair was dark and flowing in that wavy fashion of the Bard. If his chin was more pointed than the popular image, Roland had the familiar beard and moustache, the thin face, the straight nose and the heavy-lidded eyes.

One Sunday blessing was that pubs were open. That morning in The Queens as Sweeney ordered a pint, newspapers under his arm, he noticed Roland again, alone at a table by the window. A half-pint of mild sat before him and he was looking straight ahead, smoking a pipe, 'the silent sup' as his father called it. Fresh to English habits of sociability and conscious of his neighbour's reputation for privacy, Sweeney was undecided what to do. If he chose to introduce himself, would he breach some unspoken code of civility? Believing himself under no obligation and almost certain Roland would have no idea who he was (evasive justifications, he knew), Sweeney paid for his drink and was about to slink off to sit behind a pillar at the far end of the bar when he felt a hesitant touch on his shoulder.

'You've moved into the flat above me, haven't you? I couldn't help noticing you leave the house most mornings. You'll have to forgive me. I should have introduced myself earlier. My only excuse is I have been rather busy of late. Mortimer, Roland Mortimer, pleased to meet you at last.'

'No need to apologise.' Sweeney shook the proffered hand. 'Pearl told me you're working on a novel. Sweeney, Edward Sweeney, pleased to meet you too.' Roland spoke so properly – a word Sweeney's mother used approvingly to mean 'gentleman' – he didn't bother to offer him 'Eddie'.

'Have you have settled in?'

'Yes, thank you, and beginning to find my way around Hull. Are you a regular here in The Queens?'

Roland looked perplexed by the notion of a regular. 'No, no, I rarely come here,' he said glancing at the nicotine-stained walls of patterned paper with an assortment of framed prints. It appeared as if he'd suddenly realised where he was and wished to be elsewhere. After some initial pleasantries, Sweeney expected Roland would retreat to his table, to his own thoughts, and leave him to his newspapers.

'I wanted to mark something, that's all,' he explained. 'The novel Pearl spoke of so generously? I completed another draft this morning.'

Sweeney felt the word 'mark' a little odd. Was it modesty, the sort of English understatement he associated with British films about the Second World War? Was it that English, specifically middle-class, habit of being serious in an unserious, modest way which he'd observed frequently since his arrival? 'Congratulations!' he said, judging an emphatic, immodest and serious response was required. 'If I had a hat, I'd take it off. Well, if you are celebrating, I must buy you a drink.' He noticed the glass on Roland's table was two-thirds full but he thought it only good manners to offer. Sweeney expected him to refuse.

'That's very kind of you. Would you mind ordering me a Scotch? I feel as if I deserve something stronger than my mild.' Roland nodded towards his glass. 'Why don't you join me if you've nothing better to do? I suppose Park Road people should stick together.'

Maybe Park Road people should, Sweeney thought. 'A double Scotch, please', he said to the barmaid, dismissing Roland's suggestion that a single was perfectly adequate.

'A little ice if you would be so kind,' Roland added. When his drink arrived, he looked apologetic. 'You know, I feel guilty now about not ordering an Irish.'

'Don't be, I'm not nationalistic.'

Sitting at Roland's table, they exchanged banalities about their families and backgrounds. Roland told him his mother was French. 'It explains my Christian name, a paladin amongst men.' The father was English and owned a hotel in Stratford. 'We get Americans on their British heritage tour, coach loads up from London for a day or so, next stop York, always so enthusiastic ... and so loud.' He'd studied French at university – 'Mother was very keen, you understand' – and decided to stay on in Hull. 'I like it here. I like being out of the way. And if it's good enough for Larkin, it's good enough for me.'

Roland swirled the Scotch around in his glass and the ice clinked. 'I'm not cut out for the hotel business or hospitality management as they call it these days. I've been such a disappointment to my father. Luckily, my twin brother has all the business *nous*, all the management skills and all the patter of the good host. And if you're wondering, yes, his name *is* Oliver, the *prince heritier* while I am the *prince fainéant*. And I,' he emphasised proudly and yet, Sweeney felt, without absolute conviction, 'count myself lucky.'

So Oliver must look like Shakespeare too? Sweeney thought

it must be good for business if Americans met the Bard at reception. But he didn't want to go deeply into family matters for there was probably more to this domestic tale than he cared to know. He was surprised at Roland's willingness to confide in a stranger. Wasn't it un-English? But then Roland was half-French. Sweeney spoke cursorily about Belfast and his doctoral subject but took an opportunity to mention providence as a way to shift matters onto the abstract and impersonal.

'I like to think Hull chose me rather than me choosing Hull, however absurd that may seem. I think the same about the flat in Park Road which I got only by good fortune when I met Raymond Blanche. It was as if it had been predestined. Fate has brought me here you might say.'

Roland listened as he fixed his pipe, tapping the hot tobacco with his stainless-steel tamper. He re-lit and puffed a few times. He said nothing for a moment, picked up his glass of Scotch and contemplated its colour. Sweeney wondered if Roland thought him a fool.

'It must be very comforting to believe things in your life are destined,' Roland said eventually. 'I suppose it relieves you of the agonies of choice. No, let me put that another way. It avoids all the pointless regret about how things might have been, pointless because they cannot be otherwise – oh, if only I'd done this or, if only I hadn't done that. We go round and round in circles of self-reproach, regretting making a decision as much as not making one. I understand all too well.' He looked at Sweeney directly. 'Does this belief in providence make you an optimist, Edward? Do you think all is for the best in the best possible of worlds?'

Sweeney took a sip of his bitter. He caught Roland's literary reference. He didn't remember much from Voltaire's *Candide* but he did know of Dr Pangloss.

'Am I Pangloss, you mean, or maybe Pollyanna? No, I'm not

so naïve. Anyway, I hope I'm not. It's just I like to think in a universe indifferent to most things there are exceptions now and then – and a few exceptions find me and take me by the hand.'

Roland laughed appreciatively, Sweeney thought. He puffed his pipe, took it from his lips and turned the stem towards him. 'What about a fatalist then, Edward? Someone prepared to suffer things in life when he could simply walk away, someone who feels trapped but simply carries on?' His opened his eyes wide. 'You're not married, are you? I trust that's not an insensitive remark.'

Sweeney laughed in turn. 'No, coming to Hull isn't my version of joining the French Foreign Legion.'

'I'm so glad I haven't put my foot in it. I didn't think you were, but some of my contemporaries at university married young and regretted it. You've met Pearl and Simon, of course. They've been living together happily for ages ... but then they're not married. Quite a few I know ...' his voice trailed off. 'Let me put it this way. Do you tolerate situations or remain in places you find uncomfortable because you believe they have been somehow preordained?' He returned the pipe to his lips. It had gone out once more.

It was partly true. Sweeney probably did too often try to make the best of a bad thing, adapting to conditions others would change as a matter of course. He was never sure if it was laziness, stoicism, pride, or simply stupidity. Whatever the reason, he knew it wasn't a virtue but he wasn't going to admit that to Roland.

Sweeney remembered his French teacher, Miss Bell. She appeared the embodiment of the liberated sixties, young, confident, independent. She wore mini-skirts, walked tall, drove a Mini Cooper S and smoked Gitanes. She told them she was an existentialist, a word which, when she explained its meaning, appealed to adolescents looking to justify their self-importance and to make sense of their troubled souls (even if, like Sweeney, most of his classmates weren't troubled at all). They imagined (at least he had) sitting in a Parisian café with Miss Bell, being sophisticated, living beyond convention, drinking red wine, smoking Gitanes like her, talking philosophy and, above all, being modern; or they dreamed of being with her, like lovers in some French film, in an open top Citroen 2 CV, bright blue skies, tree-lined roads, motoring from Paris for *le weekend* with the theme of *Un Homme et une Femme* as soundtrack. Ah, yes, dreaming of a foreign land with Miss Bell was the fastest way out of Belfast.

She was teaching them about Albert Camus, making his words seem the most important thing in their lives and making them feel the most important generation ever. 'Like Camus, you probably feel life is absurd,' she said. 'Maybe it's difficult to find meaning in the world around you.' She paused for effect. 'Of course, you shouldn't trust a word anyone over thirty tells you, isn't that so?' They laughed. 'Luckily for you and for me, I'm under thirty.' They laughed again, doing a swift mental calculation of the age gap and wondering if Miss Bell would wait for them (at least he did). 'So listen up. The world may seem indifferent to you. Your parents may not listen to you. Society may ignore you. No matter how pointless everything seems, it is you' – she pointed around the room – 'who must make life worth living. Here's the message from Camus I want you to take away.'

She turned to the green chalk board and wrote in large letters, 'Be like Sisyphus.' Standing to one side of the board she said, 'Repeat after me. Be-like-Sisyphus, come on.' They responded. 'Again! Louder!' She tapped under each word as they shouted, 'Be-like-Sisyphus' as if possessed by the Holy Spirit of existentialism. 'We could go on all day at this rate,' she smiled, 'just like Sisyphus and his rock.' They had clapped and cheered. It

HERE

was the only time in all his years at school this had happened. Here was Sweeney today, not in a Parisian café but in a Hull pub, not with Miss Bell but with Roland Mortimer, trying to be as sophisticated as he could, drinking beer, not wine, smoking an Embassy Regal, not a Gitane. 'Let me answer your question this way,' and he told Roland his story about Miss Bell. 'Let's say I'm optimistic about pushing my stone up that hill, pessimistic about it falling back down again, realistic that nothing in life is an unmixed blessing. You might say I accept life as I find it without bothering too much about its meaning apart from whatever meaning I choose to give it or it chooses to give me.'

Roland placed his pipe in the ashtray. 'You say well, Edward.' He swallowed the rest of his whisky in a gulp. 'Yes, you say well indeed.' There was a long silence before Roland added, 'I can buy you another pint of bitter' – pointing at Sweeney's almost empty glass – 'or I can invite you back for a decent drink at mine. What do you *say* to that?'

Sweeney wasn't sure if it was a good idea. He was reluctant to become trapped, however agreeable Roland's company had been to that point. Normally he was good at excuses but could see no way out of accepting. Moreover, he felt obliged to do so in the spirit of neighbourliness, all that stuff about Park Road people sticking together. It also occurred to him that Pearl and Simon could be mistaken about Roland's desire for a cloistered existence. Perhaps he was desperate for company, at least the company of those who 'say well' (which flattered him). And it was Sunday after all and the rest of the day loomed uninvitingly. Since he couldn't think of a pretext to say no, he asked, 'Are you sure I won't be disturbing *you* this time? Pearl told me how much you liked peace and quiet.'

Roland tapped out dead tobacco from the pipe bowl into an ashtray advertising Ricard. 'She did, did she? I've always thought it wise never to contradict Pearl.' He smiled wanly.

65

'I'm not being facetious. She is a woman much to be admired and respected. Simon is a lucky man.'

'I agree with you there.'

'In my case,' Roland continued, 'she happens to be absolutely right. I would only add in my defence – if mine is a preference which needs defending – that my writing demands it. Today the writing and I have agreed to take a break from each other. So please, I'd be happy to return your kindness.' He held up the empty glass of Scotch. 'Maybe I can provide some lunch as well. Nothing special, bread and cheese if that's acceptable? The local wholefood store, the one on the corner of Princes Avenue and Spring Bank West, do you know it?'

'I've heard of it.'

'It has an interesting selection of cheeses. I have to admit I indulge myself now and then. Shall we go?'

The Queens was filling up. A group of sporty types, likely a football team, had gathered and the pub's former quiet was disrupted by raucous laddish guffaws. So they went.

. . . .

Roland's living room had the same gas fire and tiled fireplace as his own with similar armchairs arranged on either side. Before the window was an impressive mahogany writing table, the desktop inset with green leather. It looked antique and probably expensive. On it sat a typewriter Sweeney associated with newspaper offices, not the modern sort used by Robert Redford and Dustin Hoffman in *All the President's Men*, but the heavy black metal sort made famous by Joseph Cotton in *Citizen Kane*. Was there some literary virtue attached to these machines? Sweeney didn't know because he'd never owned a typewriter of any description. He relied on pen and ink.

To the left of the typewriter was a thick pile of typescript which he assumed was Roland's novel. Beside it lay an open cardboard folder with a scattering of handwritten pages. A black Anglepoise lamp hovered over everything like a bird of prey. In front of the desk and leaning against it was a tall, cushioned, straight-backed chair, giving the impression Roland felt obliged to reserve his place. On the floor nearby, a wicker basket was filled with discarded and crumpled pages. Set into the alcove between the window and fireplace were shelves on which Sweeney could see a turntable, a set of speakers and an impressive collection of long-playing records. Jazz, Sweeney guessed. That's all he'd ever heard Roland play.

All these artefacts, however, seemed incidental. Sweeney thought he'd entered a second-hand bookshop, though a bookshop dispensing with any sense of order. Books covered almost every space. There were books in bookcases and on top of bookcases, books stacked in piles of varying sizes placed randomly on the floor, books lying on the dining table and chairs, books set precariously on the mantelpiece and even books placed around the base of the floor lamp. Sweeney was in awe and it must have been obvious.

'"Books come together in vast flocks of variegated feather, and have a charm which the domesticated volumes of the library lack",' Roland said, pleased by the impression his room had made. 'Virginia Woolf wrote that. She thought books, second-hand books, that is, were homeless books. Most of these you see are second-hand too. I have given them a home. In my little corner of Hull they've found peace, as have I – and as Anthony Powell knows, books do furnish a room.'

Sweeney smiled. 'Yes, of course,' hoping his words were said convincingly enough to hide the truth he'd never read any Powell. He *was* impressed but wondered where Roland had space to live in this 'home for books'. He thought of his own meagre collection, paperbacks mostly, and felt inadequate. He warned himself not to ask the philistine question, 'Have you read all of these books?'

'If you are wondering have I read all of these books, no I haven't. Quite a few of them I *have* read, the novels, the short stories, the memoirs, but a lot of them I haven't. Quite by accident I came across the word for my habit. It's called *tsundoku*, a Japanese word as you've probably guessed. It means combining the reading of books and the piling up of books unread.' He waved an arm around his room. 'In large stacks, in small stacks, in this pile, in that pile, how you do it is irrelevant. It is my version of installation art. I practice *tsundoku* the way others do firebricks on the floor of the Tate.'

'They get paid handsomely for it, though.'

'That's a mere mercenary consideration, Edward. A brick is always a brick but I can pick a book, any book you see here, and suddenly a new world opens up. There is no need to read everything, just a chapter, a page, a paragraph, even a line will do. Or I can find again an old friend I thought was lost forever, rediscovering the original pleasure it gave me. Or I am looking for inspiration, can't find the right word, phrase or image, and by chance there it appears as I flick randomly a book of aphorisms, a collection of verse by some obscure poet, a history of Europe no longer fashionable, a study of modern jazz … I could go on. You know those things you were saying about providence? Maybe my serendipitous practice of *tsundoku* is a form of providence too.'

'It could well be.'

Roland looked at the ceiling for a moment. 'Hmm, I need to think about that.' He turned on the gas fire and lifted armfuls of books from the chairs. 'That's enough idle chat for now. Do have a seat and I will bring you that lunch I promised.'

Lunch appeared on a low fold-away table which Roland carried in from the kitchen. On it was a circular wooden board with a variety of cheeses, small pats of butter, slices of fresh bread laid neatly on a willow-pattern dish, plates and cutlery. He returned to the kitchen and came back with a bottle of red wine, a corkscrew and two glasses.

'I hope this will be satisfactory,' he said. 'It's modest, I know, but the wine should make up for the meagreness of the food.' He uncorked the bottle with a practised flourish and poured two generous glasses. 'People in England say you should leave wine to breathe but I've never heard it said in France. When mother visits my grandparents she loads the car with a cache of bottles, the good stuff you *won't* get in an off-licence here. They live in Aquitaine. It's a small village near Montaigne's birthplace, you know.'

Sweeney had never heard anyone say wine should be left to breathe for no one he knew drank it. He had only a hazy idea of where Aquitaine was. He had heard of Montaigne though never read him. 'I must re-read Montaigne at some point,' he lied. His self-confidence ebbed again. He worried he was an ignoramus.

Roland held up the bottle for inspection, pointing out that it was unlabelled. 'So good the locals keep it for themselves, so good you're guaranteed not to suffer a hangover. It's all to do with purity. He raised his glass in a toast. '*A votre santé*. What's your opinion, Edward?'

Sweeney's knowledge of wine was non-existent, his experience limited to a glass of Liebfraumilch or Black Tower, both of which had made him feel queasy. He sipped the wine gingerly. Roland appeared to take his caution to demonstrate seasoned appreciation. The wine was smooth and tasted of blackberries. Sweeney rolled it around his mouth as he imagined wine tasters would do. He could say honestly, 'This is excellent, the best wine I've ever tasted.' He couldn't tell if Roland thought he was speaking truthfully or not but he did seem childishly satisfied.

The bread and cheese were excellent too though he was

glad there was no soft French variety. His parents only bought Cracker Barrel, his father describing everything else as tasting and smelling of 'sweaty socks'. They ate awkwardly with plates on their knees and Sweeney was tempted to rest his on top of a nearby stack of books. Three down from the top was Camus' *La Peste*, the novel Sweeney had studied with Miss Bell. Like everyone else, he'd cheated by reading the English translation.

When they'd finished eating, Roland lifted the table back into the kitchen and fetched an ashtray from his desk. This one advertised Dubonnet. He set it down between them and refilled the glasses. 'We might as well polish off this bottle,' he said, 'a little French *bien être et bien vivre* on a tedious Sunday in Hull.'

Sweeney had no objection. 'It really is superb,' he said and, for the moment at least, the wine gave him a taste of freedom, with notes of sophistication and hints of culture. He offered Roland one of his cigarettes but he gestured refusal with his pipe.

'You said earlier you'd finished writing. Have you finished a chapter? Or have you completed the manuscript?'

An innocent question, Sweeney thought, and to which he expected a straightforward answer. Instead, Roland's expression changed, as though Sweeney's question revealed a misunderstanding so profound it bordered on insulting. He had a disturbing apprehension that maybe Roland had a split personality. Had Blanche hinted at such in his letter? Did it explain Simon's reluctance to speak positively about his neighbour? The look seemed to presage an outraged reproach – 'Are you really so stupid to ask such a question?' Just as suddenly, Roland's features relaxed. He ruffled his beard, put his pipe in the ashtray and shook his head. When he spoke his tone was apologetic, as if he'd read Sweeney's mind.

'Truth is the novel will never be finished. No, that's not right. The novel *is* finished but it will never be completed. Can you understand that distinction?' Before Sweeney could answer, his response delayed a little by the effect of the wine, Roland went on. 'Most people would think it crazy, I expect, which is why I rarely discuss my work with anyone. But then most people never turn their minds to writing in the first place.'

He poured more wine into Sweeney's glass, looked at what remained in the bottle, and added it to his own. 'You mentioned Camus earlier and your inspiring schoolteacher. And the story you told? I thought what a coincidence! You talked about providence too and for once I thought it can't be *mere* coincidence. You see, writing my novel *is* like the myth of Sisyphus, at least as Camus understood it. I type it up to the top of the hill. There it stands right now' – he lifted his arm – 'and that's where you find me today. Tomorrow' – he let his hand fall – 'my novel will be down at the bottom again and that's where I will be too. Does the prospect of tomorrow depress me? I can say honestly, no, it doesn't. Joy comes in the morning too. What is unfinished becomes unending. You do understand, don't you?'

'Be like Sisyphus!' Sweeney said more loudly than he intended.

'That's it exactly! My story – I can't remember how it first started and I will never discover how it finally ends. Your teacher, what was her name again?'

'Miss Bell.'

'She rang out the truth, Edward … at least for me. Can you see why your story in The Queens had such an effect? Do you remember the final lines of Camus on Sisyphus? "The struggle towards the heights is enough to fill a man's heart. One must imagine Sisyphus happy." Well, you must imagine me happy. I am my own hero! God's absence is replaced by my creative mind!'

Sweeney couldn't help stretching out his hand and running his fingers along the spine of *La Peste*. He remembered the civil servant Joseph Grand and his obsessive desire to write the flawless novel, the one which would make a publisher stand up, call in his colleagues to say 'hats off'. He recalled his preoccupation with an exact adjective. It had stuck in his mind because he thought it the perfect description of Miss Bell – *svelte*. It was perfect for Julie too. His attention slipped from Roland to an image of walking hand in hand with Julie on a moonlit summer's evening somewhere in the South of France. Roland's voice dispelled his daydream. It seemed to come from such a distance that Sweeney failed to catch the words. 'I'm sorry. I didn't hear what you said.'

Roland nodded at the copy of *La Peste*. 'I'm not a Joseph Grand if that's what you are thinking. I find it easy to get beyond the first line. The truth is' – he finished off his wine and ran both of his palms around the bowl of his glass – 'it's not a matter of finding each and every *mot juste*. Well, it's not only that. The story has become my life and I don't want it to end, of course. I'm sure you know the French word for novel is *roman*. I think of myself as a romantic in that my life is a novel.' Roland said these last words with such seriousness that it didn't occur to Sweeney to make some dismissive remark. 'When I said joy comes in the morning, it's true. I don't want to leave my world of imagination. I am more at home there than anywhere else.' For the first time Roland struggled to express himself. 'Let's just say I can edit, reconsider, revise, change, whichever word you choose, and make my absurdity bearable. Everything there *is* providential, Edward, every character, every scene. It's not a case of me needing to say something. I want to say everything! And it's best dealing with everything on paper than bothering the lives of others, don't you think?' Before Sweeney could answer, Roland said, 'Look, come over here.'

Sweeney got up groggily and followed him to the desk. It had a set of three drawers on either side. Roland opened them one by one and stood aside. Each drawer was filled with type-scripts, each one tied together with string. On the top page of each draft he glimpsed lines scored out, sentences in minute handwriting added, words scribbled along both margins. He couldn't guess how many drafts there were. Half a bottle of red wine had addled his brain. Roland picked one, undid the string, and flicked though the pages so Sweeney could get an impression of his revisions. As far as he could judge, the amendments were copious.

'You never intend your work to be published?'

Roland looked disappointed by this question. He tied up the draft again, put it back in place. He then closed the drawers one by one. '*Ama nesciri* is a venerable wisdom.' He could tell Sweeney didn't understand. 'Love to be unknown, especially in our fame-obsessed age.'

When they sat down again, Sweeney sensed Roland with-drawing from him, returning to a world where he was no longer welcome. It wasn't that he couldn't comprehend what Roland had told him. The truly inane question would have been, 'What is your novel about?' Why not spend your time creating and recreating a life on paper, especially when you consider how most people actually do spend their time and with so little to show for it? Nor did he dismiss Roland's behaviour as 'ther-apeutic' as psychotherapists understood it. His novel wasn't about coping with life. He'd been honest. It *was* his life. In truth, Sweeney considered Roland luckier than those who would think him weird. How could he dismiss Roland's way of life when his own solitary days probably seemed inconceivable to others? He was certain that he didn't have the courage to live like Roland. But he did think it unusual for someone so young to forgo all ambition, to reject all desire for fame, all desire for recognition. Sweeney would love to become a published author, to be 'known', if only to impress Julie. He pictured himself handing her a copy of his novel and when she opened it, finding a dedication to her. Ambition could be as base as that, like Disraeli seducing England.

'I was selfish to waylay you in order to indulge my little celebration,' Roland said at last. 'Tomorrow the work of Sisyphus begins again.' He smiled. 'At that point you will have to forgive me being as anti-social as before. I am grateful to you for your company today – and to Miss Bell, of course. I take it you were in love with her.'

'All the boys were.'

'I can imagine. Everyone needs their Miss Bell. Both of you will appear in my next draft … if you don't object, that is?'

'Not in the least, I love the thought that Miss Bell and I will be joined together at last.'

'I like your sense of humour. Is it typically Belfast?'

'I used to think the only thing typical of Belfast was the rain. Hull has changed that.'

'That's probably a typically Belfast thing to say.'

There was a longer silence which Sweeney took to mean it was time to go. Anyway, he was tired. The wine had made him sleepy. 'Thanks for lunch. If you get the chance, thank your mother for the wine – oh, and happy rock pushing. I'll know things are going well when I hear jazz.'

'You're gracious, Edward. I'm happy to have you as my neighbour.'

As Sweeney walked slowly and unsteadily up the stairs, Roland called after him. 'If you are planning on an afternoon nap, make sure to drink a glass of water beforehand. I promise you will wake up without a hangover. Remember, it's the purity.'

'Will do,' Sweeney replied.

He awoke a few hours later, hearing faint notes of jazz below. He didn't have a hangover and Sunday was almost gone.

CHAPTER FOUR

The morning bustle diminished as Sweeney climbed the university's bare concrete steps to the doors of the Faculty building. Excited chatter faded along corridors as students filtered off to lectures or seminars. A door slammed somewhere, a boy's voice called out, a girl laughed in response, then silence.

He stopped at the postgrad room, took a deep breath, adjusted his army surplus canvas shoulder bag used since schooldays and walked in. He expected three pairs of eyes to look his way, anticipated greetings and introductions, but the room was empty. Relief was replaced by irritation at the thought of explaining himself three times rather than once.

Blanche's presence had imparted style to this room, the neat order of pens in the dish, the glass ashtray, the photograph, that colourful tea mug. Today the room looked bare, impersonal. No books or papers lay about. The box file he'd seen in July had gone. Only a small, disposable aluminium ashtray sat on each desk top. The chair by the window had a couple of cushions in bright floral fabric, one on the seat and one on the back. So that desk was taken. In the metal bin beside another he saw a few discarded and crumpled pages along with the wrapping of a Cadbury's Bar Six. Inspecting the third, he saw a prominent plastic sticker, a blue cockerel atop a football, and around its edges printed in gold lettering Tottenham Hotspur F.C. Blanche's desk had been left for him. It was something else Sweeney had inherited. The upholstered swivel chair had been replaced by a standard moulded plastic one.

Setting his bag on the table, he extracted the form he needed along with a lined writing pad. He wrote his name on the first page of the pad and put on it his paperback copy of Waugh's *Men at Arms*, opened and face down, to give an impression of work interrupted. He took off his wet cagoule, gave it a shake and hung it from the single hook on the back of the door. Two convector radiators ensured the room was pleasantly warm. Sweeney took a moment to stand against one, drying his trousers and warming his hands as best he could. Rain beat against the window, the clouds curded black and grey. He needed to visit the departmental office.

Outside the office door he hesitated again, ran his hands through his hair, checked the collar of his green plaid shirt – 'You'll need a heavy shirt to keep you warm,' his mother had said – and straightened his maroon jumper – 'and don't forget to wear a jumper'. The prospect of seeing Julie excited and troubled him in equal measure. He knocked politely and entered. Two women were at their desks, one typing and the other sorting through pages in a yellow cardboard folder. Both of them, Sweeney guessed, were in their early forties, both with hair in buns. The woman typing wore a red, long-sleeved top and didn't look up. The woman with the file wore a dark blue dress and glanced sternly over the top of her black-framed glasses. There was no sign of Julie. Sweeney introduced himself, apologised for the interruption and explained his purpose. He held up the form needed to complete his registration. He spoke quickly, nervously, but deferentially, willing to acknowledge the secretaries' authority. The woman's manner changed immediately. She removed the glasses, put them on the desk and smiled. Her colleague stopped typing, looked up and smiled too.

'Our new PhD student, of course,' the secretary with the folder said. 'If I seemed a bit off-putting it's because undergraduates normally don't enter our Holy of Holies. Postgrads have privileges. Raymond Blanche thought we were his personal assistants, isn't that right?' She looked across at her colleague. They seemed good sports (a nice English expression, Sweeney thought).

HERE

'I met him when I was here in the summer. He told me his flat was vacant and that's where I'm living now.'

'Well, aren't *you* the privileged one, Mr Sweeney,' the woman continued. 'You inherited his flat but don't expect to inherit his two personal assistants.' The secretaries laughed. 'My name is Jan, by the way, and this is Jo.'

'Hello,' Jo said, 'pleased to meet you.'

Sweeney greeted them. 'I'll do my best not to bother you.'

'That's what we like to hear,' Jo smiled.

When he handed over the form, Jan placed it on top of her in-tray with a pat as if to assure him processing was a priority. They asked how he was settling in, what he thought of the university, did he like Hull, could he make sense of the accent.

'Everything is fine, thank you. I like Hull, still finding my way about. It's the same with the university. And I love the accent.' He pointed to the telephone on Jo's desk and said, 'foehn'.

'You'll be speaking like a native before long,' Jo said.

'Do you know if Mr Dawson is in this morning?' he asked.

'I haven't seen him,' Jan replied. 'Have you, Jo?' Jo shook her head. 'I can check his teaching schedule if you like?'

Sweeney was about to say it wasn't important, he could see him some other time, when the door pushed open and Julie entered backwards with a stack of booklets in her arms. She was wearing a neat blue denim skirt and a multi-coloured tank-top. When she turned, he could see her cheeks were slightly flushed, blonde hair falling across her eyes. Sweeney was so stunned by her looks he couldn't move fast enough to help before she dumped the booklets in a heap on her desk.

'Julie this is Edward Sweeney, our new PhD student,' Jan said.

Julie's blue eyes appraised him as they'd done in July. She hesitated for a second, 'You were here in the summer to see Mr Dawson.'

Sweeney was dismayed at the lack of warmth in her voice but managed to blurt out, 'Yes, that's right.'

He realised he'd better stop staring. He wasn't sure how women teased each other, but he imagined when he was gone the older secretaries saying something like, 'You've got an admirer there, Julie, the young man couldn't take his eyes off you.'

'Julie, you haven't seen Mr Dawson this morning by any chance?' Jo asked.

'I saw him go into his office a moment ago.' Without looking up, Julie set about putting the booklets in order and Sweeney recovered his poise.

'Would you like me to see if he's free now, Edward?' Jan put her hand on the telephone.

'If that's no trouble, thanks – and please call me Eddie.'

Jan looked at him coyly as she put her glasses back on. 'It's no trouble at all … Eddie.' He noticed Jo smiling at her performance. Yes, I'm definitely going to like it here, Sweeney thought.

'It's Jan, Mr Dawson. Are you free this morning?' She held Sweeney's eyes as she spoke. Dawson must have been giving an account of a busy schedule. Sweeney remembered Blanche's remark about him being difficult to pin down. 'Your new postgraduate student Mr Sweeney has arrived. He wondered if he might have a word.' Dawson's response was not a simple yes. Obviously he disliked being put on the spot. Jan kept looking at Sweeney and he had the feeling she was enjoying Dawson's awkwardness. 'He's here in the office. Shall I send him along?' She smiled at what Sweeney took to be hesitation, possibly reluctance, on the other end. 'I see. Yes, I'll tell him, yes, straight away.' She put down the phone with the satisfied look of someone who'd won a minor skirmish. Jo was grinning as she typed. 'Mr Dawson has a meeting to prepare for later this morning but he can fit you in now. Do you know his office?' Jan explained its location. Sweeney thanked her with exaggerated boyish gratitude (thinking he might need to look to both secretaries for motherly protection at some stage). Julie sighed at the booklets in front of her, ignoring him as he left.

· · · · · · · · · ·

'Come in,' he heard in response to his knock. Sweeney saw a portly man of medium height with thinning grey hair, dressed in a heavyweight herringbone suit, white shirt and burgundy tie. He was standing by a bookcase which took up most of one wall, returning a volume to its shelf. Sweeney couldn't help thinking this pose had been staged. 'Mr Sweeney, I presume. We meet at last.'

'Thank you, Mr Dawson. I'm sorry for the intrusion.'

'Not at all, not at all. It is I who must apologise for not being here when you came in July. It was just one of those things, I'm afraid.' He left the explanation hanging and shook Sweeney's hand. While the movement was done with apparent confidence, the handshake felt uncertain. There was a scent of expensive cologne. Sweeney noted Dawson's features were remarkably smooth and unblemished for a man of his age (mid-fifties he reckoned). 'Or may I call you Edward? The personal formalities of the academy are loosening, as you probably know. I put it down to student activism in the sixties. We had an occupation here. It was outrageous … but you're not allowed to say so in these democratic times, are you?'

'Yes, of course, Edward is fine.' He avoided confirming Dawson's complaint.

Dawson didn't volunteer his own Christian name. Sweeney didn't mind. He felt uncomfortable using the Christian names of older people.

'Please have a seat, Edward.' He pointed to the standard plastic chair in front of his desk. When Dawson was seated, he said after some thought, 'It's also the American influence, of course.' His look became guarded and, Sweeney couldn't help thinking, resentful. 'Like the current obsession with PhDs, that's an American import as well. Soon you won't be able to consider an academic career without having Doctor in front of your name.' *Mr* Dawson looked suddenly embarrassed, perhaps at the idea he may have sown unintentionally about his own lack of status. 'Call me old-fashioned, but I fear sometimes it puts a paper certificate before ability … but I suppose it's better than going down the German route, wouldn't you say?' He sniffed as if no one in their right mind would want to go down the German route.

Sweeney had no idea what the German route was but felt obliged to say something. 'As a student, I suppose you don't think much beyond passing exams. Now that you mention it, yes, I see what you mean. Things can become formulaic rather than creative, restricting rather than encouraging intellectual enquiry.' He thought it sounded good.

It must have, for Dawson tapped his desk. 'I couldn't have put it better myself. People my age are often not listened to at all.' Sweeney remembered Miss Bell – no one over the age of thirty. Was this another of his supervisor's insecurities, a feeling of being out of time already, only one 'workman-like' book to his name?

'I much enjoyed your *Memories of Things Like This*,' Sweeney lied. 'I thought it would be a great template for my thesis. Not the subject matter obviously, but the way it's composed, the putting together of text, commentary and critical assessment.'

'Why, thank you. It was a modest contribution to the literature,' Dawson replied self-effacingly but unconvincingly. 'If I may put it this way, modest but enduring, one against which future work on the subject will be measured.' He may be uncertain but he was also proud, Sweeney judged.

'I'm sure it will be. It sent me back to the trilogy. I'm reading it with new insight this time.' Dawson seemed appreciative of these ingratiating remarks and Sweeney was grateful he wasn't pressed on precisely which new insight.

'Now to more pressing matters, Edward. I have read your proposal – unfortunately I haven't got it with me this morning – and I believe it has the makings of an excellent thesis.' Dawson steepled his fingers like Mr Trammer. 'Of course, you are only at base camp, not even in the foothills, and your map is still without detail. There will be all kinds of paths, many of them dead ends or false trails. The only way to reach the top is to start climbing, the only way to learn is ... to find out for *yourself*. There is no magic formula, whatever those American "How to write a PhD" cribs would have you believe.' Making a fist for emphasis, he went on, 'You have to make it your own, stamp your creative imagination on the material. In the end, no one can do that for you.' His fist fell limply on the desk top. Sweeney almost expected him to end with 'and don't expect me to do it for you'. Dawson was more subtle than that. 'You know, Edward, I've always considered the role of a supervisor is to provide a shoulder to cry on – if necessary, that is. You know, when things aren't going right and a little encouragement is required.' Dawson's tone became solicitous. 'It can be a lonely old enterprise, academic research – fulfilling, yes, but definitely lonely.' He may have considered his prognosis too negative, encouraging Sweeney to cry on his shoulder too often, for he quickly added, 'But I have every confidence in your ability, every confidence. You come highly recommended. It's good that you have chosen Hull.'

'Thank you. Hull was highly recommended to me.' This was true. 'And yourself of course.' This wasn't.

Dawson nodded slightly. It was a dignified acceptance of the compliment. After a brief pause, he spoke of the facilities the department could provide, his own responsibilities as supervisor, Sweeney's as student and opportunities in the future to take some classes. When Dawson finished, he asked, 'Do you smoke?'

'Yes, I do.' He was about to take out his packet and offer one to Dawson when his supervisor put up a hand to stop him.

'No, Edward, allow me. After all this business so early in the day, I think we deserve a *proper* cigarette.' Sweeney smiled at the use of his father's expression. Dawson opened a silver box and offered it. 'I expect you will enjoy these. They are Turkish, best quality, I get them from an exclusive supplier in London.'

Delicately, Sweeney selected one. They were unfiltered – like his father's – and the tobacco seductively dark. Dawson pushed across a Ronson desk lighter. Sweeney moistened his lips carefully, recalling one of his aunts telling him as a child when she allowed him a puff of her Gallagher's Green, 'Don't make a duck's arse of it, Eddie'.

'Well, what's your judgement?'

'Exquisite, they must be expensive.'

Dawson waved away the remark. 'Sometimes you have to ignore expense and think only of pleasure.' I suppose you do, thought Sweeney. Both smoked for a while in indulgent silence.

The telephone rang. There followed a staccato exchange as Dawson rummaged awkwardly in a leather briefcase by his chair, pulling out a few sheets of paper, checking them over in a fluster as he spoke. When he put down the receiver, he apologised and excused himself. 'I must get these copied for my meeting. I will be back shortly.'

After he left, Sweeney reached across to inspect a framed photograph on the desk. He had expected a family snapshot, a wife, a couple of children, perhaps a Labrador. Instead, it was a black and white print of a cricket team, all young men, possibly a university eleven. There was a large silver trophy before the seated front row. He looked closely to see if he could pick out Dawson. Yes, there he was in his whites, sweater and hooped cap. He sat at one edge, smiling broadly. He replaced the photograph precisely. He didn't want to be thought prying. Around the room was more cricketing memorabilia. A hooped cap sitting atop a cabinet by the door he assumed was the one in the photograph. There was a stylised painting of a match on a village green as well as three sketched caricatures of cricketers bearing what looked like authentic autographs. Perhaps he should prepare something conversational about cricket for their next meeting? However, Dawson didn't appear to be a man for 'regular' meetings and the next three years, Sweeney thought, promised almost complete autonomy.

Leaning over the desk, he stubbed out his cigarette in the ashtray, at the same time trying to stub out Julie's earlier indifference. He had no time to dwell on her, for Dawson returned still in a fluster. Contrived or not, Sweeney couldn't tell.

'I'm going to have to cut short our meeting,' he said, waving his sheaf of papers. 'I must read through these additions to the agenda.' He sighed. 'Didn't I say how things are so bureaucratic these days?'

'I understand.' Sweeney tried to sound as sympathetic as possible and stood up to leave.

'I suggest you take some time to familiarise yourself with the library, Edward. You know, Larkin's done a wonderful job. The library has become the university's greatest asset. I recommend putting together a bibliography of sorts, list of essential works for your thesis, that sort of thing.' Dawson ran out of suggestions. 'Early days, early days, but feel free to drop by when you're more on top of things.' He sighed again, waved his papers again. Sweeney was dismissed.

. . . .

In his absence from the postgrad room, a damp donkey jacket had been left over the back of a chair by the desk with the Tottenham Hotspur sticker. Sitting on it was an equally damp box file (possibly the one he'd seen in July). A cigarette butt smouldered in the tinfoil ashtray. Sweeney could tell from the positioning of his *Men at Arms* someone had taken an interest in his arrival. He was considering a visit to the library and making a start on his 'bibliography of sorts' when the door opened abruptly.

'Sorry, people tell me I don't know my own strength.' The accent was unmistakably London. The speaker was a tall, well-built man, Sweeney's own age, mop of curly dark hair, dressed in denim jeans and a chunky grey sweater. 'Foul weather, isn't it? God's own country my arse, don't know how many times I've had a soaking these last few days. My name is Alan, by the way, Alan Brown.'

'Edward, Edward Sweeney, Eddie will do.'

'Yes, I noticed from the pad on the desk, couldn't help having a butcher's. That's a Belfast accent, isn't it? How've you been coping with the locals?' Before he could answer Brown added, 'I wouldn't worry if they treat you strangely. I'm from London and I might as well be from Outer Mongolia. By the way, don't ever mention North Humberside.'

'So I've heard. And I thought people from home were obsessed with identity.'

'Oh boy, don't you believe it, Tykes through and through here, man and boy, woman and girl. I love winding them up.' Brown gave the impression of being a bruiser if you got on his wrong side. 'Eddie, are you busy right now? What about a coffee? I need something to warm me up. This damned weather is killing me.' He went to the window. 'It looks like it's stopped raining for a bit.'

Early days, Sweeney convinced himself, early days. The

library could wait. 'Yes, of course.'

As they queued for their coffees in the Students' Union, they discussed their research. Brown was doing something on Larkin's poetics. What that something was, Sweeney didn't hear in the echoing noise of voices, the clatter of cups and saucers. 'Larkin's the reason I'm here,' Brown continued. 'In the end it was pointless trying to see the great man in person. He sent me a note, polite, civil and to the point, telling me everything I need to know is in his poems. Fair enough, I suppose. The closest I ever get to Larkin is seeing him at the bar in Staff House.'

'Are you not tempted to have a word?'

'Eddie, my son, you never disturb a man who's having a quiet drink at lunchtime. I heard he sometimes hangs out at Ye Olde Black Boy in town. Then again, you never disturb a man on a night out either.' Brown asked him what he was working on.

'It's "Imagining Northern England in Twentieth-Century Literature". That's only a provisional title at the moment.' He got no further before they reached the cashier.

'These are on me,' Brown interrupted. To the woman at the till, he said, 'Sandra, let me introduce my fellow scholar and gentleman, Eddie. He's from Northern Ireland. He told *me* he's come all the way to Hull to find someone with a bit of imagination. I told *him* it's a hopeless task. Hull's the most unimaginative place on the planet. Isn't that so?' He winked at Sweeney.

'Noooo! We just put up quietly wi' bores like you.' Sandra slapped change into Brown's hand.

'She tries to hide it, Eddie, but she can't get enough of me. Her insults are a gesture of love. Isn't that the truth, Sandra?'

'Ah shut up, you.'

Sweeney wished he had Brown's jocular ease. Maybe that was something he could learn too.

Over coffee, he enquired about their fellow postgrads.

'Patsy and Toby, Toby and Patsy, our own yin and yang, Toby Milne and Patsy Richards, you'll see what I mean. They appear to have opposing views of the world but only in the abstract. You know what? I'd put my money on them being the perfect couple. That's why I say yin and yang and I pride myself on my betting instincts. The thing is, deep down they know it too. You've come across people like that, haven't you?'

Sweeney couldn't think of any. The people he knew tended to share the same views on everything or nothing, abstract or not.

'Patsy is one of those poor little rich girls. No, I'm being unfair to her, she isn't self-pitying. Anyhow, she's from Esher. You know Esher?' Sweeney shook his head. 'It's in Surrey, leafy suburb, stockbroker belt. It wouldn't surprise me if her house is called Wisteria Lodge. You know the Sherlock Holmes story?'

'Yes, I've read it.'

'Patsy went to a private girls' school, like a long list of privilege, isn't it? Hers is a story of rejecting that privilege … in the abstract. And the reason for rejection, I'm afraid to say, is the man she's living with, one of the biggest shits I've ever known and I've known quite a few. Keith Mitchell is his name.'

'Who's he?'

'Would you believe he's also a public school boy? He lectures here at the university, sociology of course. He became a revolutionary Marxist at Winchester or wherever. You would mistake him for a merchant banker, always kitted out in the best gear, clothes made-to-measure, fit in a treat at the Piper here in Hull. I don't think.'

'What's the Piper?'

'You must have seen it on Newland Avenue. It's like *The Wheeltappers and Shunters Club*, you know on TV?'

'Workingmen's club you mean, like the one on Princes Avenue?'

'I don't think any Tories are members of the Piper. Mitchell owns a posh house on Marlborough Avenue, nothing but the best. His accent is posh too. For some reason he has left-wing guru status and Patsy's been snared into his little sect. They never seem to have any impact beyond a few turgid articles in Hullfire.'

'Hullfire?'

'It's the student newspaper. Not a bad rag otherwise.' He paused. 'You must think it very English, Eddie, workers taking a lead from their public school betters – the long march of everyman, don't you believe it.'

'I was told to watch out for the idiosyncrasies of the English class system.'

'Idiosyncrasies … I suppose you could say that.' He sniffed. 'But Patsy, she's too good for them and certainly too good for Mitchell.' Brown shook his head and looked down at his cup. 'Fancy another one of these?'

Sweeney said it was his turn, queued, paid, wasn't recognised by Sandra, and returned with two fresh cups.

Brown pulled out a packet of Gold Bond. 'Coffin nail?'

'Thanks.'

He slung a cigarette across the table to Sweeney and put another to his lips.

'What about Toby?' Sweeney asked

'Toby's Lincolnshire gentry, from a well-connected county family. He was intending a career in the army at one time, discovered literature and then – here's the interesting bit – got religion, found God, or whatever the term is. Hard to credit, isn't it, in this day and age? Church of England, intending to take Holy Orders – or is that only for monks?'

'I think the term is ordained.'

'But he's no Derek Nimmo like in *All Gas and Gaiters*. And I'll tell you something, he will do more good in this world than Mitchell. He works with the homeless as far as I know, helps out with some C of E mission in Hull.'

'Are you saying Patsy would make a good vicar's wife then?'

Brown ran the tip of his Gold Bond around the edge of the university's tinfoil ashtray. 'It would be better than being the moll of a wannabe Bolshevik, all gas and no gaiters. It won't last, believe me. Well, if there is any justice in this world, it won't ... Oh, I don't know. I'm rambling on.'

'Have you mentioned anything to her?' This was the first time Sweeney had ever discussed someone's love life. It felt strange, gossipy and quite salacious.

'I have hinted as much. Oh look, I suppose it's really none of my business. When you meet Patsy you can judge for yourself.' He'd said all he wanted to say. Sweeney wondered if Brown had an eye for Patsy. He was intrigued to meet her.

They changed the subject to life at university, things to do, things to avoid.

'For you, Eddie, there's the Celtic Cultural Society.'

'As the old joke goes, tried it once, didn't like it.'

Brown laughed, 'I haven't heard that one in a while. I suspect it's a cunning English plot to encourage the Scots, Welsh and Irish to beat up each other and not us.'

Brown had some entertaining stories to tell, skewering neatly staff peccadillos and pretentions, Dawson being one victim. 'I think Dawson feels a bit of a yesterday's man, stuck in the fifties, hasn't adjusted to the sixties and loathes the seventies. The young members of staff tend to ignore him. They think he's out of touch and doesn't pull his weight.'

'I did sense some resentment on his part when I talked to him. But I found it hard not to like him.

Brown shrugged. 'I'll give you that. He's likeable enough. Here's the important question. Have you made a good impression with the secretaries?'

'I did my best. They were helpful. Jan and Jo seem

super-efficient.' Sweeney paused. 'And Julie is very nice too.' In that pause he knew he'd given himself away. He felt like cursing.

Brown picked at one of his nails and was silent for a moment. Looking at the nail rather than Sweeney, he said, 'I don't know what girls are like in Belfast but you've got to watch yourself in Hull. You go out with a local girl once, maybe twice, and they'll want to take you home to meet their mam. I speak from experience.' Sweeney imagined being invited back to meet Julie's mam and blushed slightly. Brown glanced sideways at him. 'The swinging sixties gave Hull a bypass, I fear. Girls are charming, yes, attractive, yes, that blonde, blue-eyed Scandinavian look sexy, yes, but definitely traditional. Marriage, that's their thing, put you in a book of wedding photographs. You don't need it, Eddie, son, you really don't need it, believe me.' Sweeney didn't think it such a bad fate to be beside Julie in a wedding album. Brown kept his remarks general but Sweeney was convinced he wasn't fooled.

'That sounds like good advice,' Sweeney said and he offered Brown an Embassy Regal. They said nothing more on the matter. Brown switched subject to the performance of Tottenham Hotspur, which seemed closer to his heart than local women and their mams.

'I'm hungry,' Brown announced after a while. 'Let's get some lunch. We'll brazen it out and go to Staff House. The food's a little better.'

Sweeney looked doubtful. 'Are you sure we're allowed in?'

'Don't worry. You stick with me. They get postgrads to teach for them, you too at some point, so technically speaking we *are* staff. Who knows, we might even see old Larkin.'

And they did see him. A tall figure, more corpulent than Sweeney had expected, the glasses, the domed bald head, glass in hand (it looked like gin and tonic), standing alone, his back to the bar, gazing over the others, and smiling, as if waiting for someone. Sweeney felt an instinctive sympathy, was tempted to have a word, but was now aware of an English custom – never disturb a man having a quiet drink at lunchtime.

. . . .

Brown and he developed an agreeable rapport, having coffee when convenient, meeting for dinner in the student canteen and, the odd time, sneaking lunch in Staff House, Sweeney learning by observation (as he'd hoped) some of his new friend's sociable techniques. He recalled Brendan Behan writing that the first rule of being a good liar was to have a good memory. Sweeney saw it applied in equal measure to being good company. Brown remembered what others liked, what football teams they supported, what ailments they had, what music they enjoyed, little things which Sweeney often never noticed, didn't think important, or forgot. He was improving, aware that seriousness wasn't necessarily a virtue or quietness attractive, and that a large degree of silliness was essential for well-being. So he got into the habit of asking Jo and Jan how their kids were doing at school, Pearl and Simon how their bridge was going, and Roland, when he saw him, about his mother's trips to France. He discovered life was accordingly more agreeable and it didn't require greater self-disclosure. The opposite was true. People liked to talk about their own lives, remarkably indiscreetly at times, which allowed him to remain non-confessional. It was a form of self-protection too. Those he pleased with his attention he also encouraged to be pleased with him. He sensed the small change of life accumulating to his advantage and settled into a comfortable sociability, becoming woven into the fabric of the place, Hull's elsewhere becoming home. The one negative was failure to make any impression on Julie.

Attempts to draw Julie into his orbit were futile. When he

passed the office at lunchtime, she would be going off with two or three girlfriends. Leaving at five, she was always in a hurry, pulling on her coat, hitching up her shoulder bag. Even when she did speak to him, there was no evidence of anything beyond polite civility. Childish, that's what he thought of himself. Here he was in Hull, enjoying his independence and yet ludicrously incapable of asking out a woman his own age. Of course it would be embarrassing to be rebuffed and perhaps uncomfortable thereafter, but should he not make a first move? He hadn't done so and reckoned this timidity a true measure of immaturity. Brown's daring sense of the possible, his conviction that desires were there for the taking, hadn't rubbed off on him.

. . . .

It was half way through Michaelmas term before Sweeney met Toby and Patsy. He'd spent the afternoon in the library and when he returned to the postgrad room, he found two men, one sitting at a desk, the other standing by the door, and a woman leaning against the heater at the window. Sweeney introduced himself. It was Toby at the desk and Patsy at the window. The other man was Keith Mitchell.

'Sorry if we are disturbing you, Edward,' Mitchell said in the voice of someone used to taking control of situations and of people. He was dressed in a dark blue three-piece suit, white shirt and red tie. Over one arm he carried a mohair coat and at his feet was an expensive-looking leather briefcase. Mitchell had a round freckled face, reddish hair, and a heavy build which good tailoring flattered. 'Patsy and I are on our way to a meeting,' he explained. 'We're a bit early. We won't interrupt for long.' His tone implied nothing could be more important than being in the presence of Keith Mitchell. Sweeney immediately understood Brown's antipathy.

'You're not disturbing me. If *I'm* interrupting something, I don't mind leaving and coming back.'

Both Toby and Mitchell rejected his offer volubly.

Sweeney looked at Patsy, who smiled at him, shook her head, but didn't speak. She was tall, pale and willowy, waif-like perhaps, her thinness masked by a baggy sweater and loose-fitting jeans. Her face was long, her nose straight, her eyes dark, her black hair unusually styled. Well, it was for Sweeney. She wore it close cropped at the front and sides but long at the back. Her bearing struck him as indolent yet spirited, her look intelligent yet uncertain. The only word to describe her was captivating. Not as pretty as Julie but – captivating. She reminded him of Jane Birkin. He understood Brown's concern too. It was the way she looked at Mitchell as he spoke, attentive, fixed, and yet, he suspected, deeply insecure. He imagined their bond, Patsy in love with this egotist, Mitchell in love with himself. In the groves of this relationship, at the end of every vista, he could see only pain for her. At the same time, he couldn't be sure if this impression was at Brown's suggestion.

Mitchell talked as if in lecturing mode. He turned directly to Sweeney. 'I was saying earlier to Toby we need to rally all progressive forces in the face of political reaction. It is a critical historical conjuncture, don't you think? The old order is collapsing all around us, Labour, Tories, the lot of them. You have to be blind not to see it. Our enemies know it too. If we mobilise effectively, we can shift the balance of power for good. But we need leadership and the correct strategy. Some people *won't* see it.' He gestured with the practised timing of a demagogue towards Toby. 'They can't read the signs. They can't recognise the arc of progress. They want to cling to a fantasy of Middle Eastern sheepherders a few thousand years ago. Isn't that right, Toby?' Mitchell looked back at Sweeney. 'In a few years he will become a cassocked drug peddler – if you please vicar, more opium for the masses.' He laughed at his own joke. Sweeney noticed Patsy didn't join in.

Toby sat impassively, not rising to Mitchell's provocation. He could look after himself, Sweeney judged. He was broad-shouldered and muscular though in a natural and not gym-fashioned way. Perhaps he helped out on the farm in Lincolnshire, lifting hay bales, chopping wood, mucking out stables or whatever it was landowners did these days. His healthy complexion was not the ruddy-cheeked sort he associated with rural life (Sweeney was thinking of characters in *Emmerdale Farm*) and definitely not the anaemic look of urban life (he was thinking of himself). He possessed poise very different from Mitchell's.

'Keith,' Toby said finally, 'I was expecting you to say God is dead. Did no one tell you Marx and Engels are dead too?' Sweeney thought it a good reply. He could have sworn Patsy stifled a giggle. 'Have you ever considered your political gospel requires greater belief in miracles than mine? Ideology always needs its own creed.'

'Please, not that old chestnut again, Toby – Marxism as the new religion.' He waved his hands around dismissively. 'I've no blueprint for the future. But it *will* be socialist, you can be sure of that.'

'I thought you always did carry a blueprint around in that bag of yours. I just happen to prefer C.S. Lewis to V.I. Lenin, that's all.' Toby looked at Sweeney as he said this and winked. Mitchell must have suspected he was trying to recruit against him.

'The North of Ireland shows the conjuncture I'm talking about. You'll be aware of that, Edward, the British state using the crisis as a testing ground for repression. Our group supports the anti-imperialist struggle' – he struck the edge of one hand against the palm of the other – 'for it will break the chain of power at its weakest point. When we get the troops out, the revolution will spread here. What's your take from the front line, as it were?'

Sweeney was on the spot, all eyes on him. He felt angry being put in this position. It was why he hated politics. He could never see the point in all these debates because, in his experience, opponents never reconsidered and supporters never doubted. The clash of truths was impossible to arbitrate, he thought. Even when political beliefs proved failures, there was little evidence they ever disappeared. Similar questions and similar answers recurred irrespective of history or experience.

Sweeney's only rhetorical facility was deflection and he knew the value of pressing both sympathy and flattery buttons. 'It's a painful subject, Keith,' he said. 'Being working class like me, some things are difficult to talk about. I don't have your political vision for a start. Coming to Hull may sound like an escape but it's a chance to get a different perspective.' He considered the right buttons had been pressed. He judged he could now be as evasive as he liked. 'All I can say is people at home haven't attained your level of theoretical sophistication. The simple truth is this. It would come as a blinding revelation to most of them.'

Sweeney glanced at Toby, who was grinning broadly, and then at Patsy, who looked to be puzzling through his meaning. Mitchell beamed.

'False consciousness, how right you are. Perhaps you'd like to come along to our meeting? I can always expand on our Irish policy.'

'Thanks, but I'm afraid I have to see someone later,' Sweeney lied. Fearing it might appear an obvious lie, he added, 'And it's not seeing a man about a dog. It's seeing Alan Brown about a book.'

'Brown could do with some political education. His cynicism makes him no better than a Tory.' Mitchell's features tightened briefly as he seemed to recall a past exchange. He became affable once more. 'Another time perhaps?' He didn't wait for Sweeney's reply. 'Patsy, we'd better go.' He picked up his bag. 'It was nice to meet you, Edward.' Mitchell pulled open the door but couldn't resist a final shot at Toby. 'Forgive us leaving you in such deluded company.'

Patsy gathered her coat, gave Sweeney an affectionate pat on the arm as she passed and said softly, 'See you some time.' It was the first words she'd spoken. They captivated him too.

. . . .

There was an unspoken agreement to keep quiet until Patsy and Mitchell were well out of earshot. When Toby stood up he was much taller than Sweeney had expected. He came across to shake hands, a strong, affable grasp.

'How do you find living in Hull?' he asked.

'I'm enjoying it. I think I'm adjusting to the way of things now.'

Toby eyed the door once more. 'I can see you are,' he laughed. 'I thought it very English the way you dealt with Keith. If you don't mind me saying so, it's the kind of polite rebuff he's unable to grasp. "Our eyes shall see thee, which before saw dust; Dust blown by wit, till that they both were blind". That's George Herbert, if you're wondering. In Keith's case the dust is blown by ideology, not wit, the blind leading the blind.'

'I've seen ideology justify murderous tendencies.'

'That's my view too. I don't wish to be unkind, Edward ...'

'People call me Eddie.'

'Eddie ... Keith is puffed up by the empty deceits of politics without the wisdom to be silent on things he's little knowledge of. I mean, it takes a high level of intelligence to be as stupid as he is, don't you think? Of course, Patsy's not like that at all.'

'It definitely takes a high level of intelligence to be that insensitive. Didn't it cross his mind those being sacrificed for his anti-imperialist struggle – *so-called* anti-imperialist struggle – might be friends or relatives of mine?'

Toby put an arm round Sweeney's shoulder. 'You're permitted righteous anger now and then.' He took a step back. 'And I have a feeling you don't have anyone to see this evening. Was that another English evasion too?'

'Was it that obvious? And no, I've nothing on this evening.'

'Not to Keith it wasn't,' Toby laughed again. 'I see you *are* learning quickly. In that case, what do you say to a quick beer in the Hayworth or Gardeners?'

They had more than one beer across the road in the Gardeners. They talked about life at the university, about work in progress, about supervisors, the usual stuff. But it was all preliminary to what was on Toby's mind. What was on his mind was Patsy and for much the same reason she was on Brown's.

'You'll remember what C.S. Lewis said about love. It's not about affection or desire but a steady wish for a person's ultimate good? When I look at Patsy that's what I feel.' He swirled the dregs of Hull Brewery bitter around his glass.

Sweeney had never read any Lewis apart from *Out of the Silent Planet*, a book he'd never finished. He couldn't help thinking Toby wasn't being entirely honest in what he said. Sweeney assumed modern women were like Miss Bell or Pearl Spencer. Surely if there really was a problem with Mitchell it was one for Patsy to sort out? Wasn't she capable of making her own choices? Wasn't that what liberation involved? He didn't want to sound quarrelsome or to challenge Toby's concern and asked in a non-confrontational tone, 'Do you think Patsy doesn't know what's best for her?'

'I worry about her self-abasement to false promises, that's what. Oh, I suppose Mitchell's not the worst in the world but

I know him by reputation. He assumes mastery of Marxist jargon brings privileges. I take it I don't have to spell out what those privileges are?'

'I think I have a good idea.'

'Mitchell was going on about desert sheepherders earlier. Well, I wouldn't want Patsy to become one in his harem, would you?'

Sweeney knew there was a distinction between respecting someone's freedom and ignoring one's own responsibility, between accepting another's choice and permitting wrong to be done. Even so, he couldn't help thinking Toby was being overly protective and, yes, paternalistic. But since he owed Mitchell nothing, he replied, 'I hope Patsy sees through him before too long.'

'Indeed … I enjoyed tonight.' Toby slapped Sweeney on the back, knocking him forward. 'Sorry!'

Sweeney feigned injury. 'It must be all those hay bales you throw about down on the farm.'

Toby laughed, 'It's where I'm going next week. There's a horse I want to look at.' He noticed Sweeney's surprise. Owning a horse was well out of his league. 'It's a Lincolnshire thing. Alan Brown would call it one of the privileges of the gentry.' He patted Sweeney softly this time. 'We'll be seeing each other a lot, I hope. Thanks for the friendly ear tonight.'

. . . .

The first part of term drew to its close. Sweeney had seen Dawson once more when he handed in a vague outline of how his thesis might be organised, a provisional chapter outline, along with an extensive bibliography. He didn't think it much to show for almost four months' work. He was concerned Dawson would think him a slacker.

Instead, Dawson responded with, 'Marvellous, you've been industrious I see. I'm glad there's no trade union for students. They would send you to Coventry like – what's his name – Ian Carmichael in *I'm All Right Jack*. He's from Hull you know.'

'I didn't know that. Peter Sellers was my favourite as Fred Kite. "Russia ... all them cornfields and ballet in the evening". What a great film!'

'Quite so.' Dawson didn't seem so enthused about Russia. He took the handwritten pages from Sweeney and promised to get back to him. 'Once things have quietened down, it's been hectic this term one way and another'.

In the office, the secretaries made an effort to mark the approaching 'festive season' as Jo called it. 'Sometimes academics forget what time of year it is,' she explained.

In one corner they put up a small artificial Christmas tree hung with tinsel and around the walls arranged coloured paper garlands. A staff lunch was booked at a restaurant on Beverley Road. Jan recommended it. 'The food's fab and you get loads.'

The postgrads were invited. Sweeney thought it a nice idea but the others weren't keen.

'I was hoping to get away early,' Toby said.

'It's not really my thing,' Patsy said.

'I couldn't face being sat next to Dawson,' Brown said.

Sweeney was prepared to accept the consensus but when he admitted, 'I've never been to one of these sorts of dos before' the others agreed it was probably a rite of passage and they should go as a group.

'That's very comradely of you,' Sweeney said, and the others looked immediately to Patsy.

She raised her fist and shouted, 'Solidarity with Eddie!'

That lunchtime they were seated at a long table in 'The Humber Suite'. On its walls were framed prints of ships from different eras, negotiating the estuary. It was an occasion when academics, at least those few who attended, were self-consciously 'having a jolly good time', cheerily patronising the secretaries (or so Sweeney felt). Jan, Jo and Julie, who definitely knew what time of year it was, enjoyed the attention. Julie in particular was radiant, wearing a tight knee-length black dress with chiffon sleeves. Sweeney thought it might be an appropriate occasion to make a first move.

When the main course was cleared away and before dessert arrived, Dawson stood up and tapped his wine glass with a spoon. Brown leaned over and whispered to Sweeney, 'God help us all. Dawson is going to make a speech. I thought things had gone too well.'

'Ladies,' Dawson bowed to the secretaries and to Patsy (Sweeney could hear Patsy groaning) 'and gentlemen' (Brown nudged Toby, 'Squire Milne, he means you' and Toby pushed him away playfully). 'I believe a toast is in order. I have been informed that our lovely young secretary Julie has received a proposal of marriage. Is my informant, who shall remain nameless, correct, Julie?'

Julie put a hand to her mouth in surprise, affected or not Sweeney couldn't tell, but with obvious delight. His heart sank.

'I will take that as a yes.' There was a round of applause. Julie was hugged by Jo and Jan, waiters took the signal to pour some wine, and there were words of congratulations around the table. Julie held up for admiration her ring with its tiny diamond cluster.

'Ladies and gentlemen please!' Dawson tapped his glass again.

'He loves this, just loves it,' Patsy mumbled.

Dawson raised his arms like a priest giving a blessing. 'Ladies and gentlemen, let's be upstanding.'

As the chairs shifted in the general commotion, Sweeney heard Toby tell Patsy, 'It seems men regularly propose at Christmastime.' He noticed how she smiled.

'Let's raise our glasses. Julie, we are lucky to have you in the department,' Dawson bowed slightly, 'and your fiancé is even luckier you have accepted him. Here's to a happy engagement, to your future wedding, and to a wonderful marriage. Everyone … Here's to Julie!'

When they had drunk their toast and sat down again, Brown said to them, 'I have to admit old Dawson did a good job there, no cricketing analogies, bowling a maiden over or some such. The mind boggles. What do you say to our own party later? We can give our best wishes to Julie back in the university and head out when the pubs open again?'

'I'd love to,' Patsy said, 'but Keith's arranged a meeting tonight on workers' control of industry.'

'God Almighty, Patsy, can't the revolution do without you for one day?'

'But I promised and don't want to let him down. Tony Benn's advisor is coming. Keith thinks we can change the Labour Party's whole agenda.'

Brown shook his head. 'The Gnomes of Zurich will be shaking in their boots tonight. Toby, are you up for it?'

'I can't, sorry.' He didn't explain why and Brown didn't ask.

'It looks like it's you and me, Eddie.'

'I'm your man.'

So began a night he'd never experienced before, a night of carousing, the sort of night students have enjoyed for centuries, the sort of night the Troubles had deprived him of. They went from pub to pub in the Old Town, Burlington Tavern, The George Hotel, The Bonny Boat, Ye Olde White Harte, Ye Olde Black Boy. The last one Sweeney could remember was the King William. Afterwards, things became hazy.

'Here's to glorious deliverance,' he said loudly.

'In all honesty, my son,' Brown said to him, 'I think you have been delivered. Julie, I'm talking about.' Sweeney started to protest but Brown waved it away. 'You can't fool me. I knew from the first day we met. You know what worried me most? That you'd become like Tom Courtney in *Billy Liar.*

'A complete fantasist you mean? Oh, come on!'

Brown spreads his hands. 'Stranger things have happened … he's from Hull, you know.'

'Who is?'

'Tom Courtney.'

'Something else I never knew.'

'Live and learn, my son. After lunch I asked Jan who the lucky man was. Turns out he's the Hull Kingston Rovers' full-back. Eddie, you *never* had a chance … and from what I could see, your instinct was right not to try.'

Sweeney knew it wasn't instinct but cowardice.

Brown patted his shoulder. 'To Julie from an East Hull estate that's like marrying royalty. Maybe I'm exaggerating but you see what I mean? We might not think it much but she has status now.' He raised his pint to Sweeney. 'And you're smart enough to know what's what. You could have got *swine* drunk as Chaucer would have said, wallowing in melancholy, but you aren't that self-indulgent. So I think you've chosen to be *ape* drunk and make the best of things. See, I did learn something from my course on Early Modern English.'

Deep down, Sweeney knew he was right. He did feel release from a strange, Arthurian, enchantment. He knew Julie had been his fantasy. 'You must think me an idiot.'

'A fool for love, that kind of idiot you mean? When you're in love, even if you only *think* you're in love, you don't examine why. So no, I don't. Haven't we all?'

Sweeney sang the line, "I'm a Dreamer, aren't we all?"

Brown looked surprised, 'My old man used to sing that song!'

'Mine too. Despite what you say, I am a complete fool.'

'Don't be so hard on yourself. There are other fish in the sea.'

Brown looked around him with feigned alarm and whispered, 'Maybe I shouldn't say that out loud in Hull these days.'

'I think that's wise. And remember – no North Humberside. And thanks mate. I feel much better already.'

'That's the spirit, Eddie, my son. Finish up your ale, *mate*, we've a few more pubs to crawl. And if we're up before the magistrate tomorrow what's our story …?' It was an Irish joke Sweeney had told him, one Brown esteemed greatly.

'We only had the one drink …'

'And where did you have that one drink?'

Together, they shouted, 'Sorry, Your Honour, can't remember. We had it in so many pubs.'

PART THREE

Wants

CHAPTER FIVE

In Belfast for Christmas, Sweeney experienced the pull of elsewhere. His parents detected a change.

'Are you sure you're getting enough to eat?' his mother asked with a coddling eye.

'You look as if you could do with a feed … but then you always do,' his father said.

It wasn't how he looked because in truth he looked no different. His manner must have seemed more distant to them, more reserved, less familiar, for that's how he felt.

He returned to Hull in a pair of lined tweed trousers his mother had run up, essential protection for winter she'd told him.

'Hull isn't in the Arctic Circle,' he'd replied.

'You'll be grateful for them – and don't be cheeky.'

He had to admit they looked surprisingly good and felt remarkably comfortable. What's more, they did protect him from the winds off the North Sea which blew along the flatlands of East Yorkshire and gusted down the streets of Hull. No 'westron wynde' blew 'smalle rayne downe' but cutting north-easterlies whipped stinging rain horizontally along the estuary. Though the weather in January was as dismal as in September, he no longer felt oppressed by it. He was no longer *trying* to live here. Hull was *where* he lived. The naïve but liberating effect of that thought pleased him when he stepped off the train at Paragon Station and knew where he was going, what he had to do, which people to meet again. Welcome back to Sweeney-land, he thought. And he'd come bearing gifts.

For Pearl and Simon he brought a bottle of Bushmills whiskey.

'Eddie, there was really no need. That's very kind of you.

105

Aw, thank you,' Pearl said, drawing out the 'you', hugging the bottle to her like a precious object. 'Simon, look what Eddie's brought us.'

Simon appeared out of the kitchen wiping his hands on a dish towel. 'What's that, love? A bottle of Bushmills, that's wonderful, you're a star.' He slapped Sweeney on the shoulder.

'I'm still very grateful for all you did for me my first night here.'

They both looked at him with the same expression, appreciative of his gesture.

He brought another bottle of Bushmills for Roland. Sweeney knocked on his door but there was no response. He was half-way up the stairs when the door opened cautiously. 'Roland, Happy New Year!' Sweeney called from above, bending his head over the bannister.

'Edward, you'll be the death of me,' Roland put a hand to his chest.

Sweeney came down and handed him the Bushmills. 'As a man who appreciates the best, I thought you might like this.'

Roland took the bottle, ran his hand over it, inspecting the label with great care. He held his breath like someone experiencing shock, his words tumbling. 'Why ... why ... this is a surprise,' he said, stroking his Shakespearean beard. 'I never expected ... well, this is wonderful. I've never tasted Irish whiskey.

'I remember you feeling guilty about not ordering one in The Queens. So you can have a drink whenever you like now.'

'It will be a treat. I'm afraid I've nothing in return.'

Sweeney put up his hand. 'There's no need, Roland, no need. It's to thank you for your hospitality.' Roland's hooded eyes suggested he didn't know what this meant. 'You gave me lunch with your mother's excellent wine, remember? How can I put it, the kindness of a stranger?' It was a cliché but there was a place for clichés (he'd learned that from Brown too).

WANTS

Roland nodded, on his face the same look as Pearl and Simon.

. . . .

He had the perfect gift for Brown too. Under his bed at home he'd stashed the collected fragments of childhood. In the bottom of a cardboard box full of random copies of *The Victor*, ephemera about *The Man from Uncle* and *The Avengers* and old school magazines, he'd pulled out a football programme of Tottenham Hotspur versus West Ham United. It was dated 8 April 1966, priced at three pence. It was from a rare visit to English relatives, East Enders who had moved after the war to Harlow (as a boy Sweeney had considered Harlow the epitome of English modernity). Sweeney could remember nothing about the match. What he did remember was a raging toothache brought on by biting a Riley's Chocolate Toffee Roll from a quarter pound bag his father had bought on the way to White Hart Lane. He didn't feel he was betraying his father by giving away the programme. He'd done his bit according to the Fifth Commandment by not complaining about the pain and spoiling his father's enjoyment of the football.

'Where did you get this?' Brown asked.

'I was there. Not that I can remember anything about it. I was suffering from toothache.'

'Yes, I forgot you told me your uncle is a Spurs fan. What a team we had back then, Gilzean, Greaves, McKay, all the greats. We're struggling this season. I watched the New Year's Day match against the Hammers. We won, just about. I went to the next game against Palace. We lost. Damned inconsistency, there's the problem. But a fan's a fan for all that, as Rabbie Burns never said. I never expected something to lift my spirits this bleak mid-winter. Look, it's very good of you. I'll add it to my collection. Are you really sure you want to part with it?'

'It was under my bed. Better a good home where it's cared for.' He thought of Mr Trammer as he said that. 'Football's not really my thing.'

'There was me thinking every boy in Belfast wanted to be George Best. So you'll not be going to Boothferry Park at any time soon? You know Billy Bremner's playing for Hull these days?'

'You can put that in the thick file labelled "that's news to me".'

'Last season I went to cheer on Hull against Chelsea. Had to put on a terrible Yorkshire accent in case the locals thought I'd wandered into the wrong end. It was a bit hairy. Hull lost. Division Two football isn't for the faint-hearted.' Brown put his hands together in supplication. 'If there is a God, please let Spurs avoid relegation.'

'Couldn't you watch Spurs up here if they were?'

'I see you know nothing about footballing passion, Eddie. Let's just leave that question there, shall we? Anyway, I owe you. All I can offer you is a gasper'. He handed Sweeney a Gold Bond and lit it for him.

. . . .

However, Brown did return the favour by introducing him to parts of Hull life Sweeney wouldn't have encountered on his own. On Friday nights they got into the habit of 'drinking down to town' as they called it. They would often start at the Latus fried fish shop, tucked away on a side street off Newland Avenue. 'You need a good lining in your stomach for a night of dissipation' was Brown's justification.

On cold nights, what could be more tempting as the light of the shop spilled onto the footpath? Inside, the sizzle of hot fat, the smell of vinegar, the chatter of those waiting to be served, the rising steam behind the metal and glass fryer, filled their senses. The portions were heroic, battered cod curving in a bag of chips and all wrapped in newspaper. They would eat as they walked, the paper warming their hands, fingertips plucking out the first few mouthfuls, blowing them cool enough to eat. It was a simple and fulfilling pleasure reminding Sweeney of Alf Tupper. They would drink in pubs along Beverley Road, each one busier, noisier and smokier than the last, and into town. They always ended up on return in the Polar Bear on Spring Bank.

The first night, as closing time neared, Brown said, 'Eddie, my son, I'm going to show you one of the hidden delights of this northern town.' He guided him across Princes Avenue and into a side street where a small queue had gathered at the entrance to a factory building.

'What's this place?'

'It's the back of Arnott's Bakery. Are you hungry? You can't call yourself a man until you polish off a fadge on a Friday night.'

'What on earth is that?'

'Just you wait and see.'

The queue was composed of revellers, some young, some middle-aged, couples, singles, all light-hearted, all sharing an expectant mood.

'You got to time it right,' said Brown, 'otherwise you don't get the bacon.' He gestured to those joining the end of the line. 'What you don't want after all this waiting is cheese in your fadge. It's a bad way to start your weekend.'

They entered the building to a long wooden counter behind which was a series of industrial ovens. The aroma of freshly baked bread being slipped out on wooden peels and cooked bacon on large metal trays was irresistible. The girl behind the counter seemed incongruously scrawny amid the abundance she was serving, her features gaunt, a few strands of brown hair from under the netting cap straggling across her forehead.

'A bacon fadge if you please, Alice, and another for my pal Eddie here.'

'You've a pal?' Alice looked at Sweeney. 'You have my commiserations.' There were traces of flour on her cheeks and nylon bib. Sweeney couldn't get over how fragile she looked. He wanted to be protective, to give her a hug. It must be the beer, he thought.

'I don't know how you stand him, I really don't', Alice shook her head. 'As a reward there's extra bacon for you.'

A fadge turned out to be a soft round bap about the size of a dinner plate. Alice sliced theirs open, buttered the insides and filled them with hot bacon. Very deliberately, looking at Brown, she added two extra rashers for Sweeney.

Out in the street again Brown said, 'Alice fancies you.'

'You really think so?'

'I saw how she looked. A few more fadges and she'll ask you home to meet her mam. You could do a lot worse than Alice.'

No, Alice didn't fancy him. Her boyfriend worked at Arnotts too, a hefty, amiable lad. Sweeney knew immediately that Alice was the love of his life and he of hers when he saw them talking and sharing a cigarette by the bakery entrance on another visit.

'Love on the Roll, I've read the novel,' Brown laughed when Sweeney told him what he'd seen.

'That's the worst pun I've heard in a long time.' Brown took it as a compliment.

. . . .

His Saturday routine was predictably adequate to keep boredom at bay but its effectiveness was never assured. The predictable could become monotonous. Monotony could become melancholy. Beyond melancholy hovered futility and that was to be avoided at all costs. Brown's companionship wasn't available on Saturdays because he spent his day in a William Hill or a Ladbrokes, sometimes going to race meetings at Doncaster, York or Beverley. He was pleased to tell Toby of his wins but never spoke of his losses.

Toby would ask him, 'Have you no interest in horses apart from bookies' odds?'

Brown's response was always a variant of 'I don't need to know how they work, only if they can win.'

Sweeney's father was also a horse-racing man. He liked to rate the tipsters in different newspapers but always relied on his own judgement. Only on Saturdays did he put on a bet for he was in all things a man of moderation, wise enough to know sin lay in the curse of baseless expectation – 'my luck is bound to change' – and the path to damnation in seductive regret – 'I should have put more on the winner.' Sweeney remembered how, as a boy, he waited outside betting shops while his father put on his Yankees and Canadians. He could smell tobacco smoke billowing under the multi-coloured plastic slats at the entrance, catch murmurs and exclamations of punters inside and hear the tinny broadcast of a loudspeaker giving live commentary, glimpse beaten dockets torn and discarded on the concrete floor. Being on the doorstep of that male world should have enticed him but he never felt any desire to cross over. He only recalled being bored, for his father was a sociable man and lingered to hear another story of good fortune or bad luck. Sweeney couldn't share Brown's obsession with the track or the attraction of betting shops.

One Saturday morning, about to leave the house, he met Simon returning with bags of groceries. 'Eddie, just the man I wanted to see. Are you doing anything this afternoon?'

'No, I've nothing special planned. I was only going to visit the bookshop in Hepworth Arcade.'

'I'm going with a friend to the Hull game. I thought you might want to come along?' (He wondered if that bottle of Bushmills had put Simon in his debt).

Sweeney wasn't sure if he meant rugby league or football. 'I've never been. Who are they playing?' thinking he could work it out by the name of the opposition.

'It's Whitehaven.'

It was rugby league. 'Sounds great, what time are you leaving?'

'Around one-thirty, kick-off's not until three. But we'll have a pint or three along the way. Bring your student card. You get a discount at the gate.'

'Great! See you, then.'

Delighted to have an alternative Saturday, Sweeney went to the wholefood store on Princes Avenue. He mingled with the 'hippies' who looked un-hippy to him, though he did detect the scent of patchouli from the young woman in a turquoise headscarf, matching gypsy skirt and woollen poncho at the cash desk. He bought a piece of organic cheddar and a crusty loaf, thinking it best to put something solid in his stomach before 'a pint or three' in the early afternoon.

They stopped off in the Polar Bear. Simon's friend Chris was also a Labour Party member, an official of the Transport and General Workers' Union. He was in his late thirties, beginning to put on weight but still compact, solid. His nose had been broken at some point and he reminded Sweeney of Jean-Paul Belmondo. Two of his front teeth were missing, another consequence of playing amateur rugby league Chris said.

'How're you finding Hull, Eddie?' he asked.

'I like it. It's coming to feel like home. As Roland who shares the house with Simon and me said, if it's good enough for Larkin, it's good enough for me.'

Chris laughed. 'Those words may not be as complimentary as you thought, Eddie. There's a local story, don't know if it's true, but you can imagine it. A young up-and-coming singer is booked for a night in a workingmen's club in Yorkshire – might as well be Hull. She's shown backstage by the manager but finds her dressing room disgusting, smelly and damp, with a door which won't close properly. So she turns to the manager and says, "I can't possibly be expected to work in conditions like these." And he replies, "Listen lass, if it was good enough for Kathy Kirby, it is good enough for you."'

'I like it,' Sweeney said.

'I'm sure that story has never reached Roland's ears,' Simon added. 'He's probably never heard of Kathy Kirby either.'

'I'm sure it hasn't and you're probably right about Kathy,' Sweeney laughed.

Chris and Simon began to discuss Hull's fortunes this season and agreed the team had a good chance of promotion.

'If we make it up to the First Division we get derby match-es again,' Chris explained to Sweeney. 'Hull against Kingston Rovers, it's unique.'

'One of our secretaries got engaged to the Kingston Rovers' full-back.'

'I suppose someone had to,' Chris replied.

They had a manly chuckle and Sweeney ordered the same again.

'As students, Pearl and I went together to a local derby,' Simon said. 'Fans from both sides walked to the game together, families often with different colours, friendly banter, no trouble, a festive atmosphere we thought. Inside the ground, for the entirety of the match, nothing but abuse, things you wouldn't want your mother to hear, and no prisoners taken. The match over, everyone walked back home happily enough, as if it had been therapeutic somehow. You know what? Pearl and I agreed for once. It made us proud to live in Hull.'

Chris laughed. 'Up to a point – family differences can be

pretty deep n' all.' He turned to Sweeney. 'Are you a league fan, Eddie?'

'I used to watch matches on TV every Tuesday evening, *Floodlit Rugby League*. We were all fans of Eddie Waring at school. We repeated the sayings, you know, "up and under", "early bath" … actually that's about it. The only player I can remember is Billy Boston. But I think he was Wigan, not Hull?'

'We'll allow you Billy Boston,' said Chris, 'and yes, he was Wigan. We'll give you bonus points for *Floodlit Rugby League*. But I draw the line at Eddie Waring. A lot of fans, me included, think he plays to southern prejudice about us northerners, "e's just up from t'pit", that sort of nonsense, everything a bit of a joke.'

'I never knew that. I see what you mean – though I have to say, as an outsider, I enjoyed his commentaries.'

'Eddie, my friend,' Simon intervened, 'you've opened up a can of northern worms this afternoon and something for you to ponder in your thesis, no doubt. Let's leave that *particular* Eddie for another time and another place.' He looked at his watch. 'Now, shall we have another pint here or get one closer to the ground?' They voted to have another.

They walked down Argyll Street and onto Anlaby Road where supporters wearing black and white scarves thickened into a crowd. At Airlie Street and the turnstiles, the lines were deep.

'Welcome to The Boulevard,' Simon said. 'Did you remember your student card?'

Sweeney patted the zipped pouch on his cagoule. 'I have it here, safe and sound.' It was bitterly cold. He was glad of those lined trousers.

They stood in The Well of the Best Stand at eye level with the action. Chris pointed to the stand opposite. 'That's The Threepenny Stand. Only hard-core fans allowed, you have to prove yourself to gain entry. That's why I can't take you two.

WANTS

They'd smell the blood of fair-weather friends right away.'

The match was hard fought. Sweeney winced at the fleshy thud of bodies hitting one another at pace. And the mud – within a short time the team strips became almost indistinguishable. This sporting life, he knew, wasn't for him and his mind wandered easily even if the match wasn't entirely without interest. He enjoyed saying faintly 'up and under' when the ball was kicked high, which brought a chuckle from Chris. He also recognised one of the players and pointed him out.

'I've seen him a few times cycling up Newland Avenue.'

'That's Alf Macklin, one of the best wingers we've ever had,' Chris told him. 'If you want a working-class hero, look no further.'

'Be like Alf,' Sweeney said. They asked what he meant. 'Be like Alf … Alf Tupper, Tough of the Track, a character from a comic, a runner not a rugby player, another working-class hero. But it could just as well be Alf Macklin.'

Simon said 'That's good. "Be like Alf" should be Labour's next election slogan.' Chris thought it was a brilliant idea.

To loud cheers Hull won. 'We're still on course to win the division.' Chris rubbed his hands. 'We need to keep our noses in front of Dewsbury. That's Eddie Waring's old team, by the way. What did you think of your first live match?'

'I enjoyed it,' Sweeney said. 'I like the working-class hero bit, Alf Macklin and the rest playing for local pride.'

'That's the socialist spirit we like in Hull,' Chris told him.

Sweeney mentioned the Marxists at university.

'That wouldn't be Keith Mitchell and his crowd, would it?' Simon asked.

'Yes, that's them.'

'What a shower they are, a complete bunch of opportunists,' Simon said with genuine anger. 'They love to spout "theory" – he made the quotation sign with his fingers – 'but they've never done anything useful, not one eff'n thing. Labour does its best to help people, but Mitchell and his lot? For them, workers are only theory-fodder. People know it too and won't listen to them. I've heard they're planning to infiltrate Labour in Hull and take over the party. No chance! Isn't that right, Chris?'

Chris touched his nose. 'No chance, I can sniff them a mile off, like outsiders in the Threepenny Stand.' He looked at his watch. 'I'm going to have to head off, lads. The wife's going out with the girls tonight and I'm on child-minding duty. Eddie, any time you want to come see the Black and Whites, let us know. You brought us luck and, who knows, you might make it into the Threepenny Stand one day.'

. . . .

As the winter of 1977 struggled towards spring, Sweeney worked hard and entirely on his own initiative. Dawson did prove inventively elusive but he was happy left to his own devices. His supervisor's shoulder could remain un-cried on. The question he wrestled with seemed obvious and yet was difficult to answer clearly. The north of England was distinctive but what, if anything or anyone, was representative of 'northern-ness'? That can of worms Simon had mentioned was a problem for him. He sought out Mr Trammer.

'I've always thought if you want to know somewhere, read the popular writers. They're popular for a reason and the reason is they capture well people and place. There's a great tradition of travel writing you could look at. Now, I have good editions of J. B. Priestley's *English Journey* and H. V. Morton's *I Saw Two Englands*. Let me fetch them.'

Mr Trammer did that strange shuffling of his around the shelves. Sweeney heard him pulling out a few books and blowing dust. He returned with copies of Priestley under one arm and held up in his other hand Arthur Mee's *Yorkshire East Riding*.

'You may like this one too, plenty of local flavour.' He slumped in his chair and opened the copy of Mee. 'Oh, you'll *definitely* like this. It's on the first page. Let me read it.' He put on a pair of half-moon glasses. '"Every Yorkshire boy will tell you that Yorkshire has an acre for every letter in the Bible, and some over". Let's say every Yorkshire boy *used* to be able to tell you that,' Mr Trammer sniffed. 'It probably isn't taught in our schools any longer, more's the shame. Mee also writes this. "We may say perhaps that man has made it what it is, for the Spirit of the North is the most vital thing industrial England has". Though how long it remains true is anyone's guess. But it makes you proud, doesn't it? "All are shadows – all are passing – all is past." That's, Mrs Gaskill by the way, in *North and South*. You should read it too if you haven't already.'

'I haven't, but I will.'

'I don't have a copy unfortunately ... but maybe she was right and the world of Darkshire, of Milton-Northern has become past already, heritage not reality.' He set the book down and repeated the words about the Spirit of the North and industrial England. 'Anyway, it's that "Spirit of the North" you're trying to get, isn't it?'

'I'm exploring how novelists imagine that spirit, yes, and how it helped to make the modern world.'

'Don't forget industrial England is only one part of it. Think of all those acres in God's own country and elsewhere. Most of them are rural. You need to capture that spirit as well.' Mr Trammer placed both palms on the desk and pushed himself to his feet again. 'I can only advise you to be careful of clichés – pigeon racing, whippets in the field, ferrets, brass bands, rugby league, and workingmen's clubs. Of course, they go down well with the media in London. As Orwell knew, it is also how some northerners like to see themselves too. Most of it I find either patronising or, like Orwell, pure cant.'

Sweeney was about to say something but Mr Trammer put his hands up to ward off a challenge. But he was only going to ask Mr Trammer what he thought of Eddie Waring. Mrs Gaskill's Milton-Northern reminded him of a rugby league team.

'I won't try to tell you what to do, but one final comment. Locality, the north, is important, local customs are important, but life's problems are general. Eccentricity, weirdness, even perversity, are as common up here as they are anywhere else. I should know. I live here. The human condition, whether in Hull or London or your Northern Ireland, is universal. It's what Larkin's poetry is about, the everyday, the little things, which make the big picture. It's what all good literature should be about.'

'That's the best advice I've had since coming to Hull and I'm not trying to flatter.'

Mr Trammer's look suggested he was flattered. He tapped the Priestley, Morton and Mee. 'I have plenty similar in stock and, as you know, I'll always do you a good deal.'

And thus grew his collection of books week by week, filling the alcove shelving by the mantelpiece and spreading along the floor towards the window. He couldn't say yet he was performing *tsundoku* but he liked to think he was apprenticed to the art.

. . . .

Pleasant it was this scholar's life. Days were spent in his carrel on the sixth floor of the library. It had a view over Cottingham Road towards Newland Park, where Larkin lived. To others this small room might have seemed a prison of books. For Sweeney it provided a homelike refuge in silent communion with words, insulated from life's weariness and innocent of responsibility. The irresponsibility lay in following his own thoughts rather than the demands of others (he couldn't imagine working in an office nine-to-five like Pearl). When he felt in need of human contact he took the lift to the mezzanine, sat in one of the armchairs, read a magazine or journal article, immersed in murmurs and echoes. A short walk away was the Students' Union where there was life, energy and sociability. It was a disciplined existence qualified by only periodic indulgence like his Friday night sessions with Brown. Through a dismal winter he waited for spring in the naïve belief that good things were fated to happen, somehow.

Copious notes he translated into arguments, attaching to each equally copious quotation. Before him he kept Dawson's book on Waugh. Workmanlike, he told himself, if I'm workmanlike nothing much can go wrong and inspiration will come. As he read over what he'd written, he had a sense of achievement and left his work with an explanatory note in Dawson's pigeonhole. He felt he was crossing a shadow line from student to academic. Meeting Brown later, he told him it was time to celebrate and they spent a few hours in The Goodfellowship Inn enjoying, well, good fellowship.

Some weeks later, Sweeney was passing the departmental office when Jo waved to him. 'Eddie, Mr Dawson called just now. He'd like to speak to you. He's free for the next hour if you want to pop in.'

Suddenly all his intellectual self-confidence drained. He imagined the pages he'd submitted covered with heavy red lines of criticism – 'your methodology is weak', 'your ideas are clichéd', 'your sources are poor', 'your conclusions aren't justified' – and a final, fatal, comment requiring him to re-think his thesis. He might need Dawson's shoulder to cry on. How transient intellectual vanity can be, he thought.

'Edward, do come in and have a seat. As is our custom' – Dawson offered Sweeney the box of Turkish cigarettes – 'a civilised way to begin proceedings, don't you agree?'

He did, but 'proceedings' sounded like an execution and the 'cigarette' an offer to a condemned man.

It would be Dawson's way to convey bad news in polite circumlocutions and Sweeney thought it best to be direct. 'Did you have a chance to look over the work I submitted?'

Dawson exhaled smoke luxuriously and opened the top drawer of his desk. He drew out a manila folder. 'I have indeed,' he tapped the folder, 'and I have to say I'm very pleased with your progress. The foundations have been well and truly laid. That's the hard part. Where are we, only about eight months into your scholarship?' Dawson took another drag of his Turkish. 'I like the way you've developed your thesis, how you've used literature creatively to substantiate your points. There are some infelicitous expressions, one or two contentious assumptions. You would expect those comments from a master to apprentice, or a captain to cadet as they might say in Hull, if you also forgive the rather crude associations.'

Sweeney forgave them with a smile of appreciation and relief.

Dawson pushed the folder across the table. 'I had Julie type up my remarks and suggestions. I think it best to do these things systematically rather than scribbled notes in the margin. They're often hard to follow and my handwriting has become rather crabbed of late.'

Sweeney opened the folder. Pinned to his manuscript were eight or nine pages of closely-typed commentary. He was surprised and impressed. Dawson hadn't been evasive this time. He had been diligent. 'Thank you, you've been very thorough. These will be immensely helpful,' he said glancing through the comments.

Dawson stubbed out his cigarette and pushed across his desk the ashtray. 'No need to bother with all that now. Take your time to digest and reflect. By the way, I particularly liked the theme of northern cultures as representative of the human condition, the universal significance of the everyday, the small things of life different, yet part of something general. Reference to Mrs Gaskill's *North and South*, yes, I liked all that. Some of the authors you cite are new to me – fine detective work by the way – and there was some good use of travel writing.'

'I was trying to set out the key ideas, see how they stood up to scrutiny. I'm pleased you think they make sense.' He didn't mention Mr Trammer's guidance.

'It's all very good and very pleasing. Take time to reflect on my comments.' Dawson stood up and walked to the window. He looked with some distaste at the wet mist shrouding the campus, the rain clouds and the enveloping gloom. 'On another matter, perhaps you can help *me* with something. The staff-student cricket match will be upon us soon. I like to think it one of the highlights of the year. Raymond Blanche used to rustle up a team but, of course, he's no longer here.' Dawson coughed. 'I would be very grateful if you could step into the breach. You did say you play?'

Sweeney couldn't remember if he'd boasted any skill. 'I used to, yes. Nothing special, I'm afraid.'

'You don't have to captain or anything like that. Blanche was only captain because Milne, sound chap that he is, didn't press his claim. Brown will play, though his batting style is agricultural. There's three already.' He walked over and pressed Sweeney's shoulder.

'I will do my best to get a squad together,' Sweeney promised.

'Good man! I knew I could rely on you. I'll arrange everything else. Don't worry about bats, pads and such. The university team lends us the gear. But do try to get as many as possible to wear whites, shirt at least, trousers if they can.'

'That should be easy enough.'

'I'll confirm a date. Maybe you chaps can get in a few nets beforehand. We can only hope the weather improves over the next weeks.'

Later, Sweeney talked it over with Brown. 'I have some good news and some bad news. The good news is that Dawson likes the work I submitted so the last few months haven't been wasted.'

Brown congratulated him. 'And the bad news is?'

'He wants me to get a team together for the staff-student cricket match.'

'God, it's not that time of year is it? He loves his traditions, does old Dawson.'

'How should I go about it?'

'Squire Milne is the man for the captain's job. He was too much of a gentleman to deprive Raymond, who thought himself a cross between Ted Dexter and Colin Cowdrey. Last time we roped in some of the history boys. The theatre studies crowd supplied one or two. They're used to standing around and making arses of themselves. I can do wicketkeeper like last year and then hit a quick half century.' He played a couple of air shots. 'Don't worry, Eddie, my son. We'll a get a team together somehow.'

'Dawson suggested we get in a few nets beforehand.'

'Do me a favour! Only Dawson's that keen. He would love to play all day, enjoy the lengthening shadows, all that nonsense. He's a romantic. But not so romantic that he wants the best side to win. The staff side *always* wins because he smuggles in a few outside players.'

'Blanche did mention it.'

'Too right he did. At least it's only twenty-five overs a side. It'll finish before pubs re-open. Oh, and the staff side gets to bat first. The other way around and it could be over in under an hour.'

'He requested we do our best to turn out in whites.'

'See what I mean about romantic?'

WANTS

Toby agreed to be captain and put the word around the Arts faculty. In the end they scraped together eleven players, most of unknown quality and most suspected of doing it for a laugh. Sweeney posted home a cheque to cover the cost of his parents sending him his old school whites – a pair of cream cotton jeans with shadows of grass stain, an Aran sweater and a white nylon shirt. He found they still fitted. The beer he'd drunk, the fadges and fish suppers he'd eaten, hadn't added anything to his waistline, at least not yet.

. . . .

The sun shone on match day, East Yorkshire in exquisite stillness. It was hot, almost like the summer of 1976. The students were a ragged bunch, some in shorts and T-shirts, others in tracksuit bottoms, nearly all of them with rowdy mates who'd brought along six-packs of beer. Brown was in his normal clothing, only bothering to put on a pair of plimsoles and even they were black. Toby had a proper set of cricketing whites and wore a dark blue crested cap. Apart from Sweeney, only two others had traditional gear.

The staff side mostly looked the part, only a few younger members without whites. Dawson wore his hooped cap. His trousers, Sweeney couldn't help noticing, had been let out at the waist more than once. His face radiated enthusiasm, making him look twenty years younger.

Toby recognised a couple of players on the staff side from the local Zingari club. 'We can only do our best,' he said to Sweeney. 'I'll tell the conscripts to enjoy themselves.' From the raucous laughter and chink of beer cans on the boundary edge it looked as if they didn't need to be told. Toby whispered, 'It must seem to you a bit like a scene from *England, Their England.*'

'When in England, do as the English do.'

'I'm expecting you to do better than that. You're our man to stop as many boundaries as possible. You don't mind patrolling the outfield? Looking at our team, it will be the most important position.'

'I'll do my best.'

Dawson opened the batting with a paunchy middle-aged colleague. Both were competent enough, but laborious runners. It was just as well. When they hit the ball with any force, Sweeney had to run around to stop fours. The ground was dry and hard, the boundaries short. Every time he picked up and threw in to Brown's gloves, he would tot up the runs he'd saved. A group of young women had turned up to spectate, sitting apart from the beer drinkers, clapping and cheering when the student side fielded the ball – most often Sweeney – and laughing when, more often than not, something went comically wrong. Sweeney was certain one of them was taking special interest in him and that pleasant thought counteracted his fatigue as the match dragged on.

Dawson put the older members of staff up the order so that they could have a knock. Half way through their innings Sweeney reckoned the staff would be lucky to get to sixty runs. Dawson stuck around unbeaten as partners came and went but scored only fifteen runs. He then retired, probably considering it a captain's innings, tiring out the opposition or boring them into submission. The Zingari big guns came to the crease and it became a different game now. Formerly gambolling infielders leapt out of the way as the ball flew quickly to all parts. Sweeney had little chance either and the staff score shot up quickly. Now he reckoned they'd get close to one hundred and fifty. It was too easy and too demoralising for the students. Whatever enthusiasm they once had was fading quickly.

Another bad ball was bowled and the batsman smacked it hard. The shot sounded sweet, an infielder leapt out of the way and the young women at the boundary prepared to scatter. Sweeney ran as fast as he could and stretched out his foot. The ball hit a divot, bounced up and cracked him on the ankle. He wanted to cry out in pain, to swear, but the presence of the women and his pride stopped him. In anger he picked up the ball and flung it towards Brown as hard as he could. The batsmen must have expected a boundary and, surprised by the accuracy of Sweeney's throw, one of them was stranded mid-pitch. Brown whipped off the bails. The batsman was out. Sweeney's special fan clapped wildly and gave him a look as if to say 'I knew you could do it'. She really was attractive, he thought. He bowed to her, hoping his ankle wasn't broken.

The remaining Zingari was frustrated as the batsmen who followed added little to the score. But when he was on strike the total accelerated once again. Toby decided to bowl as a final roll of the dice. Zingari number two swept his first ball in the air and it arced high in the bright blue sky. At first, Sweeney wasn't sure where it was going. He then realised it was headed straight for him. He reached up to catch and was hit on the middle finger of his right hand. For a moment he thought he'd dropped the ball, but there it was, firmly in his grasp. His team mates cheered and he heard Brown shout, 'You've hands like buckets, Eddie.' His special fan blew him a kiss and he waved to her. His finger was swelling already and he couldn't bend the top joint. At the end of their innings, the staff had scored ninety-seven.

Brown congratulated him. 'You were a star today, my son. Dawson will be a worried man.' He looked over to the T-shirted and tracksuit-bottomed teammates helping themselves to cans of beer and sighed. 'Scrap that. We haven't a hope in hell.'

Toby asked about his injuries.

'My ankle is banjaxed, but only bruised. I think my finger is broken, though.'

'You've done your bit, Eddie, so there's no need to bat.' Toby looked at the beer guzzlers. 'I can't see our boys making a go of it.'

'If I'm needed, I'm happy to play up and play the game,' Sweeney said.

'You really *are* more English than the English.'

Sweeney sat with Brown who was padded up to go in number three. 'That finger looks nasty,' he said. 'Shouldn't you go and get it seen to?'

'I'll wait and see what happens. You never know. I may be needed.'

'You're an optimist, I'll give you that.'

After three balls and no runs the first wicket fell. Brown pulled a face, 'Still feeling optimistic? Well, a few hours to play and the next man in. I'll see you soon'.

Brown played and missed the next two balls, then connected with a great swipe for four.

Because of his finger Sweeney couldn't clap but shouted, 'Bravo!'

'Hello. Were you playing so well in order to impress me?' It was the girl from the boundary edge. She stood haloed in bright light, a full, round face with wide-set blue eyes. Her hair was long and blonde, tied with ribbon in a high ponytail. She sat beside him and clasped her knees to her chest. 'Please tell me it's true.'

Sweeney, charmed, replied, 'Yes, of course it's true. How could I not?'

'You're from Northern Ireland, aren't you? I love the accent, the way you say "fill-im". A friend of mine is from Northern Ireland. She's studying drama and always going to the "fill-ims". Do you know her? Oh, why should you? It's stupid of me to ask.'

'Where I'm from we say "fill-ums". I'm not as refined as your friend.'

She smiled. 'My name is Samantha Ahrens, by the way. Most people call me Sam.' She offered her hand.

Awkwardly, he grasped it with his left. 'Edward Sweeney, but most people call me Eddie. Sorry, my other hand is out of action.'

'Was that when you took the catch?'

'Yes, ball hit me bang on the fingertip.'

'Give it here,' she said, a strong Hull accent breaking through. She caressed his finger delicately and with attention. Sweeney looked more closely at her features. He thought she was about five years older than him. She was more than attractive. She was beautiful. She touched the finger joint and he winced. 'Sorry, I'm not much of a nurse, am I?'

'I'm not much of a patient. Ahrens is an interesting surname. I like it. Is it typically Hull?'

'There's a bit of German, a bit of Danish, a bit of Dutch and a lot of East Yorkshire. I suppose, in a way, it *is* typically Hull. But I don't know anyone else called Ahrens – outside the family that is.'

'There's probably not many in Hull called Sweeney either.'

Sam laughed. 'So my instinct was right. From the moment I saw you I knew we had a lot in common.'

'Are you at the university?'

'Yes, doing English. I've seen you in the department and in the Students' Union. For some reason I was drawn to you. I can't explain why, just something about you. I felt we shared something. I wasn't confident enough to speak to you because you were doing research. But I decided to make an exception today.'

Sweeney looked confused. 'Why didn't you speak to me? Research? I don't understand.'

'You'll probably think this foolish.'

'Try me.'

'As a lowly undergrad I think of lecturers as godlike figures, academically that is.' She stopped as Sweeney smiled at this, thinking of Dawson in his trousers let out at the waist. 'You *do* think I'm foolish!'

'No, I wasn't laughing at you. I was thinking of Dawson's cricket trousers, strange as that may seem.'

Sam looked at Dawson's portly figure bending awkwardly to pick up the cricket ball.

'Yes, I do see what you mean,' she laughed. 'The truth is I thought you above me. You could say I was slightly in awe of you.'

'Of me – maybe you thought me an angel? As you can see, I'm a fallen angel, a wounded angel, but a happy one now I've met you.'

'Can I just say that sounds very corny, Eddie.'

'You may, because it's true. I'm well-known for being corny. Would you like a cigarette?'

She accepted. After her first drag, Sam said, 'I'm glad I've finally spoken to you.'

'I am too.'

They sat for a while in silence smoking and watching the match.

Brown smashed a couple of boundaries, scampered a few singles, missed quite a few and then was bowled. Trudging back looking disgusted, he saw Sweeney with Sam and veered off towards Toby. It was remarkable, Sweeney thought, how quickly two people can become self-absorbed and excluding. But he didn't feel guilty.

Sam told him she was technically a mature student. 'I hate that term. It makes me sound ancient.' She hadn't got on well at school, had left before A-levels, done a variety of dead-end jobs, studied at night class, passed her exams and was lucky to get into university. She was in her final year. 'I'm waiting for my results and feeling a bit on edge.' She told him she wanted good enough grades to do a Masters. 'Then maybe I can become an angel like you.' They laughed.

'Here in Hull?' he asked.

She looked away and said more sharply than he expected. 'Of course, here in Hull, I don't have much choice.' They fell silent again.

There was a lot of larking around the scoreboard, students making a racket with the metal number plates. In the match, Toby and another batsman were putting together a partnership. Sweeney calculated the students needed thirty- five runs to win. They had five overs and three wickets left. It was unlikely, but not impossible. Brown was becoming more animated and the cheers of the beer-can crew were getting louder.

'Your team must be winning,' Sam said.

'I hope they won't need me to bat, the state I'm in.'

'No, no, no, don't you see? That's the heroic finish *our* story demands – last man in and a match to win – life imitating art.'

He was pleased she'd said 'our' so emphatically. 'In that case, I'd better prepare for battle.' Sweeney struggled to stand up and Sam helped him. He lost balance and put his arms around her. He apologised.

'It's not every day a woman is embraced by a hero. Is your leg hurting too?'

'I got a whack on the ankle.'

'You have been in the wars and no mistake.'

Sweeney hobbled tentatively and Sam linked arms to support him.

Brown was standing by the bag with the cricketing gear. As they reached him, Toby's partner was caught. Next in was a T-shirt and shorts.

'He won't last long,' Brown said, 'and I think you should stay where you are.' He looked questioningly at Sam.

'Samantha Ahrens, Alan Brown,' Sweeney introduced them. 'Could you two help me pad up and slip on the gloves?'

Sweeney's whimpers of pain punctuated the process. 'Don't be such a big girl's blouse,' Brown said. 'Sorry, Samantha, no offence meant.' She waved away the apology. 'Now, I'll have to ask you to turn around while I insert Eddie's box, vital protection for the family jewels, but rather unromantic.'

She laughed just as T-shirt and shorts was bowled.

'Twelve runs to make,' Brown said. 'I wouldn't bother, Eddie. Game's over.'

Sweeney wasn't going to spoil Sam's story, *their* story. He waved to Toby indicating he should stay on the pitch.

'Wait, before you go,' Sam said. She took the golden ribbon from her pony tail and tied it to the handle of his bat. 'This lady bestows a favour on her champion. Ever since I read about the Pre-Raphaelites, I've always wanted to do something like this. I'm so glad I can do it for you!' She put her hand to his cheek and let it linger there. Brown looked at the favour, looked at Sam, looked at Sweeney, and for once looked dumbstruck.

Toby intercepted Sweeney hobbling to the crease. 'I appreciate your gesture, Eddie, but we should call it a day if you're injured.'

Sweeney held up his bat to show him Sam's favour. 'I'm doing it for a lady and chivalry demands …'

'Well then, we must see it through. Try to avoid getting hit, this bowler's good. He's the Zingari man you caught on the boundary, one of Dawson's plants. You have three balls to face. Whatever you do, don't try to run! Leave the final over to me.'

'Last batsman, chaps,' Dawson said. He clapped Sweeney to the crease and encouraged his team to do the same.

Sweeney watched the bowler polish the ball fiercely on his trousers. He saw Sam's favour on the bat handle and hoped it had magical powers. He managed to block the first delivery.

WANTS

His finger smarted and throbbed. He lifted his hand from the bat and shook it.

The bowler picked up the ball. 'Next time I'm going to hit you where it really hurts.' The ball was fast but without direction and Sweeney watched it pass wide of his stumps.

The man swore at him. 'Say goodbye to your teeth.'

Toby walked down the pitch. 'Is everything okay?' Sweeney assured him it was. 'One more ball, Eddie and no heroics, please.'

Sweeney looked to Sam on the boundary edge and put her ribbon to his lips. Sam put her hand on her heart. Brown put his hand over his eyes. The bowler tried to bounce the ball at Sweeney's head but failed. He'd ducked and survived.

Toby strolled down again. 'Well played. Even if we lose, I think we can claim a moral victory. Look at Dawson. He's panicking. That's a victory in itself, don't you think?'

But there was no fairy tale ending. Toby, trying to win by hitting boundaries, sliced the first ball high in the air and the wicketkeeper took the catch.

'We tried our best,' Sweeney said to Sam. 'I must return your favour dishonoured by defeat.'

'It has nothing to do with the result. I want you to keep it in memory of today and, more importantly, of me.'

Sweeney held high the gold ribbon. 'I will bear it through life like a torch in flame.'

'Said like a true hero!' Sam touched his cheek again. 'I have to go, I'm afraid. I'm late. You should get your injuries seen to. I hope we can see each other again?'

'I'd like that.'

He watched as Sam walked away, crossing Inglemire Lane and vanishing beyond trees on the edge of campus. She was painfully beautiful, he decided.

'Normally, I'd tell you to run after her and get a phone

number or an address,' Brown said. 'Unfortunately, you can't but if you hang about I'll get the groundsman to lend us a wheelbarrow and we'll push you to the nearest pub.' He realised Sweeney was in a sort of trance. 'No, mate,' he said, 'you didn't imagine her.'

It was a good night, beer aplenty, raucous good cheer. Best of all, he had the gold ribbon she'd given him, her favour his talisman.

CHAPTER SIX

He didn't see Sam again that summer and, despite Brown's confirmation, might have thought her a *Fata Morgana* if it hadn't been for her favour. In a curiosity shop on Newland Avenue he bought a small hand-carved wooden box, laid the ribbon inside and kept it on his bedside table. He looked through the Hull telephone directory but found no Ahrens listed. He wasn't disheartened. Providence, he believed, had introduced them and providence would reunite them. He liked to think each day a Grail Quest. He expected to see her coming out of a store, standing at a bus stop, or waiting to be served at a stall in the market, and they would go off together light-heartedly, like a happy ending to a French film (though he wasn't sure they ever had happy endings). He was never downhearted when none of these things happened. He was certain they'd meet again.

He continued to work hard throughout the summer, feeling the virtue of someone who'd stayed when so many fled. Brown stayed too, claiming he'd reached a critical point in his research. Sweeney knew better. Brown had a new girlfriend and his research was more amorous than academic. One morning he announced his latest affair had ended.

'Did she invite you home to meet her mam?' Sweeney asked.

'It was nothing like that,' Brown assured him. 'She isn't from Hull, but Peterborough ... where they make the bricks,' he added as an afterthought. 'I filled a gap for her, pleasant while it lasted. As *10cc* would say, "The things we do for love", eh? I can tell you, we did a lot of things.' He sighed. 'On more important matters, how would you like to make a bit of easy money, now you're a cricket fan?'

'What's the connection – not that I *am* a cricket fan.'

'Don't you know there's an Ashes series on? Don't you know

the next Test will be in God's own country? And Yorkshire's favourite son, Geoff Boycott, is sitting on ninety-nine Test match hundreds? For your benefit and mine, I've been checking the bookies' odds on him getting that hundredth hundred at Headingley. They're good. If you put on a fiver, more if you can afford it, you'll cash in. I feel it in my bones and my instinct is rarely wrong. Best do it as soon as possible. The odds can only shorten.'

Sweeney thought of all those days waiting for his father outside betting shops. 'Can you place the bet for me?' he asked and, cajoled by Brown's certainty, committed to a fiver (which seemed a lot to him). Parting with the notes next day he suppressed all interest in the Test, thinking he'd been reckless. He could ill afford to waste them.

On the twelfth of August Brown did a dance around the postgrad room singing Abba's 'Money, Money, Money.'

'Boycott got his hundred?'

'You're in Hull and you haven't heard? What have you been doing, Eddie? Let's say the bet delivered as I promised.' From his trouser pocket he fished out a wad of banknotes and counted them on Sweeney's desk. 'Five, ten, fifteen, twenty, twenty-five, thirty, and, finally, your fiver waged, no commission. Not a bad morning's work, is it? Now, if you'd put on a tenner, you could be off to the Costa del Sol.'

Sweeney picked up the notes and fanned them, thinking it would be a good story to tell his father.

'I never thought I'd be grateful to Geoff Boycott, did you?' Brown added. 'I nominate him the greatest living Yorkshireman. And don't be a Yorkshireman and save your money. The IMF will pocket it all if you do. "You can't put off being young until you retire". That's Larkin by the way. Now, what about a toast to Geoffrey?'

Home in September for two weeks, he told his father of

his betting coup and gave his mother the winnings minus the dent frequent celebrations with Brown had made. Thereafter, Boycott's hundredth hundred took on special family significance – for his father, a son who'd discovered something in the Sweeney blood (even if he hadn't), for his mother, a son who hadn't become a selfish scoundrel, and for him, a son who'd become a giver rather than a taker.

. . . .

The first Friday afternoon of the new academic year, Sweeney was sitting at the edge of a row in a lecture theatre, waiting for a talk by a novelist, an acquaintance of Dawson's, whose novel had been shortlisted for the Booker Prize. Dawson was anxious for a good turn out and had put unusual energy into advertising the event, making it clear that everyone should recognise attendance was a duty (for the good name of the department and all that). So far, few students and fewer staff had turned up. Friday afternoon didn't seem a wise choice and Sweeney was beginning to feel sorry for his supervisor. Mercifully, he heard commotion behind him as people began to filter in.

'Shove up a place,' Sam said and sat down beside him. 'Were you planning an early escape sitting in the end seat?' Before he could say anything clever, she went on, 'Too late, I've got it now.' Sweeney's delight must have been obvious. 'Yes, it *is* me, Sam. Did you miss me?'

All he could think to say was, 'Yes, of course I did.'

'And how's your finger?'

Sweeney held up his right hand. There was still ugly discolouration and a thick bump had formed over the splintered bone below the nail. Sam took his hand, caressed the finger gently and then put the palm of her hand on the back of his.

'Do you believe I have a magic touch?' she asked.

'Your magic has touched me already.'

She withdrew her hand slowly. 'That's another corny answer, Eddie, but I will take it as chivalrous. If *you* are wondering, *I* missed you too.' She told him about being accepted onto the Masters programme. 'My marks were good enough, just about. I'm excited to be back at university. I can't understand how some take it for granted.'

During the novelist's talk on plot and characterisation, Sam concentrated hard and made diligent notes. Sweeney doodled not because the talk was without interest but because he was enchanted by Sam's movements. He watched how she ended writing a line with a light flourish, how she formed her letters, how her forehead creased when reflecting on a point the novelist made, her pen hovering over the page, how she arranged blonde strands behind her ear when they fell across her eyes. He noticed how, every now and then, elbow on the bench before her, she would lean her head against her hand and how, when her face turned to him, she would smile.

At the end of the talk, as the audience clapped, Sam leaned in to him and whispered, 'I could listen to her all day.'

'Do you have time for a coffee?' he asked. She quickly glanced at her watch, an action which made his heart sink.

'Yes,' she said after a brief hesitation. She put her hand on his arm. 'That must have seemed rude of me, like fitting you in. Let me rephrase that. I'd *love* to have a coffee.' When they walked up the steps of the lecture theatre she glanced at his ankle. 'Glad I don't have to carry you all the way to the Students' Union.'

It was that empty time in university life, late afternoon Friday, when youthful energy withdrew, retreating to its lairs, regenerating itself to pour out once more into house parties, local pubs or Union bar, announcing the weekend had begun. At this moment the stale atmosphere, the drabness of their sur-roundings, the tired feel of a place winding down, the absence of the usual bustle should have affected his mood, but didn't. He told her about the Boycott windfall. He mentioned his couple of weeks at home and was glad that, like everyone else he'd met in Hull, Sam didn't fuss about the Troubles or utter a clichéd line about how terrible things must be. Life was here and now, between him and her. He couldn't have been happier. When he asked her what she'd got up to over the summer her look was sheepish, out of character, he thought.

After a pause she said, 'I went on a package holiday to Benidorm, a whole crowd of us, Brits abroad in Spain, pubs, fish and chips, disco, all the comforts of home in perfect sunshine with beach and pool thrown in.' Sweeney felt the irrational distress of a jilted lover who was neither lover nor jilted. 'I'm sure you're a museum, art gallery, and cathedral sort,' she said and he detected in her words an inferiority completely unwarranted.

'Here's an admission, Sam. Believe it or not, I've never been outside the UK – well, if you exclude day trips to Dublin. And I have never been on a plane, so Benidorm sounds exotic to me. My sophistication, if it exists at all, is entirely bookish.'

'You make me sound like a globetrotter. Now you're in Hull, this gateway to the world, you should get the ferry to Holland, though the lads I know don't go there for its cultural highlights.' She laughed. 'I'll say no more because I suspect you're innocent of such pleasures.' She had the advantage again and he was content to see the order of things between them restored.

Sweeney offered an Embassy Regal but she said she preferred her own. From her brown suede tasselled shoulder bag – 'I bought this in Spain' – Sam took out a packet of Rothmans King Size. 'I got these in duty-free,' she said.

As she concentrated on lighting her cigarette from his match, Sweeney's gaze lingered on her nose with its slightly flared nostrils and skin still bronzed from holiday. He couldn't help imagining a firm body hidden under the jacket she wore. Raising her head from the flame, she became aware of his gaze. In his distraction, the match burnt down too far. He shook it out, blowing on his finger, dropping it into the ashtray, and struck another.

'Not another damaged finger! You'll think I only bring you bad luck.'

'I'm my own worst enemy. On the bright side, I'm glad you got on the Master's course.'

'Not half as glad as me ... but thanks, it's nice of you to say so.' She took a deep drag and exhaled slowly. 'I may be out in the cold after this course. But I'm going to have a damned good try at going higher ... become an angel or even goddess.'

'I can see nothing to stop you.'

Sam smiled appreciatively but didn't respond. Instead she asked, 'How's your work coming along?'

He provided a brief summary and thought he should equal her determination by mentioning his own scholarly ambition. 'I've been given some teaching in the department this year. It'll be challenging. I'm nervous and looking forward to it at the same time.'

'That's great news. You're moving from angel-like to god-like!'

'I hope you won't stop talking to me.'

Sam shook her head. 'Those days are well and truly over. The heavens have come down to earth with a bang.'

'It's not lecturing, only a seminar, but it's a start. Dawson tells me the secret is to keep one week ahead of the students.' She closed her eyes dismissively. 'He also advised developing a professional *persona*, a bit like an actor on stage. There's me' – and he looked at her lovingly – 'and then there's this other me' – and looked at her with a poker-face. 'Alan Brown told me Larkin didn't like the thought of going around pretending to be Larkin. I suppose I'm learning how to go around pretending to be me ... if that makes sense.'

'I'm not sure it does. Anyway, if there's a choice, I prefer the first you, the one without pretence. You know, if you're not careful, you'll get the nickname "Two-Faced Eddie". I have to say it doesn't sound good.'

'I've been adopted by the secretaries too. They seem to like me. The first me that is.'

'That doesn't surprise me one bit. You *are* an angel, after all.' She touched his arm briefly. 'By the way I know one of them, Julie. Her mam lived near us on Hessle Road. They moved out to Bransholme.' She said this like it was some kind of betrayal.

'She got engaged to Hull K R's fullback.'

Sam closed her eyes again. Was it a gesture of pity or incredulity? He wasn't sure, but she didn't say anything mean.

Their knuckles brushed over the ashtray. 'Sorry,' they said simultaneously.

'If you don't mind me asking, Sam, what encouraged you back to full-time education?'

She took a sip of coffee, set her cup back down and took out another cigarette. Sweeney refused her offer. She lit it with her own lighter. 'Save your fingers,' she smiled.

'It's a story with a long history,' she went on. 'Do you really want to hear?'

'Of course I do.'

'Once upon a time ... no, that sounds too much like a fairy tale. There *was* a time in my life when I wanted to be like everyone else. When you mentioned Julie's engagement it reminded me of myself at that age. Maybe Julie wants to be like everyone else too.' She knocked ash from her Rothmans. 'Over the last few years I've thought about it a lot. When I was younger I wanted to share all the enthusiasms of my schoolmates. I wanted to fit in with conversations about boys, clothes and pop stars. Later, I wanted to think the highlight of the week was going out with the girls on a Saturday night. I wanted to please my parents who also wanted me to be like everyone else … as they tried to be themselves. I wanted all the nice things money can buy – like package holidays in Spain. All those things were true and real enough. At least, they were true in the sense of a working-class girl from Hull, *me*, accepting her place in life.'

She took a long drag and blew the smoke out slowly. 'Then one day I realised these things weren't what I wanted, not really. So you see, I have my two *personas* as well, but maybe the opposite of yours. Perhaps I pretend to be the everyday Sam Ahrens when the real Sam Ahrens is someone else. Unlike you, at least I *think* unlike you, I remain between two worlds, the world which made *me* and the world *I* am trying to make.'

Sweeney was impressed. He knew if asked to put into words why he lived as he did, he would struggle without recourse to his imaginary friend, providence. Clearly Sam had given her life serious thought.

'To answer your question, university has given me permission – yes, that's the right word – *permission* to be different. By that I don't mean rejecting my family or rejecting Hull, I would never do that. It's just that being here, meeting you now too, allows me to explore another world. It gives me permission to be myself. You must think my story silly and me even sillier.'

'No, no I don't. I don't think you silly at all.'

'Thank you for saying so, even if you don't *really* mean it.'

'Of course I *really* mean it.'

'Alright then, so long as you aren't practising Mr Two-Faced Eddie.'

'I assure you of my authenticity.'

'You're good for my ego. I believe we are good for each other' – she touched his hand – 'if you can only stop damaging those fingers of yours.' She glanced at her watch. 'And now I'm afraid I must return to my other world and leave you in yours. Thanks for the coffee and apologies for rushing off yet again.'

She stood up abruptly, her chair screeching on the floor of the near empty refectory.

'I'll walk outside with you,' he said.

The evening had closed in. It was misty now, cool and still, an evening typical of autumnal Hull. Lights had come on across the campus. He took courage and asked if she'd like to go out somewhere this weekend.

'I can't, sorry. My other world can be demanding.' She started to leave, but turned back to him. 'Eddie, life can be difficult sometimes.'

'What about next week. Can we meet up then?'

'Yes, I'd love that.' She waved to him and headed between buildings towards Cottingham Road. Sweeney watched the energy of her body, her purposeful stride, the way she adjusted the bag on her shoulder, the way her hair moved.

. . . .

He didn't meet her the following week or the weeks immediately after that. He went to two disappointing Hull matches.

'Bloody Hell! The lads are going to go straight back down again, I can feel it in my bones. Last season's promotion was a flash in the pan,' Chris complained.

He had a long chat one afternoon with Pearl, who asked him how his work was progressing. When he told her about doing some teaching she said, 'I can see it now. You're going to find Hull as hard to leave as the rest of us.'

He exchanged a few words with Roland in the hallway about his novel. 'Have you ever heard of Sir John Cutler's stockings?' Roland asked him. 'They were darned so often they changed from silk to wool. My story started off as the roughest wool and is becoming the finest silk … *becoming*, I should stress, not *is*.'

'Do you mind if I steal that Sir John Cutler story?'

'Life is plagiarism, Edward. So please be my guest.'

At university, Brown had gone missing again and he'd really only said hello and goodbye to Toby who, being the gentleman he was, apologised for the brevity of his company. 'I'm trying to break the back of my thesis before Christmas.' He promised to be more 'collegial', saying they both should get together 'when I'm more on top of things'.

Sweeney hadn't seen Patsy for some time either. Indeed, since arriving in Hull he'd hardly seen her at all. So he was surprised, returning late one afternoon from the library, to find her in the postgrad room indexing handwritten pages into a well-filled ring binder. She seemed preoccupied by something more complicated than indexing, but he wasn't sure if this was Patsy's normal enigmatic condition. He always imagined her having an air of absence as if she really belonged elsewhere.

'Long time, no see,' he said. 'How are things with you?'

She closed the ring binder and stood up. 'It *has* been a long time. I'm fine, I'm fine' but she spoke too quickly to be entirely convincing.

Sweeney remembered thinking her willowy, but this evening she appeared much thinner, her body not masked this time by loose-fitting clothing but revealed in her fitted cotton shirt and tight jeans. Black hair only accentuated the paleness of her features. Under her eyes were shadowed rings suggesting lack of sleep. Patsy seemed to him almost without physicality at all. He still found it impossible not to be fascinated by her, yet she was so untouchable to him as to be in another world – that word again. Was it the distance between his working-class Belfast and her middle-class Esher? The social gap didn't prevent compassion for her – and wasn't compassion only another word for desire?

She surprised him by asking, 'Do you fancy going to the Union for something to eat? I haven't had anything all day. I've been trying to catch up on work. I've fallen behind, lost nearly all of the summer.'

'I'm hungry too. I was about to suggest the same thing.' In truth, he would never have suggested such a thing to Patsy.

'Thanks, Eddie, I could do with some company.' Good manners made her correct immediately. 'That must sound awfully selfish. Let me put it this way. I would be delighted if *you* could join *me*.'

'If the first was an offer I couldn't refuse,' he replied, 'the second is one I'd love to accept.'

'You've cheered me up already.'

In the noisy refectory they felt obliged to begin talking about their theses, neither of them with much enthusiasm. They'd had enough for one day. Patsy ate sparingly, distractedly, and Sweeney felt a twinge of guilt at his own healthy appetite. He tried to entertain her with Roland's tale of Sir John Cutler's stockings and an exaggerated account of the staff-student cricket match. She did laugh, especially at the bits which Sweeney's comic imagination elaborated.

'On our side, only Toby had much of a clue,' he told her.

'I can well believe it.'

'I'd say he's the only one who has much of a clue about most things around here.'

Patsy didn't respond. He couldn't fathom if her expression was wistful, regretful or dismissive.

'Has Hull met your expectations?' she asked.

Sweeney tried to explain being in Hull as matter of fate. 'Providence got me to this point and to this place. So Hull must be as expected, I suppose.'

Patsy sounded astonished. 'And it has nothing to do with your ability? I doubt that. Why do you make life dependent on other people and fortuitous events?'

'I find it comforting. It relieves me of the worry that

everything I do is meaningless.'

'Hmm, isn't that a bit naïve?'

'I think Eliot called it a condition of complete simplicity. I suppose I'm happy being a complete simpleton.'

He hoped the Eliot reference would impress her. Patsy did laugh loudly. 'Is that Belfast humour? It must be! But let me get this straight. You believe providence gives you what you need without you actively choosing it? Am I right?'

'Maybe you got it right first time, Patsy. I'm naïve. Lazy is probably a better word. I find making choices hard work. If you think everything happens for a reason or at least not *merely* coincidentally then, for me, bad things are more bearable and good things more significant. I shelter behind the word because it protects me against disappointment.'

'I grant you that. But I'm still intrigued. Providence gives you what you really *want* but never actively *desired?*' Sweeney nodded uncertainly. 'Okay. So here's my final question. Do you really *like* what you get?'

He felt rather foolish. 'When I don't have to explain these things, I understand them. When I do have to explain these things, I find I don't. I need my simple truth to protect me from such questions.'

Patsy leaned across and touched his arm. 'It's not an interrogation by Special Branch, Eddie ... or by *The Sweeney.*' She hummed a few bars of the TV theme tune. 'I'm sure you've heard that one many times.'

'Not recently, I haven't. But thanks for reminding me.' He laughed to let her know he wasn't offended. Someone of Patsy's social delicacy, he was certain, could easily be made uncomfortable and taken advantage of. He thought immediately of Mitchell.

'Forgive me,' she said. 'I don't want to force open a window into your soul.'

WANTS

'You know, your question made me see something in my soul – if that's what it is – I'd never recognised before.'

'I'm even more intrigued now.'

'I always thought my attitude to life was a form of modesty. Maybe it's not at all. Maybe it's a sign of an enormous ego.'

'What do you mean?'

'You've made me realise I go through life believing that God has faith in me and not the other way round.'

'That's one way of looking at it.' Patsy raised her arms to indicate the banality of the scene around them. 'And it was all for this, Eddie, all for this. And if that's not the greatest story ever told about Hull, I don't know what is!'

'You see, you finally get it.'

'Oh yes,' she laughed, 'I finally get it …'

'To answer your question directly and not evasively – yes, I *like* being in Hull. I should have said that straight off without all the palaver.'

'You really have cheered me up tonight, Eddie.'

'And what about you?' he asked. 'You said you were busy on other things this summer?'

'Yes, a lot was going on – politically that is – historically – maybe even *providentially*.' She smiled. 'Our party was heavily involved in the Grunwick strike. I even met Jayaben in person. She's such a wonderful woman and what an inspiration! We stayed with activists in London. Keith thinks street protest, not elections, is the way forward.' Patsy spoke of solidarity, mass activism, correct analysis, revolutionary situation, capitalism, real socialism, and Sweeney listened to her words with detached curiosity. He suspected Patsy's political message was formulaic, Grunwick, like every other protest, a sign and wonder of the revolution. This suspicion was only part of Sweeney's curiosity. He remembered street corner evangelists at home fervently speaking of salvation or damnation. Patsy didn't even sound convinced by her jargon. Her rhetoric was as Orwell had described the intellectual Marxism of his time – prefabricated phrases bolted together like a child's Meccano set.

He saw no reason to question her faith or to introduce a querulous tone, so he said, recalling Mitchell's line to him, 'It sounds like you were on the frontline.'

'We were on the picket outside the lab in Dollis Hill, yes. I did so much shouting I lost my voice. Keith used sympathy for the strikers to recruit new members here in Hull. He's keen to refresh the party, inject new enthusiasm. Most are students, but not all.' Patsy put knife and fork down on her plate. 'They need a lot of political education. These days, I rarely see Keith at all. That's why I've the opportunity to do my own work again.'

'Are you glad of the opportunity?'

'I suppose I am, yes. It feels like stepping out of one world and back into another. In the party you're part of a collective of dedicated comrades. Academic research feels so inward and private. But I love it.'

Sweeney felt like saying maybe what she needed was a break from Mitchell. Instead, he asked, 'Do you know the lines "In a world filled with friends, you lose your way?" Perhaps it's good to find your own way again?'

'Which author was that?'

'Not an author, a singer, Scott Walker, though I can't think of the song title. It's about the fear of happiness passing you by.'

Patsy looked surprised. Maybe she considered his taste in music crass? To head off any comment, Sweeney took out his Embassy Regal and extended the pack across the table.

Patsy's hand hovered briefly. 'Keith doesn't approve of me smoking, but I'll join you for one.'

'It's the privilege of the simpleton to lead good people astray.' Her remark about two worlds made him think of Sam. 'Do you mind if I ask you a personal question?' Patsy raised her eyebrows. 'Not about you, but about me?'

'Please do.'

'I met someone recently, a woman.' He coughed self-consciously. 'The two of us get on well.' He felt a flush infusing his cheeks. 'I think we do – actually, we've only seen each other twice. She's a mature student but only a few years older than me, from Hull, Hessle Road way. I couldn't believe it when she told me she felt intimidated at first by my status as a PhD student. Me!' He laughed.

'Did she really think that?' Patsy shook her head in disbelief. 'I know. Me!'

'I didn't mean *you!*'

'Sorry, Patsy, I know you didn't. Anyway, I thought we could get closer' – he was struggling and Patsy seemed aware of it – 'but she feels between two worlds, you know, that phrase you just used. She told me life can be difficult but didn't explain why. Sorry, I'm not sure what I'm trying to ask you.'

'Mature student you say? Hmm, she could mean any number of things and be reluctant to tell you. It could be a class thing. A lot of students might seem very privileged to her.'

'But I'm working class like her.'

'Yes, Eddie, but she didn't know that until recently, did she?'

'Sorry, go on.'

'There could be parents who need looking after and she feels under pressure. Maybe she can't devote as much time as you'd like because of that? She could be a single mother. She may think you'd run a mile. A lot of men would, especially those as young as you. Perhaps a man hurt her recently, maybe was physically abused, and she's reluctant to start anything serious right now.' Patsy ran her cigarette slowly around the edge of the tinfoil ashtray. 'She might be married, have you thought of that?'

Sweeney's face fell. 'You must think me a simpleton not to have considered that.'

'Look, I don't know her, I'm only speculating. Maybe it's nothing to do with any of those things. Maybe she means the trouble of balancing work-a-day things and university study, you know, the privilege we take for granted? It could just be just as she said. Life *can* be difficult at times.' She touched his arm again in sympathy. 'Don't fall at the first hurdle, don't be discouraged. Don't lose *your* way! Promise me? Is it a deal?'

'It's a deal.'

She looked quite tenderly at him. 'I want you to know two things. The first is I'm glad you felt able to confide in me. The second is you can trust me not to say anything to anyone. This evening we've become friends, don't you think? If this was one of those old Westerns we'd be nicking our wrists and becoming … oh, that's blood *brothers*, isn't it? Okay, let's stick with being good friends. A friend shall I be, call me no other!'

'A friend of your soul, call *me* no other,' Sweeney said theatrically.

'I like the sound of that,' Patsy laughed. 'Let's shake hands on it.'

Sweeney told her to be careful of his cricketing finger and they shook with exaggerated formality.

Patsy suddenly stubbed out what remained of her cigarette and furiously waved away the smoke, her expression that of a guilty schoolgirl. Sweeney assumed she'd seen Mitchell. It wasn't Mitchell but a tall student of medium build with a gangly walk, comic-aggressive thought Sweeney, dressed in a dark raincoat and wearing a black woolly hat. He didn't ask permission but set his tray on their table and sat down next to Patsy. He took no notice of Sweeney, but his eyes were suspicious, as if he'd disturbed a conspiracy.

'Eddie, this is Pete, Pete, this is Eddie.'

'Hello,' Sweeney said. Pete grunted without looking at him.

'Pete's one of our party members,' she explained. To Pete she said, 'Eddie is working on his PhD in the department.'

Pete only grunted again. Sweeney was annoyed he hadn't taken off his woolly hat. His mother always told him it was rude to wear a hat indoors, especially at the table. He wanted to reach over, snatch it and say, 'Manners!' He expected Pete's voice to complement his proletarian appearance but when he asked Patsy how things were, his voice was smooth, refined, his accent Home Counties. His shoulders and head twitched when he spoke, reminding Sweeney of Jack Douglas. After a brief exchange of banalities from which Sweeney was excluded, Pete asked Patsy, 'Have you been in touch with the comrades at Grunwick lately?'

Patsy told him about being busy on her research and how Keith was spending time with new recruits. Pete received her news with condescension. '*La lutte continue*,' he said pompously.

'Pete is a veteran of the picket at Grunwick too, Eddie.'

Pete preened, head and shoulders twitching. 'You could call me the Stakhanov of the workers' struggle.'

What an idiot, Sweeney thought. He remembered Rod and the image he had of him knocking helmets off policemen. 'Did you knock the helmets off any coppers?' He was being sarcastic-aggressive.

Pete's twitch this time was more exaggerated. 'You mean did I have a go at the pigs? Of course I did. "I'm only doing me job, oink, oink". I did a lot more than knock their helmets off. "I'm only doing me job, oink, oink". They deserve all they get. "I'm only doing me job, oink, oink". Try saying that with my boot in your mouth, copper!' He pointed at Sweeney. 'You're Irish, aren't you? You should know what I'm talking about.' Sweeney contemplated sticking his boot in Pete's mouth. 'If football is the ballet of the working class,' Pete went on, 'getting stuck into the pigs is the ballet of revolution.' He looked at both of them as if expecting applause. Patsy smiled rather half-heartedly. He turned his attention to his food, continuing to speak as he ate.

Sweeney wondered if Pete's behaviour was an attempt by a middle-class boy to express solidarity with a lifestyle not his own. If it was, it showed how little he knew. Sweeney's mother would have clipped him round the ear. There followed a rant, interrupted periodically by Pete swallowing portions of food, about the 'crisis of capitalism', the 'break-up of Britain', the 'struggle for socialism', and the need to infiltrate the 'moribund branches' of the Labour Party, especially in Hull. What a life, Sweeney thought, with nothing in it except the obscure dogma of Marxist dialectics. This man was depressing him.

Patsy tried to involve Sweeney in the conversation by changing the subject, but Pete was relentless. He gave up listening for these political ramblings bored him. Monomania was always boring. He tried to observe as discreetly as possible Patsy's reactions. Pete's behaviour seemed at odds with her nature. Now he could accept what Brown and Toby had told him. The world she was in wasn't good for her. That thought depressed him even more.

Irritated, he arranged his dish, cutlery and beaker on the tray, stood up and lied civilly. 'It was nice meeting you, Pete.' There was another grunt. 'Do you want me to walk back with you to the department?' Sweeney asked Patsy.

Before she could answer, Pete announced, 'There's some business I'd like to discuss with you, Patsy. Keith mentioned bringing a few speakers to Hull before Christmas. Maybe we should talk about arrangements?'

She looked at Sweeney apologetically.

'I'll see you again,' he said. 'If you want to meet for coffee sometime, I'm always around.'

'Thanks, that sounds good,' she answered uncertainly.

. . . .

WANTS

A week later, when Sweeney came into the office, Jan stopped typing and asked, 'Shall I put your name down for the departmental walk?'

Sweeney thought at first of a charity event, shaking collecting tins at people along the streets of Hull, the sort of thing he'd avoid like the plague. Warily he asked for details.

'It will be great fun, a proper day out. We used to do it regularly, but haven't done so in the last few years.' Jan didn't say why. 'It's on the last Sunday of this month. We're going to Burton Pidsea, nice and flat, country roads, the odd bridle path, and if the weather is good you won't muddy your boots.' She eyed up his Doc Martins.

'These you mean? They've kept my feet dry through all the rainy days in Hull. Country lanes shouldn't be a problem.'

'We're not going on a trek across Holderness you'll be glad to know. It's a stroll really. And the reward at the end is a pie and a pint. Shall I put your name down?' Sweeney could see on her desk a folder dedicated to the event. He imagined another occasion bathed in English cheeriness.

'I'm your man for a pie and a pint. Burton Pidsea sounds very English.'

'Very East Yorkshire,' Jan countered proudly.

'In that case I am even happier to go.'

'Good lad!' She opened the folder and added his name to the sheet. 'Can I ask you to pass on the message to the other postgrads?'

'You can rely on me.'

There was no problem drumming up support. Brown thought it was a good idea and would ask Jan to squeeze in his new girlfriend. 'It will give the two of us something different to do on a Sunday afternoon.' He gave Sweeney a wink.

Toby was keen as well. 'It'll be good to see a bit of the countryside. I'll ask Patsy when I next see her. She told me Mitchell is too busy these days to bother with her. Tell Jan to add my name and pencil in Patsy.'

Sweeney wanted to ask Sam but had no way of making contact with that other world of hers.

The Sunday of the outing was dull, no rich autumnal colours, the leaves long fallen, but at least it was dry. A university minibus was parked on Salmon Grove and around it stood half a dozen undergraduates who, like him, had arrived too early. None of them had any walking gear and looked like they were about to go shopping. The students were trying not to show any excitement but their animated chatter suggested otherwise. Sweeney hung back as nonchalantly as he could, lighting a cigarette to disguise his own insecurity. Shortly Jan, clipboard in hand, arrived with the driver. She was well kitted out for the day in her boots, gaiters, khaki trekking trousers, bright blue anorak and waterproofed wide-brim hat. She began ticking names off her list, ushering the students onto the bus. Sweeney tried to hide behind trees lining the street but she spotted him, waved and called him over.

'Are you looking forward to your afternoon in Holderness?'

'I am, yes. Are Jo and Julie not coming?'

'One of Jo's kids is poorly and Julie ... Julie's only interested in wedding preparations these days.'

'How many are there altogether?'

'Nineteen', she told him. 'This lot here,' – she pointed to the students in the bus – 'Jimmy, our driver, he's doing the walk n' all, yourself, Toby, Patsy, Alan and Anna. Have you met Anna? She's a friend of Alan's.'

'No. He changes girlfriends so regularly I can't keep up.'

'The Cockney Don Juan, eh?'

'Well, if you take him at his own estimation.'

Jan smiled and looked down at her list again. 'Then there's Samantha and a few staff as well, not too many. And there's me, of course.'

WANTS

Sweeney tried to make his voice casual. 'Is it Samantha Ahrens?'

'Do you know her?'

He held up a still discoloured finger. 'I broke my finger in the staff-student cricket match and she gave me some first aid.' He thought it sounded plausible.

'Oh, I see. If you have an accident today I'll know who to turn to,' but, noticing Sweeney's blush, she added, 'Don't mind me. I'm only joking.'

In the bus he took an aisle seat behind the undergraduates, keeping the window seat free.

Staff clambered on, an assortment of young and middle-aged who made awkward remarks to students in that formal informality peculiar to the English middle class. Dawson wasn't one of them. In the commotion Sweeney hadn't noticed Sam.

'We can't go on meeting like this,' she whispered. 'Are you keeping that seat for me?'

'Most highly favoured lady, I am.'

He stood up and she slipped in beside the window, adjusting her olive-green US army jacket as she sat. Sam's hair was tied up in her usual high ponytail. She said, 'I've missed you again. And you can say I should have found you, and you'd be right, but it's been all go the last few weeks. I know that's no excuse but ... look, it's good to see you.'

A hand patted his head. 'There he is!' Brown said. 'We thought you'd talked us into something and decided to bunk off.' When he saw Sam his tone softened, 'Hello. Samantha, isn't it?'

He introduced Anna, a small, attractive, dark-haired woman in a navy and white striped toggle jacket. 'Excuse us. We're going to the back of the bus,' Brown nodded. 'Is that where you stashed that crate of beer you promised?' Anna's laugh was a little too exaggerated.

Toby and Patsy followed behind and introductions were made once more. Patsy's glance at Sweeney was at first enquiring, but as she passed, she smiled approvingly.

Jan closed the door and sat at the front. Jimmy started the engine and they set off.

The minibus crossed the River Hull towards Stoneferry and Sutton Ings. At Bilton they were already in the countryside, flatland of open fields, sparse hedgerow, few trees and big sky. There was a gentle hum of conversation, punctuated now and then by an exclamation or loud laugh. Few seemed interested in the scenery. Sweeney was only interested in Sam. They sat silently but comfortably together. He was amazed to feel both excited and at ease.

'How's the Masters going?' he asked.

'I'm adjusting to being self-reliant. I didn't realise until now how much structure and guidance there is on an undergraduate degree.'

'I felt the same, but you'll get the hang of it.'

'And how's your new *persona* developing? Has Two-Faced Eddie made his appearance? Do students approve?'

'It's work in progress.' He told her the story of his history tutor on the chaise longue, the Moroccan slippers, the languid smoking and the talk at aesthetic tangents.

'Somehow I don't think it's you.' She considered him for a moment 'It's far too pretentious, maybe far too decadent? You're not decadent are you?' She laughed at his look. 'No, I didn't think so. You haven't lived in Hull long enough to be decadent.'

He recalled Mr Trammer's words about perversity being universal but said, 'Hull and decadent are two words I never expected to hear in the same sentence.'

'It's the hidden *persona* of the city – so hidden *we* can't find it.'

'Do you think we'll find it in Burton Pidsea?'

'You never can tell.' She leaned against him playfully.

'Seriously though, and forgive me for sounding like Billy Joel, but that alternative *persona* of yours, why not stay just the way you are?'

'And what way am I?'

'Hmm, that's a good question. My answer to that is work in progress too.'

Sweeney laughed. He told her of his faith in providence and said, 'I expect my other *persona* is already written in stars and it will find me.'

'That's interesting. And what about me – do you see meeting me as providential too? I'm curious to know.'

'I have thought about it and I *do* think our meeting was meant, me being me, you being you. The day of the cricket match – your instinct long before, remember – you felt we had a lot in common? It is the same for me. Companionship was freely chosen – you sought me out – and yet it was entirely natural, the affinity between us already there. And it feels like I've been waiting for it to happen even if you took me by surprise. Do you see what I mean? After all, I had to come all the way to Hull to find you, didn't I?'

Sam laughed. 'That sounds very Irish to me. But I like your idea of providence, especially now that it involves the story of you and me.'

'*My* providence doesn't tie *you* down, of course. I wouldn't inflict that fantasy on you.'

Sam looked out the window. The minibus juddered as it slowed through Burton Pidsea and pulled up at The Nancy Inn. She turned to him. 'And *you* don't need be tied down by the ribbon I gave you.'

They stood to get off the bus. From behind he heard Brown calling, 'Eddie, we never found that crate of beer.' Anna laughed over-enthusiastically.

In the car park, Jan marshalled everyone. She explained the

walk was about three miles, to be taken leisurely so everyone could keep up and no one would get lost. 'If you are wondering, the Nancy in the name of the pub isn't a woman, but a horse.'

Brown asked loudly, 'Have you ever ridden a Nancy, Toby?'

There was some smiling, some giggling, while Anna laughed heartily, even if her laugh suggested she wasn't sure of Brown's meaning. Patsy and Toby looked at one another and shook their heads.

'Alan's a right Cockney, isn't he?' Sam said

'That's one way of describing him,' Sweeney replied.

He couldn't recollect much about the walk. He recalled a church, St. Peter and St. Paul's (Jan told them it was twelfth century), some attractive ivy-fronted cottages, a beck, a pond, a meandering country lane and a rutted bridle path, thankfully not too muddy. The landscape in Holderness wasn't spectacular but if you were seeking tranquillity, wishing to experience, however illusory, eternal England, this was as good a place as any, the fine mist which had descended making everything appropriately dreamlike. He stayed beside Sam along the way. They attached themselves to others now and then, joining briefly in different conversations, but mainly enjoying their own company. It all felt easy. At The Nancy Inn they shared a table near an open fire with the other postgrads and Anna (whose earlier enthusiasm had ebbed during the walk), ate their pies and drank more than one pint.

When they got back to Salmon Grove, Sweeney expected Brown to suggest 'going on elsewhere'. He didn't and neither did Patsy or Toby. Goodbyes were said, excuses were made, and suddenly the cheeriness of the day vanished into the cold, hazy damp of evening. Jan made a point of thanking Sam and Sweeney for coming. Jimmy turned the minibus onto Ferens Avenue and drove away. Under the street lamp, Sam shivered and rubbed her hands.

WANTS

'Thank you,' she said.

'Thank me for what?'

'For your words on the bus, they meant – mean – a lot to me. But there's something else. I don't know how to express it properly, not sure what the right word is. We played at being chivalrous at the cricket match but I don't think "chivalrous" gets it. I thought about it on our walk. It's this. You gift your companionship to me and don't assume anything in return. Remember I said something about having permission to be me? With you I feel permission to be freely me, maybe for the first time ever. You treat me like I am as I am, if that makes sense. I'm not sure I'm worthy of something so – how can I put it – providential?'

'There's nothing to be worthy of. You, me, we have to live as we live. I'm only glad you're in the life I lead.' He stumbled over the last line. It was *almost* true but it wasn't all he wanted. 'Does that make sense?' he asked.

'This is my answer.' She gave him a hug and kissed him lightly on the cheek. 'And thank you for not pressing me about my other world. I appreciate your un-assumingness ... is that a word? I *will* tell you, I swear, but not right now. Tonight it's more difficult to leave *our* world for my other.' She hugged him again. 'Shall I see you for a coffee in the Union tomorrow? About ten-thirty? I promise to make it.'

'I look forward to it.'

Sam waved to him as she hurried away.

Watching her go, Sweeney thought, I am Sisyphus. Should I imagine myself happy?

Chapter Seven

Sam kept her promise. They spent more time together, becoming regulars at their table in the student refectory, she smoking her Rothmans, he his Regals, together in a cloud of self-absorption. They talked about everything and nothing. Sweeney never broached the matter of her other world and Sam never mentioned it, the unasked and the unexplained easy companions for now, keeping chaste harmony between them. He did learn her father had been in the merchant navy. When Sweeney said his father had served in the Royal Navy during the war she wondered if they'd ever sailed on the same convoy.

'You see, it's another example of our having something in common,' she said. 'My dad's retired now and not in good health.'

'Do you have to care for your parents?'

'Are you joking? They are stubborn and self-reliant Yorkshire people.' Sweeney struck off one of Patsy's speculations. 'Mam thinks dad's illness is as much mental as physical.'

'You mean he still carries scars from the war?' His own father never dwelt on the past and never wished to commemorate it, a man of no regrets and no nostalgia.

'Yes. But it's not as you think. His parents and younger sister were killed in a German bombing raid. Their house took a direct hit. Mam says dad always felt survivor's guilt, can you believe it?' She lit another Rothmans. 'People talk of the London Blitz but Hull suffered just as badly. You can understand why people here feel neglected.'

'I never knew that.'

'The BBC used to say the raids happened in a northern coastal town. That was us. If you're from Hull it's a big thing.'

'All death and destruction is a big thing.'

WANTS

'I was moved by the Wilfred Owen lines, you know, about war, the pity of war and the poetry being in the pity? When I think of Hull I feel pity for what people went through and all the sadness they suffered. But I also feel pride in how they got on with life. There's something poetic in that simplicity, don't you think?'

'You've given me an interesting seam to mine for the thesis.'

'You can footnote my contribution "as told to me by Samantha Ahrens" and my name will live forever.'

Talk about war, poetry, books, ideas, university made companionship sweet, but simple things revealed what he felt but avoided saying. A pair of bright multi-coloured socks she wore one day affected him so deeply he could hardly think of anything else. Each time she made a dramatic gesture, her watch would slide down her wrist and she would shake it absentmindedly back in place. When a strand of hair fell across an eye, she would flick it away with the back of her hand. Then there was her voice. Up to this point, he was shocked to realise, apart from Mr Trammer and Chris, he'd only heard Hull accents from the mouths of what could be called the 'serving' class – shop assistants, bus drivers, bar staff, university secretaries, porters and cleaners. Everyone else he knew didn't come from Hull. He thought of the university as a vast spacecraft landed here and populated by outsiders like him.

He loved how Sam said things, especially the elongated vowels as flat as the landscape but also melodic. It was the very opposite of his own – his 'car' was her 'caah', his 'fill*um*' was her 'mov*ah*, his 'here' was her 'i-a'. They never tried to imitate. Sweeney had a good ear but he was a hopeless mimic. Sam admitted Northern Irish pronunciation was beyond her. 'There's no point,' she said, 'imitating each other badly. Let's agree to be united by different accents.'

'Our time will be *accent*uated.'

Once Sam asked him, 'Why do *you* want to spend time with me? For me it's simple. When I think of the interesting things in life, I think of you.' The watch slipped down her wrist and Sweeney watched her shake it back in place. 'I mean, what do I do for you, me and all my dithering?' She flicked away an unruly strand of hair. 'And don't be chivalrous, there's no need to flatter me.'

He would have liked to ask her, wasn't it obvious? He would like to have said I want to be with you. I want you to take me home to meet your mam. He didn't because he felt insecure, not intellectually, but emotionally. 'Remember what I said in Burton Pidsea? The answer is because you are you and because I am me. You don't have to be anything *for* me. You only have to be you. Didn't you say you can be as you are? Well, that's good enough *for* me.'

Sam lit another Rothmans. 'I'm sorry. Maybe I've read too many novels recently. I suppose I thought you'd discover me *as* me isn't all that interesting, no woman of mystery and all that. But is this unassuming Eddie speaking now and not Two-Faced Eddie?'

'Truer words were never assumed.'

She laughed, allowing the subject to drop.

He convinced himself accepting Sam's two worlds meant indulging her desire to be mysterious. If he had doubts, he found it easier to suppress than confront them. They would disappear in her company only to return like a hangover when the intoxication of her presence faded. Sometimes he would be prey to suspicions and insidious thoughts. More often he would be energised to read with greater understanding, to think with greater clarity and to write with greater conviction. He felt his sympathies, now romantically invested in the reality of Sam unlike the fantasy of Julie, extended beyond their former narrow range, were more sensitive to the experience of others and no longer merely abstract. In his Sisyphus essay, Camus concluded 'there is no sun without shadow'. If his happiness was shadowed by deep uncertainty, Sweeney experienced life more brilliantly than before.

Yet, for all his pleasure in Sam's company, for all those little things about her which made his heart leap up, for all the novel intensity she brought to his life, he was conscious of something else. He couldn't avoid the truth of Sisyphus. He had to admit the relationship was also a burden, however much he willed it. At some point, his attention would begin to slip from her towards another desire – to be elsewhere and unencumbered. He felt pride in this solitariness. He knew his unassuming character was not necessarily as sympathetic as she imagined. It was an escape from being burdened with possible problems in her other world, like those Patsy had suggested. Was this wish for escape and self-protection a defect in him or was it human, all too human? It hardly seemed truly romantic. It worried him to think it was the first so he excused himself by believing it must be the second. Nevertheless, he couldn't shake entirely remorse for what he thought were emotional inadequacies, his wish to avoid responsibility, supposing they were further confirmation of his immaturity.

He would have liked Patsy as a confidante but she was unavailable. Pearl would have been a source of good advice but her life seemed busy enough to impose upon. Toby he could trust but he remained lost in Lincolnshire. He wasn't sure about the wisdom of involving Brown. However, he did try to broach his problem by asking how things were with Anna.

'There's been a parting of the ways.'

'You surprise me. You seemed great together in Burton Pidsea.'

'Appearances can be deceptive, Eddie, my son. Here's a *Mastermind* question for you. What was the original title of

Barry White's "My First, My Last, My Everything"?'

Sweeney shook his head. 'Pass.'

'It's "My First, My Last, My In-Between"'.

'You're kidding me.'

'Straight up. I was her in-between and she was my in-between, not the first and not the last for either of us. You know all that stuff about long and meaningful relationships? Anna and I had a short and meaningless one.'

Sweeney didn't know whether to laugh or to commiserate and said, 'I'm sorry to hear that.'

'There's no need. The parting was mutual. She thinks I'm a decent bloke but didn't devote enough attention to her. I think she's a really nice girl but wanted more attention than I could give. Both of us are right. It's an everyday tale. Basic attraction unites, personal expectation divides, and life goes on. The steps in the process tend to be accelerated between students, it's all up and then it's all down. She'll not be after me like Joyce McKinney, that's for sure.'

'I couldn't imagine you being a manacled object of desire.'

'You never know what goes on behind closed doors, Eddie.' Brown seemed wistful for a second and looked out the window at another rainy day in Hull. He fished in his packet for a Gold Bond. 'What about you and Sam? You've been very quiet on that front.'

'So far, so good, we're taking things slowly.' Sweeney dredged his vocabulary for all the phrases he'd heard others use in soap operas, delivered them unconvincingly, and finally stumbled out Sam's words about her being between two worlds.

Both elbows on his desk, Brown squinted at Sweeney through the smoke of his cigarette and then stared out the window again. Without looking at Sweeney he said, 'Between two worlds? That's a hard place to be. For both of you, I mean.' He took another drag. 'Have you ever had a glimpse of this other world?'

'Not yet, no.'

'It's best then, my son, not to unsettle your own too much.' Brown stubbed out the butt. 'Mind you don't fall arse over tit between her two worlds.'

Sweeney could have taken offence. He could have replied that he preferred mystery to certainty, except he didn't believe it.

Brown stood up, walked over and leaned his hands on Sweeney's desk. 'With my track record I'm a bit of a beaten docket in this game. So what do you say to a few beers later, two lads out on the town, one with his freedom restored, one with his freedom still intact?'

It was a good night, normal service between them resumed, no lingering on the subject of love, either lost or wished for.

. . . .

One morning Jo told Sweeney that Dawson wanted to have a word. 'It's possibly something to do with a progress report. He was waving a form that needs completing.' Sweeney said he'd look in. 'Thanks, you know how agitated he gets about form filling. He'll pester us the rest of the day otherwise.'

Progress report! Sweeney still lived as though time was an inexhaustible resource, but the realisation he was half way through his studentship unnerved him. Three years had once seemed infinite but the end would be upon him sooner than he wanted. Wasn't it true what they said? It's always later than you think.

Dawson didn't require a progress report, only Sweeney's signature confirming he was still enrolled in the department. 'I completely overlooked it. This form filling is the bane of my existence – got a call from someone in admin asking me why it hadn't been submitted.' He pointed at Sweeney. 'He even asked if you'd dropped out, said this' – he held up the form – 'had been sent in August and was needed urgently for the annual report. As if academics haven't enough to do and can't be trusted to manage our own affairs. Please sign on the dotted line to appease our officious lords and masters.' When Sweeney had done so, Dawson shoved the completed form contemptuously into an internal mail folder.

'Now, how's your work coming along?' He gestured for Sweeney to have a seat and pushed the box of Turkish cigarettes and table lighter towards him.

'It's on track, thanks. I expanded on some of the ideas you've seen already. Your comments were really helpful, thank you. They have improved my arguments, given them a sheen of sophistication. The original woolliness has become more silken.' Dawson's face brightened. Sweeney wasn't sure if it was because of the compliment or his shoulder not being required for crying on. It took only one Turkish for Sweeney to outline what he intended to do next. In truth, it was nothing more than an abridged version of Dawson's own recommendations. 'All in all, I feel I've got everything well under control.'

'Things do look promising, glad to see you've taken on board my suggestions. It's a sign of maturity when someone can take criticism and advice in a constructive spirit.'

'They saved me the bother of going down those false trails you warned me about.'

There followed a silence of mutual satisfaction. Sweeney stood up to go.

'Oh, I almost forgot,' Dawson raised a hand to detain him. 'There's departmental funding for a postgraduate conference later this term, a one-day affair. It's at Kings College London, students delivering papers on work-in-progress. There will also be career information, that sort of thing. Some of our new staff thought it was a good idea. They said similar events had been useful to them. I don't doubt it. Anyway, a few places have been paid for, lunch included. I think it's good to show a Hull presence.'

'It does sound like an excellent opportunity.' Sweeney was thinking of the trip to London rather than the conference.

Dawson stretched across the desk and spoke quietly. 'We always talk of a scholarly community like we're bosom buddies. But it can be cut throat, Edward. It's always good to see who and what you're up against.'

Later that week an excited Sam told him she had put her name down for the conference.

'Are you keen on networking, Sam?' It was a word he'd only heard recently.

'You'll probably not believe me,' she replied, 'but I've never been to London.' Sweeney raised his eyebrows. 'I'm ashamed to admit it. I never said to the others, was too embarrassed.'

'I've only vague memories of London from childhood.' He told her the tale of his toothache at White Hart Lane.

'Then it will be an adventure for both of us,' she said. 'I can't wait.'

. . . .

On a cold, dank Friday morning in late November, those travelling to the conference met on the concourse of Paragon Station. Getting the early train had clearly been a struggle for the two young women, both Masters students, in the company of Brown and Sweeney. Their expressions shifted between off-hand attention to what Brown was saying and yawning drowsiness. Most of the passengers for London appeared to be going on business, besuited and with briefcases, as if this was their daily commute. They presented a respectable contrast to this huddle of students, Brown in his donkey jacket, one girl, Debbie, in a hooded duffel coat, the other, Susie, in an army surplus greatcoat, and Sweeney in his cagoule over a corduroy jacket.

'Any sign of Sam?' Sweeney asked, concerned she might be trapped in her other world.

Susie, chin sunk deep in her army greatcoat, mumbled, 'She is coming. At least she *said* she was.'

Debbie nodded and yawned, putting a hand to her mouth, 'She told me too.'

Brown and Sweeney looked at each other, Susie and Debbie looked at them and they all looked up at the station clock. A cry, a wave and Sam was rushing from the ticket office window in a smart, blue coat flapping open, beneath which she wore a floral midi skirt. No word was said by the group but what was unspoken was obvious – Sam was the only one who'd made an effort.

'Sorry I'm late.'

They assured her she was in plenty of time.

Sweeney whispered to Sam, 'You look great.'

'Thanks, but I hope the girls don't think I'm overdressed.'

They heard the locomotive revving up so they moved onto the platform, getting in the final carriage. It was impossible for them to sit together and Sam said she would stay with the girls. Brown and Sweeney went further along, disrupting two businessmen already at work on their files.

Brown touched the No Smoking notice on the window and said it was always a lottery on British Rail. 'It won't be long before you can't smoke anywhere.'

As they pulled out of the station, Sweeney pointed out the advertisement for Tupper Gloves and Hosiery. 'It always reminds me of Alf Tupper in *The Victor*.'

'I took *The Victor* as a kid too,' Brown said. 'Alf was my favourite, always showing those posh boys what's what.'

The train knifed through the dark, empty landscape. When they stopped at Doncaster, Sam came down to chat. She'd taken off her coat and was wearing a white blouse under a dark green cardigan which matched her skirt. Yes, Sweeney thought, she really had made an effort. The two businessmen, who had shunned distraction until now, glanced admiringly at her. When the train moved again, Sam lost her balance slightly and put her hand on Sweeney's shoulder for support. He imagined she let it linger a few seconds longer than necessary.

At Grantham, Brown nodded at the platform sign. 'This is Squire Milne's domain, deepest Lincolnshire. Do you think we'll see him criss-crossing his lands on horseback? Tallyho.'

'I can't imagine Toby foxhunting.'

'I'm not talking foxes. I'm talking the peasants who haven't paid their tithe.'

'Aren't tithes a church tax?'

'He wants to be a vicar, doesn't he? He'll need the practice.'

Approaching Kings Cross, Brown said he always felt a surge of energy the moment he stepped off the train. And he was right. The noise of the station, the crowd in motion, the pace of London, loosed them like arrows from the carriage as they rushed towards the underground, putting their faith in Brown's knowledge of how to get about.

'We want to get to Temple,' he said, 'so if we get separated, find it on the tube map and when you get there, ask someone for King's College. Otherwise, follow my lead' and he put up his arm like a tour guide. As they rattled strap-hanging beneath the streets of London, Sam's face never lost its look of childish joy.

. . . .

Sweeney finally understood what Rod had meant about university life in London being like studying in the rush hour. The foyer of King's was hectic, full of noise, bodies moving quickly in self-contained purpose, so different from the relaxed atmosphere at Hull. Sam was not diminished, not overwhelmed, but seemed at home. Why Sweeney should find this unexpected, not only that, disconcerting, and why he should feel her obvious delight threatening, he couldn't say exactly. Perhaps it revealed deep-seated insecurity about her affections and ignorance of her character despite all his talk of accepting who she really was. Perhaps it exposed an intellectual arrogance, an illusion of his superiority. He remembered the conversation with Patsy and his epiphany of egotism. He felt troubled and ashamed in equal measure. When they'd registered, the women headed off to a session on Feminist Literature and Sweeney and Brown to one on The Movement. They agreed to meet up again for lunch.

Some papers were interesting, some were obscure, and some were plain obtuse. One in particular, which applied Freudian analysis to Larkin's poetry, made Brown indignant. 'Are you a fan of your fellow-countryman, Joyce Cary?' he whispered. 'Have you read *The Horse's Mouth*? Larkin liked the book, found it moving.'

'I haven't read the novel, but I've seen the film with Alec Guinness.'

'That's good enough. You'll know Gulley Gimson then. There's a line which sums up perfectly what we've just heard.'

'What's the line?'

Brown said a little too loudly, '"It's like farting Annie Laurie through a keyhole. It may be clever, but is it worth the trouble?" It's perfect for this paper, don't you think?'

Sweeney doubled over with the giggles and tried hard to suppress laughing out loud. A young woman in the row in front turned and looked reprovingly at both of them.

At lunch, Brown announced he didn't fancy the limp sandwiches and tea on offer. 'What about knocking off to my favourite pub round here, The Nell Gwynne?' He looked at his watch. 'We could be there and back within the hour.'

'That sounds good to me.'

WANTS

When the others joined them, only Sam agreed to go.

On the Strand, she pointed. 'Look, there's The Savoy!' She stopped as taxis drove in and away from its entrance. 'Maybe we'll see somebody famous.'

'No time to hang about,' Brown said, taking them up a narrow alleyway and into the fug of a small crowded tavern. There was soft reflection of lamps on bottles behind the bar, dark wood panelling and a few framed photographs. They stood tight together, their glasses raised shoulder height in the eager crush of office workers, young people in animated groups, knots of older professionals in serious conversation.

'I love it here,' Sam said. 'I don't think we're missing anything at the conference.' Sweeney recounted to her the 'farting through a keyhole' story. She laughed loudly. 'That could be the quote of the day. I can't imagine anything bettering it.'

Brown thanked her for the compliment. 'The Hull contingent has set a precedent. We might be ejected this afternoon for being drunk and disorderly. Speaking of which, I am going to leave early to see the parents for the weekend ... and there's a Spurs game tomorrow. It was good of the English Department to fund my trip.'

Sam looked at Sweeney. 'It's just us going back to Hull, then. Susie and Debbie are going home for the weekend too. One is from Amersham and the other is from Chesham – but I'm not sure which is which.'

'There you go,' Brown said, 'things couldn't have worked out better.'

'It sounds like a collection of stories, doesn't it?' Sam said. 'First we were the famous five, now we're the three amigos and finally we'll be only ...'

'Two souls housed in a single breast?' Brown suggested.

'No, I was actually thinking of "the two of us", you know, The Beatles' song.' Sam sang the lines, "On our way back home, we're on our way home, we're on our way home, we're going home". Don't you know it?'

'Not one of their best. But beautifully sung, I must say,' Sweeney said.

'Those Scousers were on their way out by then.'

'What a pair you two are, Belfast flattery and Cockney prejudice! Where's the "two souls" line from, by the way?'

'I'm not sure,' Brown answered, 'probably from Shakespeare like everything else.' They looked to Sweeney for confirmation.

'Yes, it was Shakespeare.' He knew it was from Goethe's *Faust*. His history teacher at school had used it to explain how Germany, a culture so rich in music, art and literature, had produced the Nazis as well. It wasn't about harmony, but struggle. However, The Nell Gwynne was not the place for literary pedantry. Anyway, why shouldn't the words have a life of their own? Why shouldn't they mean something different for Sam and him?

'Before we head back to the conference, let me get another round,' she said. 'What's everyone having?'

'No, my sense of honour won't allow a woman to pay,' Sweeney said feigning outrage.

'It's 1977 not 1677. Haven't you heard of women's lib? Still, I can appreciate old fashioned chivalry when I see it.'

'Do *me* a favour,' Brown said. 'Same again, mate.'

The afternoon seminars were poorly attended. Quite a few had decided, like Debbie, Susie and Brown, to take the opportunity for a long weekend. Sweeney became bored and cut the final session. He waited in the foyer for Sam, looking fitfully at book stalls and information desks. Eventually, in the excited and animated bustle at the end of the conference, he saw her walking beside a tall young man. He was suave, confident, carried a smart leather satchel, and was dressed in an expensive-looking three piece suit, blue shirt with a white collar. He even wore a tie. As they walked, he leaned over, pretending to listen to what Sam was saying, but his eyes searched for others more important, a wan smile on his face, patronisingly indulgent. Sweeney's inner Alf Tupper surfaced. The young man picked out someone across the foyer, raised an arm, hailed, said one word of impertinent dismissal, and left Sam standing. Sweeney had an urge to trip him up as he went by.

'Was it an interesting afternoon?' he asked her.

'Yes, I learned a lot, even if I found some of the papers' – she punched him gently on the arm – 'farting through keyhole stuff. I blame you for putting that phrase in my head.'

'Who was that you were talking to?'

'He's from one of those Cambridge colleges. I heard Slaughterhouse at first, but thought that strange. I asked the girl beside me and she said Peterhouse. Is that right?'

'Yes,' Sweeney said, remembering Tom Sharpe's *Porterhouse Blue*.

'He's a master of farting through keyholes ... a pompous arse n' all and rude with it.' Sweeney felt like cheering. 'Would you mind seeing some of the London sights?' she asked. 'I don't want to come here and only see the inside of King's College and The Nell Gwynne. I wouldn't know where to start.'

He produced his pocket map of the Underground. 'I was having a look at this while I was waiting.' He traced a route with his finger. 'If we go back to Temple, we can get the tube to Westminster. If you like we could walk up to Trafalgar Square ... to Leicester Square ... and cut across to Piccadilly Circus. The Piccadilly Line goes direct to King's Cross ... here.'

'What time's our train to Hull?'

'Half past seven is the last direct service, but there's a later one to Newcastle with a change at Doncaster.'

She looked at her watch. 'It's half-four now, gives us some time. Let's have a cigarette before we head off, shall we? Mam's always telling me it's not ladylike to smoke in the street.'

THE LAST TRAIN TO HULL

· · · · · · · · · ·

Emerging from Westminster Underground, Sweeney was taken aback. He hadn't expected, immediately in front of them, to find the Houses of Parliament and above, Big Ben. Sam turned to him as if he had conjured the sight especially for her. 'I've only ever seen Big Ben on TV,' she said. The bell struck five o'clock. Like a child, she clapped her hands with joy. 'Can we get another view?'

They leaned on Westminster Bridge. The lights of Parliament shimmered in the inky blackness of the Thames. 'Is this where Wordsworth stood?' she asked.

'I suppose it is.'

They crossed to Westminster Abbey and walked along Whitehall.

'There's Downing Street!' she said. 'I wonder if Jim Callaghan's home? Our family's all Labour, of course.'

She took his arm casually and Sweeney enjoyed the idea of passers-by, insofar as Londoners took notice of anyone, thinking them a couple. At Trafalgar Square she pointed to Nelson on top of his column. 'He must be cold up there', she said. Sam loved the lights on Leicester Square and asked if they were near Bloomsbury. 'I've heard so much about it, you know, Virginia Woolf and her set.'

'I don't know for sure,' Sweeney answered. He didn't know at all and the underground map was no help. 'I think we're actually nearer Soho.'

'That sounds very bohemian! I'm sure Virginia must have been here.'

'It's very likely.'

'What about Charing Cross Road?' she asked. 'I loved *84 Charing Cross Road*. Have you read it?'

'I haven't, no.' He'd imagined it too sentimental.

WANTS

'Maybe we could look in a few bookshops?'

'Okay, I'll ask the policeman over there if it's near here.'

'Ask him the time as well,' she laughed. 'Aren't our policemen wonderful?'

They stood before shop windows in silent contemplation before Sam said they should at least go inside one. As they browsed shelves and boxes, picking up books and setting them back, Sweeney told Sam about Roland's art of *tsundoku*. 'He has volumes in piles of different sizes in every conceivable place.' He also told her of Roland's curious way of life, immersed in his flat with his typewriter and jazz records for company. He expected her to appreciate the picture he'd painted of an ascetic life. Instead, Sam set down the hardback she'd been holding.

'That image makes me feel so sad. I thought of Julian of Norwich.'

'Who was he?'

'Not he, but she. She chose to be walled up in a cell. Anchorites like her were read the office of the dead, you know, for they had become dead to the world.'

'That seems a good description of Roland's existence.'

They were parted by other browsers and Sweeney came across an edition of *The Great Gatsby*. He checked the price. It was affordable. He paid the cashier, who looked like Mr Trammer, and wondered if all second-hand bookshop owners looked the same. He put it in his shoulder bag.

Moments later Sam sidled up. 'I suppose we should go?'

Outside he gave her the book. 'A present, I don't know whether you've read it, but you can never have enough copies of a good novel.'

'I'm ashamed to say I haven't read it – and you really shouldn't have spent your money on me. But I'm glad you did.' She gave him a hug, putting both of them off-balance, forcing pedestrians to swerve. She apologised. 'I'm always saying sorry now.'

Sweeney reminded her of Ali McGraw's line from *Love Story*. Sam said it was one of her favourite films. 'I'm *so sorry*, fill-*ums*,' she corrected herself.

At Piccadilly Circus she wanted to sit beneath Eros. Even on this bitter winter's evening a crowd of young people were there and they had to squeeze their way to a free spot. They smoked.

'Isn't it wonderful?' Sam said. 'It makes Hull seem so' – she searched for the word – 'provincial.'

'That's why people like the place. It's why *I* like the place … one of the reasons why, anyway.'

'I suppose you have to try living there.' They looked at each other, bursting into laughter.

When they finished their cigarettes, he said, 'We need to go for our train.'

Half an hour should have been time enough. But it wasn't. There was a signalling problem on the Piccadilly Line and the Hull train had left by the time they got to King's Cross. It was typical, he thought. British Rail, not known for punctuality, had run exactly to schedule. What was worse, when they consulted the timetable, Sweeney had been mistaken about the later train. The expected connection to Hull from Doncaster turned out to be a local service only, which terminated at Selby.

Sam let out a slow 'Oh nooo' and slapped her forehead. Sweeney apologised, but she wouldn't hear of it. 'It was my fault wanting to pack in as much of London as I could. What shall we do?'

'We can hang around King's Cross until the first train next morning,' he suggested, 'or we can travel to Doncaster and wait there. Another option is to go on to Selby. Whichever way, we're going to be stuck for the night. We haven't enough cash to stay in London.' He wished he had one of those credit cards the banks were always advertising. 'And I don't have Alan's phone number. I'm sure he would have put us up.'

'Don't panic, Captain Mainwaring. I need to make a phone call to let people know what's happened.'

When Sam returned, she appeared more composed. They had a cigarette, discussed things further and decided on Selby. She thought King's Cross not a safe place to linger, however much she liked being in London. Already rowdy youths were making their way through. 'Imagine what it will be like when they come back,' she said. 'I think it's best to keep travelling. I'm sure little goes on in Selby after midnight.'

· · · · · · · · · ·

They spent the journey to Doncaster reviewing the day, able to laugh now at missing the Hull train.

'*Last Train to Hull* sounds like a good novel,' Sam said.

'Better than *Midnight in Selby*, you think?'

'It has a ring to it … but I have a question for you. Do you think this journey is another example of providence?'

'I can't say yet. The journey's not over.'

'I think that's what's called an evasive answer?'

'I would say it's an example of how I don't know what I'm talking about.'

'I never knew honesty could be so amusing – or is it unassuming?'

The night air at Doncaster station chilled them and luckily their connection was on time. It took less than twenty minutes to reach Selby. They checked the platform timetable for the first train to Hull. There was one at five-thirty. Someone had pencilled in beside it the words 'milk train'. They looked at each other – how to pass almost seven hours? They explained their situation to a rotund pipe-smoking railwayman who told them the waiting room was open all night. 'It's heated. You can both kip on the bench.' He paused. 'Students are you?' He laughed, 'Nothing naughty now, we run a respectable station here in Selby.'

'This will be a long night's journey into day,' Sweeney said, glancing at the clock on the waiting room wall. The minute hand made an irritating clunk as it juddered forward. He stood against the cast iron radiator, rubbing his hands along its ribs. 'The porter was right. We should be warm enough, at least.' Sam slumped with a sigh onto the wooden bench suppressing a yawn. Sweeney imagined love declared in this unprepossessing little station. His mother liked Frank Sinatra and he smiled, remembering her singing along to 'It happened in Monterey'. Why shouldn't it happen in Selby too?

'What are you smiling at?' she asked.

He was too embarrassed to mention Frank Sinatra, who seemed old-fashioned. 'I remembered the words of an old song, that's all.'

'Which one would that be?'

His mind was still agile enough at this hour to come up with a good answer, suitably obscure but cultured he thought. 'Do you know the Flanders and Swann song "Slow Train"?' Sam shook her head. 'It's beautifully melancholic, about the closure of branch lines and stations in the sixties.' He saw her sceptical look. 'You wouldn't think it could pull at your heartstrings, but it does. They mention Selby station and the places that have vanished from our lives. Yet here we both are. And Selby station lives on.' He looked out at the deserted platform and then back at her. 'Or does it …? Maybe it *doesn't* exist. Maybe that porter was a ghost. Maybe we find ourselves in the twilight zone. Maybe …'

'Please don't say that!' Sam looked genuinely alarmed. 'I am easily frightened by stories of ghosts.' She sighed again. 'I didn't mean to snap. I know you're only joking. I'm tired. Why don't you come and sit down? You can't stand by that radiator all night.' She shifted over to make room. 'It's not what you'd call comfortable, but it's all we've got. And since you've put the idea of ghosts in my head, you're going to have to protect me now.' She looked about the room. 'Is there an ashtray anywhere?'

To one side of the bench was a battered metal bucket filled with sand and discarded butts. He manoeuvred it with his foot towards her and sat down. As they smoked, a heavy goods train laboriously clanked and screeched through on its way to Hull. They looked at each other, obviously thinking the same thought.

'I know, Eddie, for some reason I don't see us as train-hopping tramps.' She looked at the clock. 'I believe the hands are going backwards.'

'That really does sound spooky.'

Sam wagged a finger, but said less sharply, 'No more ghost talk.'

They finished their cigarettes and bent down to extinguish them in the bucket. Their hands touched, their cheeks brushed and it seemed natural for him to kiss her. Sam didn't resist and he felt her relax. The embrace wasn't erotic, no urgent passion, no breathless desire (unlike what he'd anticipated). She held him tightly and then laid her head on his shoulder. No words were spoken. How long they sat like this he couldn't say. Though bearing her weight made the pressure of the wooden slats uncomfortable, though his shoulder began to ache, there was no unpleasantness he wasn't prepared to endure. Then he felt her body shake gently, sensed that his collar was damp and knew that she was sobbing. Sweeney caressed her hair.

'What's wrong?'

Sam didn't answer at first, buried her head deeper into his shoulder and mumbled indistinctly. He continued to caress her hair, unsure what to do, despairing at his artlessness. Eventually, Sam pulled away, her face tear-streaked, her eyes puffed and reddened. She fumbled in her bag, extracted a handkerchief, dabbed her cheeks, blew her nose and shook her head as if to recompose her thoughts.

'Did you hear what I said?' she asked.

'I didn't.'

'I said I have been very bad to you when all you've ever done is show me kindness and treat me with respect. I don't deserve any of it. That vision I had, remember, at the bookshop? Someone walled up in a room? That's what I feel I've been doing to you, building an emotional wall around you for my own selfish reasons.' She saw Sweeney was about to say something but put up her hand. 'The truth is I'm married, okay? Now do you see how bad I've been?' Sam looked down at the floor. 'I'm ashamed for letting you think anything else.'

Sweeney was about to say it was the modern age, denying desire was no longer necessary, affairs no longer frowned upon, divorce was common, it wasn't *Brief Encounter*, she wasn't Celia Johnson and he wasn't Trevor Howard. Why not let things take their course? But if she knew of that film, she would know Johnson's line 'it's awfully easy to lie when you know that you're trusted implicitly, so very easy, and so very degrading.' Was this the guilt she was feeling right now?

'I was so thoughtless,' she continued, keeping her head lowered, not looking at him, 'all my rubbish about two worlds. I thought I could be an emancipated woman by day and a housewife by night. Feminist friends at university tell me I am crazy not to live as I want. But I can't. You know your line, because I am I, because you are you? Well, I am *Catholic*, Eddie, and I can't do it. Betraying my vows would be sinful. You probably think it nonsense. I'm in love with you and that's the truth, but I am wedded to my husband and that's the truth too. It's the old drama of desire and duty, can't you see?'

He took her hand. 'Does your husband make you unhappy?' It was a cliché, of course, but he knew what he wanted her to say.

'He's nothing but supportive even if my studies mean little to him. He made good money on the boats but the Icelanders destroyed that. Can you believe he never got any compensation? He's taken a labouring job on the Humber Bridge to help me through university.' She raised her hand. 'He was here.' She let her hand fall. 'He had to start at the bottom again. I can't fault Tony, he's done nothing wrong. But I never feel as happy as when I am with you. Today, when Alan said two souls in a single breast ... at the cricket match I sensed it long before speaking to you. I knew even before that. Remember me talking about seeing you around?' – she looked in his eyes – 'when you were an angel?' She snuffled an insecure smile. 'I did say I would explain my two worlds and I finally have. If you want to have nothing more to do with me, I will understand.'

'Is that what you want?'

'No, of course it's not what *I* want. I'm only being honest at last and setting *you* free, setting you free from me. If it's what *you* want.'

He imagined playing the role of disappointed lover, someone who turns instantaneously to hatred when confronted by the truth. But that was melodrama. A chaos of ill-formed thoughts possessed him like a brainstorm, disturbing and scattering all his neatly arranged ideas. He'd always suspected, but never wished to know. It wasn't Patsy who had put the idea in his head, but he'd preferred illusion. That was the harsh truth. The problem was emotional childishness.

'No, it's not what I want,' he said eventually, but was too sick at heart to know if his words were honest. He reached into his pocket for another cigarette but his packet was empty. He threw it onto the floor and swore loudly. She touched his arm hesitantly. Her hand trembled as she offered him one of her Rothmans.

'You know, that's the first time I've ever heard you swear,' she said.

He leaned back on the bench and raised his head to the ceiling. Sam's look was anxious. Did he detect a hint of fear? Had men in her 'other world' been violent towards her? Was Tony too if she crossed him? He took a deep breath and said calmly, 'Sweeney Swears in Selby has a poetic ring to it, don't you think?'

Her anxiety transformed into a suppressed giggle. She couldn't restrain it, began to laugh and he joined her. The tension of the moment dissolved. Another goods train rumbled slowly through the station. Sweeney used the distraction to walk to the grimy window. He saw wagons and tank cars heading up-line towards Leeds. When the train passed, the noise fading along the track, he stood with his back to the radiator again.

'If you're saying we should stay friends then I, being I, accept. I accept, you being you, cannot break your vows. It will be difficult for me. But I'd like to try.' He said these words confidently though he didn't trust them. He didn't trust himself. 'We can hold on to that.'

'Don't put on another *persona* just for me,' Sam said. 'I want you to stay the way you are. I want us to stay the way we were. Oh God, that sounds like a line from a bad film.'

'Fill-um,' Sweeney said.

'Fill-*um*. Look, why don't you sit down again.'

He sat and sank the cigarette butt deep in the sand bucket.

Sam put her arms around him and her head on his shoulder again as if she could only speak without looking at him. 'I am very guilty about what I've done, a Catholic thing. I need your forgiveness. I mean it. I need to hear you say you forgive me.'

'I forgive you.'

'I know in the eyes of the world there's nothing to forgive. I know both of us have behaved ... sensibly. But *I* know I was wrong. It would have been so easy for me to follow my feelings. I pray I haven't destroyed everything for you.'

'Of course you haven't,' he said, though now she had put that possibility into words, he wasn't certain at all. Sam thanked him, but didn't seem entirely reassured.

Hours seemed to have passed, but the wall clock said differently.

'A long time yet before the milk train arrives. I'm totally washed out,' she said softly. To him, her words seemed edged with defeat.

'I'm the same. Stretch out, Sam. You can use my jacket for a pillow.' He folded it across his knees. She protested, but laying her head on his lap, she fell asleep almost immediately. A lullaby of Selby, Sweeney thought. He expected to stay awake, toiling over failure, but he too dozed off. It wasn't a deep sleep for he remembered the station porter putting his head round the door at some point.

Sam wakened, stood up, stretched, bent over and kissed Sweeney lightly on the forehead. 'Our train will be here soon,' she said. 'Did you manage to get any sleep?'

'I did, but it wasn't my most comfortable night ever. What about you?'

'Amazingly well, yes, a bit stiff, that's all. Thanks for letting me stretch out.'

The 'milk train' was empty apart from a few railway workers going on or going off shift. The carriage felt chilly and the two of them huddled together, saying little. Sweeney was still too exhausted to think clearly. This is what defeat is like, he thought. One thing nagged him.

'Is Ahrens your married name?'

'I made it a condition to keep my family name, except for legal purposes. I didn't fancy being known as Mrs Houghton. Doing what everyone else did only stretched so far.'

'And you don't wear a ring?'

'I do on occasions – but only as a favour.'

PART FOUR

Love

Chapter Eight

Sweeney's routines followed their normal pattern, but nothing was the same. What happened at Selby had shaken him. It had undone the precious equanimity of his solitary world. He experienced a strange mental lassitude. Time congealed and weighed heavily on him, simple things appeared tiresome, important things irrelevant. There was disconnection between how he engaged with others and how he felt. It wasn't that he'd suddenly become capable of saying one thing and thinking another. His hypocrisy stayed within its normal boundaries. This disconnection was different. His smile became broader, his greetings more fulsome, his laugh louder, his manner brisker, behaviour at odds with the debilitating melancholy he felt.

Meeting Sam for coffee the Monday after their London trip, he invented an appointment with Dawson to cut things short, disclosing his manic condition by behaving light-heartedly and flippantly. It was gross duplicity and she was too intelligent not to notice, witnessing his exaggerated gestures and receiving his lie about Dawson without comment. She stayed at the table, silent, lighting another Rothmans, as he dashed off self-importantly. Afterwards he raged at his foolishness but collapsed easily into self-righteousness and self-pity. Wasn't he the one who'd been betrayed after all? He revisited incoherently all the hopes and desires placed in her.

Favourite stoical stratagems didn't work. He told himself he'd only known Sam for a few months and, like lines of the song, he got along without her before he met her and would get along without her now (this had worked very well in Julie's case). The problem was he didn't want to get along without her. He also tried convincing himself present troubles would amount to nothing for *in the end* nothing matters much, all was hocus-pocus. This was no help either because he wasn't at the end. Time wouldn't solve his problem. Time without her was the problem, rising up like an infinitely tiring mountain. Time was his sickness. He tried indifference (what was she to him really?) and that proved futile too. Stoics had lied. Sadness seemed infinite to each heart. It happened to be his heart this time and not some philosophical abstraction or fantasy. Escaping through work became impossible for the books around him lost their souls. Books were a load of crap. I must be depressed, he told himself, for his mind dwelt on old shames and insecurities, dredged up suppressed self-loathing. He felt like weeping. That 'brainstorm' in Selby hadn't subsided. It still raged.

Brown wasn't fooled by his disguises and asked him what was wrong. 'I know something is, so you might as well tell me.'

Sweeney tried to explain his woes as best he could – about what happened with Sam at Selby and the complication of her Catholic vows.

Brown tapped his pen on the desk and leaned back in his chair. 'Selby, bloody Selby, Selby, that gateway to romance. I can see she'll not ask you back to see her mam.' He apologised immediately. 'I don't mean to make light of things. But it was the first thing I said to you about Hull women – and you've used it against me as well, haven't you? And Catholic vows?' He shook his head. 'That sounds too *Brideshead Revisited* for me. I can't comment on religion. Like Larkin I don't do church well. In fact, I don't do church at all. Maybe Toby could advise you – but he's C of E, isn't he, not Catholic ...' Brown stopped talking and offered Sweeney a Gold Bond.

'You're not having much luck with women are you, Eddie, my son?'

'That's one way of putting it.'

'I'm going to be straight with you and it may not be what you want to hear right now. Shall I go on or shall I shut up?'

LOVE

'Now you've started, you'd better finish.'

Brown stood up from his desk and walked over to the window, his habit for thinking out loud. Though late morning, it was one of those winter days in Hull which never seemed to lighten between dawn and dusk.

'Here's my view, for what it's worth. I don't know Sam well but what I know I like. From what you say, it seems she's acted faithfully, if that's the right word. What I mean is she's put others before herself. I can tell the way she looks at you it is love – don't ask me why, you're hardly Robert Redford or Clint Eastwood.'

'Thanks very much.'

'If you can't be rude to your friends, who can you be rude to? Seriously, she's even put *you* before herself, God help her.'

'She's put me first? How do you figure that?'

'Just hear me out. It would have been easy for her to have an affair, for her to play away, as they say, in this "other world" of university life. She did say that, didn't she?'

'She told me she felt caught between two worlds but …'

'Okay, no matter. It would likely have been cost free, knowing the gentleman you are. Now don't deny it! I couldn't see you making a scene or threatening to tell the hubby … or some Father Flat-Hat priest. She could have strung you along, but she didn't. She could have made a complete fool of you, but she didn't. She could have hung you out to dry, but she didn't. She could have behaved treacherously, but she didn't. She behaved honourably. That's how I see it anyhow. She's no Phyllis Dietrichson, that's for sure! Look mate, people can't help who they're attracted to, married or not. Didn't I say something like you're two souls in a single breast? I think you'd be crazy to lose all that because she can't take you home to meet her mam, that's all. Surely you can sort things between yourselves? A woman like Sam, you don't want to lose her even if, well, she can't be yours – if you know what I mean.'

Sweeney thought over these words as he smoked. 'I don't know who said you must behave as foolishly as your character demands.' Brown spread his arms to show he didn't know either. 'Thanks for the advice. And I can see what you mean.'

'Mate, it's easy for me to say don't get things out of proportion. But you're a level-headed bloke, though given to high flown romantic notions about women. Now, don't deny that either!'

'So you're telling me to keep on seeing her?'

'You both might find it hard to keep passion at arms' length but you can at least try. Sam's a great girl. To answer your question, yes, I think you should.' His tone became laddish. 'And it would stop you being such a miserable sod. I'm the one who should be miserable. Second Division football's no fun. Spurs need promotion this year.'

. . . .

Sweeney sought but couldn't find Sam. Brown told him not to stress. The Christmas vacation was approaching. There were plenty of parties so why not have a good time? 'You know Sam's not going anywhere. Put your romanticism to one side for a change and give hedonism a try, women earthy-style rather than heavenly-style. You'll find it and them much more satisfying. I do anyhow. What do you say?'

'It's not really my thing – but why the hell not?'

'That's the spirit. There's bound to be something on somewhere,' Brown assured him, 'Cranbrook, Auckland, maybe Marlborough. I'll check my sources.'

At these house parties he did give hedonism a go, lots of loud music (Tom Robinson Band, Boney M, Elton John, Queen, Bee Gees, others he didn't recognise), lots of shouting, lots of bouncing up and down, lots of arm waving, lots of beers, lots of cigarettes, lots of inane chat with girls and about girls, lots of sweat and lots of insincere laughter. Sweeney's enjoyment was conspicuous yet mainly bogus and after only a few nights out, he felt partying was a lie too.

'You've not given it time,' Brown assured him. 'Here's an offer you can't refuse and to make sure you can't, I've paid for it already.' He waved a pair of cheaply reproduced paper tickets advertising a Christmas Party at the Hull Circle Cricket Pavilion. 'Before you ask, no, it's nothing to do with cricket. The English Society hired the place for the evening. It's their do.'

'Do you think Dawson is going?'

'Can you imagine him disco dancing? He'd get his googlies in a twist.'

It was a cold December night, frosty and still. They rendezvoused at The Hull Cheese before heading down Anlaby Road. Sweeney was surprised to find a cricket field so close to the city centre.

'Yorkshire used to play a few matches here, but no longer,' Brown told him. 'Just think, you could have seen Geoffrey in the flesh and thanked him for making you all that money. He'd probably ask you for a percentage. That's Yorkshire for you!'

The lights of the pavilion guided them to a set of steps leading up to the entrance. It was a venerable building, steep tiled roofs with a team balcony either side of mock Tudor frontage. The interior was down-at-heel, the wooden flooring creaking to the step, noticeboards advertising functions long past, matches long finished, the scruffy décor only marginally brightened by some half-hearted Christmas decorations. The pavilion had the unmistakable odour of generations of leather, woolly jumpers and linseed oil. Here were echoes of old glory. Sweeney loved it.

The main function room wasn't crowded, its atmosphere muted in the absence of dancing bodies. The DJ was a student, pestered and distracted by requests for records he didn't have.

At the bar Brown scanned the room and Sweeney was reminded of Larkin that lunchtime in the Staff Common Room.

'Are you expecting someone?' Sweeney asked.

'You never can tell.'

This seemed vague for Brown and Sweeney was convinced his friend had contrived some 'accidental' meeting between him and Sam. He began preparing things he should say.

'You've gone quiet all of a sudden,' Brown said, swirling beer in his glass to improve its head.

'I was just thinking. I've never properly thanked you for everything you've done for me recently, trying to cheer me up and all that, even the sore heads.'

'Especially the sore heads,' Brown corrected him.

'We might as well continue killing our brain cells in the spirit of Christmas cheer.' He ordered two fresh pints.

Brown whispered, 'I think our evening is looking up.'

Sweeney looked around, expecting to see Sam, but there were Susie and Debbie, dressed exactly as they had been on the trip to London. Brown waved to them, they smiled back and approached confidently.

'And how was your spell in the tropic of Ruislip?' Brown joked. 'Remind me again. Which of you is council estate and which is posh?'

Susie made a swish with her army greatcoat. 'You should know Ruislip is far too common for Debbie and me. There are a few exclusive golf clubs and country parks between us and the plebs.' She put her arm around Debbie. 'No outside toilets or coal in the bath for us, isn't that right Debs?'

'Glad to hear it. We boys' – Brown put his arm around Sweeney – 'have our standards too. So what'll it be, gin and French, gin and It? My friend here is buying.'

'We're slumming tonight,' Debbie said, 'so get the pints in.'

'That's what we like to hear, isn't it Eddie?'

LOVE

The pavilion filled up but never became crowded. The music got louder, the students noisier, everyone drunker and yet somehow the atmosphere remained restrained, as if there were a maiden aunt present no one wanted to outrage with unseemly conduct. The four of them had found a table. They chatted amiably, danced awkwardly to a few songs, and an unspoken but unmistakable pairing had taken place, Sweeney with Susie, Brown with Debbie. For the first time in his pact with hedonism, Sweeney admitted to having a good time.

The DJ put on The Jackson Five's 'Let me show you the way to go'.

'This is our song,' Debbie and Susie said simultaneously.

And clearly it was. The few others on the dance floor moved aside as the two of them danced fluidly, miming the words, fists as microphones.

'Look,' Brown said with astonishment, 'they have all the moves, the gestures, the twirls, the walk, it's incredible.'

'It's certainly not *Come Dancing*.'

'No, it most definitely is not. That's some double act right there.'

They watched speechless for a while, then Brown nudged Sweeney's arm. 'Don't be offended but I'm going to ask Debbie if she'd like to go on somewhere, see what happens. But looking at them dance together they may be inseparable. If she does say yes, would you mind looking after Susie?'

'Was this your *beau* stratagem from the start?'

'Just let's say I didn't rule it in and I didn't rule it out. What happens may disappoint us but then again, who knows?'

When the Jackson Five song ended there was spontaneous applause from everyone. Debbie and Susie bowed, blew kisses all round and returned to the table. Sweeney and Brown stood, held back their chairs as the girls gave a final wave before sitting.

'Where did you learn to dance like that?' Sweeney asked.

'You'd be surprised what people in our part of Buckinghamshire get up to,' Susie laughed.

'Especially as the winter nights set in,' Debbie added. Even their humour, Sweeney noted, had become a double act.

'Nothing can top that performance,' Brown said, 'and I'm sure my colleague would second that judgement?' Sweeney nodded. 'Anything else in this place of dreams would be an anti-climax.' The girls giggled, not only because they found the description funny but also because they were still high on their moment of success.

Walking along Anlaby Road, the pairing was fixed and when they reached Park Street, Sweeney and Susie turned left in the direction of Spring Bank as Brown and Debbie continued towards the city centre.

The night had become much colder and Susie sank her chin deeper into her greatcoat. In his corduroy jacket, which had been warm enough earlier, Sweeney shivered.

'Your coat looks very cosy,' he told her.

'I'll let you try it later. Not out here, though. It's too cold.'

They stopped on the Park Street railway bridge and leaned together briefly on the parapet. The lights of Paragon Station pitched an ethereal glow, the lamps on the platforms haloed in the frosty air. A local passenger train stood at one platform, engine idling, carriages shuddering noisily. At the near edge of another, a Deltic locomotive waited, its cabin lit, its yellow nose smeared with days of oil and grime.

They walked on and Susie took Sweeney's arm, pulling him tight to her coat. 'It's hard to feel safe these nights,' she said. 'At least women in Leeds are marching in protest. Yorkshire Ripper on the loose and the police are advising a curfew for women! Where are our rights?'

He didn't know how to respond. He couldn't understand this murderous brutality which haunted the county. He could have said something about terrorists at home but thought it too self-referential. It wasn't about him but about every woman's fear. To mumble agreement was inadequate. He didn't have the feminist jargon either. Sweeney stayed silent and held her tighter, hoping to make her feel safe and convey solidarity. It seemed to work for she changed the subject.

'I don't know this part of town,' she said, 'but it looks authentically Hull.'

'I feel at home here. I like to think of it as my patch now.'

She looked at him with genuine surprise. 'I don't think I could ever feel at home here. It's nothing to do with the Ripper. It's because Hull is drab in every way. Once this year is over, I'm moving back south.'

Sweeney was equally surprised by her disaffection but saw no point in making it an issue. Susie had tried living here and found it not to her taste. 'Where did you do your undergraduate degree?' he asked.

'I was at Bristol. I didn't do well enough to get on their Masters course. So here I am, reluctantly.'

Sweeney took her to The Polar Bear and since it was Friday night, across to Arnott's Bakery for a fadge. He enjoyed some banter with Alice about Brown's absence.

'This is really interesting,' Susie said insincerely. 'You seem to get on well with the locals.' She thought a fadge too much for her and wondered if he wouldn't mind sharing.

'Since I live nearby, do you want to go there and eat?' Sweeney suggested. 'I'll put on a pot of tea to warm us up.'

As they sat by the gas fire eating, she hesitantly, he hungrily, he explained to her the fine art of *tsundoku*.

'I like the idea of *tsundoku* but I can think of a better one.' Susie smiled at him differently. She still wore her greatcoat, stood up, took it off and held it out. 'I did promise you could try it.' When he put it on she slipped her arms inside the coat and around his waist. 'Why don't we warm each other?'

'Is this what people in Buckinghamshire get up to on a Friday evening?'

'There is only one way for you to find out.'

He did find out. She fell asleep in his arms, telling him as she did how much she loved his duvet.

Early next morning, Susie announced she was going back to Amersham for Christmas, needed to sort out a few things before she did and maybe she'd see him sometime. She disappeared with a swish of her greatcoat. Sweeney didn't feel snubbed. Instead, he admired her easy manner *à la mode*. He discovered Brown's story with Debbie had been similar but at least he had her telephone number in Chesham.

'Actually, she's not as posh as I first thought, unlike your friend Susie.'

'It doesn't surprise me,' Sweeney told him.

. . . .

The university term dragged to its close, corridors echoing with absence. Sweeney left off another draft chapter of his thesis with Dawson. 'Splendid,' his supervisor said. 'I will treat this as my first Christmas present'.

Exchanging books in the library he bumped into Toby for the first time in over a month. 'I've been busy with one thing and another,' Toby told him, 'but then we all have so that's no excuse.' He nodded at Sweeney's armful of books and held up his own. 'Christmas reading sorted for both of us.'

'Something to protect us from the *Morecambe and Wise Christmas Special*,' Sweeney said.

'There's always that, certainly!' Toby smiled but his look became serious. 'I don't know if you've heard but Patsy was injured recently.'

'No, I hadn't. What happened?'

'Mitchell's lot happened, that's what. They were protesting against the National Front at some demo in Hull last month.'

'Have the police arrested the one who did it?'

Toby scoffed. 'It wasn't the NF. It was one of her so-called comrades. In a scuffle with police, he accidently whacked her in the eye with a placard. It could have been serious. Mitchell wanted her to claim police brutality and take a case against the Chief Constable. Can you believe it?'

'I can well believe it. I met one of her so-called comrades a while ago.'

'Anyway, I've been helping to nurse the patient. Patsy wouldn't lodge a complaint and Mitchell's sulking about her refusal. He wasn't too pleased to see me come round either, probably thinks I work for MI5.'

'And how is Patsy?'

'She's on the mend, still in quite a bit of pain and a bit vain about her black eye too. I read for her, which she likes. Well, says she likes.'

They walked back to the department, Toby worrying through Patsy's health. In the postgrad room he stopped abruptly. 'I've been talking nonstop about my own concerns. Forgive my bad manners. How are things with you? The walk in Holderness seems an age ago now. How's Sam doing? I forgot to say, Patsy asked me if I'd heard news about your two worlds. She wouldn't say anything more. She likes to keep things mysterious.'

Sweeney outlined his story as briefly and self-protectively as he could.

'Maybe it's something we should discuss over a cup of coffee? Staff House is still open,' he said. 'Let's bluff our way in like Alan tells me he does.'

Staff House was quiet. Sweeney offered Toby a cigarette but he said he'd quit. He told him of Brown's advice and Toby looked surprised. 'Well, well, I never credited him with such sensitivity. He keeps it well hidden. What he said makes good sense to me.' He thought for a moment. 'That night we went drinking in the Gardeners, didn't I say something about C.S. Lewis and love, that it's not about affection or desire but a steady wish for a person's ultimate good? It seems to fit your case too.'

'What do you mean?'

'You look unconvinced, I can tell. I suppose "ultimate good" sounds too wishy-washy. We're accustomed these days to think love must be sexual otherwise there's something wrong with us. It all started in 1963, as you know …'

They both looked around in case Larkin happened to be passing.

'In my opinion, and it's only my opinion,' Toby assured him, 'Sam seems to have a steady view of your ultimate good and of her own as well. Me wittering on about your ultimate good probably sounds like advising you to give up smoking. You do see what I mean, though?'

'But really, is there any possibility of finding this ultimate good? I mean, for flesh and blood creatures like me or you, and not some fair idea in Lewis's mind?'

'It can work the other way, can't it, friends become lovers and all that? Only a switch from love to hate would rule it out and I don't think you're capable of it.' Toby waited while Sweeney lit another cigarette. 'Get wisdom and get insight, The Book of Proverbs says. You're wise enough but what does your heart tell you? Does knowing Sam enrich your life? Being in her company, is that a gift you never expected? If the answer to both is yes my next question is this – why deny yourself by denying her?'

Sweeney took another drag, exhaled the smoke slowly and said, 'You mean I would only be killing myself.'

Toby laughed. 'Patsy was right. You do have a unique sense of humour.'

'The humour is on me now as they say at home.'

'I like that. What's it mean exactly?'

'It was one of Ruby Murray's songs. Do you know her?' Toby shook his head. 'Belfast's finest, the Donna Summer of her day. My father liked to sing it. It means the intention or wish to do something – in the words of the song, to get married.' Toby raised his eyebrows. 'And then to regret doing so. I suppose the joke would be on me …'

They laughed. Sweeney wasn't sure what he was laughing at and thought it the same for Toby. But he felt a lot better for laughing nonetheless.

As they were leaving Staff House, Toby said to him, 'By the way, the Proverb I mentioned ends "do not let go; guard her, for she is your life." That would be my advice, Eddie.'

. . . .

How to get back in touch? The secretaries could not give out contact details but he thought he'd buy a book from Mr Trammer and ask Julie, as casually as he could, to contact Sam with the plausible line, 'She asked me for a loan of this, said it might be useful for an essay.' He would insert a sealed note asking her to meet him. It had to be Julie. Jan or Jo would see through his ruse immediately.

'This is a surprise, a mid-week visit.' Mr Trammer shuffled along from the back of the shop. 'A pleasant one, I hasten to add. Are you looking for anything in particular?'

'I'd like a nice edition of a novel or collection of poetry by a woman, something I can give as a present.'

'I see,' Mr Trammer said. 'Is it for a young lady? Don't tell me, I can see that it is.' He stood thinking for a while. 'She's at the university? Is her interest modern? I mean twentieth century?'

'I think she likes Sylvia Plath.'

Mr Trammer disappeared, returning with a copy of *The Bell Jar*. 'It's the best I can do. It's not mint condition, but attractive, dust jacket only slightly worn. I think she'll be suitably appreciative.'

When he got back to the department he discovered on his desk a small white envelope with his name on it. It contained a notelet, a photograph of a table on which sat a cup of steaming coffee, an open book and beside it, a fountain pen. There was a message from Sam saying she'd called in, was sorry to have missed him and would be in the library until three. If he got the message and wanted to meet she'd be on the fifth floor. The letters were neatly formed, the words evenly spaced and the sentences neatly arranged. She'd taken some care and hadn't dashed it off (he thought of her finding him absent, going to the bookshop, patiently choosing the appropriate notelet, sitting in the Students' Union, mulling over a few phrases, deciding on the ones she'd written, and sealing the envelope.) This image conjured in him a confusion of joy and sadness.

He found her easily, an A4 pad on her lap and books on either arm of a soft chair. She stood up when she saw him, pad falling to the floor, one of the books toppling over, and ran to meet him. They held tight to each other.

When they parted, she said, 'Let's never do this again. I was miserable the last few weeks thinking you didn't want to see me.'

They could talk as freely as they liked. No one else was on their floor. They both sat and he told her he'd been stupid and childish.

'I thought all sorts of crazy things,' she said.

'What sort of things?'

'I thought it might have been a religious thing, Protestant and Catholic, you know ...' and looked at him deeply repentant. At Sweeney's look of astonishment she grabbed his hands and said, 'I know, I should never have thought that of you. It was well out of order. But I was angry. I thought you were only interested in one thing and then dropped me like a hot brick. That last coffee we had and you rushing off the way you did, all my insecurities ...' The faster she spoke the more pronounced her Hull accent became. 'But you had every right ...'

He interrupted her, 'Stop! Stop! In the spirit of Christmas let's start again.'

'Gerreer,' Sam said and gave him another hug. 'Let's get a cuppa. I could do with a ciggy.'

The only coffee available in the Student's Union was from a machine. The refectory had closed. They smoked companionably in one of the lounges and joked about Selby, sharing the release which only making fun could bring, finding relief at understanding restored. Sweeney had no reason to hide anything but was glad Sam seemed to know nothing about his night at the Cricket Circle.

'I have something for you,' he said.

'That sounds interesting.'

They walked across an empty campus to the postgrad room.

'I want you to close your eyes and hold out your hands, palms up,' he told her.

'That sounds exciting.'

Sweeney placed the book on her outstretched hands. When she opened her eyes he said, 'Merry Christmas.'

'Oh, thank you! It's wonderful. It's so kind. How do you know I want to write my dissertation on Plath?'

Sweeney tapped the side of his nose, grateful that life seemed providential once more.

'I love it. But I have nothing for you.'

'Yes you do.'

'What do you mean?'

He pointed to the red ribbon in her hair.

'This?' Sam flicked her ponytail twice. She set the book on

his desk, undid the ribbon, shook her hair down and handed it to him 'My favour for thee only.'

'Fair lady, this thing of beauty will be my joy forever.'

Sam burst out laughing. 'How silly we are. How wonderful it is to be silly with you.'

. . . .

Hull seemed to be waiting for spring. In the New Year, the weather was again windy, cold and wet. It stayed that way for weeks, days of permanent semi-darkness, of scurrying from one place to another, of dodging showers, of leaning into gales, of listening to rain beating against window panes, of seeking refuge in the library warm and bright, of talk overheard in pubs about when things might get better, old men, former sea dogs, recalling when there'd been no let-up until May. They were days of seeing Sam over coffee and cigarettes, enjoying each other's company relieved of anxiety. They had arrived at a pact of forgiveness and freedom which brought them closer. Sweeney was too inexperienced to know if this relationship was unique. So whenever Sam would say she couldn't believe how lucky she was and how happy he made her, he would repeat his line, 'because I am I, because you are you.' It was a line which always pleased her and he almost believed it.

He bumped into Susie a few times. She was pleasant, they chatted amiably and their meetings always ending with her having 'to dash'. Neither of them mentioned the night under the duvet and she didn't offer the possibility of repeating it. Here were his own two worlds, the superficial world of Susie and other women he met and the world of Sam and all its emotional depth. He discovered to his surprise that enjoyment of these two worlds was not mutually exclusive.

Pearl, in her dressing gown, met him in the hallway one

Saturday afternoon. She'd been sorting through the post. 'Eddie, I haven't seen you for ages. Are you well? By the way, no post for you but there's a circular for a Mr Michael Charmley who, I guess, hasn't lived in your flat for yonks.' She held up the envelope and tossed it onto the dusty pile on the junction box. She didn't wait for Sweeney to tell her about his health. 'There's something I want to ask you. Come to the flat and I'll make you a cup of coffee if you're not rushing off. With the price of a jar these days it's like offering top quality champagne.' She whispered, 'I don't want to speak outside Roland's door. I'll explain inside.'

After making coffee, Pearl produced a packet of Benson and Hedges and offered him one. 'I must apologise for all the mystery,' she said.

He took that as Pearl's cue for him to ask, 'Is something wrong?'

'No, no, there's nothing *wrong*.' She swung her foot and the slipper balanced precariously on her toes. She began to giggle. 'I shouldn't laugh.' She made an exaggerated gesture to compose her features into seriousness. 'The reason I wanted to have a word is to invite you to a jazz concert at City Hall not next Tuesday evening but the Tuesday after.' She reviewed the date in her head. 'Yes, that's right, not next Tuesday evening but the Tuesday after.'

'Yes, of course, I'd love to. I've nothing on, as usual.'

'It's intended as a house social, house meaning you, me, Simon and Roland.'

Sweeney thought of what Roland had said about Park Road people sticking together and agreed. 'It would be good for neighbourly spirit.'

Pearl assumed he was joking. 'Your sense of humour hasn't changed' and she giggled once more into her coffee. 'Simon and I see it more as an act of penance – not in your case of course. It's Roland. Forgive me if you think you're being roped in under false pretences.'

'I don't think that at all, but I'm curious. What's Roland done?'

'He hasn't done anything. He never does anything. This is a two-cigarette story so I'm glad Simon isn't around to frown.' Sweeney offered her one of his as she rearranged her hanging slipper.

'What happened is this. Before Christmas, it was a Friday evening, there was no bridge game. We thought it a nice idea to round up the house and go out for a drink, all that festive stuff. Well, *I* thought so. Simon said Roland would be a wet blanket and why not just invite Eddie.' Pearl pointed her cigarette at Sweeney as if he doubted who she meant. 'Roland of course was in and found it impossible to refuse. You weren't, so it was just the three of us. There we were – the most uncomfortable threesome imaginable, Simon with nothing to say to Roland, Roland unable to communicate at all and yours truly called on to break the mournful silences. Where were you in our hour of need, eh?'

Sweeney thought it could only have been the night at the Cricket Circle. 'I'm not sure,' he lied.

'After starting at The Queens and walking in the freezing cold to The Station we stopped off at another pub on Beverley Road on the way back. I can't remember the name, the one near the public baths.'

'Do you mean The Bull Inn?'

Pearl pointed at him again in confirmation. 'There was a drunk there who shouted across at Roland. "Hey you, I know you!" Poor Roland didn't know what to say. "You, yes you, I'm talking to you. I know you, don't I?" Then the drunk shouted to everyone in the bar. "Hey, look! It's William Shakespeare!" Roland was mortified. To make things worse, the drunk staggered over to shake his hand. Simon intervened to calm things and, as you know, he's big enough not to be messed with.'

Pearl took another sip of coffee. 'If that wasn't bad enough, the drunk became pally, offered to buy "Shakespeare" a drink and said he'd a Christmas present for him. He returned with a plastic bag full of porn mags. Can you believe it? He said he worked on the ferries, got them in Holland and would do Roland a good deal. Simon – he's good in these situations for it could have got nasty – walked the man back to the bar, porn mags and all, sat him down on a stool, bought *him* a drink, and ushered us out pronto.'

'It sounds quite dodgy.'

'We laugh about it now but Roland was in a state of shock, as you can imagine. He didn't say a word afterwards but disappeared a few days later. We feared it might have pushed him over the edge. Simon thinks he has mental problems, you know.' Pearl stopped. 'I said it was going to be a two-cigarette story. I'm going to need another one,' she sighed. 'And I'm going to have a refill, half a cup maybe. Do you want another coffee?'

'No thanks, but you go ahead.'

When she returned from the kitchen Pearl said she wouldn't detain him much longer. 'We thought we'd try to make up for the first misadventure by inviting Roland to the jazz concert, patch things up if we can. You can't help noticing he's a jazz fan, can you?' Sweeney raised his eyebrows. 'And you like jazz as well?' He nodded. 'That's great.'

They stood up. 'Thanks again for the invite,' he said. 'How much do I owe you for the ticket?'

Pearl waved away the offer. 'Don't you keep us supplied with that Irish whiskey of yours? You've got us addicted to Bushmills.' She put her hand on his arm. 'Gosh, I should have offered you an Irish coffee.'

'Irish coffee is only for American tourists.'

The jazz evening, traditional and modern acts, proved a success. Sweeney's presence worked to put Roland at ease which in turn helped Simon to feel more comfortable. It allowed Pearl to do what Pearl did best and be the animating presence of the evening. Mr Trammer was at the concert too. In the interval he introduced his wife, a lively woman who looked elfin beside her husband's bulk. Sweeney wondered if Larkin was also there, thinking perhaps he'd wandered away before the modern jazz began. Brown had told him one of Larkin's liberating discoveries was you *could* walk out of concerts during intervals.

When they got back to Park Road, Simon thanked Sweeney for coming. 'If you want to go to The Boulevard any time just knock on the door. I think we're going to be relegated this season so the Black and Whites need you!'

. . . .

Hull was relegated. Sweeney had joined Simon and Chris for a few matches. He was still not partisan enough or West Hull enough to be in the Threepenny Stand. In those foul winter months, huddling in the crowd, rubbing hands, stamping feet, pulling up collars, retreating from the rain, they followed the poor performance of the squad, mud-caked, steaming, pushing up-field, retreating, and struggling with a soapy ball. The final whistle blown, supporters would shuffle out of The Boulevard after another defeat, expectations dashed, a drop to the lower division ever nearer, individual players rated and slated. Yet they would return, for a win might transform morale, form could change, who could tell? In the course of one post-match discussion, Sweeney said supporting Hull reminded him of Sisyphus. Chris and Simon looked at each other. He quickly explained the myth, at least as Camus retold it.

'Sisyphus in Hull, that's a new one,' Chris said and thought for a moment. 'Sisyphus in Hull, I like it.' He nodded his head. 'I can't say it makes *me* happy right now. But we can dream of glory next season.'

He told Sam he'd been to watch a few Hull games.

'There's something else we have in common,' she said. 'My family are all Black and White fans. I was never interested myself. But you can't avoid local loyalties no matter how hard you try.'

'I like the culture of the game,' he said, thinking of Alf Macklin and of faithful supporters, old and young.

'Well, that's a new one. I've heard it called many things but I've never heard it called culture.' Sweeney was about to protest but she said, 'Next time I see dad, I'll tell him. It will cheer him up to think he's been cultured all these years, swearing blue murder at the ref and wanting his lads to knock seven bells out of the opposition. But don't let me put you off. Remember there's no need to go full-on Hull to impress the natives. This one loves you as you are – because I am I and you are you, isn't that right?'

'You couldn't be righter, Sam.'

. . . .

He saw little of Brown who was, as Brown himself admitted, 'seeing a lot of Debbie'. Sweeney thought his friend had become softer, the spiky working-class edges smoother, the self-conscious Londoner-in-the-provinces demeanour less obvious, his look almost blissful – almost, because Brown was putting up a struggle against it. He never struck Sweeney as a candidate for true romance but, then again, who did?

'Have things been sorted out with Sam since I last saw you?'

'Yes, let's say we've reached a *modus vivendi* which suits both of us.'

'I'm glad to hear it,' Brown said, 'but is there anyone else on the go? I'm curious. All this purity can't be good for a healthy young man.'

He could satisfy Brown's curiosity by mentioning Jennie, a girl from Chesterfield he'd met in the library, Becky, a girl from Bury he'd met at a poetry reading and Rachel, a girl from Sheffield he'd got talking to one evening in the refectory queue. He didn't mention Susie. Each encounter had been superficial.

'You're happy enough, then?' Brown asked.

'Happy enough,' Sweeney replied, an answer almost true.

He didn't see Toby again until the first week of May. One evening he found him standing in the postgrad room, hands clasped behind his back, looking out the window. It had been a glorious day (those old salts had been right about the weather) and the room was uncomfortably stuffy. Hull had arisen from darkness into light, its citizens seeming dazed by the return of sunshine and blue sky, women once more in cotton frocks and blouses, men in shirt sleeves, one or two even so bold as to wear shorts. Toby was dressed in cool white linens, impressing Sweeney for whom hot weather meant wearing less of the same. He had the feeling Toby was waiting for someone. It turned out to be him.

'Eddie, the very man, I hoped you'd still be around. Such a beautiful evening I thought it would be a shame not to enjoy it. What do you say to a walk to Skidby village? Do you know it?'

'No. I'm ashamed to say I've kept myself to the mean streets of Hull. Burton Pidsea is the only exception.'

'It's charming little place, its claim to fame a windmill. It has an excellent pub as well. Not too far, take us less than an hour.'

'It sounds the sort of thing for an evening like this.'

'You won't regret it, well worth a visit. Leave your stuff here and collect it in the morning. You won't do any more work tonight. How's it going, by the way?' As they left the university grounds and walked onto Cottingham Road, they discussed academic matters as best they could above the noise of evening traffic. 'Let's cross here,' Toby said and they turned into Bricknell Avenue. 'There's a short cut with the wonderful name of Snuff Mill Lane.'

Almost immediately they left behind the noise of commuter traffic and town became country.

'What a transformation!' Sweeney was genuinely surprised. 'It reminds me of the paths at Burton Pidsea.'

'East Yorkshire is full of such surprises. The locals call this a snicket. Have you heard of it?' Sweeney shook his head. 'I suppose you'd call it a back path, all hedgerows and trees, birdsong and nature, makes me feel like I'm at home.'

'The way you always describe it, Lincolnshire sounds idyllic.'

'You must visit some time.'

Sweeney felt uncomfortable seeming to angle for an invite and Toby must have sensed it. 'I wouldn't say it if I didn't mean it. We have loads of space – an old rambling farmhouse, a cottage done up for tourists in holiday season, or you could doss down with the horses in the stable. I think that's where Alan imagines we'd put *him*. How is he by the way?'

'I believe he's fallen in love and doesn't want to admit it.'

'Really? I thought he tried too hard to give the impression he was only in love with loving, as it were. Good for him.'

'By the way, I wanted to thank you for your advice about Sam and me. Your confessional worked a miracle.'

Toby smiled. 'I take it you have made peace with each other?'

'Yes, the peace of the virtuous, you could say.'

Toby patted him on the shoulder.

They walked across fields, traversing a railway level-crossing before entering Cottingham. Skirting the student residences at The Lawns, Toby took him to the mill on the rise, its white sails sharp against a blue sky now tinged with orange and hinting at twilight. They finished up at the Half Moon, its whitewashed walls hung with flower baskets.

'I think we could really do with a drink,' Toby said, taking off his jacket as they stood at the bar.

Sweeney asked, 'What will you have?'

'No this one's on me. I owe *you*.'

'Me? Have I done something?'

'Not that you're aware of, I'm sure, but a favour nonetheless.' Toby ordered two pints of bitter and they found a corner to sit.

'Cheers!' they said together.

'Nice beer,' Sweeney said. 'I'm intrigued about this favour I did you.'

'It's a small part of a story which involves bad news and good news, well bad news which is also good news. I trust it is at any rate.'

'Now I'm bemused as well as intrigued.'

'Forgive me for being oblique. I'll give you the bad news first. A few weeks ago Patsy caught Mitchell *in flagrante*.' Toby took a deep draught of beer as if to wash away the indelicacy of the phrase. 'She came back from the university one afternoon to the house on Marlborough Avenue and found him in bed with one of the new party members, a first-year student she tells me. Apparently, it had been going on for some time. Mitchell behaved shamelessly, told Patsy he was tired of her *bourgeois* – no *petty bourgeois* – attitudes, how commitment to revolution also meant commitment to subverting capitalist family values or some such rubbish, shouted he'd had enough of her moods, her possessiveness and was tired of her emotional dependency. He threw her out. Can you imagine? He threw her out like a broken toy. After all the time Patsy wasted on *him*, I mean. And the braggart talks about capitalism turning people into commodities!' Toby took another drink, his anger barely suppressed. 'She was humiliated in front of that other poor girl and came to my place in tears, talking about giving up her studies, going home, forgetting about everything.'

'Where's Patsy now?'

'She's with me, fallen on the Jericho Road. What could I do but ask her to stay at my place, at least as a temporary refuge. Mitchell never bothered to find out where she'd gone. She was surplus to his requirements. I had to go round to collect her stuff. He had some guy in a woolly hat beside him the whole time for protection. He needn't have worried. I wouldn't lower myself to thrash someone like him – either of them for that matter. He'd shoved her clothes into plastic bags and her files and books into boxes.'

'You did predict it happening, remember, that night in the Gardeners. But that's no good to her or to you, is it?' Sweeney stubbed out his Regal. 'But where do I come into this story?'

'That's the good news. One morning I brought a cup of coffee to her bedroom, my bedroom that is. I'm sleeping on the couch. For the first time she seemed perked up – forgive the unintentional pun. When I asked why she was in such good humour she said before falling asleep she'd remembered something you'd said.'

'I'd said?'

'That's what she told me. That night she had a dream about being lost in a crowd so tightly packed she couldn't see where she was going. People's faces were stern and their bodies claustrophobic. All of a sudden they vanished and she found herself on a path across fields, the air fresh, the sky clear, and she heard birdsong – a bit like our walk here this evening. Most importantly, she felt herself again. I asked her what you'd said. She only smiled and told me to mention Scott Walker when I met you.'

Sweeney laughed. 'I did tell her a line from one of his songs. She'd seemed sad and I suspected the reason was Mitchell.'

'What's the line?'

'It's "In a world filled with friends you lose your way". I'm sorry losing her way turned out to be so brutal. But from what you say Patsy *has* found her way again. That is good news – for her and for you both.'

'Like the parable of the sower, your words – Scott Walker's words – fell on good soil.'

'Can you ask Patsy if she's changed her mind about providence?'

'That's another intriguing message.'

'Patsy will know what I mean.'

'Okay I'll ask her. I'm hoping she'll spend part of the summer in Lincolnshire. Perhaps we can encourage each other to finish our theses. Then there are the horses. I know she'll love the horses. We'll see. But for now,' he slapped the table lightly, 'I think it calls for another drink.'

'It's my round.'

'Your money is no good tonight. These are all on Patsy and me. She said you helped her more than you can imagine.'

'In that case, who am I to argue?

CHAPTER NINE

The departmental cricket match would be the anniversary of his meeting Sam.

It was Sweeney who raised the subject with his supervisor. Initially Dawson had greeted him warily, his unscheduled appearance intimating a problem, a wet shoulder possibly, but when Sweeney asked about arrangements for the match, his manner changed. He invited Sweeney to sit.

'Excellent idea, Edward, it's best to get things sorted in good time. Last year's match was something of a classic, wasn't it? It went down to the wire.' Sweeney had the impression Dawson considered going down to the wire something to be avoided. 'I'll have to keep my boys on their toes this time.'

Dawson got around to asking about the thesis.

'I'm confident it'll be finished by summer next year.'

'I must say your diligence is exemplary – well, from what I've heard from colleagues about their own charges but, no names, no pack drill, isn't that it? I suppose I should arrange for you to give a paper to the staff seminar. Also, let's see about placing an article somewhere. As you know, I have useful contacts and I'm sure if I give my imprimatur ...' He left unspoken the extent of his influence. 'Important things first, of course,' Dawson smiled. 'I'll let you know about a date for the cricket match and will rely on you to do the needful.'

There was to be no match. On the day arranged, the weather turned cool and it rained non-stop. Another day was agreed but it too was foreboding, clouds heavy and menacing. The players assembled but as the stumps were being knocked into the pitch a downpour sent them scurrying for cover and that was that. Since the pubs weren't open yet, everyone drifted off, Dawson disconsolately and nearly everyone else relieved, his colleagues especially.

Sweeney gave Sam a copy of Marilyn French's *The Women's Room* to mark the occasion. She'd mentioned the book to him a few times. 'I remembered too,' she said and from her bag took out a little package wrapped in gift paper. 'It's not much but I hope you'll like it or appreciate the thought at least.'

It was a leather drawstring pouch containing a small pewter medal. On one side was the image of St Christopher and the inscription on the reverse read: *Protect us on our travels wherever we may roam, keep us safe and guide us always safely home.* 'It will make me feel better to know you are safe wherever you roam.' There was another ribbon too. 'I chose white this time,' she explained. 'I like to think of us bound together in purity and innocence.' Images of those few nights with women in his 'other world', Susie, Jennie, Beckie, Rachel, flashed across Sweeney's mind and he felt not pure, but worldly, even decadently so.

. . . .

Sam and Sweeney enjoyed together the few good days of that miserable summer. One morning they strolled around Pearson Park. To impress her he'd memorised lines from an old book on Hull he'd browsed at Mr Trammer's. Putting on a theatrical voice he recited, 'Arranged in vistas fair and pleasant glades, Lake and fountain, bowers and leafy shades, Adorned with statues, by a master hand, Of that great lady, who now rules the land.' He gestured as they walked by the glades, the pond, the fountain, the trees and the imposing figure of Queen Victoria.

'Did you write those lines? I will see the park differently now.'

'See it for better or for worse?'

She laughed, 'Oh for the better, of course, how could I not after such deathless poetry?'

'Unfortunately, or fortunately, they're not my words. They

were written by a certain Samuel Woodhouse. Have you ever heard of him?'

'Never.'

'They're from a poem called "The Queen of the Humber" … let me get this right' and he stopped to concentrate for a second. 'The full title is "The Queen of the Humber or Legends, Historical, Traditional and Imaginary, relating to Kingston upon Hull". What do you think of that, Sam?'

'I think it's quite a mouthful. Where on earth did you come across it?'

'I found it in the Aladdin's Cave of obscure books. You know the one in Hepworth Arcade?'

'You are a regular I take it?'

'It's part of my routine as the man alone in Hull.'

'Those words make me feel sad,' she said, taking his arm. 'I don't like to think of you alone like that.'

Sweeney shrugged. 'There's no need to pity me. I enjoy my solitary times. At least I'm not walled up like Julian of Norwich.'

'I can't help it, but I do. And I feel responsible.' They sat on a park bench in the shade of a tree and Sam lit a Rothmans.

'Sometimes I can't help wishing we'd never met,' she blurted out. 'No that's wrong, stupid of me to put it like that. I love every moment we're together. I love the thought of you living in this mucky old town. And I love the thought of you thinking of me. Yes, yes, I know, those words sound cornier than what you usually come out with. They sound like something you'd find in *Jackie*. "Sam Says" sounds about right for my column. What advice I could give!'

Sweeney watched her brush away a strand of hair and shake back the watch on her wrist. 'I feel I'm to blame, that's what I meant to say. It's all about me, me, me. For *your* sake rather than mine I sometimes wish we'd never met. Maybe you think that's more of my Catholic guilt?'

'I don't think Catholics have a monopoly on guilt.'

'But you can't understand it. You're not Catholic.'

'No, my family is Church of Ireland. I know little theology but I remember in confirmation class being told we were both Protestant *and* Catholic. At home, Protestants think it's too Catholic and Catholics think it's too Protestant. Is that the best or worst of both worlds? I can't say. But I might have your Catholic guilt and my own Protestant guilt.'

'Hmm.' Sam didn't sound convinced. 'I can't get out of my head the image of you wandering the streets, like someone walking the square inside Hull Prison. I feel I've put you there when you could be enjoying life with someone else.'

How could he not think this? But fate having arranged this situation, it was typical of him to do nothing to change its course. He accepted the delicacy of Sam's position and had no intention of pushing her towards anything unconscionable. Indeed, such was the self-contained pleasure of the world they inhabited he had little curiosity about her life outside it. Nor had he any interest in her husband. His existence seemed irrelevant when he and Sam were together and their marital bed he didn't want to imagine when they weren't. What of his worlds – the one of solitude, the one of random affairs, this one of purity and innocence – did they make him happy? All he knew was they composed a life more interesting than anything he'd ever known.

'Don't think that way, Sam. Do I look like Mr Miserable to you?'

'I overheard Susie talking about you.'

Sweeney coughed. He hadn't been expecting this.

'And I'd no right, but what she said ... I felt insanely jealous.'

'And I feel insanely guilty.'

They looked at one another and burst out laughing.

'As for being selfish,' he said, 'both of us were that night. You might say Susie and I parted emotionally intact, still wrapped in our different solitudes. Susie being Susie didn't want it otherwise and I being I didn't want it either. I'm even surprised she mentioned it again.'

'What a pair we are. Shall we just enjoy the pleasant glades and leafy shades or was it the other way round? Oh, who cares?'

As they strolled and talked, the day had become much hotter and Sam said she felt tired. 'It must be this weather. We're not used to the sun in Hull these days.' He told her his flat was nearby, she should come in, have a cool drink and rest for a while. 'I think that's a good idea,' she said.

She sat down at the table while Sweeney got her a glass of water, wondering if he shouldn't ask Roland if he had some brandy.

'So this is your bachelor pad? I see what you mean about the art of *tsundoku*,' she said, nodding at discreet piles of books around the room. 'I'm impressed.'

'It's nothing compared to Roland in the flat below me.'

'The eccentric novelist you mean?'

'Yes, the very one,' said Sweeney. 'Park Road's *unpublished* eccentric novelist I should add.' Sam sipped her water. She looked ashen and listless. 'Why don't you lie down for a bit on the couch and I'll get a pillow from the bedroom?'

He helped take off her denim jacket. When he returned from the bedroom she was already asleep. He sat in the armchair watching. After about half an hour she awoke and he knelt beside her, rearranging strands of hair fallen across her face.

'How do you feel now? Any better?'

She raised herself up on an elbow and looked at him apologetically. 'I don't know what came over me, not much fun for you. Thanks, I'm feeling a bit better now.'

'I'm going to ask you a very English question.'

'At least I know it won't be an attempt at seduction.'

'Would you like a nice cup of tea?'

She smiled. 'Yes, a *nice* cup of tea would be just the thing.'

Taking a first sip, she told him, 'You make a very nice cup of tea indeed, for someone who's not English at all.'

'It's according to the Sweeney family tradition, a cuppa strong enough for the spoon to stand upright.'

'That's another thing the Sweeneys and Ahrens have in common then.' She smiled, but her eyes were tired.

'Shouldn't you see a doctor?' he asked. What he meant was she really *should* see a doctor.

'I'll be alright, honestly. I've had a lot on my mind.' She stretched a hand to touch his. 'And don't look worried, you're not the weight on my mind. I've been working hard on my dissertation, thinking about what comes next. If anything, all the usual stuff you know.'

'Are you hungry? I could make you something?'

'No, I don't think I could eat anything.'

Sweeney told her she could rest as long as she liked. 'And I'll get a taxi for you when you're ready. There's no way you're walking or taking a bus. I can use the phone in The Queens.'

She protested about the taxi, but he was unusually insistent, and finally she relented. 'There's one thing I could do with,' she said.

'What's that?

'I'd love another of your *very* nice cups of tea.'

. . . .

When he saw her again a few days later she still looked drawn, dark rings under her eyes. He asked her if she'd made that doctor's appointment but she assured him things were much better.

'I have a request,' Sam said. 'Look upon it as a way of me dealing with my guilt.'

'What do you mean?' He had a vision of visiting her parish priest.

'Do you mind me coming along on one of your Saturday routines? I'd like to see Hull as you see it.' She began to tick with her finger as the watch slid down her wrist. 'We've seen the university together, we've seen Burton Pidsea together, we've seen London together, we've seen Selby together – well, the inside of the railway waiting room – and we've seen Pearson Park together. Hull, the town, we haven't seen together.'

The image of a priest vanished. 'Of course,' he said. 'It won't be *Whicker's World* but Sweeney's world.'

'I prefer Sweeney's world. I'm happy there.'

That Saturday they met outside Paragon Station.

He joked, 'Today I'm grateful for the company of a native old Hullian,' singing the last four words to the tune of Odyssey's 'Native New Yorker'.

She said, 'That's one of my all-time favourites.'

'It's a song with a melancholy edge, I think.'

'Well, being a native of Hull isn't a barrel of laughs either.'

They meandered around his usual haunts while Sam related stories from her past. In a building near the station she told him she once took ballroom-dancing lessons. 'Mam was in a local team, loved *Come Dancing* and wanted me to follow in her footsteps, literally I suppose. But I was never any good.'

'I have two left feet so I couldn't comment.'

'You have the figure for it, though,' Sam said.

'If I danced I'd be a figure of fun.'

'That's the first corny line of the day.'

She pointed out Bailey's above the Co-op 'where me and the girls went to the disco, when we were young and far too innocent for our own good. But you learnt quickly.'

'I was reading Mrs Gaskill recently,' Sweeney told her. 'I found her a little old-fashioned, but she was right about one thing.'

'And that is?'

'Northern lasses are independent-minded and not to be messed with.'

'I wish I'd known that at the time.'

'Well, you know now.'

The Punch Hotel, she told him, was where she had her first drink. 'It was a glass of white wine' (she pronounced it 'waaht waahn' to emphasise a girlish Hull accent) 'and it was awful I can tell you.'

'In that case we must go in again to see if the selection has improved.'

'I'm much more sophisticated these days, what with all those holidays in Spain.' She ordered a 'drah waaht waahn' and Sweeney, a pint of bitter.

'Well,' he asked, as she sipped her wine thoughtfully, 'what's your sophisticated opinion?'

'It's zesty, lemony with a hint of gooseberry, certainly dry, tart even, but definitely drinkable, undoubtedly an improvement on my first time here.'

'I *am* impressed.'

'You see,' she said, lighting a Rothmans, 'Hull people *can* be sophisticated.'

'When we finish our drinks I'm going to show you something to make you doubt that.'

'Oh yes, and what would that be?'

He took her to the *Band* of Green Ginger. Sam put a hand to her mouth. 'You know, I never noticed that before. Has it been done recently?'

'It's been like that since I arrived.'

'Okay, I'll row back a bit on sophistication. Have you ever read the novel *The Land of Green Ginger*? It's by Winifred Holtby.

Sweeney remembered a copy of Holtby's *South Riding* on Rod's office bookshelf but he hadn't heard of this novel. 'No,

I only know the street from a short story we read at school.'

'She wrote that the Land of Green Ginger is a gift of fortune – a "mysterious road to Heaven", I think she describes it. What do you think of that?'

'When I write the great Hull novel I'll call it *My Time with Sam Ahrens* and I'll use those very words.'

'That's number two. The ability to come up with the corniest lines will be your literary strength.'

In the bookshop Mr Trammer adopted with Sam a manner Sweeney could only describe as landed charm, no longer owner speaking to a potential customer, but country gentleman welcoming a weekend guest. His shuffle was less pronounced, his shoulders less hunched and his paunch less prominent. When Sam began to browse, Mr Trammer stood beside Sweeney.

'I like your lady friend,' he whispered.

'Friend,' Sweeney replied, 'is the appropriate word.'

'Oh, I see,' he said.

Sam returned with a copy of Holtby's *The Land of Green Ginger*. 'I'd like to buy this for my Hull guide here.'

Mr Trammer looked surprised. 'I thought from your accent you'd be the guide.'

'I'm seeing Hull as others see it. And now I have. I never knew our most famous street has become the Band of Green Ginger.'

Mr Trammer looked confused. Sweeney told him to have a look when he had a chance.

He said he certainly would. 'Oh, before you two go.' He shuffled to the back of the shop and returned with a copy of Shakespeare's *Sonnets*. 'This is for you.' He handed the book to Sam, 'I'm sure you'll find the right words in here. Shakespeare is a good guide to those things we find hard to say.'

As they strolled along Whitefriargate Sam said, 'What a lovely man. That was such a nice thing for him to do.' She nudged his arm. 'He really likes you.'

'The truth is,' Sweeney said, 'it's *you* he really likes. How could he not?'

'That's number three ... but you do know how to flatter a girl.'

. . . .

The best day was their visit to Beverley. A brilliant sunny morning, they were sitting over a coffee at university, smoking, chatting when Sam asked, 'Why don't we catch a bus to Beverley? It's a sin to be inside when we can see somewhere else together.' She ticked off on her fingers Burton Pidsea, London, Selby, Pearson Park, and Old Town. 'Look – I'm on another hand now – Beverley. What about it?'

Just around the corner from the Haworth Arms they caught a bus. They climbed to the upper deck, got seats at the front like school kids playing truant. The bus took them past housing estates, rows of small shops, lonely petrol stations, into farmland and market gardens, weaving past Woodmansey, the upper deck brushing tree branches, and into Beverley. They got off almost in the shadow of the Minster and walked along Keldgate to the common.

'Mam and dad used to take us here for picnics on Sundays. I wish I'd thought of a picnic.'

'I will treat you to lunch if you like.'

'It would have been nice to sit and eat on the grass like we used to. I must sound to you like an old woman trying to recapture her childhood – or should I say like a mature student?'

'Searching for lost time is what everyone does, no matter what age they are.'

'You always find the words to make things okay, even if they *are* corny most of the time.'

'Maybe I should become a psychotherapist.'

LOVE

'Or a priest, you could become a priest'.

'That's one thing the world doesn't need, me in a pulpit.' She gently elbowed him in the side.

There were only a few dog walkers as they followed a path through lush pasture. Sam pointed out the Minster and the tower of St Mary's, 'You wouldn't think you're only a few miles from Hull, would you?'

'Is this where the racecourse is? Alan Brown visits when meetings are on.'

'Yes, it's on the far side. Dad used to go. He liked to have a bet but mam kept him in order, that's for sure.'

Sweeney laughed and said, 'There's another thing we have in common. My dad was a dedicated follower of the horses but my mother only allowed him a bet on Saturday.'

'Maybe in another life you and I were joined at the hip? Two hips don't sound as good as two souls though.'

'No … but you can replace a hip, not my soul.'

'Hmm, I'm not sure if that's corny or not.' After strolling for a while, she said, 'There's a place our family used to go. It doesn't sound too great, Newbegin Pits, but there's shade, a beautiful tree I remember, and we can sit down.'

In the shade of her beautiful tree, they smoked for a while, Sam with her knees up to her chin, Sweeney lounging on his side, idly pushing his foot at the odd twig. 'I'm not a great fan of the outdoors,' he said, 'but it is lovely here.'

She smiled, leaned across and stroked his hair. 'You know what you were saying about time lost? Right now I feel as if I've found it again.' She waved her cigarette in a grand circle. 'It's as if my past and my present are one. It's hard to explain. As you know, I can be a worrier. And sometimes I worry about time passing – and me wasting it. Right now, I don't think that at all. Here's a confession, Mr Psychotherapist, or is it Father Edward?' They heard the bell of the Minster chime the hour and she had her answer. 'So be it, Father Edward. When I'm with you sometimes pleasure is spoiled by my imagination, me worrying yet again, thinking you'll leave Hull, you'll leave me, and I will only have time past, time lost … it's selfish I know. Yet sitting with you here there's nothing of that. Today will be a sacred memory and remain in my heart. It's like time past, present and future reconciled.'

'That's very poetic, Sam, and very Eliot.'

'Maybe so but, like most people probably, I've blundered through life, making mistakes *all the time*, but this doesn't feel like a mistake. It feels right and true and … godly.' She crushed out her cigarette, lay back and looked at the blue sky through swaying leaves. She hitched herself up on an elbow suddenly, 'I suppose I'm still liable for penance, Father?'

'I'm not sure if melancholy of anticipation is a sin. Now that I think of it, you could call it sorrow for things that may never happen.' He felt he was becoming didactic, preaching perhaps, his alternative *persona* in action. 'Anyway, I'm hoping Dawson will retire, I can get his job and stay here.'

'Is that a real possibility?'

'If providence wills it …'

'Ha!' Sam wasn't convinced. 'What was that phrase you used, the melancholy of imagination?'

'No, it was the melancholy of anticipation.'

'The melancholy of anticipation,' she repeated, as if savouring the sound. 'I was struggling to think of a title for my dissertation on Plath. Maybe your phrase describes her best – maybe it describes *me* best.' She sighed and lay back on the grass. 'And I feel so tired again I could sleep.'

'Why don't you rest? Here, take my jacket for a pillow.' He stood and rolled up his corduroy.

'Your Selby pillow – but only if you don't mind, it's only for a few minutes, I promise. I have these waves of fatigue recently.'

LOVE

Sweeney slipped his jacket under her head. Sam was asleep almost immediately. He prowled around where she lay, leaned against the tree for a minute then sat again. No one passed by. He looked at her tenderly, reminded of Ophelia, not the painting by Millais, but the one by Waterhouse, Ophelia lying in a tree-lined glade, Ophelia blonde, not dark, Ophelia in T-shirt and jeans not a white dress. It was a vision of beauty nonetheless. There was also a sense of, yes, melancholy, melancholy of this moment's perfection ending. He was pondering layers of melancholy and joy, of bitterness and sweetness, himself drifting towards sleep in the silence, drowsing out the brief warmth of summer, when Sam woke.

'I really do test your patience. I think you should be elevated to sainthood and bypass priesthood.'

'I was your angel once, remember and with you, in Heaven already.' It sounded so silly that they could only laugh.

'That's worthy of a B-movie romance,' she said. 'Just as well for you I like B-movies, especially romances.'

'Is that true? You like B-movie romances?'

'No, it's not true, but I think I'd like one where a man said that to a woman.' She rubbed her eyes, shook her head and took a deep breath. 'Shall we head back to Beverley?'

'Don't forget I promised you lunch.' He was hungry despite romantic melancholy.

'Yes, you did. I don't have much appetite but I could do with a drink.' She pulled a few times at the neck of her T-shirt. 'It's so warm.' She got to her feet, handed him his jacket and shook her own.

They walked slowly into town, taking the shaded side of streets, and ended up at the King's Head. Sam agreed to share the sandwiches Sweeney ordered. The sleep hadn't refreshed her. Sweeney noticed her eyes were filmy and her shoulders slightly drooped.

'I don't want to nag, but are you going to see that doctor? I'm asking not as a psychotherapist or a priest, but as your friend. Maybe you can get some vitamins or iron tablets. My mother swears by iron tablets.'

She looked at her plate and pushed around a quartered cheese sandwich. 'It's the old too busy excuse. But I will do. I promise.' She looked at him tenderly. 'Thanks for caring about me.'

He was going to say that's all he did these days, for it was nearly true. He didn't because he thought it might sound bold, possibly confrontational. What he did say was, 'If you're fishing for another B-movie line, I'm all out of them.'

'You can't blame a girl for trying.'

. . . .

Sweeney arranged to go home for a couple of weeks at the end of August. Sam was holidaying in Spain at the same time. It was a big family affair she said, her parents' ruby wedding anniversary. 'I don't know if I'm up to it, what with the dissertation hanging over me and feeling tired all the time.' Sweeney did his best to sound sincere when he said the break would do her good. It was difficult to live sincerely in acquiescence and renunciation when it meant envisaging her happy without him. Love wasn't always a wish for a person's good, despite what C. S. Lewis wrote and Toby believed. He knew it was capable of the lowest, not the highest, motives.

One morning before he left for Belfast, Jan handed him a letter. 'More fan mail for you.'

'David Cassidy must be getting worried.' For once even Julie appeared to find his remark funny.

The envelope was franked 'Lincoln' and inside was a postcard with an image of the cathedral. It was from Toby and Patsy. *Just a short note to say both of us are in Lincolnshire working hard*

(?) when not working harder (!) with the horses.' Toby invited
Sweeney to come down and stay if he was *at a loose end.* He
gave an address in Hougham. *Take the train to Grantham and
I can pick you up there.* At the bottom of the card Patsy had
added the lines *I didn't believe it when you spoke to me about
providence (remember?) but you were right. Our little chat helped
change my life.* There was an 'x' after her signature. Sweeney
leaned back in his chair in the postgrad room. It was Toby *and*
Patsy now. Matchmaker was another profession he could add
to psychotherapist and priest.

Brown told him he was staying in Hull to finish his thesis but
Sweeney knew the real reason. Debbie would be here another
couple of months. His friend's usual nonchalance had become
edged with a lover's anxiety. Not even Spurs' promotion to the
First Division could hide it. When Sweeney passed on the news
about Toby and Patsy his reaction was polite but offhand.

Brown had taken to rolling his own cigarettes. He opened
a tin of Golden Virginia, lifted shards of tobacco and placed
them delicately onto a Rizla paper. It took him some time to
get things right. Finally, he raised the paper to his lips, licking
along its length. Neither of them spoke as he went through
the motions. When Brown was about to light up, he hesitated,
'What is it?'

'What's become of the Gold Bond?'

'I'm trying to save money. My grant runs out at the beginning of September so needs must.' He contemplated his roll
up. 'These aren't bad, you know. Welcome to the new me.'
He drummed his fingers lightly on the table, a sure sign that
something *was* up. Sweeney waited it out.

Eventually Brown coughed and said, 'I have a big favour
to ask. I'll understand if you refuse, so there's no pressure. It's
altogether out of order.'

'For goodness sake, out with it man!'

'I find it difficult to … bugger it, would it be possible for me to stay at your flat for a month or two? It would help me out a lot – to finish this damned thesis, that is. I wouldn't be around most days anyway. I'll be in the library. What I really need is somewhere to kip.' Sweeney ran his hand through his hair and Brown must have read it as a negative sign. 'And if you're worried, no, I'm not looking for what tabloid journalists call a "love nest". Debbie has her own place but the other girls are against having a man about the house. It wasn't that bad in the TV show. All very Platonic between Robin, Chrissy and Jo, wasn't it?' Sweeney looked blankly and Brown became more agitated. 'The truth is I don't have enough of the readies to pay the rent on my own place.' He rubbed a thumb and forefinger together. 'It's as simple as that.' He looked like a man expecting the worst.

Sweeney couldn't resist letting him expect it a few moments longer. Then he said, 'To paraphrase the song – do you think I would leave you lying when there's room in my flat for two?'

Brown jumped up, rushed over and slapped Sweeney on the back. 'Thanks, you're a real mate. I won't forget it and you'll have no cause to regret it.' He laughed. 'At least I won't end up like Fenwick-Clark.'

'I've heard that story.'

'You see, you've saved me from becoming a hatchet-wielding maniac.'

'There's one problem. I've only one bed. The sofa's not big enough for a decent night's sleep – for someone as big as you, anyway.'

'I'm ahead of the game there. I saw a foldaway bed in a second-hand shop on Newland Avenue. Solid steel frame, good set of wooden slats and it comes with a mattress, would fit away in a corner. And I promise there'll be no hanky-panky on it, that's for sure. I just need to transport it. But you can leave that to me.'

'I'll get an extra set of keys cut before I go home to see the parents. You can move your stuff in while I'm away.'

'Trust me, you won't notice any change. And you can throw me out any time.'

'You better believe it.'

. . . .

When Sweeney returned to Hull, a foldaway bed stood discreetly in one corner and over it Brown had draped a tartan blanket. One suitcase, some books and three box files indicated his presence.

'As you can see,' he said, 'minimum disruption, minimum fuss. And you'll find in the kitchen cupboards and that dodgy fridge of yours, evidence that I don't intend to eat you out of house and home.'

'What is it, bubble and squeak and jellied eels?'

'You'd be so lucky, mate. By the way, I've met the couple from downstairs, Pearl and Simon, told them you were putting me up for a bit. They were really nice, had me in for a gin before they went off to a poker game.'

'They play bridge.'

'Your other housemate is a queer fish. I couldn't believe it – William Shakespeare!'

'Roland is okay. He's reclusive, spends his time writing a novel and listening to modern jazz.'

'I'll take your word for it. Debbie sends her best wishes. We'd like to invite you tomorrow night to the Indian on Anlaby Road.'

'There's really no need.'

'I'm getting used to being a kept man,' he laughed, 'but honour demands it. Can you believe Debbie and me have become such a couple?'

'Toby and Patsy and now you and Debbie. I've become a matchmaker'

'I can see it now, Edward Sweeney as Sidney Bliss.'

So began a flat share which could have been a re-run of *The Odd Couple* if it hadn't been for the fact that Sweeney and Brown were broadly compatible in character, neither of them Oscar Madison and certainly not Felix Ungar. They managed to work around each other's idiosyncrasies. Brown said he felt guilty about not paying rent and offered to make roll-ups for two. As a result, Sweeney got into the habit, abandoned his Regals but, uneasy about smoking Brown's precious horde of tobacco, took to buying his own Golden Virginia. Nevertheless, each morning he would find a few roll ups on the table as an honour gift.

When he saw Sam and mentioned his new living arrangements, she also mentioned *The Odd Couple*. Despite what people called a 'healthy tan' from her week in Spain, Sweeney thought she had lost weight.

'How was your holiday?' he asked.

'It was all go. I tried to find some peace and quiet to do some reading but it was impossible. Having a rest was hard enough. Mam enjoyed herself, dad as well despite his poor health. They were like a couple of kids so it was worth it. You know what they say. You need a holiday from your holiday.' She took a drag on her Rothmans. 'I was going to bring you a carton of Regals from duty-free but we'd used up our allowance. Half of Hessle Road is smoking what our family brought home.'

'Not to worry, I've switched to roll ups.' He lit one of those Brown had left for him that morning.

'You look a regular bohemian, Eddie. Or is that another alternative you?' she smiled. 'What have you been up to?'

'I'm adjusting to having new faces in the postgrad room. There's Rick who was at Cardiff, but isn't Welsh. He's from

LOVE

Portsmouth. There's Cathy who was at Newcastle, but isn't a Geordie. She's from somewhere near Nottingham. They are both interested in literary theory. They think me old fashioned, a yesterday's man. How can I put it?' He knocked the thin ash off his roll up, 'They are cheerily, not rudely, dismissive.'

'Their loss, or as we say, you can't educate pork.' She paused. 'Cathy, is she good looking?'

'You know Olive from *On the Buses*?' Sam nodded. 'That's Cathy.'

'Oh dear,' Sam said, but looked pleased rather than sympathetic.

. . . .

Pearl intercepted him one evening as he entered the house. 'I've been listening out for you. Come with me.' She led him to her flat. He could hear Simon clattering pans in the kitchen, singing along to the radio playing 'Matchstick Men and Matchstick Cats and Dogs'. Pearl called out, 'Simon, I want a word with Eddie, can you turn that down a bit?'

Simon popped his head round the door, saluted Pearl and said hello to Sweeney. She shook her head. 'He thinks that song should be the Labour Party's anthem.' She held up her gin and tonic. 'Would you like one, or a beer maybe?'

'No thanks. I had a pint in The Queens on the way home.'

'Right then, take a seat. I've something to tell you. Actually, to warn you.' She sat in the chair opposite and lit a Benson and Hedges, extending the pack to him. When he refused and was about to explain about his roll-up habit, she said, 'I think you better have one.'

'Why? What have I done?'

'That's the thing. You haven't done anything. But Mrs Herdecka believes you are subletting your flat. She left about ten minutes ago. Luckily you weren't caught cold. She asked me to pass on a message. She's calling to see you on Saturday morning.'

He was stunned. 'But that's ridiculous.'

'I know. It's daft. I told her your friend was only staying a few weeks.'

'Who could have put that idea into her head? Do you think it was Roland? Has Alan been annoying people?'

She laughed at the idea of Roland being a snitch. 'No, it certainly wasn't Roland. He probably hasn't noticed anything different. And no, Alan's been good as gold ... for a southerner.' She tapped the ash off her cigarette. 'One thing I want to make clear. It wasn't Simon and me.'

Sweeney waved away the suggestion. 'I would never think that.'

'I wouldn't want any doubt to fester and poison. Anyway, I'm sure who *did* tell her. It was her son. Have you met him?'

'No. I don't think so.'

'I think the term is "built like a brick shithouse". Chris knows him from his rugby league days. He was good enough to get on Hull's books but never made it. Are you sure you've never seen him? He's a quiet lad, always wears a woolly hat, does repairs around the place, cuts the hedge at the front of the house, that sort of thing.'

'Never seen him – and I've never seen Mrs Herdecka either, would you believe?'

'Well, he obviously knows who you are. He was doing some work here last week and must have seen your friend coming and going, using his own key, and jumped to the wrong conclusion.'

'Do you think she's going to throw me out?' He thought of Fenwick-Clark.

'She can be difficult. Beneath it all she's a good person. I told her you were the perfect neighbour. Explain things, be your charming self and appeal to her better nature.'

Simon came in wiping his hands on a dish towel.

'I was telling Eddie about Mrs Herdecka.'

'Her bark is worse than her bite. That son of hers has obviously got the wrong end of the stick.'

Sweeney smiled, but was deeply unsettled. He knew bad things happened without good reason. Thus far providence had spared him the worst but that was no guarantee.

Next day he mentioned his problem to Sam, worrying through the possibility of eviction. He mentioned his landlady's name.

'Mrs Herdecka? She goes to St Wilfrid. I know her only slightly but mam is friendly with her in a churchy sort of way. I think "formidable" is the word.' She noticed Sweeney's look of despair. 'Don't worry. It's providence again, you lucky boy! Mam can put in a word for you.'

'What if she doesn't see her before Saturday?'

Sam thought for a moment and smiled. 'Here's Plan B. If she doesn't see Mrs Herdecka, I'll call round to your place on Saturday morning. I'll say you're helping me with my dissertation like a good Catholic boy! Didn't you say your Church is half Catholic or something?'

'Up to a point …'

'Well, on Saturday you're going to be entirely Catholic. Mrs Herdecka's very faithful, over the moon about a Polish Pope. Leave it with me.' She tapped Sweeney on the arm and her watch swung loose on her wrist. She was definitely losing weight.

When they met on Friday, Sam said, 'Mam hasn't seen Mrs Herdecka so it's time to put Plan B into action.' She handed Sweeney a Jacksons bag.

'What's all this?'

As he pulled out each item, Sam gave commentary. There

was a decorative plate of the Sacred Heart of Jesus with an accompanying stand – 'That's a present gran brought back from Lourdes' – a set of rosary beads – 'Mam got them for dad but he never uses them' – a statuette of the Virgin Mary – 'Now this one is from Paddy's Wigwam in Liverpool. I thought you'd appreciate it' – and finally a copy of *Time* magazine with a cover photo of John Paul II – 'I saw that in a newsagent's this morning'.

'Thanks,' he said. 'But what am I meant to do with all this stuff.'

'Here's what you do. You put them around the flat, but not too obviously. Mrs Herdecka is nobody's fool. Make sure she sort of *stumbles* on them. Don't stick them all in one place and don't forget that St Christopher I gave you.' Sweeney fished it out of his pocket to show her. 'The very one,' she said. 'Hold it tight when she arrives. It'll keep you safe until I appear.'

'What if she asks me to do something Catholic?'

'For goodness sake, Eddie, we aren't the Masonic Order! I'll see you Saturday morning.'

That afternoon he spread his Catholicism around the flat. When Brown got in, Sweeney asked if he wouldn't mind being absent in the morning.

'Are you turning the flat into a shrine?'

'A cunning plan to make sure we keep a roof over our heads. If you ever pray, pray it works.'

'I will make an exception tonight. I'll kip on the QT at Debbie's so you won't have to rush me out the door like in some French – or Polish – farce.'

Sweeney was up early. He checked the placement of the religious artefacts again and thought they were noticeable, but not blatant. *Time* magazine he left conspicuously on the table. He'd memorised the Catholic Chaplain's name in case Mrs Herdecka asked. There was a knock. He opened the door, astonished to see Flora Robson. But it wasn't Flora Robson. It was Mrs Herdecka, dressed in a herringbone tweed coat and the sort of cloche hat he'd only seen in 1950s films. She was tall, still with a good figure and yes, she did look formidable.

'Edward?' she asked. He was expecting an Eastern European inflection, but Mrs Herdecka's accent was definitely Hull.

'Mrs Herdecka?' She nodded imperiously. 'Please come in.'

He stood aside as she entered, a brief but appraising glance into the kitchen (which he'd tidied up) and a rather majestic sweep of the front room (he'd done something about those piles of books). He wasn't sure if she'd seen the Virgin statuette, the rosary beads draped over it, or the Sacred Heart of Jesus but her gaze lingered on the copy of *Time*. She put her finger tips on the cover image of John Paul II.

'There's some excellent coverage of the new Pope,' Sweeney said. He wasn't sure if that was the correct expression. Should he have said Holy Father? 'If you haven't read it, you can have my copy.'

Mrs Herdecka looked at him as he imagined Flora Robson would have done, quizzical and somewhat superior. She ignored his peace offering.

'Is it true, Edward, that you are subletting?'

'Pearl told me about your suspicions, but it's not true, Mrs Herdecka. Yes, someone is staying with me temporarily, a friend in need so to speak.' Here came the big lie. 'We know each other from the Catholic Chaplaincy – at the university.' She was staring hard at him. 'His grant ran out in September and he needed somewhere to stay to finish his degree. It's only until the Christmas vacation at the very latest. I felt it my duty to help him out.'

'I see.' Her eyes fell on the foldaway bed in the corner. 'He's not paying *you* any rent?'

'No, he's not. Well, that's not entirely true.' She raised an eyebrow. 'He makes me a few roll-ups, said it was a point of honour that no good deed should go unrewarded.'

'Hmm …'

Sweeney asked nervously if she would like a cup of tea or coffee. She didn't answer and walked slowly to the window, standing with her back to him. There was a banging on the front door. He said he should go down to see who it was. Mrs Herdecka remained haughty in her silence. He prayed it was Sam and there she was.

'How's it going?' she whispered.

'Not very well …'

'Just leave things to me.' She waved a blue manila folder as they went upstairs. 'Be sure to introduce me. Don't forget I've never been here before.'

'Mrs Herdecka, Samantha Ahrens, Samantha, Mrs Herdecka. Samantha's leaving off her dissertation for me to have a look over.'

Sam pretended surprise, but Mrs Herdecka's was genuine. Sweeney tried to act the confused host. 'Do you two know each other?'

The atmosphere changed to sociability and Sweeney retreated to one side. Sam and Mrs Herdecka exchanged news about families and mutual friends. He offered coffee and tea once more.

'You know, I'd love a cup of tea,' Sam said. Mrs Herdecka agreed to join her.

'Please have a seat while I put on the kettle.'

In the kitchen he could hear snatches of gossip. He was relieved to escape the eyes of his landlady.

When he handed Sam her tea she said, 'You make a very nice cup of tea, Eddie. Thank you.' Sweeney sat at the table pretending to scan the photocopied pages in Sam's folder.

'You can look at my scribbles later,' Sam called to him. 'Come over and join us.' As he sat on the couch, she said to Mrs

Herdecka, 'Eddie has been a great help to me this year.' She offered her packet of Rothmans. 'Do you smoke, Mrs Herdecka?'

'I really shouldn't,' but with girlish relish accepted. She allowed Sweeney to light it for her and he fetched the Ricard ashtray.

'This is a nice flat,' Sam made a point of saying. She looked around appreciatively. 'You're lucky. You should see the student accommodation friends of mine have to live in.'

'I know,' he responded. 'It was an act of providence.'

They both looked at him for a second then resumed their conversation. The statuette of the Virgin on the mantelpiece reminded Sweeney to look virtuous and the rosary to pray for a happy outcome.

When she'd finished her tea, Sam glanced at her watch. Sweeney was alarmed at how fragile her wrist appeared. 'I'll have to go. I'm meeting mam in half an hour.' She turned to Mrs Herdecka. 'I'll leave you two to your business.'

'Our business is all sorted, Samantha. It was mainly a courtesy call. So Edward,' she turned towards him with a smile this time, 'I forgot to ask if everything is in order.'

'Everything is fine, Mrs Herdecka, thanks. Only the fridge can be a bit dodgy sometimes, just like the water heater over the sink.'

'I see ... I will borrow your magazine if you don't mind.' Mrs Herdecka picked up *Time* and looked admiringly at John Paul II. 'I can give you a lift, Samantha. Danny is waiting for me in the car. It'll save you getting a bus. It looks like rain again.'

'Thank you. Mam gets annoyed if I'm late.' Sam pointed to her folder on the table. 'Eddie, I appreciate the help. But don't spoil your weekend on it. He tells me he's a Black and Whites fan, Mrs Herdecka, so I can't have him missing a match, can I?'

And they were gone. Sweeney flopped into an armchair. He couldn't help laughing. A knock on the door moments later made him spring up anxiously. It was Pearl.

'I saw Mrs Herdecka,' she said. 'Well, how'd it go?'

'I seem to have put her doubts to rest. At least I hope I have.'

Pearl gave him a hug. 'That's good news and no mistake. Is it too early for a celebratory gin?'

'After that performance, I'm up for anything.'

'Great! Come on down. It'll give me an excuse and Simon can have no complaints.'

The following Tuesday, Brown told him some 'brick shit-house' in a woolly hat had come round to install a new fridge and repair the water heater. He met Sam on Wednesday to return the Ahrens family's religious objects. When he told her about the new fridge she said it didn't surprise her.

'Mrs Herdecka thought you overdid the Catholic thing a bit, said it was hard not to laugh and was glad I turned up when I did.'

'So she knew all along?'

'She did … well your bit she did.'

Sweeney said they'd played their parts well, like Bogart and Bacall.

'Let's hope we don't have to play it again.'

'I would never ask you to play it again, Sam.'

CHAPTER TEN

'I made that appointment with the doctor,' she told him. 'Two weeks' time is the earliest I could get. And we have a Labour Government!'

A fortnight later she said the doctor had referred her for examination. 'He doesn't know what the problem is.' Sam made a face. 'It's the Royal Infirmary for me. Blood tests and I don't know what else. It scares me. I never said before but when I was a child I took very ill. I was in hospital for some time. I don't know if I imagined this or not but in my head I can hear a nurse in the ward telling noisy kids, "Keep quiet, this little girl is dying." Would a nurse say something like that? I don't know. As you see, I survived. But I've always wondered if death was denied its due back then. Maybe the grim reaper was checking the ledger and thinking, "You know what, I need to go back for that little girl." Tell me I'm wrong, Eddie.'

'You are wrong.' He said this with as much certainty as he could. He wasn't certain at all.

She stretched her hand to touch his. 'All this moooanin'll only do me 'ead in,' she said, exaggerating her accent.

'If you want me to help some more with your dissertation, I'm happy to do so.'

That Sam accepted immediately without quibble and told him how worried about her health she really was.

. . . .

Brown had finished his thesis on Larkin, 'bar a few missing references.' He shook his head. 'I'll give you one piece of advice. Keep a good record of your sources, for I didn't. Otherwise it'll drive you bonkers, like it's doing me.'

'Dawson recommended keeping alphabetical file cards for everything.' Sweeney showed Brown the red plastic box where he kept them.

'It makes you think, doesn't it? Years of your life contained in something that small … anyway, let's not dwell on that. I have another piece of news. I've got a job interview.'

'Congratulations!'

'It's not full-time, only for a year, a member of staff is going on sabbatical in January so they need a quick replacement.'

'Where is it?'

'Oxford, old bean,' Brown said in his best Noel Coward accent.

'Wow! You've really hit the jackpot – you lucky bugger.'

'I thought I'd leave it there for a moment before I told you it's the polytechnic and not the university.'

'Even so, Oxford is a great place to be.'

'There is that, yes, but how's your geography?'

'What do you mean?'

'Oxford's not too far from Chesham, that's what I mean. Debbie's going home soon. If I get the job it couldn't be better.'

'Pity it's only temporary.'

'If you're not in you can't win, my son. And you never refuse a job. You don't want to make the mistake of that sad bastard Robinson.'

'Who the hell is he now?'

'Let's say Robinson is an object lesson for us all, maybe *abject* lesson. He's a legend, if not quite in the Fenwick-Clark league. You really haven't heard?' Brown lit up a roll-up. 'He was a couple of years ahead of me, thought a lot of himself and let you know it. Arrogant is the word. Robinson believed he was destined for great things. He got interviews at Polys, got offered a couple of jobs, and turned them down. You see, he'd word of a job coming up in Durham where he'd been an undergrad.

LOVE

He thought its prestige matched his talent. The post was finally advertised and he applied ... didn't even get an interview.'

'Where'd he end up?'

'He's teaching at a comprehensive school in Sunderland. It's where his wife's family live. I'm sure it's not the end of the world but rumour has it he's a disappointed man. And I mean *very* disappointed. Hubris, is that a deadly sin?'

'Isn't that the theme of *Paradise Lost?*'

'Now that you mention it, appropriate title, don't you think?'

Brown got a letter a few days after his interview offering him the Oxford job.

'I take it you're not going to do a Robinson?' Sweeney asked.

'Damn sure I'm not.'

They arranged to go out for a night's drinking to celebrate. Sweeney called it Brown's farewell tour. They settled on the same pub crawl they'd done in 1976. 'At least those pubs we can remember,' Sweeney joked.

'We only had the one, your Honour,' Brown laughed.

They wandered the Old Town, slithering on greasy cobblestones. The rain fell steadily, driven by a bitter wind off the Humber, as it had the first time.

'One thing I'll not miss about Hull is the weather,' Brown cursed, wiping rain from his forehead as they stood at the bar of The George Hotel.

'I was seduced here by the summer of 1976.'

'Costa del Hull ...'

'What *are* you going to miss?'

His friend thought for a while, every now and then about to give an answer but shaking his head each time. The pantomime went on for about a minute. Finally, Brown said, 'Nothing in general and everything in particular is as good an answer as I can give you. I've spent three years here studying Larkin. I now realise my answer is the clue to his poetry. Why the hell didn't you ask me when you first got here?'

'You were too busy warning me off Hull girls and meeting their mams.'

'Too right, my son,' he laughed. 'Seriously, what I learned from Larkin and what Hull confirmed for me is simple. The banal can be beautiful. It has all the making of great poetry. The bizarre and the zany, the exceptional and the extraordinary, in life as well as art, can become tedious. Here's the irony. They can become tediously predictable. I never found Hull tedious … maybe because Hull doesn't do irony.'

'You mean the mundane is magical and the ordinary, mysterious?'

'You're a romantic after all! You should write poetry too, Eddie.'

Within the week Brown was packed and ready to go.

Sweeney helped take his stuff to Paragon Station. 'I want to make certain I've got rid of you,' he told him.

As they hung about the station concourse Brown said, 'When I get myself fixed up in Oxford you must come and visit. You can dine at my high table.'

'That sounds good.' Somehow Sweeney felt it would never happen.

'I'll be back in Hull at some point, like a dog returning to its vomit – my thesis that is, not Hull.' He looked around furtively. 'Did anyone overhear me? They can be sensitive up here. But you know how much I love them, really. Speaking of which, is there any news about Sam?'

'No news. I worry about her.'

Brown grasped Sweeney's arm. 'Wish her all the best from me – for your sake too. Look, I'd better be going. I'll keep in touch and send you my new address when I have it. By the way, you can keep the foldaway bed.'

He waved, showed his ticket at the barrier, lugged his baggage through, struggled along the platform and got onto the London train. Sweeney hoped he'd found a seat in a smoking carriage.

. . . .

Brown had gone, Toby had gone and Patsy had gone. Rick and Cathy, having found him in possession of the postgrad room, ignored his presence. They had no time for what had been or who had been. There were another two worlds now and Sweeney wasn't part of theirs. He hadn't seen Sam for days. He went to the office, holding the door open to let Julie pass with an armful of papers.

'You're a gentleman,' she said.

If Julie only knew what ungentlemanly thoughts he'd had.

He asked Jan if Dawson was available. She removed her glasses. 'Now there's a coincidence. Mr Dawson called me only a moment ago to ask if *you* were available.'

'I wonder what it's about.'

'I have no idea. He didn't appear agitated, more upbeat, a touch of John Travolta maybe? Let me check if he's still in his office.' She rang Dawson. 'He says to go along.' As Sweeney turned to go, she sang softly, 'You're the one that he wants ...'

'Come in, Edward. Have a seat.' Dawson had a copy of *The Times* spread on his desk. He folded it up and put it in a drawer. 'I was checking on the England tour of Australia. First Test starts next week. I fear I'll not be able to follow things in *The Times*, another so-called industrial dispute in the offing. The country's in chaos, what with these strikes, inflation, economic crisis and all the rest of it. It's enough to make you despair. Anarchy it feels like. But what can one do apart from getting on with one's own work as diligently as possible?'

Sweeney thought of Dr Rieux in *La Peste* but he couldn't really picture Dawson as an existential hero.

'How are things with you, Edward?'

'Just thinking about the future, if any jobs come up, maybe add to my CV some way, make myself more marketable.' The word 'marketable' made Dawson wince. 'Alan Brown got a temporary post at Oxford.' Dawson looked astonished. 'Oxford Polytechnic,' Sweeney qualified. Dawson subsided with what looked like relief rather than disappointment.

'That *is* good news. Pass on my congratulations when you see him.'

'He's left already.'

'Oh well, it's good to see Hull spreading its intellectual influence. About your marketability' he coughed at the word, 'it's the reason – coincidentally – I wanted to have a word. I've been meaning to make a suggestion. I had a call with my publisher recently about gaps in the literature. I took the opportunity to propose something I've been toying with for some time. It was prompted by work you've been doing, regional imagination, northern writers, where literature and culture meet, to paraphrase Larkin. You'll be pleased to know he thought it an attractive idea. Here's my suggestion. What do you say to a joint publication? Your focus is on post-war England whereas I have looked previously at war and pre-war literature. I see no good reason why the different elements can't be worked up together. I had in mind a survey of the English novel in the twentieth century, one looking at history, culture and society too. It would be attractive to students, don't you think? My publisher certainly thought so. Now, a book contract would do a lot for your *marketability.*'

Sweeney was hesitant not because he couldn't imagine such a book, but because he hadn't been expecting anything so providential. Dawson mistook hesitancy for suspicion.

'To be clear, I'm not suggesting it would be your work and I simply put my name to it, no, no. That's the sort of chicanery that goes on in some other countries – or so I'm reliably informed. An honest to goodness collaborative effort, I think we could do a good job together.' He tapped his desk gently with both hands. 'We can set a submission date for the manuscript to suit both of us. Having the contract though, Edward, that's the prize.' Dawson smiled in a way he must have considered winning. 'Cyril Connolly talked about the joy of potential. He also talked about the agony of delivery. We don't need to worry about delivery yet. And your CV will scream the joy of potential. What do you say?'

Sweeney had never seen Dawson so enthused about anything other than cricket. Did he feel exhausted of inspiration and was looking to feed off his youthful energy (such as it was)? He couldn't imagine Dawson as Dracula either. Wasn't he right after all? Whether the book ever came to fruition was irrelevant. Wouldn't it proclaim the unknown Sweeney to be a scholar with 'potential'. Dawson was a friend of promise, Sweeney decided, not an enemy of youth.

'It would be an honour.'

'I don't know about honour,' Dawson said, accepting it as his due. 'I'm glad you agree. I will deal with the publisher. It would be good to have a contract in the New Year.'

'I'm happy to leave all those things in your hands.' He certainly was. He had no idea about the publishing world.

'I think this moment calls for a little celebration … which I don't expect to be premature.' Dawson opened the bottom drawer of his desk and extracted a bottle of brandy. He felt around and produced two tumblers. 'I'll do the honours, shall I? Let's toast our joint venture.'

'To my marketability and to our future success,' Sweeney said and Dawson smiled benevolently. They touched glasses. The brandy was exceptionally smooth.

'And I think we should have a Turkish. They were made for moments like this.'

. . . .

Sweeney wished he could speak to someone about this unexpected turn of events. It would be delicious to slip casually into conversation with Rick or Cathy except they never did talk with him. Not for the first time he missed Brown. He wished Sam was here and imagined her wandering the corridors of the Royal Infirmary. The vision chilled him. Then he thought of Mr Trammer.

When the brass doorbell sounded, Mr Trammer shuffled from the back of the shop. Sweeney told him of Dawson's proposal.

'That is welcome news, something to brighten this drab day.' He shook Sweeney's hand and slumped into his chair. 'I take it you can trust your supervisor?'

'He may be elusive but I don't doubt his honesty.'

'Being published is an intimation of immortality.' When Sweeney said 'Hah' as if Mr Trammer was joking, his expression became stern. 'I'm being serious.' He looked at the books cluttering his desk, lifted a new hardback and tapped the cover. 'There is birth. A review copy a local journalist sold me. You'd be surprised how few are opened, never mind read.' He set it back and lifted a battered copy, its spine ragged and split top to bottom, title lettering illegible, the covers partly mildewed. 'And there is death.' He laid it down carefully. His arm swept the bookshelves. 'You might call this place their cemetery, rows of headstones for lives sacrificed to literature.' He waited a moment before saying, 'And then there is resurrection.' He held up another hardback. 'Someone comes in here, picks out a book, blows dust off the pages, begins reading and the author lives again – new eyes finding what old eyes once read.'

'You sound like a prophet of the book trade.'

'If only there was *profit* in the book trade! I suggest we go for a drink if you're agreeable.'

LOVE

'I was going to suggest that very thing myself.'

Mr Trammer retrieved a rectangular cardboard sign from his desk drawer with an adjustable window. He set 'be back in' for one hour, hung it on the door, threw on a grubby trench coat and locked up. A short distance from the arcade they turned down the alleyway to Ye Olde White Harte. The pub was quiet and they sat by the open fire. Sweeney ordered a pint of Old Peculier and Mr Trammer a double Scotch, no ice, a touch of water.

'My bladder's not what it was. Here's a toast to your future book.' He sighed as he sipped his whisky. 'It's a bit early for me. I'm normally a strict sun-downer. But since the sun never seems to come up in Hull these days ...' He took another sip. 'Some fire inside me and a roaring fire beside me, just what an old man needs.'

'I'd say it's what everyone needs.'

Mr Trammer nodded around the bar with its flagged flooring, its oak panelling and stained-glass windows. 'Do you know the history of this place?'

'Only vaguely, I'm afraid.' He meant not at all.

'This is where on St George's Day 1642 the local worthies refused Charles I access to the port and arsenal. That's the legend anyway. They also plotted here in 1688 to support William of Orange.'

'Cheers to that,' Sweeney said, raising his glass.

'Hull people are an independent lot as by now I'm sure you know. Maybe like the people where you come from too.'

'Queen's rebels and republican rebels – yes, you are quite right.'

Mr Trammer finished his Scotch. Sweeney pointed to his glass and asked if he'd like another.

'You are here at my invitation,' Mr Trammer protested.

'It's only proper to share a salute to my prospective immortality.'

245

'Then I will have another. You don't have to do much persuading to buy a Yorkshireman a drink.'

Ye Olde White Harte began to fill up with lunchtime drinkers, all cheeriness and banter. Distracted by loud laughter at the bar, Sweeney missed something Mr Trammer said. 'Sorry, I didn't catch what you said.'

'I said I'm thinking about selling up. *Sic transit gloria Hepworth.*' He smiled. 'My wife told me it sounded like a Hollywood actress found drunk in a van. She has a good sense of humour, my wife.'

'That's *Two Ronnies* quality.'

'She'd appreciate you saying that. They're her favourites.' He took another sip of Scotch. 'The business is a declining asset. Times change, don't they? It's closing time in the bookshops of England. A way of life is dying, I fear. We are no longer a literate country. The new owner will probably be a travel agent. People always seem to have money for package holidays. I don't blame them. Mrs Trammer says we should retire to Spain. I know she doesn't mean it. I can't see her – us – ever leaving Yorkshire.' He sighed again, finished his Scotch. 'I should be getting back. Congratulations once more. I knew from the beginning you had promise.'

'Those whom the gods wish to destroy, they first call promising.'

'Now, now, you should accept an old man's compliment.' He shrugged on his trench coat.

As they parted on Silver Street, Mr Trammer asked. 'How are things with that young lady friend of yours?'

'I really need to find out.'

. . . .

Pearl knocked his door unexpectedly on Saturday morning. She handed him a letter.

LOVE

'It was in the post so I thought I'd bring it up, personal delivery by your favourite neighbour.' Sweeney recognised Sam's handwriting and his stunned look confused Pearl. 'I'm sorry, maybe I shouldn't have …'

'No, it was very kind of you.' He tapped the letter on the back of his hand. 'I was surprised that's all, wasn't expecting this. Come in. Would you like coffee? It's only instant I'm afraid.'

'A coffee would be nice. I won't stay long.' Pearl nodded at his random stacks of books. 'Your flat reminds me of a garden with wild plants growing here and there.'

Sweeney began rolling a cigarette and explained the origin of his new habit. 'Would you like one?'

'I'm sorely tempted to say yes. I haven't smoked one since my undergraduate days. Don't tell anyone, but they weren't all tobacco. Oh, go on then.' Sweeney passed over the one he'd made, rolled another and lit them both.

'Bringing up your letter was just an excuse to give you a bit of news. Hold the front page. I'm going to have a baby.'

'That's wonderful news. Congratulations!' He said it with as much enthusiasm as he could. His mind was on Sam's letter.

'Unexpected, but after the initial shock both of us are delighted. Simon's become all health conscious. If he knew I was smoking he'd hit the roof.' Sweeney thought of Simon wringing his neck. 'Don't worry. I won't say a word. I can't imagine holding out completely without gin and fags until the sprog appears, can you?' Sweeney couldn't imagine it either. 'Being the modern man, Simon has agreed to keep off the booze in solidarity. He doesn't smoke, damn him, so he's only in for half the battle.' She took another drag. 'Me, a mother, it's hard to believe. But I suppose that's what everyone says the first time.'

'I can't imagine a better mother.'

'Thank you, Eddie. You could have a job as a parent counsellor or whatever the term is. I'm sure you're wondering why

I'm telling you this. It's to alert you to the possibility of Simon and me moving at some future date.'

'First you give the good news and then the bad news.'

'We've only begun to talk about it. I love it here in Park Road but Simon thinks the flat will be too cramped for three. Nothing can be done until after New Year and with all the economic chaos these days who knows? Anyway, I thought you should know.'

The days of Pearly Spencer were nearly run. 'Are you leaving Hull?'

'Didn't I tell you Hull is a difficult place to leave? So no is the answer.'

Sweeney held up his *Golden Virginia*, 'Do you want to sneak another one?'

'Get thee behind me Satan! I'd ask you for a peppermint if it weren't so obvious. I'll swirl the coffee around my mouth and maybe it'll do the trick.' She sniffed her fingers. 'If I can wash my hands, it would help too.'

Pearl said there was one more thing. 'My head is away with it at the moment, probably hormones raging if that's what hormones do. We want to have a small party when things are more certain. You, Roland, a farewell do while we're still all together in the house.' She said she'd keep him posted.

. . . .

Anxiously, Sweeney opened Sam's letter. Inside were three handwritten pages. When he lifted them out he found a blue ribbon within the fold. He sat down at the table and began reading.

She apologised for not having been in touch sooner, was glad to tell him she had finished her dissertation and thanked him again for his help.

LOVE

I never knew that my "favour" the day we met would bring such reward. I know you will say it's only "you being you" but I feel blessed because it is you being you for me. You've helped me to see things differently, especially Hull !!! I suppose it had become invisible to me. You show me its charms, can you believe that? How easy it is to run down your own place because it's no great shakes compared to London or Paris. But the small things I take for granted you look on with great affection. You will probably feel embarrassed if I use the word "love" but I can't think of a better one (and I have an English degree ha ha). So here you go. Your love for ordinary run-down Hull makes me feel good living here. Does that seem silly? I won't think of Selby in the same way again either!!!

Sweeney remembered what Brown had said to him, how he would miss everything in particular and nothing in general. It was true, he thought, happiness did lie in small things.

I want you to know I think about you a lot and never take you for granted. I identified with Sylvia Plath as you saw when you read my dissertation, someone who was in "two worlds" if more creative than my own, fitting in with expectations but feeling out of step, appearing settled but not wishing to be trapped, superficially happy but staring into the abyss, putting on a face but feeling empty. Unfortunately, I can't express myself as well as she could. We bottle up our souls (the priest would never fathom it in confession) because we feel vulnerable or fear being mocked (it's what I feared most when I was younger). How hard it is to put our feelings into words even when it does become possible. Mr Trammer's Shakespearean Odes have helped me a bit. He was right about that. You know, when I was with you I cursed myself for the words that came from my lips. They were so feeble. I cringe at what you must have thought.

What had he thought? He thought she'd opened a window onto life for him.

You know Larkin's "High Windows"? Mam looked over my shoulder one day when I was reading it and was outraged by the language. "Is this what passes for poetry these days? Imagine teaching you that at university!!!" Our lecturer said the poem ends with the thought there can be no true freedom. He told us that was pessimistic Larkin pouring cold water on everything. I never read it that way. The thought not of words but of high windows I found exhilarating. Seeing beyond those windows to deep blue air, clear and endless, I imagined my soul soaring to something beyond the physicality of the other verses (they are very male, you know). I've probably got it wrong. But even if I am wrong, I want to keep that image close to my heart. Do you know why? Because it is how I feel when I'm with you, beyond fear, beyond time, beyond limits and out in that clear blue air, full of excitement and yet amazingly peaceful. With you I'm Sam Ahrens, I'm me and I am free. I only hope you can say when we're together "I'm Eddie Sweeney, I'm me and I am free". I need to tell you these things because they give me courage.'

At the top of the third page she had drawn an eye with three teardrops.

I do need courage. My tests aren't good. I won't go into details for one word is enough: cancer. Just writing it shocks me.

Sweeney read those lines again to make sure he wasn't mistaken. He closed his eyes for a second and looked once more. The word was unchanged, a word he couldn't wish away. He looked at dark clouds through the flat's rain-speckled window. He imagined them opening only onto endless death. He shivered.

Last time I was complaining about the health service. Everyone's been great this time. The hospital consultant has scheduled an operation immediately. He was honest about my condition. Family is clutching at prayer. Everyone wants to look on the bright side. They want me to be hopeful. I suppose I must be. Faith should make these things easier but it doesn't. It should keep you in good spirits, but it can't. Faith only helps the living not the sick or dying. God forgive me.

LOVE

Sweeney thought of sixth-form in school and his English teacher (who happened to be Welsh) in his sepulchral tone reading Dylan Thomas's 'Do not go gentle into that good night'. It had been comforting for a robustly healthy youth to hear those words of rage against the dying of the light, comforting because such a moment seemed unimaginable, like a sad song when happy, a remembrance before an enjoyable toast, or a funereal allusion during a delicious meal. Now he sensed his own tears of rage. There can be no comfort in death. But there must be hope, surely? Modern medicine, scientific advances, technological progress, new drugs … it was 1978 after all! Surely there was hope?

Two worlds won't leave me alone. This time it's another two. There's my new world of doctors, nurses, medicines and hospital, then there's my old world with its mundane things. Here's one mundane thing. I need to be at university on Tuesday to hand in a copy of the dissertation with my name proudly on it. I suppose you can guess its title? Yes!!! 'The Melancholy of Anticipation'. Can we meet in our usual place at ten? I may not get another chance to see you before Christmas. It would mean everything to me.

She signed her name and beside it, *xxx* and a lipstick kiss. Sweeney ran his finger lightly across the imprint of Sam's lips. There was an arrow pointing to the back of the page. He turned it over.

PS I enclose this blue ribbon for your collection to symbolise my soul soaring above you, the lightness of spirit I have around you, and the depth of love I have for you. As the old song goes, they can't take that away from me. Sam xx.'

Sweeney set the page aside to stop tears falling onto her handwriting.

. . . .

He longed for Tuesday. He dreaded Tuesday. He feared appearing inadvertently insensitive or irritatingly solicitous. Who knew what to say in these circumstances? Did the priest and the doctor in their long coats? He didn't. At ten o'clock he sat at their table in the Students' Union, mouth dry, thinking about getting a glass of water. Then there she was – Sam. He looked for signs of illness, in her face, the shape of her shoulders, but he could detect nothing special. She seemed the same as ever. And yet she wasn't the same. He decided to be open about his uncertainties.

'Sam, I'm probably going to ask and say a lot of stupid things. Put your hand up and stop me when I do.' He touched her hands resting on the table, 'How are you feeling?'

'There are good days and bad days. This is the best of days.' She took out her packet of cigarettes. She noticed his look and said, 'I don't think it's going to make much difference, do you? It feels like I'm shaking a fist at fate and not letting cancer beat me. Anyhow, I enjoy smoking, so to hell with it.'

He fetched their coffees. For a while, they sat amidst the hubbub around them as if it was just an ordinary day. And then with an urgency he'd never witnessed before, she ran through the Kafkaesque trials of diagnosis, tests, examinations, consultations, procedures, the planned operation, her prospects for recovery. Sweeney never said a word, just listened. When she finished, she looked exhausted. The refectory had become noisy and hectic.

'Is there somewhere quiet we can go?' she asked.

They found a television lounge at the top of the building. Three women students were intently copying notes. He sat with Sam on a soft and lumpy sofa pockmarked here and there with cigarette burns.

'Hold me,' Sam said.

He put his arm around her and she rested her head against

him. She began to weep. He laid his cheek against her hair. The women stared at them for a few seconds, glanced at one another, collected their notebooks and left quietly. Now and then there were loud voices in the corridor, the odd guffaw, but no one disturbed them. He felt the damp of tears but her body remained still, her breathing calm. She squeezed his arm as tears flowed more quickly and he stroked her hair, but nothing was said. After a while she raised her head and pulled apart from him.

'I must look a right sight,' she said running the back of a hand across wet cheeks. 'What must you think of me?'

He almost laughed at the absurdity of the question.

Sam closed her eyes. 'Sometimes I'm terrified by this dark thing inside me.' She opened her eyes again and Sweeney saw submission, which broke his heart. He was about to hold her again when two lads burst into the room, shouting and wrestling over possession of a bag of crisps, falling across a chair and rushing out again. 'It's time to go,' she said.

As they walked, he apologised for having so little to say.

'Don't. Everyone comes out with words of comfort. There are no words of comfort. If my operation is successful, I will welcome all the comforting words in the dictionary.' She moved closer to him. 'Holding me the way you did, that's what I needed more than anything. And do you know why? My tears were tears of self-pity, yes. But amongst them were tears of happiness. Both things are true.'

Sweeney's expression showed he didn't understand.

'Don't you see? This is what it is to feel sorrow. This is what it is to feel happy. To know life's contradictions, isn't that what literature is all about?' She kissed him on the cheek, told him she was being collected by car on Cranbrook Avenue (he didn't ask) and they parted.

. . . .

His parents were disappointed he didn't want to stay longer at Christmas.

'Hull must be some place, you're so keen to get back,' his father said, 'swopping your mother's cooking for a tin of baked beans. Does everyone there smoke roll ups?'

His mother suspected a girlfriend at best, English decadence at worst. 'You need to be careful' was all she said, five words freighted with so much assumption and conjecture.

He appeased her by seeking advice on a suit, one he would need for job interviews (if he got any). 'You can't go wrong with Donegal tweed,' was his mother's considered view. They found a contemporary style discounted in the January sales. She told him he looked a proper gentleman. His father told him he looked like a bookie at the racetrack.

Returning to an England of industrial disruption, he managed to avoid a rail strike and made it to Hull. The winter was severe. Heavy snow and freezing temperatures made life miserable. Some nights Blanche's duvet wasn't enough to keep him warm and the flannel pyjamas, never worn until now, made little difference either. Some days were so cold he didn't venture out and sat blanketed for hours by the gas fire, grateful for the bounty of the North Sea. A lorry drivers' strike meant food disappeared from the shelves as well. Hull was an easy place to cut off. When ambulance drivers, hospital staff and even gravediggers went out in protest it felt like Dawson's edge of anarchy cutting deep. Sam was in the middle of all this, but he'd heard nothing.

He asked Simon what was happening. His shoulders slumped. 'I'm afraid the labour movement is at war with itself, Eddie. The government has lost touch with the trade unions, the party has lost touch with the government and some unions have lost touch with the people. And you know what the result will be if we can't sort out this mess? We will hand power to the Tories for the next ten years.'

'I have a friend in hospital needing cancer treatment. Do you think she'll be affected?'

'Don't worry on that score. The tabloid headlines tell you Hull is a city under siege and the docks are blockaded. Chris says don't believe a word of it. T&G officials will make sure no one suffers.' He saw Sweeney didn't look convinced. 'I know Mitchell and his crew of agitators think Hull has become a revolutionary soviet. Don't believe them either. Does it feel like Russia in 1917 to you?'

Sweeney felt like saying it reminded him of Belfast in 1974 during the Ulster Workers' Council strike. What he did say was, 'No – and I hope it never will.'

'The NHS won't let down your friend. You can trust me on that.'

A few days later he received a short letter from Sam telling him she'd had her operation and was recuperating in the Royal Infirmary. Simon had been right. She gave the ward number and the afternoon visiting time. She wrote it would be better to visit then because in the evening loads of family came. He knew exactly what she meant.

Arriving at the hospital, he sensed an unmistakable monotony – of waiting, of convalescence, of illness. Everyone spoke in absorbed monotones. Porters moved slowly, their casualness adding to an impression of universal tedium. Here normal English cheeriness felt weighed down by apathy. He went up in the lift. The faces of visitors registered fulfilment of duty with anticipation of escape. Outside might be freezing, miserable and strike-bound but it beckoned with life and freedom. Their animal instinct did not fail them.

He asked a nurse for 'Samantha' rather than 'Mrs Houghton'. She pointed to a bed half curtained at the far end of the ward.

The others were occupied by women of various ages and Sweeney felt an interloper. He peeked round the curtain. Propped up, Sam was wearing a plain white T-shirt and over her shoulders was draped an unbuttoned cardigan with flower motifs. She smiled, moving her head to indicate the chair beside the bed. Her eyes were vague and dreamy. Sweeney assumed it was a lingering effect of anaesthetic and not his angelic presence.

'Eddie!' Her voice was husky. He found it seductive and was shocked by this primitive impulse, his own animal instinct. 'I must look awful,' she said.

'You look lovely as ever.'

'That's a corny Eddie-ism for "you look awful". You can't sweet-talk me.'

He spread his hands, laughed and said she knew him too well. 'I come bearing gifts,' he told her. 'I thought grapes too traditional and I imagined you'd have lots of flowers – but I see there aren't any at all.'

'Flowers are frowned upon in this ward, for some reason. Anyway, I'm glad you didn't. They remind me of funerals.'

Sweeney had never considered this aromatic association. He felt in his canvas bag and pulled out two packets of Rothmans. 'I don't know if they are allowed.'

She nodded at the ashtray on the bedside table. 'You're a lifesaver.' She closed her eyes and said, 'Isn't that what you need in hospital, a lifesaver?'

'Your humour is intact, I'm glad to see. Oh, and I got you this.' It was a collected volume of three Françoise Sagan novels. 'You mentioned Paris in your letter. So I thought, why shouldn't Sam go there when she's in hospital?'

'Aw,' she said, 'that's so kind of you.' He put the hardback and cigarettes on her table.

'Hide the ciggies in the drawer, would you? Mam has become puritanical all of a sudden.'

LOVE

Sweeney opened the drawer, saw layers of underwear neatly arranged, and slid the packets as discreetly as possible underneath.

'Can I have your lighter as well?'

Sweeney fished it out of his pocket. 'I'll put it in with the fags.'

She closed her eyes and breathed deeply. 'I'm still pretty woozy from the medication.' She opened her eyes again. 'Thanks for coming.' She reached for his hand and squeezed it softly.

Sweeney had considered in advance how he might talk to her, had run through different tones from jaunty to solemn but feared they might sound ridiculous in their different ways. Sitting by her bed he was lost for words yet again.

'I won't speak about the operation and all that stuff,' she said. 'It would be as uncomfortable for you as it was for me.' Obviously Sam could read him like a book.

'You are feeling better, though?'

'Let's say the answer to that question is – I have felt better.' There was no edge to her voice, no self-pity. 'One thing I did find out.'

'What's that?'

'You know all that romantic stuff about being half in love with an easeful death?'

'Keats,' he said.

'Yes, Keats, I can tell you it's a load of crap. There's nothing romantic about it, easeful or otherwise. There's nothing poetic about it at all. The other women in here will say the same. So let's not talk about death. Tell me what you have been up to. Tell me about life instead.'

He told her about Brown's job and his book with Dawson. She told him to pass on her congratulations to Brown and pressed his hand, saying it was great news about the book.

'I haven't heard anything more on the contract. With inflation, strikes and all the rest, the publisher may think twice.'

'Aren't you a great believer in providence? You know – I know – it will all work out for you. I'm certain of it.'

'You bestow the favour of believing in me.' He raised her hand and kissed it. 'I suppose my biggest piece of news is I got myself a suit in case I ever get a job interview.'

'What sort of suit?'

'It's a three-piece Donegal tweed. My dad says it makes me look like a bookie.'

'That's the sort of comment my dad would come out with too,' she laughed, 'yet another thing we have in common.'

'And that's about it,' evidence, he couldn't help thinking, of how sheltered and uneventful his life really was. 'The weather has been awfully cold so I rarely go out – it's really warm in here. Oh, and there are food shortages in the shops. At least you'll get enough to eat.'

'Obviously you've never tasted hospital food.' Sam turned her head away and was silent for a moment. She looked back at Sweeney. 'You know what? I already feel as though I have gone through Larkin's high windows.' She closed her eyes again. 'It's … it's like looking down on life from above rather than being part of it. Can you understand?'

'Are you sure it's not just your operation, the effect of your medication, maybe even the hospital food you're eating?'

She shook her head. 'It's not that, or not only that. It's hard to put into words. Being ill like I am … I don't know … it's as if I'm absolutely at one with myself and also completely beyond myself. That sounds contradictory, but it's so real. I think Plath must have felt exactly the same way. It's like I have knowledge *of* something, not simply a feeling *for* something. My problem is trying to tell you what that something is.' She swallowed hard. Her face relaxed, abandoning any attempt at explanation. 'I loved what Alan said in that pub in London. Do you remember?'

'How could I forget "two souls in a single breast"? It was the one occasion he said anything with a hint of romance, typical Londoner, unlike people in Hull.'

'Oh yes, we're nothing if not passionate.'

The curtained partition was disturbed. Sweeney expected a nurse but it was a small woman in a heavy coat with a faux fur collar, plain scarf around her neck and hair tucked under a black woollen beret. She showed no obvious surprise at Sweeney's presence though it couldn't have been anticipated. He knew at once it was her mother and withdrew his hand from Sam's. He stood up with muddled emotions – betrayal of their bond, embarrassment at being discovered, self-loathing for lack of moral courage.

'Mam, I wasn't expecting you. This is Eddie from the university. Eddie, this is mam.' Her mother had seen everything but chose not to remark on it.

'Pleased to meet you, Mrs Ahrens,' Sweeney stepped to the end of the bed, stretching out his hand, the one which hadn't been holding her daughter's.

She shook it lightly and quickly. 'Sam has mentioned you a few times.' Though her greeting wasn't warm, her tone was pleasant. She hadn't smiled at him but her manner revealed no hostility. Mrs Ahrens placed a large Marks and Spencer bag on the metal rail at the foot of the bed and pulled out a long floral print cotton nightdress, draping it for Sam to see.

'Oh, Mam, put it away. You'll only embarrass Eddie. He's a good Catholic boy.' Sam gave him a wink her mother didn't see. Sweeney played the part by looking at his feet.

'You can't wear T-shirts all the time,' Mrs Ahrens said as she refolded the nightdress.

'I'm not ungrateful, mam. I will wear it. It's just Eddie is here …'

'Actually, I think it looks very nice Mrs Ahrens.'

'There, you see,' her mother said

Sam looked at him, narrowing her eyes, pouting her lips and slowly shaking her head. The awkward moment had passed. Sweeney asked Mrs Ahrens to take his seat and he moved round to where she'd stood at end of the bed.

There was family-talk – 'your dad sends his love' – church talk – 'Father Finnegan will pop in to see you tomorrow' – and health talk – 'you look much better rested today'. Sweeney contributed nothing during this time. Now and then Sam looked at him apologetically. A nurse passing along the ward told them visiting time was ending shortly.

'I'd better be off,' he said. 'It was nice to meet you Mrs Ahrens.' He asked her to pass him his canvas bag.

'I'll walk out with you.' She kissed her daughter and said her goodbyes.

Sam held up her hand for Sweeney. Awkwardly, he squeezed by her mother to clasp it. 'Come and see me again.' When Mrs Ahrens turned her back, she gave him another wink and blew a kiss.

From the lift they walked silently towards the exit among the departing visitors. When they reached the main doors, Mrs Ahrens touched Sweeney's arm and motioned him to one side. 'I have to know. Is there anything going on between you and my daughter?' If her look had been aggressive, her voice accusatory, Sweeney would have denied everything. But she was matter-of-fact and her directness gave him permission to be honest. He needed to expiate the shame of dropping Sam's hand earlier.

'I won't lie to you. If by "anything going on" you mean are Sam and I having an affair, the answer, Mrs Ahrens, is no, absolutely not. You know your daughter would never betray her vows.' He stopped to judge the impact of his words but her face remained impassive. 'If you mean do I love her the answer is yes. And because I do, I would never ask her to break her vows either. You must believe that. It's true.' Her look was unchanged. 'A good friend of mine described us as two souls in a single breast. Sam loves that description. And so do I.' More visitors leaving the hospital jostled past them, commenting on the snow falling outside. He paused to let her think of that image. 'It's just how we are together. It's a spiritual love, not a physical one. As I said, two souls as one, Mrs Ahrens, not two bodies.' He made a final pitch for her acceptance. 'It is a blessing. Neither Sam nor I have anything to be ashamed of.'

The press of departures over, the Royal Infirmary returned to its normal sluggishness. Mrs Ahrens kept her eyes fixed on him. They reminded him so much of Sam's he had to look away. She touched his arm again and her features had softened. 'I know I've not read enough books to understand everything you said but I believe you're being truthful. I worry enough about Sam, you can imagine ...'

'Understanding doesn't depend on books, Mrs Ahrens.'

'For what it's worth you have *my* blessing to see her. I saw how you two got on – as if I couldn't tell.'

'I would give anything for Sam to be well again.'

Mrs Ahrens' allowed him to take her arm along the icy, snow-caked, pavement of Anlaby Road. It was a sign of her acceptance. As they walked, she asked, 'Where do you live, Eddie?'

'Park Road – it's beside Pearson Park and it'll be a very cold flat when I get back.'

When they reached Walton Street she said, 'Go up here to Spring Bank West. Turn right at the junction and it'll take you to Princes Avenue.'

He thanked her and asked, 'Are you okay to get home on your own? Or do you want me to walk with you? These pavements are really icy.'

'Council workers are on strike again! I'm Hull born and bred. Don't worry. A bit of ice and snow won't stop me.'

PART FIVE

Going

Chapter Eleven

At the junction of Walton Street and Spring Bank West, he passed the old cemetery, overgrown and disordered. Headstones visible from the footpath were badly weather-beaten, names removed by time, the dead gone to endless nothing and nowhere. They didn't lie. Here was no deep blue air, only brooding cold and darkness.

He thought what he'd seen in the cemetery was no *mere* coincidence. His intuition was equally dark when visiting Sam again. Her face was paler, her eyes duller, her gestures slower, and she spoke from behind a veil of tiredness, but her spirits appeared good, at least they did in his presence. And yet he knew.

He'd bought her an antique silver cross and chain from a jewellery shop in the Old Town.

'Can you put it on for me? Mam will be so pleased to see it. She thinks you're a good boy, you know.'

As he bent over to fix the clasp, she raised a hand to brush his cheek. Despite the cloying warmth of hospital ward her touch felt cold, and Sweeney remembered again those dead on Spring Bank West. He shivered faintly.

'What's wrong?' she asked.

'Nothing's wrong. You tickled me.'

He rubbed his cheek as if brushing away an itch, smiled at her as convincingly as he could, caressed her hair and stood back. 'It looks good on you,' he said. She was as lovely as ever and yet more distant than ever. He behaved with gentleness, spoke with tenderness and showed compassion, all of which could leave her in no doubt about his feelings. And yet her touch aroused in him a deep-seated despair. If his behaviour expressed love, fertile with life, his instinct spoke of fear, barren with death.

265

· · · · · · · · · ·

On the Saturday he braved the bitter weather to go to Mr Trammer's but when he got there the shop was closed. No sign on the door showed a time of return. Maybe he'd really had enough of watching the 'country going to the dogs'. His locked door added to Sweeney's deepening gloom. He went to the Prospect Centre where at least it would be warm. The mall was full of shoppers, some bustling from store to store, some sitting on wooden benches, watching and waiting. Here the wisdom of English cheeriness found refuge against a daily diet of misery, strikes and shortages. He liked this spirit of resilience – 'bugger it, let's just enjoy ourselves'. It seemed very Hull and his mood improved.

In W. H. Smith's nearly every space before a wall of magazines was occupied by customers who flicked through glossy pages on classic cars or steam trains, football or fishing, stamps or caravans, gardening or home decoration. Sweeney envied those (even if he had no wish to be one of them) whose hours were spent arranging stamps in a collection, tinkering with fuel pumps of old cars, recording numbers of trains or planting perennials in the garden. He picked up a copy of *Horse and Hound* for no other reason than its cover boasted an article on Lincolnshire. Someone tapped his shoulder. It was Rachel, the girl from Sheffield, wearing a W. H. Smith jumper and blouse.

'I didn't know you were a horsey person.'

He returned the magazine to the rack. 'Unfortunately, I can't get near *Trainspotter Weekly*.' Rachel nudged his arm and smiled. 'And I didn't know you worked here.'

'It's a Saturday job. The money's not great but it comes in handy. The way the price of things is going up these days is mad.'

'To tell the truth, I'm only in here to escape the cold.'

'Oh, poor you,' she laughed. 'I didn't think I'd say it but

this winter I'm glad to live in university accommodation. It's always toasty.'

'Oh, lucky Rachel, how I envy her! You suit the W.H. Smith look, by the way.'

'Why, thank you.' Rachel hesitated and said, 'Look, most of the girls in my house are away this weekend or stuck at home because of the bad weather. It can be spooky with only one or two around. You're welcome to warm yourself this evening if you'd like. We've even got a television.'

'That sounds perfect. You don't mind being the Salvation Army for the evening?'

'Bring your own tambourine,' she laughed. 'You remember where it is on Cranbrook?'

'I remember it well.' She'd been honest with him that night they'd had together, told him she was having a fling because her boyfriend had cheated on her, but intended to get back together. They must have broken up again. Sweeney found Rachel good-looking but in an uninteresting way.

'Make it about eight, okay? I don't finish here until after five. I could make spaghetti Bolognese. If you're lucky, that is!'

'I feel lucky already. Anything else will be a bonus. I'll bring a bottle of wine.'

'Fine … uh oh, I see the manager is giving me the evil eye. I'd better get back to work. There's no union for part-time staff, more's the pity. See you later, then.'

When he arrived at Rachel's, his hand half frozen to a bottle of red wine, there was one other girl in the house who introduced herself as Katy. She made a point of saying, 'I will leave you two alone' despite Rachel's protest she was welcome to join them for dinner. Katy put on her coat, threw a heavy scarf around her neck, pulled a hat over her ears and, without turning, waved a hand in the air. 'Thanks, but I promised to see Alison. She's got man trouble again so it's a girlie thing. Enjoy your evening.' The front door slammed.

'Katy's very thoughtful,' Sweeney said.

'She likes to think she's worldly but she's an innocent really. And her friend Alison – her trouble with men is she can't get one.' Sweeney made a mental note not to get on the wrong side of Rachel's sharp tongue.

If he really had been a good boy like Mrs Ahrens believed him to be, worthy of her daughter's favour, true in heart and pure in soul, he would have said goodnight when dinner was over, the bottle of wine empty, the *Parkinson* show on TV over and the last cup of coffee drunk. He didn't say goodbye. When she said casually that he could stay, he did. Remorse he would confront another time. That night he wanted to affirm life and renounce death.

Much later, wakened by Katy's footsteps on the landing, he lay on his back staring at the ceiling. From under the covers, Rachel murmured. Her hand appeared, felt for him and touched his cheek. 'For a moment I thought you were gone,' she said. 'Hold me,'

. . . .

'I finished those Sagan novels you brought. They were addictive, like a schoolgirl's dream of sophistication, so light and easy.' Sam was happy and told him she expected to be out of hospital soon.

Realising his visits were no longer needed, Sweeney couldn't help feeling resentment at being pushed to the margins of her life once more. The memory of Rachel's hand searching for him, her desire for his touch, conjured a grievance against his passive relationship with Sam. She was too acute not to notice.

'Eddie, I want you to know I appreciate everything you do for me.' She shook her head. 'No, that sounds pathetic. It's much more than appreciation. "You are the secret voice speaking straight out of my own bones."' Sweeney looked surprised. 'It's a line from *The Bell Jar*. When I read those words I thought immediately of you and me. It's maybe even better than two souls. Don't you think so?' At her look of pleasure his grievance vanished, as did all thought of Rachel.

Next time he arrived at the Infirmary Mrs Ahrens was waiting by the lift. 'Sam has gone for more tests today,' she told him.

'I hope it's nothing serious,' he said more casually than intended.

She suggested they go the hospital café. Sweeney got two teas. Mrs Ahrens didn't drink coffee.

She took a sip and looked at her cup disapprovingly. She stared at it for a while and Sweeney sensed what she was about to say. He gave her time to find the right words, if there were any right words.

'The news about Sam isn't good, I'm afraid.' She was still looking at her cup, then pushed it gently away. Never before had he seen anyone 'wring their hands', but in her anguish this is what Mrs Ahrens was doing. 'The consultant was business-like and non-committal. I suppose he has to be. "We need to make sure we haven't missed anything, nothing to be too worried about yet." Those were his exact words. It's not very reassuring, is it? He must think I'm stupid not to notice "missed" and "too" and "yet". Our hopes were up. It feels like we have to start from the bottom again. I prayed everything would be normal after her operation.' She looked up at him, as if for spiritual reassurance, and he remembered the day in Beverley, Sam joking about Father Edward.

She was no longer wringing her hands. They were clasped tightly on the table. He placed his hands on either side of hers. A moment later Sweeney felt a warm tear fall on his thumb and Mrs Ahrens pulled her hands away, seeking a linen handkerchief from within the sleeve of her coat, exactly like his own mother. She always kept one there. It made him feel filial, above all, protective. For her sake he should be a good boy. She daubed her eyes, wiped her nose, shook her head at this show of emotion and glanced around the café to see if anyone had noticed.

'I can't find any words,' he said.

'Your touch meant more than words.'

'I'm not much good at it, but I promise I'll pray for Sam.'

'Pray as you can, Eddie, not as you can't.'

Sweeney gave Mrs Ahrens his address and asked her to send him any news. She promised. He walked home along Argyle Street this time, avoiding the cemetery on Spring Bank West.

. . . .

Brown wrote to say he'd found some *grotty digs* in a house in North Oxford. They were *nothing as posh as Park Road. I'm really a lodger with a certain Miss Boynton – and no, she's not young and attractive, she's like Margaret Rutherford in one of those Miss Marple films.* He was getting on well. The local beer was drinkable and it was easy enough to see Debbie *'who sends her best wishes'.* He hoped Sweeney could get down for a few days *if you can drag yourself away from the fleshpots of Hull.* He asked about Sam. Sweeney wrote back telling Brown about Sam's condition, his dark premonitions about her well-being, but felt he couldn't pour out his heart. He couldn't imagine his friend being a *Jackie* agony aunt.

Dawson called him in to say the book contract had arrived. He'd never cried on Dawson's shoulder and wasn't going to confess his worries about Sam. Sweeney could imagine Dawson's profound discomfort if he did.

Simon called up one morning to tell him their farewell party would have to be earlier than expected. 'There's a general election coming so I'm going to be busy.'

Sweeney had forgotten all about the party. He feigned interest and said, 'I heard them talking about the election on the radio. They were saying the polls don't look good for Labour.'

'Don't remind me. Callaghan should have called an election last autumn. He waited too long at the damned church! I'll be busy canvassing, looking for a job *and* house hunting. Pearl thought it best to have the party asap. Saturday at eight ok? There'll be plenty of food so don't fill up beforehand.'

'I'll be there, thanks.'

They could hear Pearl talking to Roland downstairs.

'I thought I'd leave Roland to her,' Simon whispered. 'I think he's a secret admirer.'

Aren't we all? Sweeney thought. 'I'll see you Saturday,' he told Simon even though his heart wasn't in it.

After nearly three years in Hull, he'd adjusted to the English habit of eight o'clock really meaning any time between half past eight and nine, perhaps even later. When he arrived on the half-hour Roland was already there, since eight on the dot probably, seated primly, a glass of red wine in one hand and his pipe in the other. Simon was in the kitchen. Pearl was moving about the sitting room arranging dishes and glasses.

'Eddie!' Pearl said, kissing him on each cheek. 'Isn't that how the French do it, Roland?' Before Roland could answer she went on, 'I think now we're in Europe there are a few continental customs we should adopt.' She raised a glass. 'Wine with every meal is one.'

'Go easy on the booze, love,' Simon called to her.

'As you see, Eddie, we haven't started our new health regime yet. It begins from tomorrow. Simon's become such a fusspot about this baby,' she said running her hand over a belly that hadn't become noticeably bigger. 'I hardly touch the stuff these days, more's the pity.'

Sweeney set the bottle of wine he'd brought on the table. Pearl offered him a glass of red. 'Roland brought this one. You must try it. It's delish. I know you shouldn't open your guest's wine but Roland did insist.' She raised her voice towards the kitchen. 'Simon, isn't Roland's wine delish?' From the kitchen came a grunt of affirmation.

She poured Sweeney a glass. He toasted everyone. 'The wine is excellent,' he said. 'Are you allowed a cigarette?'

'Simon and I had a confab earlier. We agreed I could finish my last packet of B&H. There are only a few left. And that will be that until the baby arrives.' She repeated the gist of this agreement towards the kitchen and there was another unenthusiastic grunt of acquiescence from Simon.

Pearl opened a drawer in the sideboard, retrieved the packet, flipped the top and held it out for Sweeney and Roland to confirm there were only three left. 'Father,' she said, pointing to the kitchen, 'Son,' pointing to her belly, 'And Holy Smoke,' pointing at the packet. She took out one of the cigarettes and twirled it above her head. Like a diva acknowledging the bravos from her audience, Pearl bowed in response to Sweeney's and Roland's laughter. It set the scene for a surprisingly convivial evening, dispelling for a time Sweeney's sorrows. The food Simon prepared was also delish and Pearl made the most of her licence to smoke and drink. It was Roland who made a surprise announcement.

He took the pipe from his lips and set it carefully in the ashtray by his chair. 'I think I should say that I will be leaving the house shortly as well.'

Simon asked a little too keenly, 'Do you mean for good?'

Pearl and Sweeney gave each other a knowing look but Roland was insensitive to Simon's tone.

'Indeed I do. Mother's finally had enough of England. The weather and strikes this winter pushed her to a decision. She's returning to France and I'm going with her.'

'What about the rest of your family?' Pearl asked.

'Mother has had enough of father too. My brother – I assure you he'll be happy to see the back of both of us.'

'I'm so sorry to hear that,' Pearl said.

Roland replied, 'I think it's for the best.'

'I thought you liked it here?' she continued. 'Won't you be sad to leave Hull?'

'I'm happy to support mother. I'm also happy to leave England. I don't see much future here. And France, yes, I've come to realise France is my spiritual home. The English are incapable of great culture today.'

Simon choked at these words. Sweeney noticed Pearl putting a hand on his thigh to stop an outburst.

'What about your novel?' Sweeney asked.

'My novel has exhausted itself in this country too, Edward.' Roland lifted his pipe and scrutinised what remained of the tobacco in the bowl. To this enigmatic answer he added, 'It's not a question of art or truth. It *is* exhaustion, even disgust. Life in England no longer inspires. I need France to put life back into my work. Edward, you'll understand this. Everyone should imagine me happy.'

'Roland we *are* happy for you,' Simon said. 'I'm sure I can speak for everyone here.'

Sweeney had to look away. Pearl, the perfect hostess, kept a straight face.

. . . .

At the beginning of March, lectureships were advertised at universities in Wales and Lancashire as well as the Polytechnic in Northern Ireland. Sweeney applied and was shortlisted for all three. Dawson had been right. The book contract seemed to give him a patina of 'promise'. He felt things were looking up. Maybe he'd been too pessimistic about life, misreading the signs about Sam. Medical science, perhaps he'd been wrong to doubt the 1970s. Then a brief letter from Mrs Ahrens arrived.

She wrote to tell him how devastated the family had been when new tests showed Sam's cancer had spread. She *trusted he understood* why it was best for her not to have many visitors at hospital but Sam had *asked about you* many times. The consultant spoke of a new combination of drugs which he wanted to try so *we are still hopeful*. The hopelessness of hope, Sweeney thought, as he read that line again. He was certain Mrs Ahrens knew there was no hope. Hope was another lie. You can become sick from hoping. *Our family is grateful for your prayers.* But he'd said no prayers, not once, not ever. He was good alright, good for nothing. Below her name – *Carol (Sam's mother)* – she'd written: *Here is our telephone number. We finally got one installed last week. Sam will be out of hospital soon. I will care for her mornings and afternoons. Ring in a few days. I'm sure she would like to talk to you.* He wrote the number on an index card which he put in the breast pocket of his jacket.

He rarely suffered phobias but telephone boxes provoked unusual anxiety – the sticky feel of the receiver, the thought of waxy lobes pressed against the earpiece, spittle lips against the mouthpiece, the faint odour of urine and disinfectant on the concrete floor. Ever since he'd watched the film *La Cabina* he would use one heel to keep the door slightly ajar. In Hull telephone boxes were cream, not red, but they provoked the same irrational response. He decided to use one of the wall-mounted telephone booths in the Students' Union, noisier certainly, but likely cleaner and less claustrophobic certainly. Under a soundproofed hood (which made no difference whatsoever), Sweeney placed a few ten pence pieces along the ledge, took out the index card and dialled the number.

GOING

After five rings a woman's voice answered. He didn't recognise it immediately.

'Hello, I'm calling to ask how Samantha is doing.' His own voice sounded odd to his ear. There was silence. 'It's Edward Sweeney.' He thought the line had gone dead. 'Hello?'

'Sorry! Eddie! I didn't recognise you.' It was Mrs Ahrens. He couldn't possibly call her Carol and didn't think she would appreciate it either.

'I wasn't sure if Sam is with you, Mrs Ahrens, but thought I'd call anyway to find out how she's doing.' Whether Mrs Ahrens was preoccupied or his accent was difficult for her to decipher on the line he couldn't tell, but there was another silence. He heard what sounded like a door closing.

'She is here, yes. Tony leaves Sam off each morning for me to keep an eye on her.'

Her matter-of-fact use of 'Tony' troubled him. 'Tony' made him sound all too real and his marital status all too exclusive. Sweeney felt shrunken within the hood of the telephone booth. Mrs Ahrens still hadn't said anything about Sam's health.

'And how's she doing?' he asked again.

'She's not as well as we'd like.' There was another silence. 'Sam's not responding to treatment in the way the doctor expected ... or told *us* he expected. He's reviewing the drugs again,' a further pause, 'and we have to keep praying, don't we?'

He felt absurd mumbling affirmations into the receiver and began to punch softly the soundproofed hood. A young woman walking by looked at him quizzically. Embarrassed, he gestured towards the handset, implying the person on the other end was being difficult. The girl made a face in solidarity and walked on. Sweeney felt guilty for disrespecting Mrs Ahrens.

'Is there anything I can do?' he asked.

'It's nice of you but ... just a moment.' He heard the phone being set down, picturing it on a semi-circular metal table in the hallway just like the one his parents had. A muffled conversation was taking place. Since he didn't know how long this interruption would take, he pushed another ten pence piece into the coin box and the voices were interrupted by the pips. More students were about now, distracting him with their commotion. Finally, the phone was picked up again.

'Eddie! I hoped it was you. Mam has become overprotective as well as puritanical.' Mrs Ahrens must have been standing close by because he heard her say something. 'Speaking on the phone to Eddie won't do me any harm, mam.'

'You sound tired Sam,' Sweeney said. 'Maybe you shouldn't overdo things.'

'Don't you start n' all, making me feel like one of those women in a Victorian novel with tinctures, herbal teas and bottles of pills.' She laughed. He doubted if he would be up to laughing in her position. 'No sad songs for me, please, tell me what's happening with you.'

He told her about the interviews – 'though they're not for some time yet' – and she seemed pleased. He mentioned how his house would soon be emptied of Pearl, Simon and Roland – 'leaving me like the mad one in the attic ... or your Julian of Norwich.' He told her about Brown, Miss Boynton, and the invitation to visit.

'That's another one of your coincidences! I grew up near Boynton Street – in Hull that is, not Oxford. I've always wanted to see Oxford.'

A few students yelped and whooped as they passed by the rank of phone booths.

'Where are you? There's a lot of noise.'

'I'm in the Union.'

'It's hard to hear you.'

Sweeney was going to say he'd call some other time but could hear another muffled discussion between Sam and her mother.

GOING

The pips went and he pushed in another ten pence.

'Do you have mam's address?' Sam asked.

'No, I don't.'

Sam gave him the street and number along with directions. Sweeney repeated them to confirm. 'That's right. Can you come over tomorrow morning?'

'Of course I can. I'd love to see you.'

'Mam will make you one of her famous cuppas, won't you, mam?'

He imagined Mrs Ahrens shaking her head and wagging a finger. 'Are you sure it's no bother for your mother?' he asked.

'Oh, it's no bother, is it mam?' he heard her say. 'I can't wait to see you,' she whispered.

. . . .

At half-past ten the next morning, he knocked at the terraced house on Somerset Street. He'd bought a few pastries on the way in a Skeltons bakery. The door was opened by Mrs Ahrens dressed in a green-check tabard overall, exactly like the one his mother wore. He followed her along a short, wallpapered hallway. The telephone table was as he'd imagined it, a replica of the one in his parents' house. She pushed open the door to a neat red-carpeted living room. On each side of the coal fire was a grey-clothed armchair. On the window, white Venetian blinds were louvered three-quarters shut and in the corner by the TV, a standard lamp with a tasselled shade was lit. On the wall were a few framed prints of ships. Sam was lying on the couch before the fire, pillows at her back. On her head was a white turban. It reminded Sweeney of Elizabeth Taylor in a film he'd once seen. But her face wasn't at all like Elizabeth Taylor's, full and fresh. Sam looked gaunt, her skin sallow, much frailer in the flesh than her voice had sounded on the phone. She grimaced trying to prop herself up.

'Hello stranger,' she said.

Her mother went around the couch helping her, plumping up the pillows and pulling a blue crochet blanket under her daughter's chin.

'Have a seat,' Sam said when she was settled. 'Are you ready for a *nice* cup of tea?'

'That would be great. It's freezing outside. Winter is running well into spring. I brought some pastries along.' He handed the bag to Mrs Ahrens.

'That was thoughtful of you, Eddie,' Sam's mother said. As she went out of the room, she looked back at her daughter and then at Sweeney. He still wasn't sure if she approved of his visit. The door closed slowly. Sam looked at it for a moment. In the kitchen they could hear cups and plates being arranged.

Sam turned to him and said softly, 'Come here and give me a hug.' She raised her arms from underneath the blanket. 'I'm always chilly these days and never seem to warm up.'

Sweeney bowed down so she could embrace him. He put his hands on her shoulders. They felt bony and thin. About her there was an odour of antiseptic, peppermint and freshly soaped flesh, not unpleasant, but with every association of illness. He suppressed his instincts as best he could.

'What a state you find me in,' she whispered. She patted her turban. 'Under here I look like Yul Brynner. You don't want to see the truth. This disease is humiliating me as well as killing me.' She saw Sweeney was about to remonstrate but put a finger to his lips. 'No, don't say something only to mollify. That would add lying to the list. You may be corny, a charmer at times, but you are not a liar, at least not with me.'

'But I can be a sneak.' He took from his pocket a packet of Rothmans.

'Here, quick,' she snatched the cigarettes and slipped them

into the pocket of her dressing gown. 'I'm policed here like we're in East Berlin, not West Hull. But it's not my lungs which have cancer.'

'Will smoking not affect your treatment?'

'My treatment's not working. It's as simple as that. Death is hard enough so why make life harder?' She said this in such a matter-of-fact way Sweeney didn't comment. 'Thanks for the ciggies. I'll call them my Eddie stash, to be smoked when I'm not under mam's bell jar – which isn't all that often these days. There's "a silken web, enervating and soft which isolates me". That's Françoise Sagan in *Bonjour Tristesse*. I memorised the line. It's what my illness feels like.'

Sweeney heard the rattle of cups on a trolley. He let go of Sam's hand and returned to his chair.

'Mam's got dad to care for as well. Today's one of his bad days so he's in bed. It's like a cottage hospital in here sometimes.'

Mrs Ahrens wheeled in a tea trolley. It was exactly like the one his parents owned as well, copper-coloured metal and two-tiered. On top were cups, saucers, side-plates, bowl, jug and tea pot, below an oblong tray with biscuits, slices of fruit cake as well as the pastries Sweeney had brought. What was it Sam had said? In another life they'd been joined at the hip? Sweeney could only wonder about these coincidences.

Mrs Ahrens parked the trolley at the side of the couch. She poured three cups. 'Do you take sugar, Eddie?'

'No thanks, Mrs Ahrens.'

'He thinks he's sweet enough as he is, mam,' Sam added. 'Milk?'

'A wee taste, please.' He could see Mrs Ahrens hadn't understood. 'Just a little, thanks.'

Her mother handed him a cup and then passed one to Sam.

'I'm taking one up to your dad,' Mrs Ahrens said to her. She put one of the small cheesecakes Sweeney had brought on a plate. 'He loves these, don't he Sam? He's not feeling the best today, Eddie, so I told him to stay in bed. I'll leave you to it – and see if you can make this girl eat something. I'll be down to join you soon.'

Sam's spirits seemed to improve and she was happily animated by their playful chat under the indulgently if watchful eye of her mother. An hour or so passed pleasantly.

When he was leaving, Mrs Ahrens hesitated before opening the front door. 'Your visit did her the world of good, Eddie. But you can see how easily she tires. I'm sorry if I seem protective but I'm sure you can understand. Please feel free to come over anytime. I mean that. You're very welcome. Just call in advance. I'm still getting used to having a phone in the house, you know.'

. . . .

He visited regularly. Sam never talked of dying, not because it was too hard to bear, he thought, but because it was too certain. Sweeney didn't sense she was being 'brave' by not burdening others. Larkin was right about that. Being brave lets no one off the grave. Hadn't she told him the comforts of faith were for those left behind? That wasn't a lie. What he experienced during those visits was startling clarity, the privilege of knowing life in its purest essence. The prospect of death concentrated the mind on the gift he possessed. Death unmasked life, leaving nothing hidden other than life itself. In that little parlour in that nondescript house on that commonplace street, he thought he was saving his soul. It was a strange sensation but he thought it true. He believed Sam felt the same.

He would bring her books from Mr Trammer's, who had recovered a hesitant optimism after the Conservatives had won the General Election in May.

'As you know, I considered quitting last winter but I will give

Mrs Thatcher a chance. Her father was a shopkeeper so maybe she understands the likes of me.'

He was genuinely upset to hear the news about Sam and did something out of character. He put his arm around Sweeney's shoulder and after a short silence said, 'Old men do forget. But they don't forget how it felt to be young and in love. I am so very sorry, for her and for you.'

Mrs Ahrens provided a chaperoning presence when Sweeney visited. Mr Ahrens was either resting in bed or down with old pals at his social club. Maybe he didn't approve of these visits? He didn't know, but never sensed any ill will in that little house on Somerset Street. Sam and Sweeney talked about his future as if life went on regardless which, she told him, it would do.

He told her he'd been interviewed for a post in Cardiff but hadn't been offered the job. 'The person who got it was teaching part-time there already. Anyway, there's another one coming up at Manchester. Let's see how things go there. I've got to be optimistic, don't I?'

When he visited the day after that interview, Sam was excited to know the outcome.

'It was a disaster,' he said and it pleased him to see that she and her mother were genuinely disappointed. It was like he was one of the family.

'Why, what went wrong this time?' Sam asked.

'I travelled on the hottest day of the year. The train was stifling and the hotel room was like an oven, even with the windows open. Pearl and Simon are from Manchester.' He explained to Mrs Ahrens they lived in the same house in Park Road. 'I only mention that because Simon is always talking about how good Boddingtons beer is and how Hull Brewery is nothing by comparison.'

Sam snorted and her mother said, 'Well, of all the cheek.'

'I went out to get something to eat in the evening and beside the hotel was a Boddingtons pub. I went in for one but was so dehydrated I stayed for more.'

Sam put a hand to her mouth. 'No! Please don't tell me you turned up for your interview with a hangover? These Irish boys, mam, what can you do with them?'

'The hangover was only half of it. I was doing alright until the pounding started.'

They said simultaneously, 'The pounding?'

'The pounding, yes, they were laying foundations for a building across the road. My interview must have started when the workers were on their tea break. Then pile drivers began ... piling, a muffled boom, boom, boom, but too loud for me. I thought my head was going to explode.'

Mother and daughter looked at each other, seeming to add together hangover, interview and pile driving.

'The chairman of the panel asked later if I was feeling ill. He said, "These things can be nerve-wracking. We were rather concerned you were going to be sick." Blame bloody *Boddingtons* I felt like saying – oh, sorry for swearing Mrs Ahrens.'

'My husband was on the boats, remember.'

'That's quite a story,' Sam said, 'and I'm not sure if I should laugh or cry.' But she did laugh and so did her mother. 'Put it down to experience and stay off the booze in future.'

'Well, tell us,' her mother said. 'Was it better?'

'Was what better, Mrs Ahrens?'

'The Boddingtons of course?'

'Was it 'eck!'

'Spoken like a true local, Hull and proud,' Mrs Ahrens said.

'If it wasn't for the accent and words like fill-*um*, you would think that, wouldn't you?' Sam added.

. . . .

GOING

He telephoned her mother one morning to ask if Sam could go with him to Pearson Park. It was a beautiful day. 'Only an hour at most,' he promised. 'We'll go by taxi and sit out under the trees for a short time, make the most of the sunshine while it lasts.'

Mrs Ahrens hesitated, but agreed eventually. 'Don't overdo things, Eddie. You know how delicate she's become.'

He assured her, but asked, 'Only don't tell her it's Pearson Park? I'd like to surprise her.'

When he arrived at the house, the taxi driver wanted payment for the first part of the journey. He said he was sorry for sounding suspicious but he'd had a few runners lately.

Sweeney helped Sam into the back seat which was hot to the touch already. 'You won't need your blanket today,' he told her.

'Where are we going?'

'Not far.'

'Pearson Park!' she said as the taxi pulled through the archway off Beverley Road. Her voice registered surprise and, he feared, disappointment.

'I promised your mother not to take you far.'

He paid a second time and arranged a pick-up with the driver who assured Sweeney he'd be there in good time. The driver apologised again for earlier and nodded to Sam. 'Look after her, won't you?' He knew.

Sweeney took her arm and they walked slowly across the green. There were a couple of joggers running the perimeter but otherwise the park was almost empty. They reached the path Sweeney took to the university most days. Their closeness wasn't intimate, more like patient and carer. He asked her if she was comfortable walking.

'I've still got the use of my legs, just about,' Sam replied. 'There is one thing I'd love to do.'

'And that is?'

'Have a cigarette.'

'Now that is something I expected, which is why we're heading for the bench by that large tree over there.' He stopped and took out a packet of Rothmans. Next, he pulled out a pack of Trebor mints. 'I thought these might come in handy too.'

'You can't fool mam. She knows about you sneaking the fags into the house n'all. She's resigned to me smoking. She knows it makes no difference. She's resigned to everything now. She's assented to me dying, as I have done.'

He avoided her eyes, too conscious of his inability to respond. He ran his hand over the surface of the bench under a birch tree to make sure it was dry. It was slightly damp with dew, so he took off his jacket for Sam to sit on.

'Ah, Sir Walter,' she said. He lit two cigarettes and passed one to her. 'It's lovely here,' she said, 'the leaves, the grass, the scent of the air, the flowers, the birds singing, you beside me, all my senses so alive.' She looked at him with what he hoped was joy.

But he knew death haunted everything here too. The summer would pass. The leaves would fall. The birds would be gone. The flowers would decay. Yet he couldn't deny the splendour of this moment. 'It is beautiful,' he said. 'And so are you.'

Sam smiled, but didn't reply to his compliment. She exhaled slowly. 'You know how I went on and on about my different worlds? I suppose they all end with me now.' She gestured to the park 'All of it ends with me. But *this* world still goes on – this world with *you* in it.'

A woman walked by with a Golden Retriever which looked up at its owner with what seemed like an adoring look. Sam's eyes followed the dog. 'I suppose only humans are cursed with such morbid ideas.'

'I do know one thing.' He corrected himself. 'No. I know two things.

'And they would be?'

GOING

'I *know* you will take part of me with you. And part of *you* will stay with me. Romantic poets would call that part the heart. I suppose it's another way of saying love.' She didn't answer. 'You met Toby, didn't you, my fellow postgrad?' She nodded. 'We were at a pub in Skidby and he said something I'll never forget. He was at home and dragged along to the midnight service one Christmas. During the familiar ritual it dawned on him that this isn't a cold, indifferent universe. He knew, just *knew*, he'd come from love, was made by love, that love begins with love, and that God *is* love. And suddenly everything made sense to him. I told Toby I wished I had his faith. He said my wish was the first step. I've gone no further, despite you lending me the Ahrens' family relics.' She smiled again. 'But I've gone one step further than Larkin. I *know* the instinct he wrote of is true and that what survives of us is love. You know the poem?'

'"An Arundel Tomb" isn't it?'

'Yes. It's the reason I brought you here today. I have something to show you.'

'What is it?'

Putting out his hand for her to stand up, he led her to the far side of the tree. He pointed to a carving in the trunk a few feet from the ground. The bark had been removed and a heart-shaped space cleared and polished. Engraved there was 'S A and E S 1979'. Beneath were the words 'Love survives'. He supported Sam as she bent slightly to make sure she'd read correctly.

'You did that? But when – and how?'

'I did it with a Swiss Army knife bought in a shop on Newland Avenue – that and some sandpaper. It took me about a month. I'm sure it's against City Council regulations. So, like Johnny Cash's song, I did it one piece at a time to avoid attracting attention. Rainy evenings were best. I carved it on the park side so no one would notice walking by. Well, Sam, what do you think?'

285

'It's beautiful is what I think, so simple and so true.'

'What's done in love is done well.'

She rested her head on his shoulder. 'I think I'm going to cry again. I'm always crying on your shoulder, aren't I?'

They stood for a while under the canopy of their tree in Pearson Park. Then she lifted her head once more, wiped her eyes and snuffled. Sweeney felt in his trouser pocket for a handkerchief. He daubed under her eyes.

'Larkin also has a poem called 'The Trees' which ends with the line "afresh, afresh, afresh". Do you know it?' he asked.

'No.'

'When the leaves green each spring, Sam, we'll be together in Pearson Park afresh, afresh, afresh.'

'I'm all cried out now, Eddie. You've made me feel happy again.'

. . . .

It was the last time he saw her. He'd been busy preparing for the interview at Ulster Polytechnic. He hadn't been to see her the week before the interview and for some days afterwards. Relaxed about whether he got the lectureship or not – he wanted to remain in England and preferably in Hull – he'd talked calmly, authoritatively through the questions the panel asked. He even managed to share a literary joke which went down well. All in all, it had been an assured performance and he'd avoided alcohol the night before. The chairman told him they would make a decision after a few days' reflection and candidates would be contacted by post. As he flew back to Yorkshire, he tried to shake the thought that this job was *meant* for him, hoping providence had something else in mind. But somehow he knew.

Two days later the departmental office telephone rang. Julie answered. 'He's right here, actually. Shall I put him on?'

GOING

Sweeney pointed to his chest and mouthed, 'Me?' Dawson, he thought. It wasn't Dawson. It was the Dean from Ulster.

'Can you speak confidentially, Mr Sweeney?'

There was only Julie in the office. Sweeney was certain Julie wouldn't be interested in their conversation, confidential or not.

'The panel was impressed by your interview and excited about your forthcoming book. We discussed how it might put our school on the literary map, so to speak.' There was a pause. 'This isn't normal practice you understand but I thought I would ask. Are you prepared to take the lectureship if offered?' He added, 'we are keen to appoint.'

Sweeney thought of Robinson, of his life in a Sunderland comprehensive school, and replied immediately, 'Why, yes, of course. It's the job I wanted.'

'Excellent, I'm pleased to hear that. We are ambitious to promote talent in our school and I'm sure you will find the faculty congenial. I will put things in motion straight away and you should expect a formal letter in the post tomorrow or the day after.'

As he suspected, Julie had paid no attention to his conversation. When he told her the good news, she looked up briefly from a spread sheet on her desk. 'So, you'll be leaving us then?' It was a question without a trace of sentiment.

'It will be another month or two. I'll be sorry to leave Hull, of course.'

'It's nice you've got a job though,' she said and went back to what she'd been doing.

Later on, Jan and Jo showed more emotion, saying how sorry they'd be to lose him.

'But then that's the rhythm of life, isn't it?' said Jan.

Jo chipped in with, 'Go, Go, Go, Eddie and tell them everything you know.' She laughed. 'We'll miss him though, won't we Jan?'

'We will indeed.'

He would miss them.

Dawson told him he could relax. 'It's first rung on the ladder.'

'It's hard to believe three years have passed so quickly.'

'They begin to pass much quicker when you get to my age,' Dawson said cheerfully, but his look darkened immediately. 'Then I suppose everything slows again – if they cast you prematurely on the scrapheap, that is. There's plenty of life left in me yet, though.'

At the house in Park Road, Roland had gone but his flat hadn't been re-let. Possibly, like Blanche, he'd paid up to September. Unlike Blanche, Sweeney thought, money wasn't a problem for Roland.

Simon and Pearl were moving out at the end of July. 'We've found a just-about-affordable house Kirk Ella way,' Simon told him the evening of the phone call from Ulster. Pearl was visibly pregnant and slumped in a chair by the fire.

'Never mind our news. I'm so pleased for you, Eddie. I'm sorry to be a *bore* but I can't join you in a celebratory drink. In fact, this pregnancy is a bit of *bore* too so I won't *bore* you by complaining. Men know nothing about it,' she huffed.

'Pearl's loving it, take no notice,' Simon said, handing him a can of lager. 'I'm sorry there's nothing better or stronger. We haven't been buying drink recently.'

'Tell me about it – and no fags either.'

'Love, I'll allow you a glass of lager since this *is* a special occasion.'

'That's what I mean. You know I can't stand the stuff.' She sighed and looked at Sweeney. 'Sorry for moaning, Eddie. You came to us across the Irish Sea and now you're going back across the Irish Sea. I suppose it completes a circle of life.' She looked introspective. Simon and Sweeney glanced at one another, waiting for further words of wisdom. Instead, she sighed again and, suddenly aware of their look, asked, 'What?'

'Someone told me it was part of the rhythm of life,' Sweeney said. 'I think I prefer your circle of life.'

Pearl smiled. 'You always say the right thing even if you don't mean it. We'll miss that, won't we, Simon? What was it you said that first night? "Whatever you say, say something nice"?'

'I'm saying nothing,' Sweeney laughed.

Pearl slapped her forehead. 'You're always diplomatic! Now, I'm going to have to get out of this chair and make myself decent. At least I haven't had to give up my bridge.'

. . . .

He should have known it was no *mere* coincidence, all the talk about life's circles and rhythms.

When he called Mrs Ahrens next day, a different woman answered the phone. 'Who is it?' In the background Sweeney heard many voices. He gave his name and said he was calling about Sam. The voices rose and fell. 'I'll see if her mother can speak. What's your name again?' He heard the handset being set on the hallway table. Sweeney closed his eyes, picturing the scene in the front room. He pressed another ten pence piece into the coin box, resting his head against the side of the phone booth. The voices grew louder but remained indistinct. He heard the front door open, a car driving by and the sound of the door closing. He checked in his pocket to see if he had any more change.

'Eddie?' It was Mrs Ahrens. 'Sam died in the night.' That was it, no euphemism, straight and factual. 'It was peaceful. She didn't suffer, thanks be to God.'

She spoke with dignity and control and he thought it proper not to blubber. 'I am so sorry.'

'You were good to her. I know that and will always remember.

That day you took her to Pearson Park. I hadn't seen Sam so happy, ever. That's the truth. Such a small thing but it made all the difference at such an awful time.' He detected a tremor in her voice. She paused and said, 'I'm glad you called. Can I check your address in case I've lost it?'

He gave his number on Park Road.

'I will post you details of the funeral arrangements.'

'Is there anything I can do?'

'Everything is in hand.' He heard a knock on the door. 'I'll have to go now.' She repeated his address and he confirmed it. He heard women speaking together before the line went dead. He replaced the receiver in its cradle, went upstairs to the empty television room in the Students' Union and collapsed into a soft chair. He still had a half empty packet of Rothmans in his pocket.

Sam was gone, yet do we ever lose people? Was it any different him going across the barrier of the Irish Sea and her across the barrier of death? He knew this was a ridiculous question. Alive, they could have corresponded, spoken on the telephone and possibly met now and then. Yet would they have done? Wouldn't nostalgia use itself up? Would longing wear itself out? He imagined their experiences diverging, the intensity of companionship waning, their interests changing and perhaps embarrassment about the past intruding. Would 'keeping in touch' become tiresome? As he 'settled down', as his 'career developed', as he 'made a new life' – as she would too in other ways – he could imagine them filing their time together under 'youthful romanticism', disposed of in maturity. They would have wistful memories, elegiac moments certainly, but as 'responsible adults' knowing everything was unrecoverable. The sting of separation would fade in time and become too mild to trouble them. Time, which could strengthen friendship, would weaken love. Who wanted to live with regrets? Such melancholic anticipation helped him cope. It provided unusual solace.

What he wanted to believe was that now they would never grow apart. What he wanted to believe was she'd met her death nonchalantly. What he wanted to believe was she'd risen above it and, despite her mocking, found it easeful. What he wanted to believe was that her death made sense. Those moments together – the cricket match, the conference in London, the night in Selby station, the walk in Burton Pidsea, the afternoon in Pearson Park, the truancy in Beverley – they weren't subject to corruption by changing circumstances. What he wanted to believe was they were in two worlds no longer but in one world of self-cast enchantment. Death, he wanted to believe, had brought them together. Maybe this was the grandest lie of all, even further from the truth than a vulgar one. He didn't know. Most things were unknowable. Most things were lies. He wished simply to be *more*, not *less* deceived, and desiring this state he stayed strangely unmoved. He would turn grief into destiny.

This world they shared, whatever it was called – spiritual, imaginative, eternal – seemed disconnected from the terrible news Mrs Ahrens had given him. It was distinct from those voices he'd heard in the background, of family, friends, clergy and neighbours. That had never been his world-with-her. He felt he couldn't honestly share its sorrow or loss of those things he'd never possessed. For him she was Sam Ahrens, not Mrs Tony Houghton, the lady of the favour, not the daughter of Carol. Were these thoughts monstrous? He couldn't convince himself of their wickedness because in this world she would not change.

Only once did he briefly feel remorse and self-doubt. A few days after his telephone call, a black-edged card arrived, announcing the time and place of the funeral service. Inside the envelope her mother had placed a handwritten note. It read, *Sam's request was for the silver cross you bought her to be placed in the coffin. I want you to know I did as she asked.*

THE LAST TRAIN TO HULL

. . . .

On the day of the funeral service, Sweeney put on his new suit. He tied around his left wrist the gold ribbon she'd first given him – her favour – covering it with his shirt cuff. He sat at the edge of a pew at the back of St Wilfrid. Mrs Herdecka, when she saw him, gave a nod of recognition.

He knew Sam wasn't here in this place of whispered consolation and condolence. Her coffin stood at the front of the church on an undertakers' trolley wreathed with flowers. But she wasn't here. Pity for the dead, he could hear her say, was only self-pity of the living. Looking through the high windows of the church, Sweeney saw deep blue air. At the end of the service, the priest, coffin and family passed along the aisle. He imagined the silver cross clasped in her hand. He held the St Christopher she'd given him tight in his own. But he knew she wasn't here.

With mourners filing out he spoke to Mrs Ahrens and her husband, a frail man who leaned on a walking stick. 'Jim, this is Eddie, Sam's friend from university.' Mr Ahrens nodded politely but didn't return Sweeney's greeting.

She introduced on her other side a heavily-built, bearded man in his thirties, uncomfortable in his dark suit, white shirt and black tie. 'This is Tony, Sam's husband.' To Tony she said, 'Eddie was a good friend of Sam's at university.'

Tony shook his proffered hand with unexpected delicacy. Sweeney knew immediately that the barrier between Sam's two worlds had never been breached. 'Thank you for coming,' he said tearfully, distractedly, a loving man whose burden was inconsolable. Imagine Sisyphus happy? That's another lie … and yet. Like the comforts of faith, Sweeney had learned life required lying to oneself. That was why he'd chosen the most exalting lie he could imagine.

He wouldn't go to the graveyard. Sam wouldn't be there

GOING

either. He walked out of St Wilfrid onto The Boulevard. People of Hull were going about their normal business, cheerily as ever. Sweeney saw women with bags of shopping and men with newspapers under their arms. In a school playground nearby, he heard the sound of children. He breathed in the air and felt free, released, and set out for Pearson Park to sit with her by the tree. There love survived endlessly, afresh, afresh, afresh.